The Firebird's Vengeance

Novels by Sarah Zettel

* A Tor Book

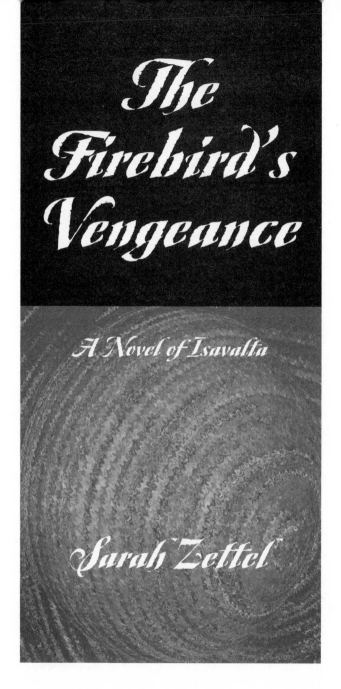

The Firebird's Vengeance

A Novel of Isavalta

Sarah Zettel

TOR®

A TOM DOHERTY ASSOCIATES BOOK
NEW YORK

THE FIREBIRD'S VENGEANCE: A NOVEL OF ISAVALTA

Copyright © 2004 by Sarah Zettel

"The Fox" by Peter Knight. Words and music by Knight/Johnson/Pegrum/Prior © 1988
Peermusic (UK) Ltd., London. Used by Permission.

This book is printed on acid-free paper.

Edited by James Frenkel

A Tor Book
Published by Tom Doherty Associates, LLC
175 Fifth Avenue
New York, NY 10010

www.tor.com

Tor® is a registered trademark of Tom Doherty Associates, LLC.

Library of Congress Cataloging-in-Publication Data

Zettel, Sarah.
       The firebird's vengeance : a novel of Isavalta / Sarah Zettel.—1st ed.
          p. com.
       "A Tom Doherty Associates book."
       ISBN 0-765-30812-6
       EAN 978-0765-30812-2
       1. Superior, Lake, Region—Fiction. 2. Mothers and daughters—Fiction. 3. Women—Fiction.
    I. Title.

    PS3576.E77F57 2004
    813'.54—dc22

                                                                          2004044086

First Edition: August 2004

Printed in the United States of America

0 9 8 7 6 5 4 3 2 1

To Tim and Alexander, with all my heart

Acknowledgments

The author would like to thank those superlative grandparents Len and Gail, as well as the tireless Aunt Julie, without whom, literally, this book would not have gotten written. She would once again like to thank the Untitled Writers Group for their valuable help and unending patience. Special thanks to Sifu Genie Parker, Si Kung (Eddie) Wu Kwong Yu, and the International Wu Style Tai Chi Chuan Federation for their inspiration.

You can hound me, now you've found me,
But I'm far more cunning than you.
I'm a shy fox, I'm a sly fox,
And I'll teach you a lesson or two.

—Peter Knight, "The Fox"

The Firebird's Vengeance

Prologue

"Grace, Grace. Have you heard? Oh, it's too awful."

Grace pushed back the curtain that separated her spartan back room from the heavily furnished parlor. Hilda Rudiger closed the door and shook a sprinkling of snow off her grey shawl. Cold and exertion had turned her round cheeks red, and gossip shone in her eyes.

"What on earth, Hilda?" Grace dried her hands on her towel. She had just finished dressing for her appointment and now wore her best emerald-green skirt, loose white blouse, and heavy gold jewelry. The gypsyish attire helped make up for her distinctly non-gypsyish blond hair and blue eyes. She glanced at the gilt clock on the shelf above the parlor stove. Mrs. Hausman would be here in half an hour, and she still needed to draw the drapes, light the lamp, and make sure she was settled and composed at her prepared table. Seeing a medium attending to domestic details ruined the atmosphere.

"You haven't heard?" Hilda trotted forward, both of her hands out to grasp Grace's. "Poor dear. It's just such a shame."

Grace gently disengaged herself from Hilda's chilly grip. "I haven't been out this morning," she said, glancing meaningfully at the clock, hoping Hilda would take the hint. "What's happened?"

The shimmer in Hilda's eyes dimmed just a little, and a little genuine concern showed through. "Bridget Lederle's gone."

Grace stared. "Gone?"

"Gone," Hilda repeated, with a nod for emphasis. "With that fisherman who was staying at the lighthouse with her. Francis Bluchard went round with the tug to pick her up because the light was closing down for the winter, but there was no one there. Mrs. Shwartz—her husband, you know, he works at the bank—she says he had orders to pay off the housekeeper, and that Bridget had pulled all her money out . . . Oh, dear, Grace, you've gone quite pale. Do sit down."

Grace dropped onto the settee with an undignified thump, but she could not seem to control her knees. She couldn't focus on the room in front of her. She could only see Bridget as she had been when they last met—tall, auburn-haired, stubborn, and looking far, far too much like her mother, Ingrid.

I shouldn't be surprised, thought Grace stupidly. *He spun her a pretty story and she went. Just like her mother.*

Ingrid Loftfield was Grace's older sister. Almost thirty years ago, Ingrid had also vanished with a stranger, leaving Grace, and their entire family, ashamed and furious. Ingrid had returned a year later, however, pregnant with Bridget. She gave birth and she died, before Grace could say another word to her. Grace had never found out where she had gone, or what had happened to her there, if she had been happy or frightened on her mysterious journey. If she'd missed Grace as badly as Grace had missed her.

Something curving and cool pressed against her palm. Grace started and looked down. She held a cup of water. Hilda stood anxiously in front of her. Hilda must have brought the cup from the jug on the washstand. Grace hadn't even been aware that Hilda had moved.

"Thank you," Grace said reflexively and took a long swallow.

"I know you and Bridget weren't close . . ." said Hilda, sitting next to her, settling in to give consolation and gather news.

She did not want to think about this. It hurt too badly to think of Bridget gone, vanished as her mother had vanished. Gone to her death too, to become another one of the ghosts that drifted through the landscape of Grace's life?

No. No. Surely not. Grace closed her eyes as if the gesture would guard her against that possibility. Not her too.

I will not . . . I cannot think of this now. Grace struggled to regain her composure. "I have an appointment, Hilda."

The other woman drew back. "Grace, you're not well. You've had a shock."

Yes, it is a shock, but it shouldn't be. I knew in my heart she'd go. Knew when her man came here, knew when she turned away from me. "Yes. A shock, but as you say, we were not close, and after all . . ." She took a deep breath. "It is only to be expected, considering my sister also . . ." *Vanished. Ran off with some man. Left me alone to face our father and brother and be thrown out of the house.* Grace waved her hand, unable to finish the sentence. "Please, Hilda. I really must get ready for my client."

"Well." In the pause following that one word waited a silent "I was only trying to help." As Grace did not seem inclined to acknowledge this, Hilda wrapped the ends of her shawl fussily over her arms and stood, her face pinched tight. "If you're certain, I suppose I had better go."

Grace touched Hilda's arm and called on her great stock of social acting skills. "Thank you for being so understanding, Hilda, and so thoughtful. I'm sure I don't know what I'd do without such a good friend."

That appeared to mollify her. Hilda patted Grace's hand solicitously. "I'll look in on you later, shall I?"

"Thank you, that would be most kind."

Hilda's pinched look relaxed and was replaced by a catlike satisfaction. "Well, I'll just show myself out." To Grace's relief, Hilda also put actions to words, making a great show of closing the door softly behind herself.

As soon as the latch clicked, Grace got up and set to work. Routine would smother thought. She hoped. She closed the shutters over the frosted windows and drew the ruffled pink curtains so that only a few thin rays of winter sun remained to set the dust motes sparkling. She added more wood to the stove. With some difficulty, for her hands were not as steady as they should have been, she lit the lamp beside her working table and replaced the fringe shade. She trimmed the wick quite low so it gave more a suggestion than the reality of light.

All the while she saw Bridget's face before her mind's eye, proud and angry, and above all lonely.

I should have told her. Grace bit her lip. *I should have told her I understand all about loneliness. I should have told her there are worse things. Far, far worse and that I know about them too. I should never have let her go. I should have . . .*

Tears stung the corners of Grace's eyes. She fought them back with a strength born of long years. *Her mother should not have left me,* she told herself. *What happens to Bridget is Ingrid's fault, not mine.*

15

Grace adjusted the long, flowered cloth that covered her worktable and disguised the fact that it was light wickerwork, easy to set rocking for dramatic effect, should that be necessary. Her crystal ball she kept covered on a separate, smaller table for when she needed to see the future or past, rather than just communicate with the spirits.

Finally, she sat in her aging wingback chair, smoothing her hair down. The pale gold of it was fading into silver far too quickly. She wondered if she might try dye to go with the marcel wave that kept its curls fresh. Her hands, which had once been slender and were now just soft, she rested on the chair arms in order to assume a pose of regal calm. Appearance was everything in her trade.

To Grace's relief, a knock sounded on the door just as the little clock struck ten. Now she could get to work, and not have to think about Ingrid anymore, or about Bridget.

"Come in," she said languidly.

Unlike Hilda, Mrs. Hausman did not bustle. She peeped in timidly, as if afraid of disturbing Grace in the midst of something socially unmentionable.

Grace gave her most serene smile. "Do please come in, Mrs. Hausman. Sit down." She gestured toward the chair drawn up opposite her. "I feel certain the spirits will be with us today." The spirits were not always ready to come when called. Somehow, the uncertain nature of the sittings made them more real for many clients.

"Oh, I am glad to hear that." Mrs. Hausman hung her coat on one of the pegs by the door. One could not expect a medium ready to commune with the spirits to do so mundane a thing as take a guest's wrap. "I am so much in need of guidance. I've been having the most dreadful presentiments that something is going to happen."

Grace smiled gently as the respectable matron took her seat and laid her handbag on the nearby curio table. Grace was always glad of an appointment with Mrs. Hausman. The woman believed implicitly in the spirit world. Some comforting words and vague hints from "beyond the veil," and she would go away satisfied. Grace would be left a dollar richer, all for a little acting, without even having to produce any spectral knockings or make her table levitate.

"I am certain you will find the guidance you seek." She gestured again. Mrs. Hausman, who knew the routine perfectly, pressed her gloved fingertips against the tabletop. Grace laid her own hands down and began.

"We call on the powers of the World Beyond," she intoned, making her voice resonate deeply. "We here are two seekers of knowledge. We ask that the Veil of Night be parted that we might see beyond. We ask that we may be permitted the presence of those who have gone before us . . ."

Grace droned on, letting the familiar words spill forth while the greater part of her mind worked on what Mrs. Hausman's dear departed would have to tell her this week. From under her lowered lashes, she surreptitiously watched Mrs. Hausman close her eyes and lift her sharp chin to show how hard she was attempting to reach the other side.

Satisfied that Mrs. Hausman was well under the influence of the dim light and atmospheric surroundings, Grace closed her own eyes.

Help me.

Grace's eyelids snapped open. The room had not changed. Mrs. Hausman still sat in her attitude of rapt concentration. No other human form disturbed the room.

". . . let us be in the presence of the spirits," she continued, closing her eyes and striving to bring certainty back into her voice. "Let them speak to their daughter, Leah Hausman, who waits here before them for their guidance."

Help me.

The voice was as clear as it was unbidden. It echoed through the privacy of Grace's mind, robbing her of her concentration.

She heard the rustle of cloth as Mrs. Hausman shifted her weight uneasily, uncomfortable with her medium's sudden silence. This was not part of the usual program. Grace mentally shook herself, squaring her shoulders and pressing her palms hard against the tabletop. "We ask that we may be permitted the presence of George Hausman," she began again. "His loving and ever-faithful daughter waits ready to receive . . ."

Please, Grace.

The sound of her name shot Grace to her feet. She stared wildly around the room, looking for the source of the voice. Startled, Mrs. Hausman threw herself back into her chair, her hand pressed against her chest.

Grace stood where she was, hands knotted at her sides. Her name. The ghosts did not speak her name. They seldom spoke at all.

"Madame Loftfield?" said Mrs. Hausman tentatively. "Are you quite well?"

Grace tried to swallow, but her throat would not open, so she simply nodded.

"What was it?" Fear and nervous anticipation filled Mrs. Hausman's voice. "Was it a manifestation? A message? Is something wrong? Was my father . . . ?"

"No, no, this was not your father." Grace shook her head and tried to gather her wits so she could make up a plausible story. The truth would not do. "When one travels on the ethereal planes, one occasionally meets with mischievous entities. Nothing truly malevolent, you understand." She touched Mrs. Hausman's sleeve reassuringly. Her comfortable patter drew her back to herself. "There is no danger in the work we do, but such encounters can be distracting, and occasionally the results can be dramatic." She pressed the back of her hand against her forehead and her cheeks, just for show. She could already feel the alarm draining from her. "I am sorry if you were unduly startled."

"Oh, not at all, not at all," said Mrs. Hausman breathlessly. She clasped her own hands in front of her, fear replaced by excitement as she realized she had witnessed a significant spiritual event. Grace suppressed the weary, ironic smile that threatened to form. She'd be the talk of the better front parlors for a month. Again.

"I am sorry that we didn't reach your father today, Mrs. Hausman." Grace dropped back into her chair and assumed a further air of exhaustion. "If you were to come back tomorrow at this same time, I'm certain we would have better success." *At least I hope we will.*

"Yes, yes, of course." Mrs. Hausman fumbled with her purse, snapping the catch and pulling out a dollar gold piece.

Grace let Mrs. Hausman lay the coin on the table before she demurred. "Oh, no, I couldn't. Not when you're leaving without answers . . ."

"I insist." Mrs. Hausman stood as if the gesture would add extra force to her statement. "Now, I must let you rest. Do not trouble yourself." She waved at Grace to stay where she was. "I can find my way."

Do not trouble yourself. Why is that always said by the ones who bring the trouble? Grace did stay as she was, pushed up straight in her armchair while Mrs. Hausman retrieved her coat and saw herself out. The door closed and she was alone again.

Except for the dead one who is here with me.

She took the dollar piece over to her sideboard and locked it in the top drawer. Then she pushed open the shutters to let the daylight back in. For a while she just stood where she was, staring out through her pink gauze curtains at the shadows of the street below, one hand resting on the chipped wood of the sideboard. Fronds of frost framed the view of the winter street. The wind blew in harsh gusts down Second Street, causing men to clutch their hats to their heads and women to tighten their grips on their shawls and coats. A faint draft worked its way under the window sash to chill the back of her hand. People came and went from the apothecary's shop below. She could hear the door opening, and the steps of shoes and boots on the bare wooden floor. Yet here she stood, apart from it all, alone with her dollar piece and a head full of things she did not want to think about.

Grace was used to seeing ghosts. It wasn't every day. Sometimes she could go up to a week without them. Then, suddenly, they'd be filling the streets—men, women, children, whites, blacks, reds. They were cold and translucent. Sometimes, they touched her, and when they did, she saw the future, or the past, sometimes the long past. On her ghost days, she could even call up real visions in the crystal ball if she wanted to. Which she did not.

But she had never before heard a voice without seeing a form to go with it, and none of those voices had ever called her by name. Not since . . . not since the first one. The one who'd tried to take her life to keep himself warm.

This voice was not his, though. Even after all these years, she still heard that voice in her dreams and she knew it intimately. "Is it you, Ingrid?" she whispered to the winter windowpane. "After all these years, is it finally you?" *Do you come to me now that your daughter Bridget is in the same trouble you got yourself into?*

What if it wasn't Ingrid? What if it was Bridget who called her? Had Bridget died so soon?

Should I have tried harder to keep her here?

Grace touched her frosted window. The ice melted under her fingers, leaving them damp and tingling. She had only two choices—wait for the voice to come again, or go in search of it. She let her hand linger against the glass, using the cold as an anchor to the real world, the practical and the hard. She had learned to make and live with difficult decisions long ago.

It had been almost thirty years. Thirty years of watching Bridget grow up, tall and distant. Thirty years of not being able to go to her, to tell her about Ingrid, because the ladies of the town from whom Grace made her living would look askance at such a thing. Bridget was illegitimate, which was reason enough for the disapproval of the respectable. Later, Bridget was brought to trial under suspicion of having murdered her own illegitimate daughter. This made it twice as impossible for Grace to speak with her niece. Bridget did not understand the difficulty, and Grace was sorry for that, but there was nothing she could do. It was not only inside her parlor that appearances mattered. Grace had learned that lesson slow and hard.

She glanced back at her chair. It would not do to attempt to seek out a real contact here. Anyone might walk in. Her clients would only accept her as long as her eccentricity had carefully defined limits. Those who came to her did not want to know what "the spirits" really had to say. Not one of them had ever been touched by a cold, desperate ghost, nor did they want to know that Grace had. They wanted nothing to do with true second sight. She knew that all too well from Bridget's example. As if her bastardy hadn't been enough, nature had cursed Bridget with visions of the future. Her inability to keep quiet about what she saw had set her even farther apart.

Grace set her jaw. Aside from her carefully decorated room, the one place she could reliably call upon genuine ghosts was the cemetery. Given the gossip that Hilda was surely spreading all across town about poor Ingrid's wayward daughter, no one would wonder at Grace going there. They would assume she had gone to visit her sister's grave. This once, they'd be right.

Grace buttoned up her stoutest boots, stuffed her hands into her knitted mittens, wrapped a shawl around her head and two more over her shoulders, and headed down into the street, directing her steps up Rittenhouse Avenue toward the cemetery.

There was no color in the graveyard during winter; only black, white, and grey. Snow lay smooth and crisp on the ground, climbing up the sides of the grey stones and capping off the monuments with white. Bare, black trees stood sentinel over them all.

Grace had not gone to Ingrid's funeral. She had, however, gone once the few mourners had left. Grace had stood at graveside and waited to see her sister, to find out after all what had really happened to her.

But Ingrid had not appeared. Even dead, her sister would not come to her.

Grace had been back to the grave only once since then, to intercept Bridget and try to convince her not to go off with the man she'd pulled out of the lake.

Grace hiked up her hems and waded through the burgeoning drifts toward the back of the cemetery. The black trees scratched at the clouds with their branches, as if to tear them open and spill out the snow. In the faint shadows of those trees waited three headstones. One for a young woman, one for an old man, and one for an infant.

Grace stood squarely before her sister's grave. Ingrid Loftfield Lederle, read the stone. Beloved Wife and Mother, March 12, 1848– October 15, 1872. Not one word about how she was also a sister, or a daughter. Grace fixed her eyes on the snow that blanketed the grave and did as she seldom did—reached into her mind and tried to open her inner eye.

Let me see you, she thought fiercely. *I'm here. Let me see you.*

In the corners of her eyes, the ghosts began to take shape. Men and women both, mostly in old-fashioned, formal clothes. Shades of who they had been, lingering above their graves, because they remained bound to the bones that lay within.

But all three graves before her remained unpopulated. Neither woman nor man came back to the place of their bones. Not even Bridget's poor little baby appeared.

Where were her dead? Grace shivered. This was wrong.

Then, Grace did see someone. Between one blink and the next, a fat, naked Indian appeared on Ingrid Loftfield's grave, whittling. He sat in the snow wearing nothing but a loincloth working steadily at a stick with his stone knife. Then, she noticed his ears. His lobes stretched out so long that they dangled across his naked chest.

"Finally," he grumbled. "Damn white women. Always making you wait."

Grace's chest seized up. Her first thought was to turn and run, but she held her ground. "Who are you?"

"Rude too." The red man inspected his work and shaved another sliver of wood from the stick.

"What are you doing here?" she demanded.

The red man squinted at his whittling. "Better," he said. "But still too damn rude. I'm waiting." He blew on the stick to clear away the chips.

It was then Grace realized what else was wrong. She could not see his breath. It was so cold that her own breath steamed up in white clouds in front of her eyes, but the fat red man in front of her breathed invisibly, as if it were the warmest summer day.

He cocked one round, black eye at her and grinned.

Grace opened her mouth and shut it tight again. Anger at his impudence burned even stronger than the fear and drew her spine up straight. "Why are you waiting here?"

"I was asked to."

This was becoming ridiculous, but Grace couldn't stop. This . . . person was not right. He was not a ghost, but he was not a living being either. She needed to know what such a creature was doing on Ingrid's grave. "Asked by whom?"

"A vixen."

"I don't understand."

"You sure don't."

Grace resisted the urge to shout in her frustration. "All right," she said exasperatedly. "Why did this . . . vixen ask you to wait for me?"

"Closer." The Red ran his fat fingers over his work. "She wanted me to bring you a message. She says the cage won't hold a second time. Think you can remember that?" He blinked his beady, black eyes at her.

"I still don't see . . ."

"No you don't." He tucked knife and whistle into his loincloth's thong. " 'Cause you're too scared to go where you need to."

Oddly, Grace felt those words stab straight at her pride. "I'm here, aren't I?"

The red man spat. "Here? What's here but the dead? It's what the living's been up to you don't want to face." He picked himself up off the snow. "Don't know what the fox's game is, but I'm done with it. You remember, you forget. You find out what's left at that lighthouse, you stay here and freeze yourself the rest of the way, it's all the same to Nanabush."

Then the pudgy red man was gone, and there was only a winter-white rabbit dashing away, kicking up glittering sprays of snow behind itself until the trees hid it from view.

Grace blinked hard and pressed her hand against her forehead. What had just happened here? Why was she standing about in the cold? There had been a rabbit on Ingrid's grave . . . No. She squeezed her eyes shut. There had been a Red. He'd had a message . . .

The cage will not hold a second time.

What cage? What was he talking about? Grace swayed on her feet. Why had she stood here having a conversation with a rabbit?

No. No. Not a rabbit. Keep your mind on what happened. Her memories were trickling away so fast she could feel them like a stream running through her mind. *There was a Red. He told me the cage wouldn't hold a second time. He said I was afraid to go where I needed to. That I needed to know what the living were up to.*

She shook her head. What did the living have to do with her? The living had left her flat, requiring that she make her own way in the world and they never once looked back to see how she was doing.

But now there was this voice, and it was asking for help, and it might be Bridget, calling on Grace in her trouble, as her mother had never done. Grace clenched her teeth. If these things were to do with Bridget, living or dead, there was only one other place Grace could possibly go to find out what was happening—the Sand Island lighthouse. Bridget's home. If her shade or her body was anywhere, it was there.

She'd have to go out on the lake to the island.

Memory rolled over her as it always did. That the terror was thirty years old did nothing to lessen it. She remembered the water pressing relentlessly against her filling eyes and ears. She remembered the taste of it in her mouth, the pain in her lungs, how her fingers stretched up to the light, how her own skirts entangled her like a net and dragged her down. She remembered the silence, and her heart hammering against her ribs.

Fear tightened her throat, turning her breath into gasps. Fear shifted the ground under her feet, and Grace caught herself against Everett's stone. The icy edge of it bit into her palm even through her mitten, reminding her where she was and in a moment she was able to stand again.

Grace pulled her shawls more tightly around her. *I could turn away. I should turn away. It would serve her right. She turned away from me.*

This time, though, the anger was a lie, and Grace knew it. It was because she was afraid. Afraid of the deep water, afraid of what lay asleep beneath it waiting for life and warmth. That was why she hadn't gone to see Ingrid while she waited in Everett's house to give birth to Bridget. She couldn't make herself cross the lake again. She had thought there would be time. She had believed Ingrid must come to Bayfield at some time, and then they'd meet and then . . .

And then Ingrid died.

Deep inside herself, Grace felt her heart stir. If this was a genuine plea for help from the only one of her family who had ever reached out for her, her heart would break again, and this time it would not heal.

Wrapping herself as well as she could against the strengthening wind, Grace took herself down the sloping road to the lakeside and the port.

Normally, Bayfield's port was a busy place, but winter's cold had brought it to a standstill. The big steamers had all left for open water and big cities to the south. The fishing boats wintering at the quayside all rested in cradles on the shore to keep them from being broken by the ice that would soon form. A few men braved the cold, but they did not linger about as they would have in spring or summer. They strode purposefully between the grounded boats, chins tucked in their high coat collars and hands thrust deep into their pockets.

Grace made her way between the curving sides of the boats, trying not to look at the dull silver expanse of water that waited beyond them. She pushed open the door to the long, grey shack that was the harbormaster's quarters, letting in a swirl of snow and cold to announce her entrance. Men huddled by the stove cursed in rough voices, looked up, saw a female form, and shut their mouths. It took them a minute longer to see which female it happened to be. Eyebrows lifted. Pipes were pulled from mouths.

Grace did not give any of the weather-roughened men a chance to make their comments. "I'm looking for Mr. Bluchard." She lifted her shawl from around her head and shook off the blown snow that clung to it, casually, as if being stared at by eight or so fishermen was a matter of no moment to her.

Francis Bluchard must have gotten down here early, because he had a spot right next to the potbellied stove. He stood up, straightening out his whole, lean length. He'd never been a handsome man, but standing against the hard work of years had given his horsey face and brown eyes a comfortable solidity and assurance.

And he remembered to call her "Miss" in public, something not many did. This raised Grace's estimation of him.

He took his long-stemmed pipe from his mouth and tapped it against his palm. "What can I do for you, Miss Loftfield?" he asked.

"I'd like a word with you, if I may." She left the "in private" implied. More than one of the men caught that implication, however, and knowing glances were exchanged. Someone sniggered. Grace held her ground. She was old enough that she was no longer an object of attraction to these ruffians. Her past, however, was well known and still good for a ripe joke.

Frank glanced left and right at his compatriots, laid his pipe on the stove, and made his way through their ranks to her. No one said a word. Frank gestured toward the office, and Grace walked ahead of him until they were both inside. He did not close the door.

For a moment they faced each other against a background of battered wood furniture and stacks of bills, notices, and receipts. Grace had known Frank all her life. He'd taken over the tug from his father. He'd been the one who took her from Sand Island to Bayfield after Father had forbidden her entry to his house.

"This about Bridget, then, Grace?" he asked, awkwardness making his voice gruff.

Grace nodded. "I'd like . . . I need . . ." Her tongue faltered. *Say it. You must.* "I need . . . you to take me out to the lighthouse."

Frank stared. He was also the one who sat by her on that last passage, as she huddled in on herself, quaking in her terror as if she'd shake herself to bits. That was something else she'd never forgotten.

Now, he shook his head heavily. "She's not there anymore."

"Yes, I know." Grace searched for an acceptable lie. "I've had a telegram from her. She left some things behind and asked me to collect them for her." If Frank thought to check at the office, he'd catch her out, of course, but somehow she did not think he'd do it.

But he did cast an eye out the office window that looked over the port, watching the pale grey water under the steely sky. Ice soon, said the water. Snow sooner, said the clouds. Even Grace could tell that much. "Well, it'll have to wait 'til spring."

But my nerve may not hold 'til spring. Grace's hands tightened around the ends of her shawl. "Frank, please. She's made another foolish decision. I have to let her know I'm her friend, so I can get her out of this before she strays beyond all salvation."

Frank looked down at her. He knew her history, and he'd never said a thing about it. Until now. "Funny words coming out of you, Grace."

Grace shrugged, but she found she could no longer meet his gaze. "Who would know better what she's letting herself in for?" Which was true, as far as it went.

Frank looked out the window again, his jaw working back and forth as if he were trying to shift the pipe he'd left on the stove. "I'm sorry, Grace. It ain't safe anymore."

For a moment Grace thought to make some tart remark. For another, she thought to offer to pay for her passage. But she was not sure which would insult Frank more deeply. He was only doing what he thought best. Not because he didn't think much of her, or because he did not approve, but for the simple, honest reason that Lake Superior was dangerous and she had told him nothing to make the risk worth it.

What would he do if she did tell him? What would he say? Grace realized she wanted to know. Would he think she was insane? What if he didn't? Frank had sailed the lake for a long time and seen any number of strange things. What if he believed her?

But the habits of thirty years were too strong to be overcome by the wonderings of a single moment, so Grace only lifted her chin. "Very well. Thank you for hearing me out, Frank."

Frank stuffed both hands in his pockets and looked toward the partially open door. "Grace, what have you heard about this thing?"

Odd choice of words. "Only what I've been told by Hilda, and Bridget," she remembered to add.

He scuffed the floor with the worn heel of one boot. "Well, when I was out there picking up the ones who want to winter on the mainland, they were telling me they saw fire up at the light."

"Fire?" Grace's hand went automatically to her throat.

Frank nodded. "Huge gout of flames shooting up into the sky folks said. Lit up the whole night. They thought the lighthouse had caught fire. Soon as it was day, they got out the boats and went round to Lighthouse Point, and there was the house, everything fine. 'Cept it was empty, and dark, and Bridget wasn't nowhere."

Trust Hilda to leave this out. Bridget vanished is the news of the day but a tiny detail like a fire . . . Grace swallowed anger and fear both. "She wasn't there when you went to pick her up?"

"Nor any sign of fire neither, except by the stove where the wall'd been charred a bit. Nothing like people said they saw."

Grace shrugged and her gaze slid sideways. "People say they see all sorts of things."

"That they do, Grace." *Especially in your family,* Grace added in her own mind, but a glance at Frank told her that if he had thought such a thing, he wasn't going to say it, for which she was grateful. "But they don't always say they've seen the same thing, nor yet do they get out the boats to go have a look at it."

"No," agreed Grace.

Frank cocked his head. "Don't suppose Bridget said anything about what that might have been in that telegram she sent you? Nor how she got off the island? Because I didn't take her, and the lighthouse's dory is still in the boathouse."

In those words, Frank told her that he knew she had lied, but he was going to leave her some dignity nonetheless.

"No," said Grace again, her determination deflating. "Bridget did not tell me any of these things."

Frank drew his hands out of his pockets, flexing them awkwardly as if looking for something to grab, or maybe to hand over. "I'm sorry, Grace. Truly."

Grace's hands tightened around the ends of her shawl. "Yes, I know. Thank you."

"I'd take you if I could, but the ice is on the way, and it's just too damn dangerous. I can't take you out when I'm not sure I can get you back." A plea for understanding crept into his gruff voice. "Soon as the way's open in spring, we'll go, if you still want to."

Grace did not reach out to touch his hand. Someone might be watching. She did manage a weak smile. "Thank you, Frank." She turned to go.

"Take care, Grace," said Frank behind her. "And if you hear from Bridget . . ."

"I'll tell her you said hello," Grace said, not letting him finish. "Thank you." That much, at least, she meant.

Cold wrapped around her and the stiff wind cut against her cheeks as Grace turned toward the grey expanse of the lake. The water was sluggish, weighted down with snow and cold. The reflection of the cloudy sky turned the water the color of tarnished steel. She stared across the bay, letting the wind raise the tears in her eyes.

They saw a fire up at the light.

It's what the living have been up to that you don't want to face.

Bridget Lederle's gone.

Help me.

"Where are you?" she murmured. "Where's your baby who should be in her grave?"

Grace clutched her shawls, trying to warm herself against a cold that came from inside her.

"What's happening, Bridget?" she asked the wind. "Where in God's name *are* you?"

Chapter One

Bridget Lederle stood under a canopy in the icy spring rain waiting for a fox.

Bridget had grown up on an island in Lake Superior. She was used to cold, or so she had thought. The Isavaltan winter had taught her a few things, however, as had the frigid flood that was spring. Her mouth quirked up into a tiny smile. Actually, it wasn't spring yet. It was *rasputitsa,* "the time of the road's undoing." She had to agree with Sakra about this. Any land, he said, that had a separate word for the time when the roads turned from ice to mud was to be regarded with caution, and to be avoided if possible.

Yet, here she stood, in the imperial gardens of Vyshtavos palace, at midnight, under a canopy that bowed under the weight of the water that had collected on it. Beside her, a tin lantern hissed and steamed as raindrops and runoff from the canopy spattered against it.

Bridget shivered, despite the fur-trimmed cloak she wore over her woolen dress. She had sent her servants, Richikha and Prathad, to wait closer to the palace. The one she came to meet would not appear before so much of an audience. So, just now she was alone in this land of cold and magic, a world away from where she had been born. Here, where she was an attendant to an imperial family, and a sorceress, and beloved.

It was a strange thing. She had gone through much of her life alone, not because she wished to, but because she felt it was the only way she could survive. Now she was surrounded by people who sought her company or assistance, and she found herself frequently wishing she could be alone again, if only so she could think clearly.

Bridget rubbed her eyes. It was a heavy night, and it brought heavy thoughts. She had been through so many changes so quickly she hadn't had time to adjust to them all. She would though, she was certain, and she would do so soon. After all, she had plenty of help.

Bridget lifted her head, and saw the Vixen sitting on the other side of the canal.

She had come in her guise as a female fox. Bridget knew she had other forms and faces, but this was the only one she had seen. The Vixen was the queen of the *lokai,* the fox spirits. Even in the gloom of the rainy night, her fur was a bright red and her chest blazed white. Indeed, there seemed to be moonlight where she was, although it shone nowhere else. She also seemed completely untouched by the freezing rain.

How convenient. Bridget immediately silenced the sardonic thought. The Vixen was powerful, cunning, mischievous, and untrustworthy, and if she was treated with anything but the deepest courtesy, she could become suddenly and permanently dangerous.

Bridget reverenced in the Isavaltan style—eyes lowered, one leg slightly extended, and her hands folded across her breast. When she looked up again, the Vixen had dropped her pointed muzzle open so that she looked to be laughing.

"You learn your lessons well, Bridget Lederle." She spoke English, and Bridget found herself startled to hear her native tongue after so many months.

It took her a moment to rally an answer in the same language. "I do my best, ma'am."

"And very properly too, I am sure." The Vixen dipped her laughing muzzle. Although she appeared no larger than an ordinary fox, Bridget had the sudden sensation of being looked down upon. "The good and dutiful daughter, and the faithful lover."

Bridget had resolved to remain calm through this interview but now she felt herself blush like a schoolgirl. True, she had not consummated her relationship with Sakra, but she had felt that desire, and it was growing stronger.

The Vixen was laughing again. Bridget struggled to regain her self-control.

"You wished to speak to me, I believe, ma'am," she said, folding her hands in front of her, a gesture from her previous life when she wore an apron instead of mantles and brocades. She remembered Prathad divesting her of her grey work dress for the last time, and how the woman looked as if she'd like to burn the garment.

"So I did." The Vixen tipped her head to one side. "I am surprised you were able to tell. I had not thought your sight to be so clear as it once was."

"What could have changed?" Bridget clamped her mouth shut, but it was too late. The words were out.

Do not ask questions if you can help it, Sakra had advised her. *Let her do as much of the talking as you can. Questions can reveal as much as answers.*

The Vixen swished her bushy tail back and forth. "Perhaps much, perhaps little." Bridget saw her green eyes gleam in her strange, isolated patch of moonlight. "Perhaps the dutiful daughter and lover has forgotten she had other duties to look to, and others who look to her."

Bridget found her mind racing backward, to the lighthouse on Sand Island, to all her long, lonely days as keeper. She had worked hard, living alone, tending the light, and warning the sailors. The man she called her father was long dead. His ghost had forgiven her for all that had happened. She'd had a housekeeper, Mrs. Hansen, and Mrs. Hansen's son Samuel . . . had something happened to them? To the lighthouse?

But why would the Vixen care? Sand Island, Bayfield, and Lake Superior Islands had nothing to do with the *lokai.* They belonged to other powers. The Vixen's place was here.

So why is she bringing up my past?

This time, Bridget kept the question silent.

The Vixen clacked her jaws and stood up, raising one paw as if to take a step. "Such eyes. Such sight, but always looking too far away. You should be looking close as skin, Bridget Lederle, close as blood."

She was being goaded, and Bridget knew it. Perhaps she should just let the Vixen leave. If she did, though, night after night, the fact of this visit would gall her and Bridget would wonder what the Vixen might have said if she, Bridget, had spoken, if the Vixen had stayed just a moment longer. Bridget had no doubt the Vixen was fully aware of that.

Close as skin, close as blood . . . that spoke of family.

"I have no one of my blood who acknowledges me," Bridget said.

The Vixen combed her ear with her paw. "No? Are you sure? Daughter and lover, niece and aunt, are you that sure of all your family?"

Oh, yes, thought Bridget. *Of that I am very sure.* "I thank you for your advice, ma'am. Was there anything else?"

The Vixen scratched her chin. "Well, that depends. Some time ago, you helped free something from your home. It has taken time, but it has returned to its own home, and it's been busy. As you once did a favor for me and mine, I'd thought to show you how busy, but since your past is of so little interest to you, perhaps you would only be bored."

Bridget's heart skipped a beat. Could the Vixen be talking about the sorcerer Kalami? Or something older, and even more deadly?

"If you please," said Bridget, trying not to sound too anxious. "I'd be glad to see whatever you might have to show me."

The Vixen scratched her chin vigorously for a moment, apparently considering. Bridget's mouth went dry. Had she misstepped too badly? But, at last, the Vixen sighed. "Very well. If you would see, close your right eye."

The Vixen turned tail and whisked away, accompanied by her patch of moonlight. Bridget laid her hand over her right eye, and watched the Vixen's departure. Although the *lokai*'s queen trotted away at a good clip, she did not appear to grow any more distant. It was as if she pulled Bridget along behind her, but Bridget did not feel herself move. The world around her faded away, and all Bridget could see was the red fox moving steadily through a place of formless darkness.

More familiar with such workings than she once had been, Bridget held still. She knew herself to no longer be in the gardens. She held tight to the idea that wherever she was, the Vixen had not brought her here to harm her. Probably.

The darkness moved. It writhed, it bulged, and in places, it lifted. Before her, Bridget saw a fantastical collection of creatures, each stranger than the last. A green, glittering serpent with a body thicker than her waist lay coiled beside a golden eagle the size of a full-grown man. There was a dragon, glowing red, gold, and silver with sharp, old intelligence in its strangely whiskered face. Beside it waited an animal Bridget could not name. It had a particolored body roughly the shape of a horse and a whiskered face like the dragon's, only larger and more snubbed at the muzzle. A single, short, green horn protruded from its forehead.

In the middle of them all sat the Firebird. Formed entirely of flame and even larger than the eagle, the magnificent creature shone so brightly that it drew tears from Bridget's eye. Despite the pain, she did not dare look away. Gold, orange, red, and white, the Firebird burned in the infinite blackness. The light of its flames shone in the eyes of the other creatures and played across their bodies.

The Vixen's purposeful gait slowed to a saunter as she approached the other creatures. All of them turned to glower at her. Either she had grown larger at some point, or the others were not so big as Bridget had thought.

"Oh, I'm so sorry," the Vixen said as she entered their circle. "Am I late? Do go on." She sat down on her haunches, her tail swishing back and forth.

The eagle turned its glaring red eye back to the Firebird. "Speak then," it said. "What is it you desire?"

"Retribution," said the Firebird. Its voice was quiet and dangerous, like the crackle of a fresh wildfire creeping across the forest floor.

The others watched the Firebird in silence. "Retribution," it said again. "It is mine to ask. I have been imprisoned and I have been unlawfully used. I may claim vengeance."

The brown tortoise raised its ponderous head. "We are guardians," it said in a voice as weighty as the earth itself. "We exist to protect. We are not furies, nor should we seek to be."

"We judge. We punish the transgressors and the impious." The Firebird spread its brilliant wings. "It is our duty. I claim that duty and that right!"

The serpent lifted itself, uncoiling its body until its eyes were level with the Firebird's. The light played along its scales, making them appear to be moving even when the great snake held itself still. "We may all see who has transgressed. But who are the impious?"

The Firebird beat its wings once against the empty night. Bridget imagined she could feel an incredible heat waft off them. "They summoned me to their need, and did me no honor. They left me in the hands of the enemy of the sacred lands, as if I were only the spoils of the war from which they begged to be saved. It cannot be condoned."

"What was done, that was done for the sake of protecting those who stood helpless against your power," said the eagle. Its voice was harsh where the Firebird's was smooth. Its feathers were like burnished bronze. "That is right and natural, and is allowed by the laws."

The Firebird crouched low and drew in its fiery wings. Eye to eye it faced the great eagle. "Not like this," it hissed. "Thirty years in a cage, always under the threat that I might be turned against my own people. No rest, no respite or quarter. There was only the pain of the bars and the binding spells, and those who owed me honor, who sacrificed and were sacrificed, did nothing to bring me ease or release. They would have permitted me to be made into a profane thing and then tried to destroy me."

The creatures all stood silent at that, but Bridget felt that they did more than imagine what had happened to the Firebird. They shared it. Each of them felt the constriction of those bars and the dreadful heaviness of whatever force could hold such a creature against its will.

These creatures knew patience and they knew duty, but they also knew mercy, Bridget was sure of it, although she could not have said why. But there was no mercy for this, none at all.

"I will not oppose your retribution," said the dragon slowly.

"Nor I," said the tortoise.

The eagle hung its great, proud head. "Nor I."

That same answer echoed around the circle of fantastic judges, until it came to the Vixen.

"Tell me," said the fox mildly, "when you have taken your retribution, what then?"

"What can that matter to you?" retorted the Phoenix.

The Vixen blinked her green eyes. "Little, little. This is, of course, only to satisfy my idle curiosity."

"We have seen your kits sport in other ruins." The snake shifted its coils silently. "I would think this deed exactly to your taste."

The Vixen opened her mouth in her expression of silent laughter. "Oh, the opportunities for such sport will be many, I am sure, and yet, that is not what I asked. I asked, when this retribution is done, what will our revered compatriot do then?"

"I will return to my home," the Firebird replied.

"Will you?" The Vixen clacked her jaws together once. "Will you, indeed?"

"Do you withhold your consent?" asked the dragon, its trailing whiskers bristling with impatience.

The Vixen turned and nosed her tail, setting the brush of it in order. "Oh, no, no. Certainly not. I only wondered."

The horse-shaped creature for which Bridget could find no name stomped its foot and shook its shaggy head. "It is agreed, then," it said solemnly. "The Phoenix may have its retribution and no guardian shall oppose or intervene."

At those words, the creatures faded back into the darkness until only the Firebird and the Vixen remained.

The Firebird stretched out its neck, towering high over the Vixen, the living flames streaming from its back and wings.

"What do you want of me?" it demanded.

The Vixen shrugged. Her coat glowed bright red in the shifting light of the Firebird, so bright it almost seemed to be the color of blood. "Nothing at all."

"You are no proper guardian. You have no right to judge me."

"You have no comprehension of what I stand guard over," replied the Vixen, and Bridget saw how her teeth shone sharp and yellow. "Take your vengeance if you must, but be wary. There will come times after your vengeance when you may yet be called to answer. Such as you cannot bring about true endings. That is for others."

"Do you threaten me?"

"Not I." The Vixen twitched the tip of her tail.

The Firebird thrust its head forward. "Then leave me to my business."

The Vixen's eyes took in the living flames and reflected them back without flinching. "Go then." She pointed with her muzzle. "I am not the one who keeps you here."

The Firebird lifted its blazing wings and launched itself into darkness, and was gone, and Bridget was back under her canopy in the freezing rain of the garden.

Bridget lowered her hand from her right eye. Her lungs heaved as if she had just run a mile. The Vixen was nowhere to be seen.

The Firebird is coming back. Bridget swallowed hard, afraid to move in case the Vixen should suddenly reappear with some last cryptic bit of news. *The Firebird is coming for revenge.*

When the Vixen did not reappear, Bridget snatched up her hems in one hand and the lantern in the other and raced across the lawn toward the darkened palace.

The Firebird was one of the four guardians of the empire of Hung-Tse that lay to the south of Isavalta. Twenty-eight years earlier, the measure of Bridget's life, Empress Medeoan of Isavalta had managed to cage the creature. Her death the previous winter had freed it, and it had vanished. The sorcerers whom the new emperor, Mikkel, brought to court had searched the realms of the flesh and the spirit and found no trace of it. It was determined the creature had returned to the fire from which it was born.

Apparently they'd been wrong.

Bridget's feet found the road up to Vyshtavos's main gates. In daylight, the palace was an elaborate octagonal stone edifice, thick with lace-like trimming and formidable gargoyles. Now, all that separated it from the night were the lanterns and torches of the guards on patrol around its walls and a few lights in widely scattered windows.

Richikha, Prathad, and the two soldiers Bridget had been assigned for this night emerged from the guardhouse. Richikha tried to slip a fresh cloak over Bridget's shoulders, but Bridget waved her off.

"I must see the emperor. Right now."

"He is sure to be asleep, mistress . . ." began Richikha.

Bridget didn't let her finish. "For this he'll wake up. I've received a vision from the Vixen."

"I'll go," said Prathad. She was an older woman. Her dark hair had gone almost entirely grey and a perpetual sadness haunted her brown eyes.

"Make sure Sakra and the lord sorcerer are told as well."

Prathad reverenced hastily and strode off to find the guard who would find the page who would find the manservant, who would have the unenviable job of waking up the emperor of Isavalta.

All of which would take some time. Bridget now allowed Richikha to strip off her sodden coat and drape a dry one over her shoulders. She had to admit it felt better.

"Thank you," she remembered to say as she strode across the cobbled courtyard. A few lights looked down on her passage. One of those lights would be Sakra. He had not told Bridget he would be waiting up for her. There was no need. They both knew it would be so. If her news was not so dire, that knowledge would have made Bridget smile.

As they reached the main doors, the guards were ready to pull open the great portals and servants waited inside with lamps to light the way up the grand staircase to the imperial floor.

Richikha deftly relieved Bridget of her new coat. "With your permission, mistress...?" she began. Bridget nodded and the serving woman scurried away toward Bridget's room to deal with both the wet and dry outer garments.

Bridget entered the imperial antechamber. The doors to the apartments themselves were still closed, but the guards and pages on duty looked quite alert. Evidently, Prathad had already completed part of her errand, because Sakra waited here as well.

Sakra was a dark man with eyes the color of amber. His long hair was parted into dozens of small braids. They spilled down his back, drawn into a tidy bundle with red ribbon. This was the mark of a sorcerer from his far southern homeland of Hastinapura. Each braid was part of some spell that would be released if he unbound it. Despite his foreign origins, he wore the clothes of a noble of Isavalta—a wine-colored kaftan and a sable sash and pantaloons tucked into leather boots.

"What's happened, Bridget?"

Bridget glanced toward the guards and held up her hand. Sakra understood and asked no more. He just touched her hand briefly in acknowledgment of the pallor he surely saw on her face.

Just then the lord sorcerer, Daren Dobrilosyn Abukanvin, rounded the corner with Prathad two steps behind. Unlike Sakra, Lord Daren had obviously been roused from his sleep. His clothes, hair, and beard were all disordered and he was attempting to smooth them down as he strode forward.

"What is it?" he demanded. "Is it the Vixen?"

There was no time for Bridget to answer. A liveried footman opened the doors and stood aside, thumping his staff once on the floor.

"Their Imperial Majesties will hear you now."

The footman stood aside. Lord Daren made one more attempt at smoothing down his wild hair and brushing his sleeves into some semblance of neatness as he entered the room. Bridget and Sakra followed close behind him.

The reception chamber of the imperial apartments was grand in the old Isavaltan style. That, to Bridget's mind, meant chiefly that it was cold and stony. The lush tapestries on the walls did little to screen out the drafts seeping across the floor. The buttresses and arches with their frescoes and divine imagery were artistically interesting but they offered no warmth or comfort. The firepit, for all it was a solid bed of coals, did little to help.

Mikkel, the young emperor of Isavalta, stood beside his wife, the Empress Ananda. Mikkel was a handsome youth—tall, fair, with broad shoulders and the beginnings of a curling beard. Ananda was from Hastinapura, as was her sorcerer, Sakra. She was dark of skin and hair. Her amber eyes slanted above her high cheekbones.

As usual, a small army of servants swarmed around the imperial couple, lighting candles and lamps, setting chairs near the firepit, decanting strong wine and mixing it with water, just in case this meeting went on long enough that refreshment was required.

Bridget and those who entered with her began to kneel, as was required by Isavaltan etiquette, but Mikkel stopped them with a raised hand.

"What has happened, mistress?" he asked Bridget. "What did you learn?"

Bridget straightened up, ignoring the look that Lord Daren shot her. He set great store by matters of protocol. "Sir, madame," the term "Majesty" did not yet come easily to Bridget. "The Firebird is still in the world, and it means to have its revenge."

Mikkel blanched white, and even Ananda looked suddenly pale.

"How is this?" cried Lord Daren. "We searched, Majesties. All across the world and through the Land of Death and Spirit. The Firebird was nowhere."

"I know," said Bridget. "But it's back now."

"The Vixen showed you this?" Ananda's fingertips touched the back of Mikkel's hand. "That power is not to be trusted."

"No, but she said she was showing me . . . this event because of the favor I'd done her family. She wouldn't lie about an obligation."

Mikkel glanced to Lord Daren. "No, Majesty, that is quite true," admitted the lord sorcerer. "No spirit power will tell a falsehood about a promise or a debt, although they may not tell the whole truth."

"Can you ascertain the truth of what the Vixen showed Mistress Bridget?" asked the emperor.

Being consulted on the matter appeared to mollify Lord Daren. "The Firebird is one of the great guardians. It could not be fully in the world and remain unseen." The statement neatly sidestepped the issue of how it had remained unseen before. "All the sorcerers of your court will bend their sight to it."

"Thank you. If the sorcerers of the land must be alerted, I do not wish to send out any false missive." Mikkel's mother had exiled all sorcerers but one from her court. He had begun to find and recall those who had served the old emperor and empress, but although none had disobeyed, it was well known some were not delighted to be pressed into service of such a family again.

"There is another point which should be considered," said Daren.

"Which is?" Apprehension touched Mikkel's words, and Ananda drew minutely closer to her husband.

"Whether this vengeance is the Firebird's own, or is sent by the Nine Elders." The Nine Elders were the sorcerers who defended the empire of Hung-Tse from all ill-intentioned magics, whether they were malevolent or merely mischievous.

Bridget shook her head. "I think the Nine Elders are in at least as much trouble as Isavalta, and I sincerely doubt they know it's coming." She shuddered at the memory of the Firebird's voice as it spoke of those who should have rescued it but did not.

"Which leaves us with the possibility that they will think we are the ones who unleashed the Firebird on them," said Mikkel. "That was ever my mother's threat."

A look of swift calculation took hold on the empress's face, and she did not seem to like the conclusions she was reaching. "Could we not warn them?" Ananda asked Sakra. "Is there not some way . . . ?"

Lord Daren was the one who answered. "There may be, Majesty, it is a question of whether there is time enough."

Mikkel drew back his shoulders. He was about to give an order, his whole stance said it. That was not always easy for him, and Bridget tensed. "Let there be no delay. Use whatever means you have to reach the Nine Elders. I will send a message by courier as soon as may be. All efforts are to be turned toward finding the Firebird and divining its movements, under your direction, Lord Daren."

Bridget softly expelled the breath she'd been holding.

"Majesty," Lord Daren reverenced, but Bridget caught the victorious gleam in his eye. It had been acknowledged in front of Sakra that Daren was the one in charge. She suppressed a sigh. Did the man never think beyond petty politics?

The empress glanced around ruefully. "I think no one will sleep much tonight, but return in the morning and we may face this trouble in the full light of day."

Dismissed, Bridget, Sakra, and Lord Daren reverenced and backed out of the doors that were closed, leaving them standing again in the antechamber with Prathad and the cluster of imperial servitors.

"Well, Mistress Bridget, you bring us grave news indeed," sighed Lord Daren. For a change, he just sounded tired and worried instead of critical. "You will forgive me if I hope this is some deception on the part of the *lokai*'s queen."

Bridget's smile was tight, and completely without humor. "Sir, if you find out I've been taken in, I will be the first to cheer."

"Hmph." There was an "I'll believe it when I see it" look to Daren as he wrapped his heavy robe more tightly around himself. "I must go rouse my fellows."

Sakra stepped forward, not quite getting in Daren's way, but making sure he was seen. "Lord Daren, I beg you to let me know how I may assist."

"I will, but I'm sure the empress will want you free to consult with her come the morning."

Which meant he would make sure Sakra was kept as far from the work as possible. Bridget felt her mouth purse in disapproval as the lord sorcerer strode out with his servants in tow. Daren did not like Sakra. He did not like the fact that Sakra was a foreigner, and he did not like Sakra's influence with the empress. He never said so out loud, but he made it plain with a hundred small slights. Bridget was well aware of this, because he played the same sorts of games with her.

Bridget looked to Sakra with a sigh. She set aside Daren's behavior. Now was not the time to take umbrage.

"I suppose I should have known there would be consequences from what happened," she said instead.

Sakra shook his head. "You are not the only one."

"If you please, mistress."

Bridget started slightly. She was getting into the bad habit of forgetting that Prathad was in the room. She met her maid's gaze.

Prathad hesitated. "Is it . . . was it . . . is this because of my former mistress?"

Once, Prathad had been lady-in-waiting to the Dowager Empress Medeoan, and she had been the last to remain loyal when Medeoan finally went mad. Not even Ananda could bring herself to give the woman a new position after the disaster that brought Medeoan down. Bridget, however, knew about bad luck, and what it was to be unwanted. So, when she was told her new status allowed her two lady's maids, she'd asked for Prathad to be assigned to her.

"If this is what it appears to be, Prathad, there will be plenty of blame to go around." Bridget sighed again. "Let's go back to the room, shall we? It's going to be a long night." She looked at Sakra as she said it, letting him know he was welcome. The truth of the matter was she didn't want to be alone just yet, although she was not sure she was ready to speak about what else the Vixen had said. Better to let it lie, perhaps. At least until she had a better understanding of the riddle.

Sakra walked beside her through the shadowy corridors. They both knew better than to talk of important things in Vyshtavos's halls. There was no knowing who was listening, even at such an uncivilized hour. Vyshtavos functioned on rumor and intrigue. In that it was very like a small town. It had not taken Bridget long to learn to guard her tongue.

When Bridget had declared her intention to settle in Isavalta, she had been made a lady-in-waiting to the empress. She was not, however, a lady of the chamber, so she had her own rooms on the imperial level, rather than having to live in the imperial apartments.

She actually had more than that, and that was something she would have to deal with sooner or later.

So much to get used to, she thought ruefully. *And now this new thing from the Vixen, whatever it means. If we don't all get burnt to cinders, I will have to try to puzzle it out.*

Perhaps I should have stayed on Sand Island after all.

They reached Bridget's door. Prathad stepped forward smoothly to open it before Bridget could even get her hand out. Having Prathad at her side proved a mixed blessing some days. She knew a great deal about the customs and the country, and she was dedicated to helping Bridget understand both. As she had once been waiting lady to an empress, however, she had a little trouble with her new mistress's more informal ways.

Inside, Richikha dozed in her chair, but came instantly awake as Bridget stepped into the chamber. She had not been idle. The firepit had been tended and now held a cheerful blaze to fight the room's chill. Beside the fire waited a covered silver pitcher of something that filled the room with the scent of cinnamon and old apples.

Sakra stopped politely at the chamber's threshold.

"Please come in," said Bridget.

Sakra stepped inside. Richikha and Prathad offered no comment. They just bustled about, bringing forward a small table, a second chair, setting out two cups for the warm cider.

"Thank you both," she said to her ladies. "You can get ready for bed. I'm going to sit up for a while."

She didn't think either one of them was actually going to retire while she was awake, but at least they might sit down and relax for a few moments. They both did reverence and retired behind the wooden screens that separated the living and the sleeping portions of the room.

"Please sit down," said Bridget to Sakra as she took her own chair and drew it closer to the fire. Even her stay in the imperial apartments had failed to take away all the chill from the garden and the rain.

Sakra gave her a sympathetic smile.

"You'd think I'd be used to the cold." Bridget held her long-fingered hands out to warm.

"I don't think it's possible for anyone to get used to the Isavaltan cold."

"You've never wintered near Lake Superior."

"A portion of your life I am not sorry to have missed," he replied blandly. He poured a measure of cider into a silver cup and handed it across to her.

"There were a few of those winters I would not have been sorry to miss either." She accepted the cup and raised it to him in a small toast. He raised his in return and they drank. The hard cider and bright spices warmed Bridget's stomach instantly. She lowered the cup, and saw Sakra watching her, waiting for whatever she had to say.

To her embarrassment, she sought delay. "Lord Daren doesn't think much of either of us."

Sakra sipped his own cider thoughtfully, but did not look away from her. "Lord Daren is uncertain of his position. He was removed from it before. Losing power is a difficult thing to face, especially for such a sorcerer as he is."

"I suppose it would be." Bridget rested her fingers on the rim of her cup. She could think of nothing else to say, and yet she couldn't say what she wanted to.

"Bridget, did the Vixen say something to you personally?"

Bridget considered telling him that she was just tired and worried about the Firebird, but then she looked up at Sakra's eyes, and saw he already knew this was not the truth.

Daughter and lover, niece and aunt, are you that sure of all your family? What did she mean?

Bridget rolled the cup back and forth in her hands. "She seemed to be interested in my family. She asked was I certain of how all my family felt about me. She said, 'Daughter and lover, niece and aunt, are you that sure of all your family?'" Bridget watched the steam rise from her cider. "Why would she care about what might be happening on Sand Island? Or Bayfield? And what has any of that to do with the fact that the Firebird's coming here?" She frowned and shook her head.

"Daughter, lover, niece, and aunt," said Sakra. "Is that all that she called you?"

Bridget thought back carefully. The Vixen played games with words. No turn of phrase was accidental. "Yes," she said at last. "Why?"

Sakra's face went very still. "Bridget, you are also a mother."

Bridget's hand tightened around her cup. "My daughter is dead."

"Nonetheless."

Bridget bit her lip. Sakra was right, of course. She was a mother. The hollow pain that took hold of her heart whenever she thought of the swaddled babe in her arms told her that.

No turn of the Vixen's phrase was an accident, neither was any omission.

"Anna is nine years gone, Sakra. I held . . ." She swallowed. "I held her body. I saw her buried. I didn't . . . I'd never even heard the word 'Isavalta' when I lost her. How can the fact I once had a child mean anything to anyone here?"

"I don't know," he answered with the quiet honesty that was the central facet of his character. "What else did she ask you?"

Bridget set her cup down on the lacquered table. Her hand had begun to shake. Yet, if she did not answer his question, it would gall her. When the Vixen set one on a path, one had to follow. She was a power, and her touch, however mild, was not to be resisted.

As best she could, Bridget repeated the whole of her conversation with the Vixen. Sakra listened in silence, his only comment the deepening furrows of his brow.

"As close as skin, as close as blood," he murmured when Bridget ran out of words. "And other duties. Bridget, I fear you are right, she spoke of your family."

"And you think she meant Anna somehow?"

Sakra nodded.

"Oh, God." Bridget tried to turn away from the idea, to dismiss it from her mind utterly. Anna was dead. Bridget had been put on trial for that death. She had stood in dock and listened to Ernie Lawrence, Bayfield's prosecuting attorney, spew invective at her for that death. It was Anna's death as much as anything else that had driven her from Sand Island and into this strange, vast, welcoming world where she now lived.

"This is ridiculous." Bridget rubbed her hands together as if she were Lady Macbeth and was afraid of seeing blood on her palms. "She's trying to distract me. We should be helping Lord Daren track down the Firebird. Surely, you and Mistress Urshila can help me bring up a vision . . ."

Sakra did not let her finish. "Bridget, have you . . . ever seen Anna's ghost?"

Bridget swallowed with difficulty. "No." Her voice was hoarse, and she did not trust herself to speak more than that one word. She had seen the shades of her mother and her father, and the man whom she had grown up with as her father. But not her baby.

"And you did not seek to." Sakra spoke the words for her.

Bridget nodded her agreement, her mouth still firmly closed.

Sakra sat silently for a moment, giving himself time to think, and giving Bridget time to collect herself. Of all the things that might possibly have brought her again to the Vixen's attention . . . this had not even entered her mind. How was it possible she was sitting here with Sakra discussing Anna?

Sakra reached out and touched the arm of her chair, his fingertips a hairsbreadth from her sleeve. "I am sorry, Bridget, but can you tell me how Anna died?"

Bridget licked her lips. Of course she could, but she did not want to. "She just . . . it was a cradle death. It was night. I woke up to help Poppa tend the light, when I came back down . . ." She could not say it. Nine years later and a world away, and she could not say it. "I tried," she said instead. "I did everything I could think of. If I'd been a moment earlier . . . If I'd done more than glance into the cradle instead of the light, maybe . . ." That was the thought that had echoed through her head the entire time she stood in court. If she'd been a moment sooner. If she'd cared for her child first and her duty to her father and the light second. If, if, if . . .

Maybe she had truly wanted the child dead, as the prosecutor had said. Maybe she was taking revenge on her lover Asa Kyosti, who took her virtue and left with nothing but a bastard daughter.

Bridget closed her eyes.

"Then there was no mark upon her body? No cause or sign?" Sakra spoke as gently as he could, but the words still burned.

"No. It's . . . something that happens." A moment sooner. If she had looked into the cradle for more than a second. Spared Anna more than just a passing glance . . .

"Yes, I know. But it is also something which may be hastened . . . or it may be made false by magic."

Bridget's eyes flew open. "What are you saying?"

Sakra had drawn his hand back and now he rubbed it across his brow. "I don't know," he admitted.

"Are you saying someone . . . a sorcerer . . . from Isavalta might have murdered my baby?" Her voice rose high and sharp. "Why? How could they? They didn't even know I existed."

"But Medeoan knew your mother existed. Who knows when she first sent Kalami across to the world of your birth, and who knows what he saw there?"

Bridget pressed her hand against her mouth as if she were about to be sick. She was suddenly glad she was sitting, because her knees would not have supported her at that moment.

"Could Kalami have murdered my daughter? Why? Why would he murder a baby? Why not me? I was the threat to him."

"The children of sorcerers are a rare breed," said Sakra slowly. "When they come into being, they are powerful. You are the daughter of a sorcerer, Bridget. Your daughter would have been the third of her line, and I don't know that there has ever been such a child. There is no telling what her powers would have been."

Rage swelled like a fire in Bridget's heart. A single hot tear ran down her cheek, but whether it was for that rage or the cold sorrow that warred with it, she could not tell.

"Murdering bastard." She clenched her fists. "Murdering bastard." She tried to control herself, without success. "How could he do such a thing? Anna was an infant. She'd barely drawn breath. How could he do it!" She pounded the arm of her chair.

"There is one other possibility." Sakra held himself very still.

"What?" demanded Bridget. "Do you think Medeoan did this? Medeoan killed my child?"

"Bridget, your child might not be dead."

Bridget stared at him. She couldn't understand. His words made no sense. "What?"

"Your daughter, your Anna, might still be alive."

"Sakra, do not taunt me like this. Anna is dead. I buried her."

"Bridget, have you ever heard of a changeling? Or a stock?"

"A changeling is a fairy child left in place . . ." Bridget's voice died in her throat.

Sakra nodded as if she had completed a full sentance. "A stock is a wooden image, made to look like a certain individual, whoever or whatever the sorcerer desires. It is then enchanted and left in that person's place. It will live a few days, or a few weeks, depending on the strength of the spell, and then it appears to die, and is given funerary rites, as if it were the real person, but the real person is still alive."

It took a moment for Sakra's words to assemble themselves inside Bridget's mind in comprehensible phrases. When they did, Bridget knew her mouth fell open, but she could not move to close it.

"That's impossible. It couldn't be."

"Why?"

"Because." *Because I have been nine years alone mourning my child. Because I stood accused of her murder. Because if she were alive for all these nine years I could have been looking for her. I could have found her. Because if she was alive, I should have been doing something other than grieving her death.*

Oh, God. Oh, God. Bridget closed her eyes. "It can't be. I would have known."

"How, Bridget?"

"Because I was . . . I am . . . I was her mother!" Bridget bowed her head into her hands. "That was my baby I held. I would have known if it wasn't. I would have seen it! I would have seen her!" Her hands clenched into fists, and her knuckles pressed against her eyes. She would not cry. She would not cry.

Silence, and then the touch of Sakra's hand. Bridget unknotted one fist and wrapped her fingers tightly around his. She stayed like that for a moment, eyes closed, holding his warm hand like a lifeline, and not saying a word.

Gradually, she was able to open her eyes and lift up her head. Sakra stood beside her, his eyes filled with sympathy and concern. She drank in his gaze for a long moment, drawing into herself all the strength he could give, she needed it all to speak her next words.

"God Almighty, Sakra, could . . . could it be so? Could my Anna still be alive somewhere?"

Are you that sure of all your family? Had the Vixen truly stressed the word "all," or was that only Bridget's fancy?

"I don't know. I only know that such a thing can be done, and that Kalami was aware of you much longer than you were aware of him."

"God, Sakra, I don't . . . I have to . . ." She took a deep breath. "What do I do? Do I try to find her ghost?"

"That is one way."

The idea made her sick with fear, and worse than fear. Fear of what failure of such a spell would mean, and fear of what success would mean. She was in no way certain she could stand to look on the ghost of her infant daughter. Ashamed of her own cowardice, she asked, "Can you do it?"

"No."

"Why not?"

"I have no tie to her, Bridget. You and I are not married."

Bridget's throat tightened. She was not sure she could speak. To see her child again, even as a spirit. To see Anna with the eye of memory and imagination, which was how one beheld a ghost, to see the little girl and the young woman she had once imagined her child would one day be . . .

"Why is the Vixen doing this to me?" Bridget choked out. "Was it something I did? Have I offended her?"

Again, Sakra shook his head. "I cannot say. We have none such as her in Hastinapura. She was banished by the Seven Mothers millennia ago. I think, though, if she meant to avenge some offense, she would find another way than this to make you pay."

Bridget got to her feet. She paced aimlessly around the firepit. The stone walls seemed suffocating now. She wanted to tear them down, to see right through them to the Land of Death and Spirit to see Anna's ghost at peace there, and she wanted to be struck blind so she never would have to see such a thing.

At the same time, this was an uncertainty she could not bear. The whole of her felt balanced on a knife's edge. Now that the possibility that Anna might be alive had been raised, she had to know for certain.

Another thought came to her. "I'd have to go back to Wisconsin, wouldn't I?"

"I'm sorry?"

Bridget turned and faced Sakra. "To be sure, I'd have to go back to Wisconsin. Otherwise, any spell I might use, even with my second sight, if it didn't reach her . . . spirit, it might just be because I can't reach far enough, or that she can't cross to Isavalta. That's right, isn't it?"

Sakra considered and then nodded. "Ties of love and blood are immensely strong, but the space between worlds is vast. Were I to perform such a working, I would want to be near the bones."

"And if I went, now this minute, and the Firebird came to Isavalta, I'd be out of reach and unable to help stop whatever this vengeance might be."

Sakra considered, his brown eyes flickering back and forth. "That is also true."

"So either the Vixen is doing me a great favor by telling me my daughter may still be alive, or she is luring me away from Isavalta when my help would be most needed."

"Luring us," corrected Sakra.

For a single heartbeat, Bridget thought to say, "What do you mean?" but she realized she had no need. Sakra meant he would go with her back home. He would not leave her to face her daughter's grave alone.

Instead of that, she said, "You may not be permitted to go." Sakra was bound-sorcerer to the Empress Ananda. His first duty lay in serving her and the bond that had been solemnized by a series of complex oaths. Bridget knew he carried those oaths in the center of his soul.

She wanted to say, "Let's wait until we've found the Firebird. Then we'll go." But the words would not come. Anna's name pulsed through her mind in time to the beating of her quickened heart. What few memories she had appeared before her mind's eye. She remembered Anna, red and wrinkled, her dark hair plastered to her skull, how her eyes had opened and shown themselves to be green already, instead of the usual baby blue. She remembered warmth and living weight and the scent of sweet milk. With these actual memories came the remembrance of dreams. All mothers dreamed of their child's future, but Bridget with her second sight had more than usual reason to think hers might be true. She remembered telling herself how beautiful, how tall, how strong Anna would be. How she'd always raise her hand in class, how she'd be so quick and clever at her chores, and how well she'd read in the evenings. She'd go on to the teacher's college, or nursing school. Anna, Bridget, and, of course, Asa would move down to Madison . . .

So many dreams and not one of them showing her daughter's death. Was that because she did not die?

Bridget knew she would not be able to wait. The world might burn down around her ears, but she would still go. If it was possible that Anna lived, if there was even a faintest whisper of that impossible hope . . .

Bridget bowed her head. If this was the Vixen's trickery, she had done her work very well.

But Sakra had other duties, and other claims on his loyalties, whatever he might feel for her, or however much he might wish to help. Bridget knew that. She always knew that.

Perhaps that was why he had not yet spoken of love to her.

Bridget brushed that thought aside. "I'll speak to the empress in the morning," she said, clasping and unclasping her hands. "She'll surely give us leave once she understands . . ."

Which was something else she had to stop to consider. What if the empress did not give leave? She knotted her fingers together. Bridget would go anyway. She would find her way back across the gulf between worlds, but what then? If Anna lived, could Bridget find her alone? If

Kalami had done this unspeakable thing, where would he have taken her? To Tuukos, his homeland? Or someplace else? She had to leave to be sure Anna was alive, but could she come back to Isavalta if by leaving she defied the empress? Or would she be giving up this new life that promised to be so sweet, for something too faint even to be called hope?

Too many questions. Bridget felt positively sick with all of them churning around her skull.

"I have to go." The words fell from her one at a time without strength. She felt only defeat and fear, fear that this thing might be true and fear that it might not. "It doesn't matter what the Vixen's plan is."

"I know," said Sakra simply. Was that sorrow beneath his voice? She couldn't tell. She was too caught up in the whirl of her own emotions. She did not want to be this way. She wanted to be able to reach out to him, but the gulf was too wide.

"We can do nothing until morning," Sakra went on, setting his cup of cider down. "Will you try to sleep?"

"I don't think I can." Bridget ran her hands over her hair, as if trying to press down the thoughts filling her skull.

"Come, you must try." Sakra mustered a small smile. "If only for Richikha's and Prathad's sakes. They cannot go to bed until you do."

"Of course, of course, you're right." She glanced across at her maids, who waited in the corner, each sewing at some piecework, pretending to ignore what was happening by the fire. She stood, smoothing her dress down fussily. "I will go to bed now."

Prathad rose and reverenced, her face betraying no hint of the relief Bridget was sure she must be feeling. With Richikha, she went back behind the wooden screens that separated Bridget's bed from the rest of the apartment. The rustling of bedding being turned down and night attire being shaken out drifted from the sleeping alcove.

"I'm almost afraid to sleep," Bridget breathed. "I'm afraid I'll dream, or see something . . . Anna's ghost, or I don't know what." To her shame, her voice began to shake. "Sakra, this can't be true, but if it is . . . I don't know which way to turn."

Sakra moved closer to her so she could feel his warmth, his solidity. Close enough so she could touch him if she wanted to. "You have nothing to fear in this place, Bridget. I will watch over you until sleep comes."

It was a highly improper suggestion that he stay at her bedside, but

Bridget only looked up at him in mute gratitude. His eyes were warm, and filled with the kindness she had come to understand was so much a part of him. But there was something else, and again Bridget thought of sadness. Her hand longed to move, to take his hand, to ask what was wrong, what he thought, whether he would help her, no matter what Ananda said, because this was about her daughter, the most precious thing she ever had, ever would have.

Because she wanted to be able to love him.

But this was not the time, nor the place, and she still had a reputation here. She had to remember that. Prathad and Richikha were not given to gossip, but still, that Sakra would stay after she had gone to bed was outrageous enough, without such overt gestures of affection, and she desperately wanted him to stay. She did not want to be alone with her fears.

She smiled at the awkwardness this kindness of his created and went behind the screens to her sleeping alcove. The bed was a huge affair, big enough to sleep five people who didn't much care for each other. Posts carved with hawks and running deer held up a canopy and curtains of moss-green velvet.

In contrast, her night dress was pure white with more lace flounces than any one garment should possess. She had spoken with Prathad about acquiring some simpler night attire, and they had met with the seamstress, but for the moment being dressed for bed involved feeling done up like some elaborate French pastry.

She was not sure she wanted Sakra to see her like this. Whatever else might be happening, she still had her pride. But she looked at the bed in the flickering brazier light and thought about lying alone for hours, staring at the blackness, waiting to see something, and afraid of what it might be.

She climbed beneath the layers of throws and blankets, stretching her toes out automatically to reach the felt-wrapped bed warmer Richikha had already placed there. Her maids said nothing about the fact that there was still a man in the room. They reverenced in silent unison and withdrew, taking the lit brazier with them. It was only the reflection of the light beyond the screens that allowed her to see Sakra come and sit beside her. His face was lost in shadow, but she could smell his scents of warmth and spice, and the faint fragrance of oranges that always seemed to accompany him. Now that there was no one to witness it, her hand moved of its own accord, reaching out, telling him with its motion all she needed, and he covered it with his own.

They sat like that for a while, holding hands, Bridget drawing strength and calm from his presence and, after a while, Sakra began to sing. It was a low, slow song, perhaps a lullabye, in some language Bridget could not understand. Perhaps there was magic in it, for Bridget's hopes and fears gradually sank toward sleep. Her last conscious thought, though, was not of Anna. It was the memory of seeing the Firebird, rising into the night sky, spreading out its flaming wings to encompass the world, and the awe she had felt at that sight.

As sleep took her, she wondered where that magnificent terror had gone.

Chapter Two

But where is the Phoenix?

Xuan, the Minister of Fire, felt his whole being strain forward as An Thao, the Minister of the North, spoke.

"The details are not yet clear." An Thao lowered her eyes slightly to indicate that she felt shame at this inadequacy. "But we do know that the Dowager Empress Medeoan of Isavalta has died or been displaced, and Emperor Mikkel has assumed the throne in full."

Her words fell heavily into the expectant air of the Chamber of Eternal Voices. All the Nine Elders of Hung-Tse, the Ministers of Directions and Elements, were assembled in their circle, sitting cross-legged on their platforms of camphor wood. The symbols of their offices glittered on their robes in the flickering light from the lanterns and braziers. Behind their tattoos, the Elders' faces wore identical expressions of composure. Xuan strove to keep his face properly calm as did all his colleagues, but in his heart he wanted nothing more than to leap to his feet and shout.

Where is the Phoenix?

None spoke in answer to An Thao's blunt statement. His life as one of the Elders had given Xuan the ability to read the weight and quality of the silences that could fill the room like water in a lacquer cup. This news of Isavalta disturbed the other ministers, and it should. They had not planned well for this contingency. All signs, all forecasts, had pointed toward Medeoan dying an early death, which would shatter Isavalta, both removing the threat from the northern border and freeing the heavenly guardian she had imprisoned with a single stroke.

What had changed? How had all the predictions of magic, spies, and politics gone wrong?

And where is the Phoenix?

But it was not his time to speak. Xuan struggled to hold his tongue. He cast his gaze down so that he did not have to look at the others as he fought to compose himself. That was a mistake, because now he saw the Phoenix, emblazoned on his hands, on his robes where they folded neatly across his knees, and even inlaid on the floor at his feet with images of the three other great guardians. It arched its trailing wings and opened its hooked beak in song. Or in a scream of pain. Or in a call to the minister of its element to be free.

Xuan wished the Chamber of Eternal Voices had a window. He wanted to see Heaven's blue overhead. He wanted to know if there was some sign, some bright star or thunderstroke to show that the Phoenix was at last free from the cage woven for it by the empress of Isavalta. But no window could be permitted here, or even any reflection. The surfaces were all of dull or rough finish. Windows and reflections could become the eyes of a sorcerer, so that they might see to create an attack. Should any be so foolish as to think they might commit an assault on the Nine Elders with the high arts.

And yet wasn't that what Medeoan had done?

"Is the spell that held their emperor broken?" asked En Lai, the Minister of Earth. Her robes were brown, gold, and green, as were the tattoos on her face and hands. The symbol of the tortoise that was her guardian was repeated over and over across her skin and clothing. Like her guardian and her element, En Lai was a long and purposeful thinker. Just to be next to her was calming and strengthening. Xuan wished she sat beside him now. Instead he sat between Chi Tahn, the Minister of Water, and Quan, the Minister of the South. Their presences spoke of heat and fluidity and only agitated him, sending his thought flaring out.

"Yes, the spell is broken," said An Thao. She delivered her news in absolute stillness. Her white robes with their embroidery of wolves and snow geese did not flutter at all as she spoke. Xuan did not believe she could feel so calm inside. Isavalta was her special study. This news could mean that the greatest threat to Hung-Tse had just intensified. There could be no knowing yet. "The Emperor Mikkel's mind is whole again."

The tale in Isavalta was that their emperor had succumbed to an "illness of spirit" shortly after his marriage. That illness was supposed to have rendered him childlike and incapable of carrying out his duties. This was the lie that had been sent in official communication to the

Heart of the World. Whatever the nobles of Isavalta believed, none in the Heart had been taken in. Here, thanks in large part to An Thao and her spies, it was well known that the emperor of Isavalta had been enchanted. The dowager had let it be believed that it was her new daughter-in-law, Ananda, First Princess of Hastinapura, who was responsible for her son's "illness." Careful investigation had shown that to be another lie.

"The broken spell is the clearest evidence that the dowager truly has fallen," went on En Lai. She spoke slowly, as she always had, as if the element she represented infused even her words.

"Are these words official?" asked Chi Tahn, the Minister of Water. Xuan sat at his left hand and could see the blue whorls on his skin and the silver dragons of his robe in minute detail. He searched Chi Tahn's face for some indication that he was about to ask the important question, the only question.

"Not yet," An Thao answered. "I received this communication from our informant early this morning. The change took place in midwinter and there was no way to get through until now." Isavaltan winters rendered road and sea impassable. It was possible, of course, to have spies in place who carried magic with them, but magic was easier to intercept and guard against than a slip of paper, a pair of sharp eyes, or a vague word in the proper ear. "But it is of course expected that Isavalta will soon send a message."

Nha My, the Minister of the East, shifted her weight. Her green and red robes rustled, giving voice to her uneasiness although her face remained composed. "If the dowager is not dead, is there a possibility that this is a temporary reversal of her fortunes?"

An Thao shook her head. "It does not seem likely. The Lords Master of Isavalta were all said to be eager to take the oath of loyalty to the emperor. I cannot imagine they would do this if there was the possibility the dowager would retake power. No, my brothers and sisters, Medeoan is dead or gone and she has an heir who is of sound mind."

"But what of the guardian?" The words burst out of Xuan. It was not his turn, it broke the order of direction and precedence, but he could not hold silent anymore. Did it truly matter who held the throne? Did anything matter but that the northern blasphemy had finally been undone? Should he even have to ask this question? Should he not know what had happened already? "What of the Phoenix?"

An Thao bowed. "I regret to say I have no word. If the guardian is free, it has not been seen by our eyes nor heard by our ears."

Xuan realized his chest was heaving. The rasp of his breath filled the chamber.

"Brother," said Chi Tahn. "Speak to us. What is it you know?"

"Nothing," said Xuan and his hands trembled. "Why do I know nothing?"

He gazed at each of them in turn. Together, they were the eternal protectors of the Red Center of the World that was Hung-Tse, and not one of them had an answer for him. They had met in this place for three thousand years, ever since the third emperor had completed the palaces that comprised the Heart of the World. There had always been answers. Always. The Nine Elders commanded the highest magics, the magics of true transformation and summoning. They were gifted by the gods with the ability to manifest on earth the power of the heavenly guardians, as had been done almost thirty years ago to save Hung-Tse from invasion by Isavalta.

But at that time, an unimaginable blasphemy had been perpetrated. Medeoan, then the girl empress of Isavalta, had from somewhere acquired the knowledge to trap the Phoenix, the gift of Heaven, and hold it in a golden cage.

Each of the four walls around them was dedicated to a different guardian. The north wall had been drawn with the tortoise, the east with the *k'i-lin,* and the west with the dragon. Xuan looked to the southern wall, where the chamber's only door was located. It was covered in images of the Phoenix—his guardian, his element brought into glorious life.

Trapped in a cage in Isavalta for thirty years.

At the base of each wall was a collection of spirit tablets. The initiation of an Elder to their place required many spells, but although they did not speak of it beyond themselves, it was never forgotten that a life was surrendered in service each time the examinations were held and a new Elder was chosen. After the day of choosing, when the bindings began, a spirit tablet was made for the one who would become Elder. It was placed in the appropriate direction beneath the appropriate guardian. There was one beneath the Phoenix for the boy Seong, who had entered this place thirty years ago to become Xuan.

Once the ceremony was done and Seong was Xuan, he remembered all the other times the ceremony had been done. He knew in mind and spirit all the other moments of sacrifice, the glory and pain of transformation, the dissolution of self into the whole that came with the magics and the highest communion of thought.

But that was not how it was this last time. This last time, part of him remained withdrawn. Part of him was lonely and afraid, as a child is afraid, and angry as that same child when he does not understand. He understood why this was, and so did his brothers and sisters. The Ceremony of Naming should have recalled the whole of Xuan into being, weaving the body and power of Seong into the whole, but it could not. Part of Xuan was caged in the form of the guardian, ten thousand of *li* away.

When its work was complete, the Phoenix should have returned to Heaven to wait for that time when its essence would again need to be drawn down to the mortal worlds. So it was each time a guardian was summoned. But it did not, and it had not, and so Xuan remained incomplete.

Xuan wondered what debate the others had held before calling for the examination. Should they wait for the full death of their brother Xuan before his new self was chosen? Could they afford to wait? Without fire represented among them there could not be harmony, so the great spells of protection could not be worked. There had to be balance, or the great ghosts and devils, held at bay for so many years, might break free.

So fire was chosen, but fire was flawed, and Xuan knew it, and so did the others. They looked at him with the composure of courtesy, but they pitied him and they feared for themselves and for Hung-Tse, and the gap between Xuan and his brothers and sisters in art deepened.

Xuan breathed deeply, trying to find control of himself, trying to gain strength from his brothers and sisters, as he had in the past. "Surely when the dowager died, the spell holding the guardian broke and the guardian rose. Such a thing could not have gone unseen."

And if the Phoenix rose, why did it not send some sign, some dream, so that I might know?

Because you failed, whispered a voice from the hollow place in his mind that none of the others could touch. *Because in all these thirty years, you could not find, could not free the gift of Heaven. Do you think to still have Heaven's favor after that?*

"The dowager may not be dead," said Qwan, the Minister of the South. He spoke without sympathy, merely reminding a colleague of a salient point. As Minister of the South, the Phoenix was his guardian as well. Like Xuan, he felt the Isavaltan blasphemy in his bones, but he was complete and he could still hold firm to propriety and right.

Xuan turned to Qwan, in danger of losing his countenance altogether. "With respect, Brother." Tension made the word tremble. "Do you believe Medeoan would relinquish power while alive?"

The Nine Elders sat for a long moment, considering and giving Xuan time to recover himself. He hated his lack of control and the division between himself and the others, as a crippled man hates his withered limb. He tried to endure, but time passed so very slowly.

If the guardian had returned to Heaven, would the part of Xuan it harbored return to his body, rejoining the rest of his spirit? Would it end his separation from his brothers and sisters? There was no precedent, and no body of knowledge to study. Xuan suppressed a shudder. It had been a long time since they had encountered something so unknown.

"What of Kalami?" asked Chi Tahn, diverting talk and attention from Xuan, giving him time and deflecting shame. Xuan was grateful and irritated at the same time, for his heart could not completely believe there was anything else they should be talking about at this time.

Was An Thao relieved at the change of subject, or was that his agitated imagination? "Valin Kalami has vanished," she said. "Word from the Isavaltan court is most confused, but it appears that a new sorceress has risen to prominence and driven him out." Her shoulders straightened minutely, a sign that she had yet more difficult and important news. "This new sorceress may be the child of Avanasy."

Avanasy. Medeoan's chief advisor, her second in blasphemy. His life had been given to make the cage that held the Phoenix. His spirit stood guard over its captivity and could not be exorcised or dissuaded. They had tried.

The Isavaltans passed the story back and forth that Avanasy had fathered a child, one who would take up the protection of their realm as he had done. It was a story the northerners told with eager hope, and that the Nine Elders heard with a mix of horror and contempt.

"Avanasy's daughter is a rumor," said En Lai, her knuckles whitening as she clenched her hands together to try to keep her anger from reaching voice and face. Despite her efforts, a flush had crept into her skin beneath her red and green sigils.

An Thao bowed her head in acknowledgment of En Lai's statement. "That conclusion may have been mistaken."

"Was not Avanasy's child to be the dowager's ally?" asked Nha My. She leaned forward slightly as she spoke, perhaps to put herself between her sisters who might be getting ready to quarrel.

"That conclusion also seems to have been mistaken," said An Thao. "If this is Avanasy's child, what is clear is that this sorceress has taken the emperor's part, and the empress's."

"A point not to be forgotten," said Chi Tahn. He ran one hand down his blue and silver sleeve, smoothing out wrinkles that did not exist. He stared into the distance as if seeking to see the winds that were his charge and provenance. "The daughter of Hastinapura also assumes the throne."

Xuan, even with his disordered mind, had not forgotten that. He was sure none of the others had either. He could see in the set of An Thao's jaw that she was glad she was not the one who had to say the words. She had delivered enough bad news. They had lost a gamble in the game of empires. The enemy to the south had a favored daughter on the throne of the enemy to the north. And the guardian was gone, or was lost, or, worst of all, was still caged and in unknown hands.

That thought cut through Xuan's weakened composure. The muscles of his face ticked and twitched. Qwan leaned minutely closer to Xuan, giving him what little comfort he could.

"Do we believe that Kalami will be able to continue with his plans to overthrow the dynasty?" asked Qwan.

"If Kalami lives, his power is sure to be much diminished, even if the dowager herself is yet alive. It is difficult to see that he will be welcomed in the new court as he was in the old."

"Is anything known of the new emperor's mind toward the Heart of the World?" Chi Tahn turned his head to look directly at An Thao. Xuan knew what he was doing. By keeping the talk on Isavalta and on politics, he kept Xuan from having to speak until he was ready to do so, thinking to save him from the shame of a quavering voice and disordered thoughts.

An Thao pulled her own composure around her like an outer robe.

Xuan felt for her. This was a combination of event she had not foreseen. In that, she too failed in her duties. "Nothing certain. All is too new."

"The emperor must be told," said En Lai. It was a poor time to be stating the obvious, and the way she dipped her eyes said En Lai knew that. Apparently, he and An Thao were not the only ones who were now deeply disconcerted by what they knew, and what they did not know.

"There is another question," said An Thao. Her words were clipped. Xuan had the feeling that if she'd had any choice, she would have left this until later. Possibly, much later, but who knew what the next days would bring?

"What is that?" Chi Tahn's voice held a frown. He was ready for this to be done.

"The child," said An Thao. "The daughter of Kalami."

Chi Tahn waved his hand with its blue and silver dragons in a gesture of dismissal. "Kalami pledged his daughter's safety against his ability to move in cause of the Heart."

"Is she to be killed then?" An Thao's voice was just a little too casual, Xuan thought. She knew the child, he remembered. She oversaw the girl's education and reported on her progress and actions.

"Surely, it is too soon to make such a determination," said Qwan smoothly.

"Yet it must be thought on." Chi Tahn folded his hands again. Xuan narrowed his eyes slightly. Why would Chi Tahn insist? He was the one whom Kalami had contacted with his bargains. He was the one who had first brought his plans before the ministers.

Therefore he felt he was the one who had failed and been most betrayed.

But to take that out on a child?

Oh, yes, Xuan reminded himself. *Especially this child. If he fears her, it is not without cause.*

"Surely to undo such potential as she carries would be regrettable waste," said An Thao. "Her tutors say she is loyal and obedient. This is the only home she has known. Is it difficult to believe she will serve the Heart willingly?"

"Is it difficult to believe that such a father as she has would try to reclaim her, pledge or no?" replied Chi Tahn calmly. "We speak of one who would help the enemy of his liege lord topple an empire. Can we allow such power as the child represents to return to Isavalta, or even to Tuukos if Kalami is still alive and working to wrest that island from the empire? Can we allow any save Hung-Tse to possess the potential of this child?"

Those words rang around the chamber, and settled heavily in Xuan's mind. Even An Thao seemed startled into stillness.

What Chi Tahn said was not without merit. Xuan remembered the last report An Thao made of the girl's annual examinations. If the child had not been a barbarian, if she'd had even a trace of the first blood in her, An Thao would have taken her to train in preparation for the examination to become one of the Elders, possibly even the Minister of Water to be their voice to the emperor.

Could they risk such power finding its way in the wilderness of the north, where all was chaos and a child queen could cage the gift of Heaven?

That thought caused Xuan's heart to beat heavy and slow. An Thao, however, tried to take refuge in old loyalty. "Can a barbarian sorcerer fallen from his place breach the defenses of the Heart?"

Chi Tahn blinked, as if he could not understand why she would say such a thing. "Can we say that the child of that barbarian will remain loyal when she learns of her father's downfall? Or what she will do if he lives and she comes to believe that he has been abandoned by the Heart? For all the teaching she has received here, she is a great and unknown power. Do we risk that power turning against us?"

It was a necessary question. Distasteful, but necessary. And yet, to destroy a child . . . any child, especially one who had the potential to do such good for the Heart of the World, out of fear and revenge . . .

Would An Thao speak the word "revenge" aloud? Would she accuse Chi Tahn of acting out of that weakness? It would be bad if she had to do so, it would be a sign of disharmony.

Disharmony brought by the imbalance of one of their number being flawed.

"Do we risk eliminating the child too soon?" Xuan heard himself ask. "We do not know yet that Kalami is dead. Now is not the time to act in haste."

An Thao shot him a look of gratitude that he had no way to acknowledge. Qwan inclined his head once, thoughtfully. "Kalami may yet serve as eyes and ears in his land. We may yet bargain with him."

But Chi Tahn was not ready to be convinced. "And he may yet claim his daughter's loyalty. Can we stifle her filial piety?"

Again, Chi Tahn's words held a core of truth, but there was something missing. Xuan felt it in his blood and in his spine. Something none of them had thought of, with all their separate cares. They were not united as they should be, not thinking as one whole. They together captured the essence of the world and held it safe in the Heart. They acted in concert or they did not act. It was true. His isolation had finally begun to pull the others apart.

"An oracle is needed," he said, almost before he realized he had spoken the words aloud. "These circumstances went unseen when the child was taken as hostage guest." *And perhaps it will tell me what thoughts I cannot seem to bring to the fore of my mind. Of all our minds.*

"Let it be done then," said Chi Tahn. Did he feel it, then? This fragmenting? This discord? "We will gather at the eleventh hour to hear what has been found. I will go with the Minister of the North and the Minister of the South to speak with the Son of Heaven and Earth."

"With respect, Brother," said An Thao. "Should I not be the one . . ."

"You are the one who has the most knowledge of events in Isavalta," replied Chi Tahn. "The Son of Heaven and Earth will wish to question you closely. Our brother, Xuan, will cast the horoscope for the child."

Thank you for your trust, Brother, said Xuan silently. He met An Thao's gaze. He tried with his silence to assure her that he would work with care, that he would find all that could be revealed about the child's destiny, and the destiny of the land to which she belonged.

An Thao bowed. Xuan and the others bowed in return. No further ceremony was needed. The meeting was done. In single file, with Chi Tahn leading them, they walked from the Chamber of Eternal Voices and descended the great, winding iron stairs. No magic could stand in the face of so much cold iron. Each piece had been cast in molds crafted by the Minister of Earth and the Minister of Metal and held sigils of purity and protection embedded in the black metal. Xuan had presided over the smelting of the ore and remembered how the workmen had labored in fixing each join, hoisting each new section into place as the tower rose around them. He remembered the pride and the wonder of it, seeing this as the truest symbol of the Empire of the Center. It was from here that they would protect the chosen of Heaven. Even incomplete, it had been a great thing.

Even incomplete. Xuan held tight to that thought as he descended the stairs with his fellows, raising a flurry of footsteps that rang like bells.

In the dragon-spiraled shadow the Nine Elders dispersed to commence their separate tasks. Around them spread the splendors of the Heart of the World. Pillars of marble and carnelian held up the carved beams of the roof. Ornaments of gold and jade, and hangings of painted silk graced the long, straight corridors. Xuan did not turn to look at any of the luxuries that surrounded him. He did not even stop to take note of his brothers and sisters, but walked to the Western doors as swiftly as dignity permitted.

Passing through red and gold portals, Xuan stepped into the noon-time sunlight, and the Garden of Heaven. Here waited the tombs of the emperors, small grey temples of granite and unpolished marble. They stood rank on rank with their open doors facing east so that their imperial spirits could watch all those who came and went from the Heart of the World. Smoke rose through the openings in each roof from the fires of incense and precious woods. Monks in robes of sky blue tied with saffron sashes passed silently to and fro on their endless rounds of tending the fires and prayers.

Xuan held a memory of each of those emperors. On his left he passed the tomb of Emperor Sai, who had been round and fat and as skilled a judge of men as had ever sat on the throne. On his right lay Emperor Quyny, who had been born female, but who had convinced the Nine Elders to turn her into a male because not one of her brothers was fit to take the throne. He had seen born most of the ones who slept in these final houses. He had seen them all ascend the throne, and he had seen them all die. He had served each and every one of them with all his craft and heart. He had sacrificed himself a dozen times, become guardian or storm, become memory and soul, become flesh again to serve again. He would do so a thousand more times if necessary. The peace of Heaven was not for such as he. He was given his power to protect Hung-Tse, the red center of the world, and he would do so with a clear head and a full heart for as long as the world stood.

But, Goddess of Mercy, I do not want to have to tell An Thao to order the death of this child.

Because she too had been deceived by Isavalta now, and he would spare her a further such wounding.

Amid the tombs of the emperors, the temples of the gods stood out like exotic flowers. Red and green like the Heart of the World, their walls were carved in deep relief with the symbols of the element, direction, day, and hour where the god held sway. Their gilded roofs shone in the sun, reflecting the light of Heaven out into the world. Each threshold was flanked by statues of the god's servant spirits who carried their tools and symbols.

In the case of the temple of Chun Ja, her two serving maids each held one hand over the door and beckoned the supplicant with the other. Chun Ja stood at the Threshold of Life and laid her hand on the head of each child as they passed. The shape of her divine palm left the impression of the individual's destiny on their skull. Since Chun Ja knew all destinies, she also presided over the creation of horoscopes and all types of personal divination.

It might be argued that Chun Ja would have had no part in the making of the destiny of a barbarian child, but she would know the destinies of those the child interacted with in Hung-Tse and therefore might be consulted on this matter.

"The cart means travel, but it can also mean release from a burden or . . ."

Xuan froze on the temple threshold, startled by the light voice. Two people crouched on the floor of the temple, overshadowed by the statue of Chun Ja on her jade altar. Their startled faces gazed up at him. An old man in the plain black coat and cap of a scholar crouched beside a child dressed in a coat and trousers of rich blue. The coat's grey cuffs and collar marked her as a hostage guest to the Heart of the World. One of the female soldiers who guarded the women's palace and the dowager's residence stood silent sentry beside the door. Behind them, the life-sized image of Chun Ja, the Goddess of Childbirth, on her carved jade altar seemed to be supervising their study.

The two immediately got to their feet, the child in a swift scramble, the old man in a stiff and dignified motion. They folded their left hands over their right fists as was proper, and bowed deeply.

"Forgive us, Excellency," said the scholar. Xuan now recognized him as Master Liaozhai. "In seeking to instill energy and virtue in my pupil, I woke her early to her studies. If we had known you would be seeking the guidance of Chun Ja this morning, we would have sought another lesson."

Xuan and An Thao bowed briefly to acknowledge this polite and pious greeting. An Thao said, "Do not concern yourself, Master Liaozhai. Is not the pursuit of knowledge worth a few extra moments of searching?"

Master Liaozhai bowed his head. "His Excellency speaks wisely."

The floor of Chun Ja's temple was carved and painted with the Great Star Wheel. The four guardians and the characters of the zodiac surrounded the concentric circles that held the symbols of fate: the cart, the cup, the fish, the needle, the drunkard, the soldier, and all the rest. Several neatly painted telling sticks lay across the symbols. Master Liaozhai had been teaching his student the art of interpreting divination by laying the rune sticks down in various positions and having her read the possibilities there. Xuan remembered his own tutors doing the same with him.

Normally, Xuan enjoyed the sight of a young person at their studies, but now uneasiness crept through him. Could it possibly be chance that brought Tsan Nu to this place when Xuan came to inquire of her future? Xuan glanced up at the goddess in her red silk robes, her hands extended and cupped, waiting for those who would pass beneath her.

Did you bring us all here, farseeing Chun Ja? Is this a message from Heaven?

There were only a very few moments when even the most sensitive of sorcerers could truly feel fate's delicate threads surround them. Those who were wise did not fear such moments, but welcomed them. Xuan could not raise any welcome within him, only the chill of foreboding. If this moment was shaped by Chun Ja, what had the Goddess of Destiny brought them all here to see?

The child Tsan Nu stood slightly behind her tutor, her hands folded and her eyes properly cast down. She was a slight creature, with pale skin. A lock of black hair had escaped the tidy knot at the nape of her neck and coiled like a spring over her temple. Xuan found a moment to feel pity. Whatever must happen, it would not go easily for the child.

But then, now might be his chance to take the child's measure with more than just the tools of divination. Character was vital to destiny. If there had been only one destiny for each person, then action would be useless. All would be written. But what true sorcerers knew was that Chun Ja placed both her hands on each person's head. The right hand made the imprint of the evil destiny, the left the imprint of the righteous destiny. It was up to each to choose and to work to travel their righteous path. The other waited for those who were lazy or abandoned their duty.

Two destinies, even for those whose souls were incomplete.

"I must make my devotions, Master Liaozhai," Xuan said, at last recovering himself enough to speak. "Then, if you will permit it, we will see how well your pupil has learned her lessons."

Master Liaozhai bowed again. "We would be most honored, Excellency."

Xuan knelt before the altar and pressed his forehead three times against the cool stone floor. The altar was crowded with cut flowers, bags of coins, and caches of rice or fruit. Sticks of incense smoldered in trays of sand, filling the air with their perfume. Once every eight days the Garden of Heaven was opened to the city so that all might come and honor the gods and the departed emperors. Parents flocked to Chun Ja, praying for good lives for their children, or thanking her for blessings received.

Honored Chun Ja, I pray you open the eyes of your humble servant to that which must be and that which might be.

Xuan stood and faced the child and her tutor again. He remembered the day Tsan Nu's father, Valin Kalami, had brought her here as an infant. She had been a red and wrinkled babe, with a thick shock of black hair, and thoroughly unhappy. While the baby wailed, An Thao and Chi Tahn together walked the zodiac circle and cast the telling sticks, and what they had revealed had almost caused An Thao to lose her composure before the foreign sorcerer with his infant wriggling in his arms.

Power, the telling said. Power and sight, salvation in danger for Hung-Tse. He had watched Valin Kalami, as he watched them make their silent interpretation. Kalami knew, he was sure, that the child was destined to power, but did he know how much? Could he know and still give her into the Heart as surety for his risky plans? Or did he have some plan other than the ones he had told them of?

For nine years the Elders had considered that question, and no answer had come to them. Spies in the Isavaltan court reported that Kalami did as he promised and undermined the dowager and her rule. An Thao reported regularly that the child had taken well to her nurses and her tutors.

She had shown filial respect and affection when her father visited her. Her tutors in the spirit gifts had all been instructed to inform the ministers if they discerned any unusual displays of power, but none of them had done so yet.

Xuan folded his hands and let his face be the serene mask of centuries behind the tattoos that covered his skin, protecting him and imparting to him the powers of her office. "Master Liaozhai, I would have Tsan Nu cast a horoscope for me now."

Master Liaozhai bowed in acknowledgment. "Whose future shall she divine, Excellency?"

Xuan considered. "Her own, Master Liaozhai." When the child was finished, Xuan could cast a second horoscope, and see how well the two matched. That first horoscope made nine years ago predicted Tsan Nu would have great gifts when it came to seeing and calling on the future. This would be a good test of that power. A child of nine years who could cast a horoscope that was even partially accurate would be a remarkable person indeed.

Those who knew little of magic wondered why true sorcerers did not cast horoscopes and draw birth charts constantly, as the frauds and illusionists did. They did not understand that the gods, in their wisdom, frowned upon those who spent too much time trying to see what their path was rather than traveling along it. As a result, they required deep and exhausting magics to reach past the Veil of Now.

Master Liaozhai turned to his student. "You have your task, Tsan Nu." Tsan Nu bowed politely in return, both to her tutor and to Xuan. She had learned her manners well at the very least. The child tried to remain composed, but her nervousness showed as she picked up the bundle of telling sticks from the floor and shuffled through them, looking for her year, month, day, and hour. When she found the correct symbols, she handed the remaining sticks to her tutor, glancing up at him for reassurance. He nodded slightly, his whole manner radiating calm. Xuan was certainly not the first to test the child in such a fashion and Master Liaozhai's stance and calm spoke of confidence in his pupil. This was a difficult spell, although it was the easiest of the possible horoscopes to cast, because the chart was already drawn, and it could be worked in a relatively short amount of time.

The child took the telling sticks in both hands and stationed herself on the east side of the zodiac circle, beginning where the dawn rose. She bowed once in each of the four outer directions, and bowed a fifth time to acknowledge the center. Then, she began to walk sunward around the circle, her movements each performed with the care of a child who knows very well she is observed. She completed a circuit in silent prayer to Chun Ja, and on the second circuit she began to sing.

> *"The path is unknown and*
> *Cannot be seen,*
> *But light may shine for*
> *Eyes that seek.*
> *Chun Ja, let your servant see.*
> *Chun Ja, let your servant know.*
> *The path of Tsan Nu Kalami*
> *Who stands here with humble heart.*
> *Chun Ja, let your servant see.*
> *Chun Ja, let your servant know."*

Xuan felt the air thicken around him, filling with the currents of the magic Tsan Nu drew to her. They slid across his skin like purest water, chilling and awakening his inward senses—his mind's eye and his heart's understanding. The touch was strong, stronger than Xuan expected. Warning prickled in the back of his mind, but he resolved to wait and watch.

> *"Chun Ja, let your servant see.*
> *Chun Ja, let your servant know."*

Tsan Nu completed the second circuit, and the third, weaving the pattern of song and motion. The magics thickened and strengthened and the child's voice began to shake. She completed the fourth circuit. Xuan felt the air press against her lungs. Master Liaozhai clasped his hands together, but not before Xuan saw them tremble. Only the guard by the door remained unmoved. Untouched by gifts of spirit she could feel nothing of this steady, deepening cold.

> *"Chun Ja, let your servant know.*
> *The path of Tsan Nu . . ."*

Stop her, said all the instincts born of memory and ministry in the back of Xuan's mind. *This is too much, too strong. It cannot be contained by one child. Stop her.*

But the warning came too late. As Xuan raised his hand, Tsan Nu completed the fifth circuit and tossed the telling sticks out into the air, her face elated with the power of her spell. The magic caught them and whirled them around . . .

. . . And shattered them with a sound like firecrackers bursting.

Tsan Nu cried out as if in pain. Liaozhai grabbed her shoulders and pulled her back from the edge of the circle as the splinters clattered onto the stone floor, scattering like straws. Xuan's heart pounded against his ribs. Even the guard had startled, going automatically into a ready stance with her spear in both hands.

"Excellency," murmured Master Liaozhai, staring at the zodiac circle.

Xuan looked as well, and his throat constricted. He had for an instant thought Master Liaozhai wanted him to interpret what had happened here, but as he looked down, he saw that the telling sticks were not all that was broken.

A crack ran across the temple floor, splitting the zodiac circle in two. It started at the sign of the Phoenix, and ran black and jagged to the base of Chun Ja's altar. The splintered telling sticks had fallen to either side of the crack. Not one fragment lay across it.

Tsan Nu was trembling. Master Liaozhai, oblivious to propriety, drew her close for comfort, but although the child huddled in the folds of his black robes, her tremors did not ease.

"What does it mean, Excellency?" asked the ancient teacher.

Xuan opened his mouth without speaking. His mind was awhirl. Never had he seen such a thing, not across centuries. No memory, no voice spoke to him. He looked at the splinters, saw them crossing cup and cart, book and fire, horse, crane and chameleon and a dozen other symbols. A dozen futures, a hundred, and none of them made any pattern.

The crack started at the Phoenix, emanating from its gilded breast like a black thunderbolt. What did it mean? What was his guardian, his other self, trying to tell him?

"It means death," said the child.

Xuan stared at the child, pressed close to her tutor.

"It means we're going to die," Tsan Nu said again. "All of us. It's the end of the world."

Master Liaozhai laid his old hand on her head, as if seeking to reshape the destiny Chun Ja had imprinted there, but he looked to Xuan for words. So did the child, and even the guard.

Xuan wanted to look to Chun Ja. He wanted to fall down in prayer to the goddess and ask her what this meant, but he could not. He was voice and memory, he was gate and guard, and he must act that part now.

"It is a common thing to see death in such a drama," he said, drawing himself up into a more properly composed stance. "But death comes from the earth and the north, not from the sky and the south." He nodded to the tortoise sign, which waited serene and untouched by any crack or splinter. "This is a difficult thing to read and will take time to interpret. Clearly it is a strong message . . ."

"It's death!" Tsan Nu stomped her foot. "We must all get away from here. The Heart is going to die!"

"Tsan Nu," said Master Liaozhai. "Do not shame us with this display."

She pulled away from Master Liaozhai and stood with her arms wrapped around herself. She did not, Xuan saw, look down at the broken circles. "But he's not listening! He asked me to see the future and now he doesn't want to know what it says." The pique was childish, but the fear was real.

"It is not for the Minister of Fire to listen," said the tutor, giving Tsan Nu a small shake. "It is for us to hear."

The child clamped her mouth shut, but she was clearly not mollified.

Xuan, remembering the first horoscope and the strength of Tsan Nu's magic, felt a thread of chill run down his spine. He felt certain Tsan Nu's interpretation of this . . . horoscope, if it could be truly called that, was not just an attempt to get attention. She believed what she said.

"Why do you believe it is death for the Heart?" asked Xuan. "It could be change. It could be that the new home of the imperial wisdom must be chosen." It was not permissible to speak of the death of the emperor, even among the High Ministers.

"You don't see it?" Tsan Nu frowned. "It's there." She pointed down at the shattered zodiac, the scattered splinters, and the jagged crack.

Xuan made himself look down and focus on the symbols, on the directions of the splinters, and how they crossed one another. It took all his strength to set aside the fact that the crack came from the Phoenix. "I see change and travel, fortune and misfortune both."

Tsan Nu looked at him as if he were mad. "That's just the sticks on the signs. That's not the real thing."

For the first time, Xuan felt anger's spark. Such rudeness on the part of a child would ordinarily be grounds for punishment. And yet . . . "Tell me what you see."

"Fire," said Tsan Nu. "Anger, and the golden tower's falling. It's too late and the damage has been done. The Heart has failed and will be taken down to ashes."

Fire? How could that be? That was his element and for all his trouble, his binding to his element was strong. No fire could take hold in the Heart without him.

Did this child say he was to betray the Heart? She might as well say she was going to drink all the water in the sea.

"How has the Heart failed? Who will set this fire?"

The child stared at the broken circle, stared hard as if to see through the stone, stared until she began to tremble again.

"I don't know. I can't see that far." She frowned, angry again. "I should be able to see." She moved to get down on her knees, but Master Liaozhai restrained her with a hand on her shoulder.

"Enough, Tsan Nu. It is enough." He looked to Xuan in something of desperation. *I didn't know,* his old face said. *I don't know what this means.*

But Xuan saw how the crack began at the etching of the Phoenix and ran all the way to the foot of the goddess.

Was it possible to compel the gift of Heaven? Was it possible, as Medeoan had threatened all these years, to change its essential nature from guardian to attacker? Was that why he could not feel the guardian?

And where was Valin Kalami? A powerful sorcerer, and privy to all Medeoan's secrets, whose daughter stood here and spoke of death? What was her part in this? It was not power alone that allowed her to see such a future. What did her blood have to answer for? For a moment his vision blurred with anger. What further blasphemy had her barbarian people wrought?

"I will take this matter before the Nine Elders," he heard himself say as from a great distance. "You may go now."

"But . . ." began the child. But her tutor clapped his wrinkled hand on her arm and steered her at once toward the door. The soldier shouldered her spear and hurried after her charge. Xuan had the distinct feeling the woman was glad to be gone.

When Xuan was alone, he knelt slowly, as if he were as decrepit as Master Liaozhai. He pressed his forehead against the cool, shattered stone, bowed to fate, to the goddess and the guardian.

Blessed Chun Ja, what is come upon us? Guardian, speak to me. Let me know our fault. I will pay the price, whatever it is. But come back to me. Let me know how to restore all to what should be.

But there were no more answers. Alone and in silence Xuan got to his feet and left the temple, and went to seek his brothers and sisters. Not because he felt they might be able to answer, or to help, but because he did not know what else to do.

Behind him, the future lay on the temple floor and waited.

Chapter Three

Lieutenant Mae Shan Jinn of the Heart's Own Guard walked three paces behind her charge, and wished she did not have to hear the child's words. She tried to concentrate on keeping the prescribed distance behind the little girl who had a tendency to speed up and slow down unpredictably. It was an exercise in concentration, and kept her thoughts from straying back to the crack in the temple floor.

If she had still been the peasant girl she once was, she would have instantly made the sign against the evil eye and run out to buy lucky amulets and incense from the first healer she could find. As it was, knowing she was in the center of the Heart, within yards of the Nine Elders and the Son of Heaven and Earth, she wanted to be at her prayers rather than at her duty. She had seen Tsan Nu and Master Liaozhai work magics and divination before, but she had never seen anything like this.

"He didn't believe me," Tsan Nu was complaining. Despite all her training in manners, she still strode ahead with clenched fists, her anger plain on her pale features.

"He did not say that." Master Liaozhai would have to scold her soon, as Tsan Nu was paying no attention to his example of measured steps and folded hands.

"He's not going to *do* anything."

"He is going to take the question before the Nine Elders. That is a very important thing. What is the admonition to patience?"

"It is only patience that allows both the mind and the heart to see clearly," recited Tsan Nu so quickly she almost tripped over the words. "If he believed me he would have sounded the alarm. The bells would be ringing by now."

"Tsan Nu, this behavior is undisciplined and undignified. You know better."

"We're going to die, Master Liaozhai. You saw what happened!"

Master Liaozhai sighed. "I saw strong magic and a strong reading. I saw a young student who does not yet know how to control herself."

The girl refused to take the admonishment. "You don't believe me either."

Master Liaozhai looked out across the roofs of the tombs. Mae Shan looked as well, listening for a tread or movement that did not belong to a monk or a servant. "I believe something strange and portentous happened," Master Liaozhai said, and Mae Shan let the words balance out the peasant girl fear she still harbored. "I believe you saw beyond the normal seeing. I believe it is good that the Nine Elders know all of this."

Tsan Nu turned suddenly, switching with a child's speed from anger to imploring. "Let me do a scrying."

"No, Tsan Nu."

"But I might be able to learn something else. Something that would convince the Elders." She hit on a new point and her eyes lit up. "If it's a scrying, you'd be able to see whatever I see and you could tell them too."

Mae Shan watched the shadows of the tombs around them, the fall of the light. She felt the breeze against her face. She listened for the sounds beyond the voices of her charges.

"No, Tsan Nu."

"But why not?"

"What is the truth of seeking the future?"

"You always do this."

She tried to filter out the words that were nothing to do with her and her duties. Tsan Nu was not a bad child, but she did sometimes feel the girl needed a long afternoon of hauling water or digging clay to settle her to her lessons.

"What is the truth of seeking the future?"

The child shut her mouth tight and glowered at her teacher, even as she had at the Minister of Fire. In response, Master Liaozhai simply stood silently facing her, his hands folded, clearly prepared to wait calmly until darkness fell, perhaps even until the sun rose again.

Tsan Nu's face colored red with her indignation and she turned on her heel and ran. Her tutor did not move.

"Mae Shan," he said evenly.

The bodyguard had been anticipating this. It was not the first time

Tsan Nu had attempted to escape her tutor. Mae Shan flexed her long legs. In a very few minutes, she caught up with the child, and passed her by to stand in her path and clamp a big, callused hand on Tsan Nu's shoulder. Without a word, she turned the girl around and marched her back to Master Liaozhai.

She did not let go either. She stayed at the girl's back with her hand on the thin shoulder. Tsan Nu did not try to struggle. The child had learned that was useless. Mae Shan had not lost hold of her in five years of chasing and catching.

"What," said Master Liaozhai, "is the truth about seeking the future?"

Tsan Nu sighed, loud and showy. "The act of seeing is like the tide. The harder certainty is sought, the faster it recedes." She broke off her recitation. "But it's not like that for me. You know it's not."

Master Liaozhai's face softened. He nodded to Mae Shan and she released the child's shoulder. "I know, Tsan Nu, you have been granted great gifts of spirit," he said gently. "I know that one day you may see farther and truer than even the great sages. But I also know I have seen many students with great gifts, and if they do not learn how to govern those gifts, they are ruled by them. They forget the truth they see is temporary and they go mad with their fears, burning out their souls performing scrying after scrying looking for a single immutable truth that does not exist."

That seemed to reach the child. She stood there for a moment, saying nothing, knitting her brow up tightly. "Have you really seen that happen?"

"Yes." The tutor's eyes clouded. "To a boy who was trying to find out if he would become one of the Nine Elders. His father pressed him to reach for the highest of all high positions and would not be dissuaded. I had been called to the Heart to assist with a matter of law and returned to him too late."

Tsan Nu looked down at her toes, encased in their neat black cloth shoes. "But I did see it, Master Liaozhai. What do we do?"

Master Liaozhai folded his hands again. "The hardest thing there is, Tsan Nu. We wait and we trust. Sometimes there is nothing else. Come," he added. "You have upset Mae Shan. Make your apologies and show your respect to this one who serves as you serve."

Tsan Nu turned, but did not look up from her shoes. "I'm sorry, Mae Shan."

Again Mae Shan bowed, making sure the gesture was brief, so she would not take her eyes off her surroundings, and also making sure it included the tutor. Master Liaozhai was unusual in teaching his gifted student to respect all those around her, even those of lesser rank. There were times when Mae Shan wondered if he did it because the child was a barbarian and so, despite her gifts, was in truth more lowly than any who would ordinarily be permitted to set foot in the Heart, even if they came only to scrub the floors. But though there were others who might do such things for such reasons, Mae Shan suspected that Master Liaozhai was what he seemed, a scholar of impeccable manners.

"I think you have worked hard enough this morning," Master Liaozhai went on. "You may play in the garden until the eleventh hour bell."

"Thank you, Master Liaozhai." The child sounded more polite than grateful. Her mind and heart were still full of her worries obviously, and it would take time for them to ease.

Master Liaozhai seemed to understand that. Even now, he walked close to Tsan Nu. He did not touch her, but carried his hands properly folded before him, but still he was close enough that the skirts of his coat brushed her occasionally and she could surely feel his warmth and hear the rustle of his breath and his clothing. All this making a constant reminder that she was not alone, and that was probably what she needed most of all.

The Star Garden was as filled with the sounds of children's laughter as it was with the small white flowers called star of winter. They ran about on the grass, playing tag or racing, or, to their nurses' despair, climbed the trees. The more sedate played at ball or read to each other. They poked in the brown ponds, teasing the goldfish there.

These were the children of all the palaces. The children of the nobility and the imperial ladies, the children of the scribes and scholars and the officers. A number, like Tsan Nu, wore grey cuffs and collars on their clothes, marking them as hostage guests. Some of the higher-ranked children would not play with her because of this marking. Tsan Nu tried not to let this bother her, and mostly she succeeded.

Like all the gardens of the Heart of the World, the Star Garden was surrounded by high walls painted over with sigils of protection. Tsan Nu could read most of them now. There was the warding against watching, against listening, against reaching, which took four days all by itself to paint properly. There were the signs of the crane for health, and of the tiger for strength, and the monkey for cleverness, and of course the symbols of the gods and goddesses that oversaw children, health, and growth.

The gates and doors were all locked and soldiers stood outside. Some of the children talked about climbing the walls or rubbing out one of the signs, but Tsan Nu was glad for the protection. It meant Mae Shan could take up a post beside the gate with the other bodyguards, and let Tsan Nu play on her own, even letting her out of sight.

The gate closed beside them, and Tsan Nu remembered to bow her thanks to Mae Shan, as Master Liaozhai approved of, motivated by the knowledge that he was not going to approve of what she was going to do next.

"Thank you, mistress." Mae Shan bowed in return, and took up her station beside the other guards, planting the butt of her spear against the ground, and squaring her shoulders until she looked just like a toy soldier.

Tsan Nu took off running. Her friends waved and called as she raced past them, and she waved and shouted back, but she did not stop. She had something else to do first.

In the back corner of the garden, a patch of wilderness had been left, a symbol that chaos was part of order. Underneath the untrimmed bracken was something very rare in the gardens of the Heart, a pool that had been forgotten. It was filled with thick brown water scummed over with green, that reflected next to no light. As such, it made a terrible scrying vessel, but it could serve if one was desperate.

She wondered if she should have stopped and played with the others. She wondered if Mae Shan had seen and guessed what she might be up to and was even now on her way to tell Master Liaozhai.

She'd have to be quick.

"Hey, Tsan Nu! Tsan Nu!"

Tsan Nu groaned, slowed, and turned. Yi Qin, daughter of Lady Yi Tang, trotted up behind her. Yi Qin was tall, and carefully groomed and wore robes of blue and red, emphasizing her high rank, as much as she was allowed, because despite the fact that Lady Yi Tang said that her father was Lord Pao, private secretary to the General of the Northern Borders, *he* had never said so.

Yi Qin was nosy. She liked to have secrets and hated anybody else having them. So the next question was predictable.

"Where're you going?"

"Nowhere," tried Tsan Nu.

"Come on." Yi Qin smiled at her, and looked a lot like her mother when she did. "I'll tell you what Li Tan told me about Master Bin."

Yi Qin treated secrets like strings of silver. It was almost a shame she never really knew anything interesting.

"Nowhere," repeated Tsan Nu. "I just wanted to think."

That was a mistake. "About what?"

"Nothing." Even as she said it, Tsan Nu knew that was another mistake.

"You're a liar," said Yi Qin flatly. "Tell me where you're going or I'll tell your tutor about how you turned all the white flowers red to make the dragon picture before the New Year festival." It was well known Tsan Nu had the spirit gifts, and occasionally she had shown them off by freezing a pond in midsummer or putting a goldfish into a tree. Master Liaozhai frowned on these exploits and set her to learning pages and pages of new characters whenever she did it, but the looks on the other children's faces could be worth it.

She would tell on Tsan Nu too, but Tsan Nu couldn't let her see the scrying. She couldn't let Yi Qin of all people know what she could really do. The girl would never leave her alone for a minute if she knew how much Tsan Nu could see when she tried.

She had to do something. Any moment now, the nurses would descend. They'd be scolded and made to play together. "Listen, Yi Qin, if you let me alone now, I'll give you a good luck amulet. A real one. Master Liaozhai taught me how." That wasn't true, but Yi Qin would never know.

Yi Qin considered. "What kind of good luck?"

Greedy brat. "Future luck," said Tsan Nu conspiratorily. "It'll be waiting for the time when you need it most and then . . . you'll get exactly what you want." Tsan Nu was pleased with her wording. That way if something didn't work out for Yi Qin, Tsan Nu could just say, "It must not be the right time yet." She could keep that up for years.

Yi Qin eyed her suspiciously. "All right," she muttered, "but if you don't do it, I'll make you very sorry." Yi Qin had lots of friends and the secrets she knew might not be interesting, but sometimes they were dangerous.

"I promise," said Tsan Nu again. "You'll have it by bedtime."

Whatever else Yi Qin was, she did what she said. Showing off how much the lady she was, she walked primly back to where her co-conspirators were playing "court." Tsan Nu turned and ran, praying that the gods not decide to deal with her lie by having one of the nurses or, worse, one of the tutors catch her now.

But they did not. Tsan Nu made it to the back wall and the wild patch. It was shady back here and gnats buzzed around her ears. She swatted them away impatiently and pushed her way through the screen of brambles and nettles, ignoring the pricks and stings.

The pool was only a little wider than she was, rimmed with algae and covered over with a kind of floating moss. Tsan Nu shoved that aside with a stick until she got a patch of fairly clear brown water. The stench of decay wafted up around her, and she held her nose. Then, she knelt down, leaning out over the pool, looking at the muddy swirls, and she set aside the itching, and the stink and her anger at Yi Qin, and the crack in the temple floor, and she thought about tomorrow. Tomorrow. What would tomorrow be like? She thought about the Heart, about the great courtyard and the tower that was Ah Min's Spear, and all the palaces around.

This wasn't even really magic, not the weaving and shaping Master Liaozhai taught her. This was something separate, something inside her blood that was her very own.

Fixing her mind on the Heart, and on tomorrow, Tsan Nu reached inside to where her mind's eye waited, and willed it open. She looked down into the brown, swirling water, and she saw . . .

Nothing.

Not darkness, not the black that came with night, or with closing one's eyes, but nothingness. It was as if her inner eye had gone blind.

Tsan Nu pulled back, and the mood broke, and her inner vision snapped shut, there was nothing in front of her except a pond settling back toward stillness.

Tsan Nu, though, was gasping and shaking like she'd just woken up from a nightmare. Nothing. Tomorrow was nothing. The Heart was nothing. How could this be?

I didn't ask the right question. There can't be nothing. There has to be something.*

But she remembered Master Liaozhai's story about the boy who died from too much scrying. Even if he wasn't like her, with visions that could be called without a shaping, what if she got paralyzed like he did, and all they found was her bones crouching over the pool, because she couldn't make herself look away anymore?

There couldn't just be *nothing*.

Still, Tsan Nu shivered. Biting her lip, she did what she always did when she was afraid. She took off her left shoe, slipped her fingers into a slit in the cotton lining, and brought out the flat, colorful amulet hidden there. It was called a *zagovor*'s heart, and when Tsan Nu traced the pattern with her finger, she could sometimes feel the subtle heart shape hidden in the layers of tight braiding.

Her father had given her this amulet, just in front of the bushes where she now hid. She had shown him her secret spot, and he had praised her. "Be obedient, Tsan Nu, but do not give them all of yourself," he'd said seriously. "Keep something just for you and me.

"And to that end." He'd reached in his pocket and pulled the amulet out. It was half the size of her palm, as flat as a copper coin, and braided red, black, green, and blue. "This is for you. If there is ever a time when you are truly in danger, and I mean in danger of your life, Tsan Nu—not in danger of a scolding, or of being made to practice your writing." She'd blushed, but he'd just smiled. "But if such a time ever comes, you can use this to contact me. Listen closely," and he had explained how to open up the magic he had locked into the weaving.

Now she held it tightly against her as if it were her favorite doll. Should she use it? With everything she'd seen and everything she hadn't seen, was now that emergency? Father was a sorcerer, and important, not just to the Isavaltans, but to the Nine Elders as well. He could make them listen.

But slowly, Tsan Nu lowered the amulet to her lap. No. Not yet. She'd wait until tomorrow. By tomorrow, Minister Xuan would have talked to the others. By tomorrow, things would have changed. Maybe that was why she couldn't see anything. It was all changing, maybe because of what she had already seen. Maybe it was as Master Liaozhai said, he *had* heard her, but he couldn't do anything alone. The Nine Elders always had to talk for hours and hours before they did anything.

Tsan Nu slid the amulet back into her shoe, and slid the shoe back onto her foot. She crawled out of the thicket and dusted off her knees and elbows. Then she set off running again. She needed to find Lady Pim Ma and beg some red ribbons so she could make Yi Qin's "lucky" amulet.

Everything would be all right tomorrow, and if it wasn't, then she would call Father.

In the end, it was to be Earth.

The debate was long and intense, lasting from noon until twilight, but Xuan had known through it all what would be done. There was only one choice.

If the guardian had been perverted or angered, the only one who could stand against its wrath, or answer how they might heal it, was another guardian. The only question was which guardian should be called.

It was no small thing. It was never normally done, and had never been done twice within the same hundred years. The ceremony was difficult, and called for all the Nine Elders, for Heaven itself had to be touched and implored, and the life of an Elder had to be given in the transformation.

The guardian of earth was chosen because while earth was slow where fire was quick, solid where fire was ethereal, the earth could also contain fire and so they were not in direct opposition to each other. This was no battle they sought to stage. That would be an even greater blasphemy than the northerners had perpetrated. This was a sacrifice for the restoration of harmony and peace, when all other means had failed.

The transformation could only be worked at night. They all gathered now atop the tower. The moon was a silver coin in the black sky, surrounded by the pinpricks of countless stars, white, gold, and blue. All of them flashes of fire, blue white gold and red. Xuan remembered other nights, gazing up at those stars and feeling his connection with Heaven. Where there could be no water, no earth, there was yet fire, changing yet eternal.

En Lai stepped forward alone to the altar. She positioned herself on the ancient stone, waiting, rooting herself in her element, opening her heart. Xuan saw her hands tremble as she brought them together, folded in acceptance and in prayer. He remembered how it felt to stand there, alone, waiting for the end. Even knowing that Heaven waited and that life went on, it was a hard, lonesome thing.

Chi Tahn met En Lai's eyes in silence. En Lai did not even have to nod. All there knew she had reached her moment of readiness. To wait any longer would make what must be done unbearable. They all remembered, they all at one time or another had stood on that stone.

Chi Tahn threw back his head and he began to sing. His voice was strong and pure and it went straight to Xuan's heart, drawing him close and opening him wide. One by one his brothers and sisters added their voices to the spell, raising their magics from within and from without, drawing the essence of each element and each direction into their invisible weaving until the whole of the world was within their compass.

Xuan's voice joined the others almost without his conscious volition. His song was needed, his element, his magic, and so it answered the call and wove itself with the others, rising into the air, sinking into the earth, reaching out to all the four outer directions and bringing them to the center.

Song and power swelled until all the air around them trembled. Then Minh, the Minister of the West, stepped forward, still singing, always singing. In his arms he bore the robe of transformation. Dull brown silk embroidered with ebony threads, it showed the interlocking plates of the shell, the creases of eternity and wisdom, the shelter and strength that were the Earth's guardian. En Lai's shoulders sagged beneath its weight as Minh draped it about her. Xuan put aside his wishes to comfort her, and sang on, each tone, each word, robbing En Lai of self and strength, turning her into the vessel, emptying her being to the need of Hung-Tse.

Shaiming, the Minister of Metal, stepped forward next, bearing the snub-nosed mask fashioned of gold and bronze. En Lai could no longer stand. She collapsed against Shaiming as he tied the ribbons tightly against her skull, so that her face was gone and all that remained in the moonlight was the face of the guardian. Singing that mystery, singing praise and gratitude, Shaiming lowered En Lai to the stone. The woman could not be seen anymore. There was only the shell, the great legs, the wise face, the dark eyes.

There was only the vessel to be filled.

Chi Tahn shifted the song, deepening the pitch, slowing the tempo, reaching into stone and earth where the guardian waited. Words of praise, words of pleading, words of gratitude and need. This was the greatest of all the songs. These were the words of true transformation. This was the first gift, and the last, the final duty of all who were chosen for this high office. Xuan poured himself freely into the working, spending strength, breath, and magic to shape the change, to call the guardian forth.

And nothing happened.

At first no one moved. Chi Tahn led the song still, and effort redoubled. Xuan reached within and without, bringing all his training to bear to shape the words that shaped the world. Around him, he felt the others doing the same. He had not been so close to his brothers and sisters in many years, and he gladly drew himself closer yet. En Lai lay still upon the altar, a heap of brown cloth and sparkling metals.

Cloth rustled. Eyes shifted, left and right. A note wavered. The air shivered. The song went on. Xuan shaped the words, shaped the power, but the first traces of weariness were beginning to creep in. His jaws began to ache, his breath began to catch. The weaving loosened. He could hear Chi Tahn's voice above the others, calling and calling again. He felt the pull, but it was weaker. It no longer touched heart and soul, compelling the magics. Xuan had to push them toward Chi Tahn, as if he were moving a burden up the ramp of a ship, trying to fill a hold that was too large for what he carried. The net of their magics frayed and the power began to spill away.

En Lai moaned.

They all heard her voice, muffled by the mask. It should not have been so. En Lai should have been long gone, departed but for her final essence to help the guardian shape her body. The woman should not be there to feel weariness or pain. The moan, a purely human sound, came again, and the threads of the spell snapped as if cut by a knife.

Silence fell, and the Nine Elders stared at one another. Xuan's heart barely remembered to beat. This was wrong. This was impossible. The great spells did not fail. They could not. They were part of the order of nature. They could no more fail to bring the guardian than the sun could fail to rise in the east.

Yet under the silence, power still thrummed. Something unspent still resonated in the air, making Xuan's skin shiver.

On the altar, En Lai, who was only En Lai still, lifted her head. Her pale hand reached out and pushed the mask back from her face. The inert piece of metal clattered onto the stone.

"What happened?" she whispered, but her words rang as loud as the song had. "Where is my guardian?"

She sounded lost, like a small child. But there was no comfort to offer her, no words, no learning. They stared around them, looking for answers on stones meant only for protection and prayer. Yet, there was still that something, that final spark of power, growing stronger, calling without words.

"Do you feel it?" asked Xuan. "Do you feel that?"

But none of the others heard him, they were too busy babbling out their own questions.

"Where are they?"

"Why do they not speak to us?"

"What have we done?"

There was light now, more felt than seen, a warmth in his veins. En Lai was on her feet, shedding the robe that should have become her skin. She stared at her human hands with their unaltered markings as if she did not know what to do with them. Tears streamed down her face.

She did not feel this thing. It was not for her.

Like a man in a dream, and yet at the same time utterly sure of what he must do, Xuan broke the circle. He walked to the altar. En Lai stumbled past him, moving in the other direction, seeking the comfort of the others, but he barely saw her. Thirty years ago he had walked this path. He had crossed these stones, lifted his foot, taken these last steps to the center of the altar of sacrifice, had stood with his brothers and sisters in art all around him. Thirty years ago, two hundred years ago, a thousand years ago. But they had been singing then, weaving the great spells with their voices. They had not stood mute and staring. He had been the one who stood still then, waiting for the transformation, waiting with open heart for what must be. He had not stood with his hands and eyes lifted toward Heaven. His had not been the voice to cry out.

"Come home to me! Be welcome and speak to us of your freedom! Tell us how we are to redress the wrong that was done!"

His had not been the eyes to see the golden streaks of fire across the night sky, shining more brightly than any comet's tail.

I kneel before you, he said with all the power of his mind reaching out toward his guardian, to this other part of himself and the element to which he was bound. *I offer myself for my failure.*

In his mind, he heard the voice of his guardian give answer. *Too late. Too long. I possess you already. I will have my retribution.*

Too late, the damage already done. As Tsan Nu had said.

He knew what was going to happen, knew it with his whole being, as he knew how to breathe or his heart knew how to beat. *There are innocents here.*

You knew what had been done to me. You knew and you did nothing. You feared and you schemed, but you did nothing.

Tears ran from Xuan's eyes. He reached up to the fiery form. He would have embraced it gladly and let himself burn, to be whole again. To be as he should have been. *Let us help you find the path to Heaven.*

Anger poured over him. *That is why you think I do this? You burn in my heart and you think I could not find my way?*

And Xuan saw. With heart's eye and mind's eye, he saw. He felt his wings and the rage of his own fire. He rose into darkness, the only light in the Heavens.

Free. Free. Finally free.

He stretched his wings out their whole, great length. His fire, his life, his heart and song rose for the first time in all the long, slow years. His captor was dead, dead, ash and dust behind him and the cage was gone, was gone, was *gone.*

The veil between worlds was as nothing. To enter the Silent Lands was only to return home, filling its unchanging skies and shifting illusions with his song and his fire. The powers lifted their heads and took note of his passing. Let them see. His captor was dead, his cage was ashes, and he was free. He would fly, and he would go to his true home and there would be peace and rest, and no more pain.

He spiraled higher. The sky became black and filled with fabulous stars that shone like diamonds with fire that lit up nothing but endless darkness. Those stars watched the Phoenix spiral higher. They watched comets fly beneath its wings and their own dust coat its feathers, only enhancing its brightness. Higher, and higher yet, singing out into that world where there was only darkness and fire, singing of what had been done, singing of coming home.

At last, overhead the sky paled from black to blue and all the stars fell back in reverence as the light of Heaven shone down upon them. Tears spilled from Xuan as the Phoenix cried in gladness and stretched its wings to be enfolded into the pure sapphire light that was heart and home. Soon all of Heaven would know its suffering, and its curse would fall upon its captors and those who abandoned it.

But even as he approached Heaven's light, it receded, leaving him in blackness. The Phoenix, Xuan, the Phoenix, cried out in confusion and beat its wings harder, climbing yet higher. But still the blue sky fell back, as if it were only illusion.

Frantically, the Phoenix called out. All the true names of the kings of Heaven were in that cry, Xuan knew that even though he could understand none of them. The Phoenix called out to its creators like a lost child calling for his parents. But they just turned away, pulling in the boundaries of Heaven like the hems of a silken robe, and for all that the Phoenix cried tears like small stars and for all that it called out and beat its wings, rising higher and rising faster, still Heaven retreated before it and would not pause so that it might enter.

Exhaustion can come even to a child of the gods and at last the Phoenix's wings began to falter. The ethereal realm would no longer support it and it began to fall, back into the darkness, back among the lesser stars who watched it with pity and contempt, back into the green of that space fit only to wrap up the mortal worlds and hold them in their courses.

All that long, weary fall, the Phoenix cried. It cried because it knew why it fell and it drove that understanding deep into Xuan's heart. It fell because it was corrupted. It was no longer pure in its being and its purpose. This the Nine Elders had done in their neglect. This they had left it to. Exile, loneliness, pain, and Heaven's denial because it could not rid its heart of anger.

Would you show me the path to Heaven? How? It was you who tore Heaven from me!

Xuan collapsed to his knees, tears streaming down his cheeks. He still wept as the first flames blossomed from the wooden roof beams and the Phoenix screamed out its anger over the Heart of the World.

Chapter Four

Mae Shan woke to the scent of burning.

Her eyes flew open and she was on her feet before she was fully awake, one hand on the knife in her belt. Night still darkened the nursery, but red and gold light flickered through the screens that blocked the way to the garden, casting dancing shadows on the floor.

Fire.

Now that the word penetrated her mind, Mae Shan smelled the acrid smoke and heard the crackling, tumultuous noise of a mounting blaze. She ran to the window, shoving the heavy shutter up.

Outside, she saw the familiar shadows of the Moon Garden and its heavy walls, but all was illuminated by the vicious, dancing light, turning the willows the colors of blood and brass. A talon of flame jutted over the western wall, releasing sparks to touch the topmost leaves of the garden's trees.

The great bronze alarm bells began to toll to the north. Black silhouettes raced past on top of the walls, some carrying spears and axes, some hugging clothes or bedcovers to themselves. Screams and weeping joined the clamor of the bells.

Mae Shan automatically looked eastward to the Heart of the World, with its golden tower standing sentinel over all. Flames stretched up the sides, halfway to the roof. Clouds of grey smoke billowed into the air like dragon's breath.

Mae Shan's heart froze, but reflex remembered training and duty. She had to get her charge away from here. Now.

Mae Shan ran to the inner chamber.

"Wake up!" she shouted to the two maids snoring in their beds as she raced past. "Fire! Fire! Wake up!"

As the sounds of slow waking rumbled and rustled behind her, Mae

Shan laid her hands on the rosewood door. Hot, too hot, and she could hear the rush of flames beyond it. The fire was already in the corridors. Confusion rushed through her. How had this happened so fast? Such a fire should have taken hours to start. Where was the Heart's Guard?

She had been trained to wake at the sound of an unfamiliar footfall. How could she have slept through the rising of such a blaze?

Wei Lin? Unbidden, her heart called out to her sister who slept in the companions' quarters with silken sheets and maidservants all around her.

How much of the palace burned? What if Wei Lin were still asleep?

Behind Mae Shan, one maid proved she was finally awake by shrieking like a startled kettle. Then came the clatter of a screen falling, and wordless, horrified cries. The other maid was beside Mae Shan in an instant, yanking at the door's handle with terrified urgency.

"Let me out! Let me out!"

"No, you fool!" Mae Shan shoved her aside. "The door's hot. The corridor must already be burning. Get your mistress. We'll go through the garden."

The maid stared at her, the light of the blaze reflecting in her frightened eyes. She gathered up the hems of her heavy sleeping robes and bolted again, vaulting over the screen her fellow servant had knocked down, and was out in the garden without pause for anything but her own escape.

Mae Shan gaped for a second, not believing such abandonment of duty. But then, she heard another sleepy, small voice.

"Min Lao? Mae Shan?"

Mae Shan raced back to the inner chamber. She crossed the room in three strides to stand beside the carved bed that was much too large for its tiny occupant. Tsan Nu sat up. The child pushed her waving hair out of her round, pale eyes and blinked up at her bodyguard.

"There's a fire, mistress. Come to me." She held out her arms.

Tsan Nu stared at her for a moment, but instead of running to her guard, she dove under the bed. Mae Shan gawped for a moment and then heaved the bed to one side, exposing the startled child clutching a pair of black slippers.

Mae Shan did not give the child a chance to speak another word. She snatched a coverlet up with one hand and Tsan Nu with the other, wrapped the one over the other, and threw the squirming bundle over her shoulder. She sprinted past the toppled screens out into the Moon Garden.

The flames were not here yet, but the heat was. It played across Mae Shan's skin like the flickering lights. Smoke wisps drifted through the air like the morning fog, rasping against her throat and lungs and drawing tears from her blinking eyes. The willows swayed in the unnatural wind, as if trying to pull away from the heat.

Tsan Nu's faithless maids had reached the inner southern wall, the only wall not crowned in flame. They beat upon the wooden door, struggling futilely with the bar and lock. The younger of the two cried up at the silhouettes that raced or struggled past on the stone road formed by the tops of the doubled outer walls. No one paused. No one shouted down, although they called out to each other, their voices making no more sense than the constant roar of the flames.

Disgust joined fear and anger inside Mae Shan. More voices screamed overhead, urging her to look up. She ignored them. She could not afford to look back now. She could not be frozen in her tracks. Her whole duty was to see the wriggling child in her arms safely out of this disaster. All else came later.

She strode to the edge of the nearest round pond. A soft and heavy thing hit the ground behind her, and another. The maids wailed to all the gods in Heaven. Unseen women shrieked and screamed. One might be Wei Lin, Mae Shan's beautiful, laughing, loyal sister. She closed her ears even as her heart cracked open.

"Hold your breath!" she shouted, and she dropped Tsan Nu into the water. The girl screeched, coughed, and sputtered, but Mae Shan paid no attention. She dragged the dripping child and sodden coverlet back into her arms and ran for the southern wall.

"What's happening?" screeched Tsan Nu, beating at the cover with her free hand. The other hand still clutched her shoes. "Mae Shan, what's happening?"

"Hold still!" snapped Mae Shan in reply, not caring at the moment what her young charge thought, as long as she obeyed. If she struggled too hard, she'd slow down their escape, and any delay could mean a blocked exit, or a lost chance.

Get through the Sun Garden. Make for the Heart's courtyard. All stone. Nothing to burn. No way to spread the fire.

The two maids still beat upon the wall's locked door. Mae Shan thrust a hand into her shirt to bring out the bundle of keys she wore next to her private purse. She found the right key by touch and thrust it into the hands of the older maid.

"Open that door!"

Startled, the woman shoved the key into the door's black iron lock and turned it.

Where are the Nine Elders? Where is the rain they can bring?

"Put me down!" cried Tsan Nu, fighting her way free of the soggy coverlet. "Mae Shan, what's happening?" Then, her pale eyes saw the fire leaping over the top of the walls, and her mouth hung wide open and silent.

"Hurry!" screamed the younger maid, beating her soft fists against her older compatriot's back. "Hurry!"

Mae Shan did not slap the foolish maid, although she wanted to with all her heart. Instead, as the lock snapped open, Mae Shan shoved the bar aside with her free hand, throwing open the door to the causeway between the walls.

Each palace in the Heart of the World was surrounded by three walls. There was an inner wall, then a stone causeway for carts and foot traffic, and then a doubled outer wall, which held the garrisons and basements within it and the soldier's way above. At a glance, Mae Shan saw a dozen shadows, fleeing down the causeway, outlined in flame. Behind the shadows, a section of inner wall had crumbled, allowing the fire to claw its way out. To the left, the way she had hoped to run, she saw a tree blazing above the inner wall, already teetering and ready to fall.

The younger maid saw none of this. She just squeezed past Mae Shan fleeing into the oven-hot night that lay between the inner and outer walls.

Mae Shan found she had been expecting that. "You will come with your mistress," she ordered the remaining servant. "Try to run like that and . . ."

A new noise sounded overhead—an inhuman scream that reached over even the devouring flames and crumbling stone. Mae Shan looked up without thinking, and did the one thing she had determined she would not do. She froze.

She had never seen the Phoenix in real life, and never expected to.

She had never imagined she would with her own eyes see its arching neck and the trailing feathers that were streamers of flame like the ones that reached over the walls. She had never thought to hear it scream in triumph over the tower of Ah Min's Spear as that tower cracked, so slowly, so terribly slowly, and began to fall. She had never thought she would stand and stare while heat seared her eyes and lungs as its wings curved over the whole world, claiming the night and the burning Heart of the World for its own.

Beside her, the older maid gaped like the child in Mae Shan's arms. As slowly as the golden tower had, the woman crumpled and fell to her knees. She stared up at the sacred guardian as it wheeled in the sky, its great tail blazing behind it, blotting out moon and stars.

Finally, the woman bowed, pressing her head against the ground. Her prayers poured out of her becoming a babble of noise.

Mae Shan wanted to drop down beside her. Running suddenly seemed a sacrilege. The Phoenix soared overhead—one of the immortal guardians, the protectors and avengers of Hung-Tse, a gift from the gods to ensure the final security of those who lived at the center of the world. Surely if the Phoenix was here, so too were the gods, and if they declared that the Heart should die, she should throw herself prayerfully into the flames.

"It came. I told them it would come." Tsan Nu huddled underneath her sodden coverlet, whimpering with nothing but a child's fear. Mae Shan tore her eyes from the beautiful, terrible sight overhead. She had her duty. No matter what, she had her duty, and if she was to die tonight, she would die acting correctly. "There won't be any tomorrow. I saw it."

"Come on!" Mae Shan shouted to the maid, tearing the bundle of keys from the servant's hands. But the maid just screamed and yanked herself away. Weeping, she knocked her head against the ground and continued with her wailing, babbling prayers.

Mae Shan clutched Tsan Nu tightly to her chest to protect her from the pull of the fleeing crowd. There was no room to retreat now. The surge of the crowd was too strong. Not daring to press back against the inner wall, Mae Shan held still, drew the rapidly drying coverlet over Tsan Nu's head. The girl pressed her face close against Mae Shan's shoulder. Servants and nobles, free and slave, jostled together, indistinguishable, partially clothed, smudged with soot, and reddened with fear, tears, and burns. All made for the Heart of the World and the broad stone court with its gate to the outside world. None seemed to see the tree teetering overhead.

Mae Shan did not look up. She did not want to see, did not want to think about what flew overhead. She did not want to see her death, and the death of the child in her arms, in the holy beauty of the Phoenix.

Ahead, the ancient tree gave over to the flames, and tipped slowly down to the lower causeway. Those who saw screamed and tried to reverse their panicked flight, only to plow into those who rushed up behind them. The burning branches crashed down, and the screams Mae Shan had thought could grow no louder redoubled. Now the crowd ran back, reversing its current in its desperation to get away from the sudden deadly barrier.

Now she could move with the river of bodies. Holding Tsan Nu tight against her chest, Mae Shan ran, keeping her eyes on the way ahead, blessing her height and long legs. In places, the fire had breached the inner walls, leaving piles of stone on the lower causeway to be licked by flames overflowing from the gardens.

Sweat poured down Mae Shan's face and neck. Bodies jostled her on all sides. Terrified eyes flashed in the firelight. She recognized no one. She forced herself to keep her own eyes on the way in front of her. Even if one of these was Wei Lin, Mae Shan would not see her, not disguised in soot and shadows as she surely would be. To look for her sister's face would be to waste time, to lay aside duty, to die, and to kill Tsan Nu.

Oh, my sister. I'm sorry. I'm sorry.

Finally, she spied a knot of people pounding against the outer wall. She could not hear their fists and bodies hitting the surface, but she knew they must be in front of one of the soldiers' access doors, all of which were kept locked. The Phoenix's fire came so fast there would have been no time to open them. Or maybe they were meant as sacrifices to appease the guardian's anger.

Members of the guard raced by on the soldier's road atop the outer walls, seemingly oblivious to what went on below.

"Let me through!" Mae Shan bellowed, wading into the thick crowd of bodies. "I've got a key! I've got a key!"

They heard and had enough control left to do as she said. Mae Shan shouldered her way to the iron-banded door. She thrust her key in the lock, turned it, and this time, made sure she blocked the whole way with her body.

She meant to duck through with Tsan Nu, and to shut the door behind her. To leave it open, even for a moment, was to let the flood into the garrison space inside the walls, clogging it up, possibly clogging it shut. Her duty was Tsan Nu. She had none to these who surrounded her now. Not even her own sister. She couldn't hesitate now. She didn't even know if she could get Tsan Nu out, not with the Phoenix blazing overhead and calling down the doom of the Heart of the World. She couldn't risk trying to save anyone else. Not even Wei Lin.

And still, she cried out, "Quickly! Follow me!" She flung the door wide open and plunged into the stifling darkness inside the doubled wall.

At least part of the crowd was able to obey. Their cries echoed off the vaulted stone that encased the garrison as they swarmed after Mae Shan. She did not look back. Those who could think to follow would follow.

Mae Shan's flame-dazzled eyes adjusted rapidly to the darkness. The only light came from the flicker of the fire through the arrow slits and the copper lanterns spaced evenly down the sandstone walls. None of the doors they barreled past was guarded. All the sentries had been called up and out, to do what could be done. She could hear their boots pounding as they ran past on the soldier's way overhead. Sweat dripped into Mae Shan's eyes and her lungs felt like withered leaves, but she did not slow down. She tried not to be grateful that the realization of what had brought the fire had left Tsan Nu silent and still in her arms, a burden to be carried, nothing more. She tried to compose her mind to prayer and duty. She tried not to let her thoughts veer back to lost Wei Lin, to those who still filled the causeway outside, or even to the crying strangers who ran beside her. But some of those found the ladders to the soldier's way and swarmed up them.

"No!" shouted Mae Shan to whoever would, or could, listen. "With me!"

Some listened, some did not, and she heard their cries change again as they threw open the hatches and found fire, or soldiers who flung them down to the dirt, leaving them unable to rise and run; leaving Mae Shan unable to do anything but pray the walls would hold to keep them safe from the flames.

But who will answer those prayers when the gods' servant is the one who brought the fire?

The garrison held hatches in the floor as well as in the roof. As Mae Shan hoped, one had been thrown open by some guard or soldier whose haste did not permit them to close it behind them. She set Tsan Nu on her feet and stripped off the coverlet that was now dry as if she had never doused it.

"Climb down," she ordered. Tsan Nu, mute and serious in her fear, stuffed the slippers she still carried into her sash and obeyed. Mae Shan's hand closed on her knife as she faced what was left of the crowd surging up behind her. If one of them tried to push their way down before Tsan Nu . . .

But none did. They halted, huddling together, waiting for her orders. In the dim light, she could not even tell which were men and which were women.

"Keep up as best you can." Mae Shan let go of the knife without drawing it. Instead, she snatched one of the copper lanterns off its chain and followed Tsan Nu down the ladder.

The next level down was below the heat and the smoke. Mae Shan dragged in a great breath of dank, foul air as if it were the rarest incense. There was no light except for the lantern she carried. She grabbed Tsan Nu's hand and strode forward.

Down here were the cells. She could hear the prisoners moaning and calling out behind the heavily barred doors. No one had come to let them out, and no one would. Maybe they would be safe, but how long would it be before some survivor remembered they were down here? She could do nothing. She had no keys for these doors, no way to quickly fling aside their bars.

Gods help me. Gods help me to my duty and stop my ears, and Tsan Nu's. Don't let this child realize what's happening.

Mae Shan broke again into a run. Tsan Nu whimpered as she was dragged along, but Mae Shan did not slow down.

The floor down here was lined with flagstone. An open drain, dry now, ran down the center of the corridor. That was their guide, and Mae Shan followed it like a lifeline. Harsh breath, coughs, and the sound of soft shoes and bare feet on stone followed behind.

At last, the corridor dead-ended at a wall of blank stone. The drain itself continued through a metal grating, heading into darkness.

"Now, Mistress Tsan Nu," said Mae Shan between gasps for air that were echoed a dozen times by those who had managed to follow. "A spell blocks this grate and keeps anyone from cracking it open. This is our way out. Can you break it?"

The girl's chin trembled in the pale lantern light, but she knelt down by the grating. Mae Shan held the lantern over her so she could get a good look at the riveted metal. Either the girl could find a way, or they waited here for the fire overhead to burn out, taking their chances with the other prisoners.

"I'll need your knife," Tsan Nu said, her voice sounding small and tired. "And something to tie knots in."

Mae Shan undid her sash, handing it and the knife to Tsan Nu. Although she did not want to, she faced their followers. Any one of them might try to run forward and shake the girl because she did not work fast enough, or they might try to tear at the grating. They were the immediate danger, and because she had brought them down here, they were her responsibility.

Now that she had a moment, Mae Shan found she could begin to make out some details among them. There was a tiny old woman with ash-grey hair. There was a burly man with a thin line of beard staring at the grating and clearly wondering if he could make it through. There was a willow wand of a girl, and a boy who looked to be all of a year older than Tsan Nu.

Overhead, something groaned and crumbled to the ground. Mae Shan kept looking at her followers. The doubled walls were starting to fall up there. The fire was starting to find its way inside to the garrisons. When the crowd before her realized that, they might panic. She had to be ready for them, any of them, all of them.

She had given Tsan Nu her knife, and they had all seen her do it.

Mae Shan did not look down to see what the girl was doing. She heard Tsan Nu's voice rising and falling, but did not understand one word. Tsan Nu spoke the spell language, learned from her masters who were up there now, if they had not succumbed to the flames. If they had not fled.

She will be able to do this. She saw the Phoenix coming when no one else did. If she can draw out the future, she can open the grate on a drain.

"It's ready," said Tsan Nu. Was it wishful thinking, or did her voice sound more firm?

"Thank you, mistress," Mae Shan said, hoping her own voice sounded quietly confident. "If you are willing, it would be good for you to continue now."

Mae Shan permitted her gaze to flicker down. Tsan Nu's pale eyes were wide as they looked up, but her trembling had stopped. She had slashed Mae Shan's sash into five strips. Into each strip she had tied four knots, and with a final knot she had tied them all together. Mae Shan knew just enough to know that this was how Tsan Nu had drawn up and shaped the magics she commanded. Now, she had to release them to work.

With a swift, practiced movement, Mae Shan slit that final knot. The strips of cloth fell separately to the stones. Another low rumble sounded overhead. Mae Shan's nose caught the distant scent of smoke. Someone among the other escapees whimpered.

Metal twanged sharply. Tsan Nu darted behind Mae Shan as the grating snapped, its rails falling away from the stone as the cloth strips had fallen away from each other.

Mae Shan did not waste time gaping. After the sight of the Phoenix, this was a small miracle indeed.

"I'll go in first," she said. "With luck I'll be able to keep the lantern lit on the way. Mistress, you must follow behind with your hands on my heels. You others . . ." She lifted the lantern to the small crowd.

They said nothing, but they understood. They had to follow, one at a time, as best they could. They held their places, though, and Mae Shan silently blessed them for it.

Now came the moment of vulnerability. She had to turn her back on them, and kneel down, and push the lantern into the drain. The smell of old blood and old waste was hideous, but it was preferable to the scent of smoke that was growing stronger by the heartbeat. Now they could shove Tsan Nu aside. Now they could ruin all.

But small hands grasped her heels and Tsan Nu's familiar voice said, "I am ready."

Mae Shan crawled forward, edging the lantern along the tunnel of dank stone. Damp seeped through her clothes at the knees and elbows. Something cold dripped onto the top of her head, ran down her scalp, and then down the back of her neck, making her shiver. More droplets pattered against her back and calves. After the heat and terrible light, the cold and dark were a relief at first. Soon, though, the narrow tunnel became oppressive. Mae Shan knew where the drain ended, but she did not know what came between here and the midden. Were there more grates? Had the conflagration overhead collapsed the foundations along the way? The shuffling and moans of her followers echoed off the baked clay and filled Mae Shan's ears. Summoning all the discipline she could muster, she shut the small, desperate sounds off from her mind. She kept crawling, inching the flickering lantern along ahead of her and trying not to start at the shadows.

They crawled for what felt like hours. Mae Shan's elbows and knees seemed bruised past endurance. Each breath Tsan Nu took was a whimper and one of the other children had begun to cry, softly but insistently. At last, Mae Shan looked up and saw the grey circlet that was the mouth of the pipe, and the dawn outside.

"I see it!" shouted one of the men before Mae Shan could open her mouth. "Goddess of Mercy, I see the end!"

Prayers and weeping bounced loudly off the pipe's curving sides and Mae Shan winced. A moment later, she berated herself. There was no enemy waiting for her. Did she think the Phoenix would hear their escape and come for them?

Am I sure it won't? Oh, Goddess of Mercy, do not abandon us here. At least cast your eye on the children. The children can't have offended.

Faint daylight filtered through the pipe's mouth. Mae Shan crawled out to its rough, stone lip and took a moment to blow out the lantern. Then, squinting against the grey dawn, she lowered herself into the waist-deep canal, turned, and held out her arms for Tsan Nu.

The child permitted herself to be carried to the bank and stood on her feet. There were no boats or barges on this little side channel of the main canal, but there should have been. Likewise, the one bridge Mae Shan could see was empty of pedestrians. So were the streets. Even though it was just dawn, laborers and vendors should have been about their business. The wind was hot and the air was thick with ash and the reek of smoke and worse things. Reluctantly, Mae Shan turned around.

T'ien, the city that held the Heart of the World, was a city of walls. They loomed on all sides, defining neighborhoods, market and business quarters, sheltering the streets and allowing soldiers free passage unencumbered by the traffic of carts and pedestrians. From here, Mae Shan could not see the Heart of the World. There was only a black cloud of smoke and ash rising into the brightening sky. The fire must still be burning, for the cloud's belly glowed bright orange. Sparks and burning debris fluttered on the wind, spreading out to land where they would, to start new fires in the gardens and take down the wood and earth walls of the houses where they alighted. Mae Shan swallowed. The Phoenix's work was not yet done.

"Madame soldier," said a soft voice at her elbow. Slowly, Mae Shan looked down. One of the women who had followed her was beside her. Her night clothes were soaked to the shoulder and water ran in rivulets from the ends of her unbound hair. She coughed from the ash and smoke, and her eyes were wide with fear. "Madame soldier, what do we do now?"

Mae Shan's gaze turned involuntarily back to the cloud of ruin spreading out across the city. A shiver that had nothing to do with cold ran down her spine.

I don't know. May the Heavens help us all. I don't know.

But she could not say any such thing. She was the representative of the imperial house here, however deep in ashes that house now stood. She had to know.

Where stillness is not possible, order must be primary. The voice of Mae Shan's training master echoed in her mind. Before she had been assigned to duty as a personal bodyguard, she had been taught as a soldier of the Heart, which included instruction on how to deal with civilian disarray.

"We must clear the streets," she said firmly. She looked around her, noting the markings on the closest walls and the lay of the buildings. Fortunately, there was daylight enough for her to make out what she needed. "We are in the Street of the Hospitable. That"—she pointed to the nearby cross street—"is the Street of Shining Morning." Thorough knowledge of the city's byways was required for all the Heart's soldiers. "You who have friends or relatives within the city bounds must go to them as quickly as possible. Others must take shelter in the public houses. The nearest is east down the Street of Shining Morning. Tell them you are under orders, and wait for the official directives, which will be made shortly." *So I hope.* "In the meantime, make sure all vessels are filled with water and wet down the walls and roofs of the houses."

"Yes, madame soldier," they murmured. "Thank you, madame." In twos and threes they moved away, huddling close to each other as if for warmth, despite the burning wind. They did not run, but walked weaving paths as if dazed or drunk. Mae Shan spared a prayer for them, although she did not know a single name, and hoped they would find safety.

Deep in her heart, she prayed for herself as well.

Tsan Nu had hoped when they emerged that the air would be fresh after the stink of the sewers, but it was not. The red dawn was filled with ash and hot smoke and it grated on the inside of her throat and nostrils as she tried to breathe.

Mae Shan was telling the others what they should do. Tsan Nu, however, knew that Mae Shan would take care of her, so she did not pay close attention. Instead, she looked up at the clouds of smoke from the Heart of the World, shivering as her nightdress hardened in stiff folds against her body from the hot, ashen wind.

As she had thought, the devils were rising. The cloud of smoke and bright embers that rolled endlessly into the brightening sky was beginning to separate out. The wisps and streamers took on fresh shapes and colors—an emerald, clawed hand clutching a poleax here, a pair of glaring yellow eyes there, a bright red mouth in another place. All the devils the Nine Elders had held in check for three thousand years were free now and they would soon be looking for plunder and ruin.

"Come, mistress," said Mae Shan. "Hold my sleeve. We must hurry."

Tsan Nu grasped the short sleeve of Mae Shan's nightshirt and made herself hurry along as best she could, taking three steps for every one of the tall woman's strides. Mae Shan would watch the way. Tsan Nu watched the walls. She was vaguely aware of people rushing past, some with their arms and wheelbarrows full of possessions and weeping children. Some carried buckets on yokes, running to the wells and fountains for water to protect their homes. She squinted between weaving torsos, and up past bowed heads and frightened faces to try to see the wards drawn in red and blue on the pale walls.

The blessing posts at the corners still stood, that was good. People bowed to them, weeping, that was not good. No god or ancestor would hear them there. Mae Shan would not slow down so Tsan Nu could explain that to anyone. These were only places for guardian spells. They needed to go find the gods in their temples. The smoke was getting thicker. Her hair dried against her scalp in tight coils that itched. She coughed and Mae Shan held out a handkerchief and told her to press it over her her mouth. She did, and that helped some, although tears still streamed from her stinging eyes, making it hard to decipher the runes as they ran by.

Overhead, the devils continued their work. The little ones swarmed over the larger, helping join together severed limbs to create whole creatures with skins of scarlet, night black, blazing yellow, or brilliant green. Their white fangs gnashed together and they rolled their eyes as they looked down on the ruin that was the Heart of the World. The little demons danced around them, tiny whirlwinds of color raising their pikes, or their taloned hands to rake at the smoke as if seeking to claw Heaven apart.

Tsan Nu shivered and stumbled over an uneven cobble. Mae Shan jerked her arm up a little to keep her from falling. While she tried to find her stride again, Tsan Nu looked around for a street sign, to try to see where they were. Mae Shan hurried them around another corner. The smoke seemed thicker here. Tsan Nu craned her neck as they hurried past the blessing post.

The Imperial Way, she managed to read before smoke and distance obscured the characters. Her throat seized shut. Mae Shan was circling them back toward the Heart of the World.

"No!" Tsan Nu shouted, digging in her heels. "We can't!"

The biggest of the red devils in the sky was almost fully formed now. Lesser demons and devils were running to it, bringing a finger here, and a bit of horn or whisker there so it could complete itself. At last, a whole host of little demons with paws and faces like tigers charged up to it, bearing on their shoulders a great, curved sword in an elaborate golden scabbard. The chief devil, now complete, bared all its fangs in an evil grin and drew the sword, swinging the blade over its head with the force of a whirlwind, spinning the smoke around it into fantastic shapes. She saw at once what it was doing. It was spreading out the embers of the Phoenix's fire over T'ien. That fire would destroy houses, but it would also crumble

the walls, leaving the demons free paths to descend upon the city's inhabitants, and on those who fled, like Mae Shan, and her.

"We must go back, mistress." Strain tightened Mae Shan's voice. "If
any of my compatriots are still alive, that is where they will be, and they
will know where the survivors are to be taken. The Temple of Glorious
Heaven may still stand . . ."

"No!" cried Tsan Nu again. She stabbed her finger up at the sky.
"Don't you see?" No. Of course she didn't. Mae Shan didn't have the
right kind of eyes. "The devils are out there!" she shouted. "They're free
and they'll be able to come get us where the walls have fallen!"

Mae Shan squinted up at the smoke-filled sky. The lesser devils and
demons were forming up ranks behind the great one, a surging riot of
color, claw, and blade. Black and red banners lifted up to mark their
companies.

"I see nothing but smoke, mistress," said Mae Shan slowly.

"I know." Tsan Nu tried to think past her desperation. Why did no-
body see? Why didn't anybody *listen*? "Please, Mae Shan, listen to me.
The Nine Elders kept all the demons walled up and quiet, and now
they're dead and the walls are broken. They're out, and they're as angry
as the Phoenix. We can't go back to the Heart! We have to stay between
the walls or they'll find us!"

She could see what Mae Shan was thinking. Mae Shan wanted to
join the other soldiers, because that was what she was supposed to do.
Maybe she even wanted to get away from Tsan Nu like Min Lao and Si
Yin. What would she do if Mae Shan wouldn't listen, like the Nine Elders wouldn't listen? Could she run away through the streets? She clutched
her shoes. As long as she had them, she had Father's amulet, but it would
take time and safety to make the working. Could she find a temple where
the priest or a sorcerer could see what was happening and help hide her
until she could reach Father? Could she run fast enough to get away
from Mae Shan? When she'd run away from her maids and tutors it was
always Mae Shan who caught her and marched her back.

Mae Shan took in their bearings with her quick eyes. "There's a garrison in the Street of Seven Generations Under One Roof," she said. "We
will be safe there, and they may have news of what's happened."

"We know what happened," Tsan Nu pointed out as Mae Shan started
off down the street.

Mae Shan did not answer that. Instead, she said, "Watch the walls, mistress. If we are in danger, you must let me know at once."

"Yes, Mae Shan."

Mae Shan frowned and picked their direction. Tsan Nu risked a glance up. The Chief Devil was exhorting his followers. They were all of them waving their banners and fans to send the smoke and embers pouring out across the city. More spots of orange glowed against the bellies of the clouds. More fires already? The Chief Devil threw back his head to laugh, and Tsan Nu couldn't stand to watch anymore. Instead she looked at the walls. In this street, at least, the words of blessing were still whole, as were the stones. They should be safe, for a while, anyway. The demons and their devils could not come down here while the walls were whole. While the walls were whole, the spells of protection woven with stone, mortar, paint, and hidden carving would hold and no devil could walk the streets. She remembered again how the walls fell as flames consumed the Heart of the World. She thought about Yi Qin and the fake amulet she'd said would be the other girl's good luck. Tears stung her eyes and Tsan Nu bit her tongue, as Master Liaozhai had told her to do when frightened. "You cannot show the face of fear to the devils," he said. "This will make them grow even more ferocious."

But the Nine Elders were dead, and the protective walls were crumbling. Yi Qin's ghost would surely haunt her for what she'd done, and she'd deserve it. How could she not show the face of fear?

But before long she couldn't pay attention to anything except the pain in her lungs and the way the hot wind lapped at her back. Tears filled her eyes so she could not see the walls properly. She stubbed her toes painfully against another cobble and stumbled again. This time, Mae Shan scooped Tsan Nu into her arms.

"There, mistress," she said in her deep, steady voice. "We're there."

Mae Shan pointed toward a blockhouse that stood at the juncture of four streets, the walls of the streets making up the walls of the garrison. It was a solid, square, unornamented building with slits for windows and a watchtower rising from its center.

"Without a single man standing watch," muttered Mae Shan.

Shifting Tsan Nu to the crook of one arm, Mae Shan picked up the baton for the iron bell and struck it once. The single tolling echoed loudly in the empty street. Tsan Nu winced and clutched Mae Shan's jacket, even though she knew loud noises were effective for keeping devils at bay. People should be out in the streets with firecrackers and pots and pans. She should tell someone, but there was no one left to tell.

Eventually, she saw the brief glimmer of an eye pressed to the door's watch slit. That glimpse was followed by the shuffle and scrape of a bar being pushed aside. The door opened on well-oiled hinges to reveal a gangly boy in hastily donned armor. Tsan Nu saw her guard's mouth twitch disapprovingly.

The boy pulled together a self-important air. "The curfew has sounded, mistress. If you do not clear the streets at once I will be forced to fine your family."

Mae Shan did not roll her eyes, although Tsan Nu could see she wanted to.

"Stand down, Private," said Mae Shan in the voice Tsan Nu thought of as her most soldierly. "I am Lieutenant Mae Shan Jinn and a Soldier of the Heart." She held up her left hand to display the topaz and gold ring that was the sigil of her service.

The boy gawped at the ring. "But you're . . . you're . . ."

"A guard of the women's palace and very much out of uniform." Mae Shan barged past the boy, setting Tsan Nu down as soon as they were inside. Two other boys sitting beside the clay stove scrambled to their feet. The blockhouse itself showed signs of its occupants' hasty departure; bowls and cups waited on the table and the vague scent of cabbage hung in the air. An empty wine jar had fallen on its side. A helmet had dropped from its hook beside the door and lay on the floor like an abandoned turtle. All three of the boys looked guilty and Tsan Nu wondered if they had been discussing whether or not they should run away and where they should go if they did.

"It's no good running away," Tsan Nu said, although the smoke had made her throat sore. "You need to stay between the walls or the devils will come."

The boy soldiers gaped at her. Before Tsan Nu could explain, Mae Shan squeezed her arm, a warning to keep quiet.

"What are your names?" Mae Shan asked the boys.

"Private Trainee Airic Bei," said the gangly boy who had opened the door and threatened to fine her.

"Private Trainee Chen Hsuan," said the stocky boy with wisps of hair trailing from his poorly braided queue.

"Private Trainee Kyun Biao," said the last boy who stood nearest the stove and had a huge mole on his right cheek.

"Where is the rest of the garrison, Trainee Airic?" Mae Shan asked, mustering a brisk tone, but her disgust shone plain on her face. "Where are the men who left three boys on their own in the middle of an emergency?"

Airic remembered the deference due to rank, even when rank was half-dressed and female. He pulled his shoulders back. "They've gone to help keep order at the Temple of Mercy, ma'am."

Of course. Curfew or no, the temples would be besieged with terrified petitioners, the temples of Szu Yi, Goddess of Mercy, more than any. Heaven itself only knew what the priests were saying about what should be done. Not all of them had the right kind of eyes either.

"Well, we won't be seeing them for a while," Mae Shan muttered. Then she raised her voice.

"Very well. Trainee Chen, the watch should not be neglected. You will take your turn. Trainee Kyun, this room is a mess. It will be cleaned at once. Trainee Airic." She faced the boy who had threatened her with fining. "You will show me a private room where I may wait with my charge, then you will get some rest before relieving Trainee Chen on watch."

Dazed by her sudden listing of orders, the boys did nothing but stare at her for a long moment. Then, however, they did as they had been trained to do and obeyed. Kyun began piling bowls and cups together. Chen vanished through the room's inner door, probably to grab a spear or other weapon and mount the tower stairs. Airic turned smartly, leading Mae Shan and Tsan Nu through a second door into what Tsan Nu guessed were the barracks. There were rows of cots with lumpy mattresses and rough blankets, and two other doors. One led to a spartan room that had a real bed, and a rug on the floor and a few banked coals in the small stove. More importantly, it had a shuttered window through which the street might be observed.

As Mae Shan thanked Trainee Airic, Tsan Nu climbed up on the bed and threw open the shutters. To her disappointment, she found the window barred. She gripped the bars and twisted her head sideways, trying to see as much of the sky as she could.

"Mistress, come down."

Tsan Nu ignored Mae Shan. Her heart was thundering so loudly, she barely heard anyway.

The army of devils had arrayed itself atop the roiling hills of smoke and ash. The chief of the devils waved his sword, sweeping it out to indicate the whole of the city, maybe the whole world. The demons cheered, waving their banners, pikes, hooks, and axes.

But they weren't alone anymore. The smoke still rose in grey streamers and up those streamers swarmed the ghosts of the Heart.

Many of them were soldiers, like Mae Shan, dressed in their armor and carrying their weapons on their backs. Others were officers who rode up the smoke on their horses, their servants behind them carrying their banners. Some seemed hesitant, confused, looking about themselves indecisively, but when they saw the devils they rallied at once and went to stand beside their fellows. Lords and ladies rose up on cushions of smoke, their sleeves billowing around them. Last came the emperors, borne on their platforms looking still and stern.

The Chief Devil saw all this and threw back his head and laughed, the blast of his breath making the floating ash around him boil. His followers jeered, rattling their flags and weapons.

But the Heart's ghosts ignored them and moved into their own ranks, each general taking charge of a company. The lords and ladies climbed the smoke hills and stood looking down, their hands folded. The emperors rose until they were the highest of all, their faces impassive and dignified.

This enraged the Chief Devil and he shouted and gestured madly to his followers. The lesser demons poured down the hills of smoke, brandishing their fearsome weapons. The ghosts of the Heart, though, did not hesitate. The officers gestured and called to their troops and charged the ranks of demons.

"Mistress, what do you see now?" asked Mae Shan, her voice tightening, with worry or impatience, Tsan Nu couldn't tell.

"The imperial ghosts are fighting the devils," she reported. "They've joined the battle. The Chief Devil is furious and he's trying to reach the emperors, but they're too high." The noble ones lifted up their silk and bamboo fans, waving them in elegant patterns that Tsan Nu recognized from court dances. "The lords and ladies are raising the winds to clear the smoke so the demons won't have anyplace to stand."

Mae Shan blinked. "How goes the battle?"

Tsan Nu squinted up at the shifting sea of smoke and colors. "I can't tell. I think it's too soon to know."

Mae Shan licked her lips. "Then leave it for now, mistress. Climb in the bed and warm yourself."

As Mae Shan said those words, Tsan Nu felt how deeply tired she was. The air was cleaner in here, and it was easier to breathe and see, except her sore eyes were heavy with the need for sleep.

Tsan Nu crawled under the covers. The rough fabric scraped against her skin. She wanted a clean nightdress. She wanted to swim in the lake in the Sun Garden so she could wash the awful itching feeling out of her hair. She wanted to tell Yi Qin she was sorry and that she'd make her a real amulet as soon as she had some more ribbons.

She didn't say any of this, because she couldn't have any of these things and she knew that. She clutched her shoes to her chest. She wanted Father. But she wouldn't be able to do any kind of working now. Not tired like this.

In the meantime, Mae Shan brought her a dipper of water from the bucket in the corner. She drank every drop and looked up to see Mae Shan kneeling in front of the stove.

"We will rest here and wait for news from the Heart." Mae Shan scooped up a handful of tinder from the box and laid it gingerly over the coals. A yellow flame stretched up to lick at the twigs, and then another. Watching them and remembering all that had passed, Tsan Nu winced and pulled her knees up to her chin.

"There won't be any news," said Tsan Nu bluntly. "The Heart is gone."

"The Nine Elders will have saved the emperor." Mae Shan did not look at Tsan Nu. She just reached for a stick of kindling and cracked it in two to add to the stove. The fire burned innocently, as if it were no relation to the flames that had almost taken their lives, that had destroyed the palace of a thousand years.

"The Nine Elders are dead," said Tsan Nu. Didn't Mae Shan hear her? The devils would not be free if the Nine Elders were still alive. "So is the emperor."

Mae Shan swallowed visibly. "You don't know that, mistress."

"I do know." Tsan Nu raised her chin. "This is what I saw when Minister Xuan asked me to cast that horoscope. I tried to tell him to get everybody away, but he wouldn't *listen*." Raw, shrill frustration filled Tsan Nu's voice. Master Liaozhai would have been furious. Was he up there now, fighting the devils? She hadn't been able to see his face. "They should have listened."

"Yes," said Mae Shan, looking at the fire. "They should have."

She closed the grate on the stove and stared at the formless glow it made of the fire inside. "You will tell me what you see, mistress? You will make me listen?"

"I'll try," said Tsan Nu in a small voice. Suddenly, she didn't want to see anything. She didn't want to know what was happening. She just wanted to hide her head under the covers and have morning come and be back in her bed with her maids bringing her breakfast and Master Liaozhai chiding her for being lazy.

She pressed her cheek against the pillow, tears leaking from the corners of her eyes. But sleep was heavier than sorrow and it soon took her mind down into darkness. Her last sight was Mae Shan sitting alone, lost in thought, her dagger in her hand.

Chapter Five

The spring morning dawned over Bayfield slow but blue. The puddles on the cobbled streets had thawed overnight and made miniature lakes to sparkle in the watery sunlight. The wind blew brisk and cold as Grace walked to the port, but it also held the fresh green smell that said winter was retreating at last.

Good as his word, Frank waited on the deck of his tug, a battered, square-sterned steamer named the *R. W. Currie*. His peaked knit cap had been pulled down over his ears until it almost touched the collar of his coat. His pipe, as battered as his boat, smoked in his mouth, the wind dragging the plume inland.

Finally. Today it would be over. She would finally be able to chase this voice from her head.

All winter it had haunted her. It ruled her dreams, showing her images of the shuttered and empty lighthouse, the frozen lake, and the bleak winter island. Sometimes it took her as she tried to work her trade, showing her images that might have come from fairy tales; fantastic palaces, kings and queens in their splendor, a bird of flame in a golden cage. Always, always, the same desperate voice called from the shadows, begging for help.

But never once did the owner of the voice show her its face. Not for all her searching with mind's eye and gazing crystal could she see who called out to her.

She had not slept the night through in months. Exhaustion grew heavier and the unwelcome burden of it made her increasingly frantic. She must end this. She would do anything, *anything* if this voice, this ghost, whoever it was, would just go away and let her sleep.

Even cross the lake.

Grace hurried down the dock, ignoring the blatantly curious stare from Charlie Raney, the harbormaster's assistant. Frank extended a hand to help her up over the side of the tug, looking her squarely in the eye. She had seen him once or twice in the street over the long winter. Each time he had asked how she was, and commented on the weather. She thought she had seen that he would like to say more, but he never did. Perhaps that much was just her imagination anyway. Her vision was obviously less clear than it had once been.

Now, though, she saw the question in his eyes quite clearly. "Are you sure?" he asked her silently. Her only answer was to step over the rail onto the deck. The boat rocked under her. Fear squeezed Grace's heart. She swallowed hard. Frank thrust his hand into his pocket and stepped aside, curious, disquieted, and so obviously holding back his words that she was surprised he didn't burst with what he wasn't saying. Ashamed of her cowardice, Grace said nothing, but moved away into a sheltered spot behind the tiny wheelhouse. She felt his gaze rest heavily on her shoulders, as she laid her mittened hands on the rail and stared out at the lake and the chunks of ice that still floated on its restless, grey surface. The barrier and boundary of her world for so long.

At last, she heard Frank turn away. His boots thudded on the decking, making the little tug rock restlessly. Grace gripped the rail and for a moment thought she would be sick.

And we haven't even left shore yet. She closed her eyes.

The boiler was already stoked and the steam drifted overhead. A moment later the engine chugged into life, making the deck thrum, and they were away.

The Apostle Islands sprouted in a ragged cluster around the small peninsula that held Bayfield and a half-dozen other logging and fishing towns. Sand Island and Devil's Island clung to the outer edge of the cluster. Grace had grown up with Ingrid, two other sisters, and two brothers on Sand Island. Mamma and Papa had passed on years ago. Leo still lived there with his family, fishing and doing a little farming and timbering. The others had left, making their way down to Milwaukee, or out to Chicago. She had heard nothing more of them, not for years.

The wind smelled of cold, water, and the coal and ash of the boiler. Her hands ached from clutching the rail. Fear weakened her knees and roiled in her stomach with each small bobble of the waves beneath the hull. Screams formed in her throat and she clenched her teeth against them.

Somewhere in the back of her mind, Grace recalled that in summer, the trip out to Sand Island could be pleasant enough. Lake Superior would be blue-grey under the sun and passing islands wore emerald crowns of trees on their red stone cliffs. This early in the spring, however, those crowns were evergreen and grey over slabs of bloodred stone still splattered with the stubborn white ice. No other boats sailed past with crews to raise a hand or blow a whistle in greeting. It was only them, and the water. The shifting, deceiving curtain of water that hid the dead men, the ones who waited for warmth, who promised life, if only she came back, she must come back, come down, come drown . . .

Grace stuffed her hand into her mouth to stifle her shriek and reeled toward the stern. She tore open the door to the wheelhouse and staggered inside. The boiler's warmth rolled over her, startling her and clearing her vision. She saw Frank stood at the wheel, guiding the tug with a strong but dexterous hand, chewing on his pipe stem.

Looking at her with a sympathy she'd never thought she'd see again from anyone.

"You all right, Grace?" he asked softly.

Grace could not find her voice, but she found she could dredge up some shreds of dignity. The warmth of the wheelhouse and the throaty chug of the motor that covered the slap of the waves against the hull helped. She nodded, drew herself up straight, and closed the door firmly behind herself.

"It's good and clear, at any rate," Frank said around his pipe stem. *Sailors and islanders begin any conversation with the weather.* "Should hold too," he went on. "Wouldn't want to push it, though."

You're not going to say anything. You're going to let me decide what to tell. Grace bowed her head. *Thank you, Frank.* She knew she should say that aloud, but the words would not come to her. "I don't expect to be long," she murmured instead.

"Okay then. I'm going to drop you off at Lighthouse Pointe. You can do what it is you need to while I run 'round to Eastbay with the mail and some canned goods for the store, pick up whoever's set to go. I'll be back in four, maybe five hours."

"I'll be ready for you."

"That'll be fine then." Frank clamped his mouth closed around the stem of his pipe, his attention all on the water.

Grace too stared out at the water. Only one hardy gull wheeled in the bright, brittle blue sky. The lake had no touch of that blue in it today. It was as grey as it had been the long ago day, the day the squall had come up, and the waves, so small and civilized today, had swelled into curving walls of water, and come crashing down across the deck of the old tug, wrapping her tight and hauling her over and forcing her down into the dark, into the cold . . .

Grace tried desperately to push those memories aside. She instead turned her mind to thoughts of her niece. Unfortunately, her two or three direct memories of Bridget did not give her much to chew over. She'd kept track of the doings up at the lighthouse through gossips like Hilda, or through genuine news, such as when a ship ran aground. Only occasionally had she actually seen the girl Bridget, or the woman she became. Everett Lederle had never stopped to call on Grace when he was in Bayfield, and she, of course, had never gone back to the island.

The dead had always been able to compel her more forcefully than the living.

She had met Bridget face-to-face just once. It had been ten . . . no, almost fifteen years ago. Grace had arranged a seance to try to drum up some extra business. Her clientele had fallen off and she needed to raise a little talk about herself. She hadn't been so foolish as to actually invite a newspaperman, of course, but she had advertised in the paper so that all "seekers of truth" might "receive the words of those who have gone before."

She remembered sweeping into the parlor, not in gypsy gauds that day, but a severe black skirt and blouse, and her hair pulled back in a tight bun, every inch the distant and respectable woman. She'd delivered a general message to each of the ladies sitting there, some token that she could elaborate on during the actual seance. Then, the thin girl in the face-covering sunbonnet had lifted her head, and Grace had stared into Bridget's eyes. She'd known her at once, the girl looked so much like Ingrid. She'd almost stammered then. She knew why Bridget had come. Bridget had the second sight. Everyone knew it. Her visions of the future were real, and they invariably came true.

Bridget had come to her aunt, who was supposed to have the same gift. She had come for comfort, guidance, and companionship.

And Grace had let her down.

Grace bit her lip. A stream of guilt chittered through her mind and she had to steel herself against it. It was not she, but Ingrid who was responsible for the life the girl led. If Ingrid hadn't run off, if she hadn't left Grace alone with ghosts and gossips, it all would have been different.

Usually, Grace could work up some righteous indignation to warm her cold depths with those thoughts, but not today. Today, caught between the empty sky and the grey water, she just felt tired of them.

From the corner of her eye, she caught Frank watching her. She turned her gaze toward him, and he was already looking out at the lake again.

Despite everything, Grace felt a small smile form. "Should I ask what you're thinking, Frank?" she called over the noise of the engines.

"Probably not," said Frank around his pipe. He removed the much used object from his mouth, inspected it to see that it had well and truly gone out, and tucked it into his pocket. "I was thinking 'bout you as a girl," he said.

"Ah." *Not a safe subject. No.*

But now that he had begun, Frank did not seem inclined to stop. "Prettiest thing for miles around, you were, with a smile for everybody."

As if she had forgotten that girl. "That was a long time ago."

"What happened, Grace?" A plaintive note crept into Frank's voice. It sounded strange coming from so solidly built a man. "You didn't have to go this way."

Grace's mouth twitched. She should keep silent, she knew, but she was worn to the bone with fear and cold. There was no strength left in her to hold back her words.

"What happened? Ingrid vanished with that . . . fisherman Avan, and Papa decided he was going to take it out on me. When I got to Bayfield, and I was made . . . promises, by first one young man and then another. Fool that I was, I believed my pretty face and my smile were enough to make them keep those promises. But they went off with other girls who knew better ways to make them keep their word, and had fathers who would back them up. Then, I met a man who said what he wanted from me up-front, and paid by showing me how I might earn a living for myself."

A traveling spiritualist had come to her boardinghouse. He'd organized a seance in the parlor to drum up interest in his trade. Grace had heard the knocks and rattles, and saw the automatic writing, and saw not a single real ghost. She kept her mouth shut however, and when he'd approached her later, in private, she'd told him flatly he was nothing but a fraud.

He'd smiled then, and shrugged. "So I am, but it's a good living, if you can manage it." She remembered how he'd eyed her, appraisingly, not lasciviously. "In fact, I'd say a sharp girl like you should be able to pick the fat cats of this town over easy."

He'd been right, and he'd been generous in teaching her the tricks and the patter, letting her participate in his several seances to practice her own abilities at cold reading and falling into "trances." Grace couldn't say she remembered the man fondly, but by his own standards, he'd been honest.

None of which Frank would understand, especially not with the despairing light that shone in his eye. "Couldn't you have gone into service? Or one of the shops?"

Grace fussed with the ends of her shawls rather than look at him. "Evidently not."

"Couldn't you . . ." Frank clamped his mouth down to cut off the rest of that sentence.

Grace let him have his silence. Partial payment for the favor he now did her. But she found herself recalling how Frank had no wife, and no children, and for the first time it occurred to her to wonder why.

Well, Frank. She sighed. *I suppose I could ask why you couldn't have come to me.*

But she let the silence carry that question away too. Frank went about his work, stoking the boiler, correcting the boat's course, keeping his eye on the water. Grace waited for him to speak again, but he did not.

At last, Sand Island rose from the horizon, snow-white and ice-grey. Frank idled back on the motor and eased the wheel around, putting the shore on the port side. Ice still made a ragged white skirt for the shore and bobbled in big chunks on the waves. Careful as ever, Frank kept the tug well out in open water. The shoreline grew craggier, rising up into jagged walls of red stone. Water dripped from the long, toothy icicles hanging from the cliff. Grace kept her gaze on the far end of the island, and gradually, the lighthouse came into view.

The Sand Island light wasn't one of the tall white towers they had down south and out east. It was an octagon of brown stone from the local quarry standing a bare two stories over the white-trimmed house that was the keeper's quarters. The light was dark now. The new keeper wasn't due for another week yet.

They rounded the point of land and Grace saw the boathouse and the long flight of weathered, wooden stairs that led up the cliff to the light. Frank's attention had gone entirely to the management of the tug—slowing and reversing the engines, steering carefully between the rocks hidden by the grey water and the ice that floated on its surface. Despite his care, ice still grated against the hull and Frank's jaw tightened. Slowly, patiently, he eased the tug up to the tiny jetty beside the boathouse. At the sound of the dock thumping gently against the tug's side, Grace felt ready to cry out in relief. As quickly as she could, she hurried to the rail and let Frank help her disembark.

"I'll be back for you this afternoon," he said. "I want y . . . to be safe in Bayfield before full dark."

"I'll be here," Grace promised.

Frank looked like he wanted to say something else, maybe to offer some help or comfort, but years of silence still held his tongue. He closed up the boat, returned to the wheelhouse, and fired the engines once more. The tug pulled away from the jetty.

Grace faced inland. She did not want to see Frank leave her.

Fortunately, the snow and ice on the stairs was mostly melted. Still, Grace mounted the steep flight carefully. At the top waited a sea of mud and last year's grass with a few brave, green shoots peeking up to look for the sun. The forest loomed at the lighthouse's back, still winter dark and forbidding. Grace lowered her eyes. On the other side of that forest her older brother Leo raised his family and lived his life, and never spoke her name. It would serve him right if after this she turned up on his doorstep and told him point-blank all that had happened. Let his wife and children know what sort of madness they inherited.

Madness. The idea sent an unexpected chill through her. Was that what brought her here after all? The mad heard voices, had nightmares. She had told herself repeatedly through all the long months of winter that she was not, could not be insane. But then, that was what all the mad told themselves.

Grace clutched her shawl and looked back down the muddy path marked by her own boot prints. She could go back down the stairs. She didn't have to do this. The boathouse would shelter her until Frank came back again. This was nothing to do with her. It might not even be real.

Why did I even come?

Because someone told me I was afraid to. Because someone else told me I was uncaring. If I leave now, which of them will I prove right?

Grace squared her shoulders and mounted the three snow-speckled steps to the front door. She put a hand on the knob. Part of her hoped to find it locked, but no, it turned easily under her touch.

The door swung open silently on well-tended hinges. As she stepped inside, Grace noted that whoever was the last here they had not bothered to sweep up. Several pairs of boots had tracked in mud and left it to dry where it fell.

No sound issued from within. Whoever had left these traces was no longer here.

She repeated that fact to herself firmly, several times, but Grace still hesitated. It was wrong for her to be here, she felt that keenly. This was no business of hers.

It's what the living are up to you need to find out. Who had told her that? Why had she believed them?

The front room was sparsely furnished. She could gain no appreciation of the quality of those furnishings, because they were all hidden by the pale drapes of dust cloths. Incongruously, pieces of hemp rope lay beside the sofa. The wall beside the square, iron stove was stained with black, as if it had been scorched. It even seemed to Grace the scent of smoke still lingered in the air.

She drifted to the heap of rope and picked up one of the fragments. The hemp pricked at her fingers. A red ribbon had been twisted into it. Apart from that, it looked like any other length of rope, but it felt wrong, not to her skin, but to her mind. Grace let it fall.

What happened here? Bridget, what have you done?

She thought again about retreating to the boathouse, to wait for Frank. Why should she care what anyone thought of her? She had her life and it kept her warm and fed, and safe from such strange things. That was surely all she required.

No. It's already gone too far for that. I must at least try to see. If I do not, it will start gnawing at me, and who knows when that voice will come back. I cannot live with that voice in my head.

Grace turned to face the room and drew herself up to her full height. Mrs. Hausman and her other clients would all be stunned if they could see what was coming next. There was no chanting, no pleading, no dim light or gazing crystal.

"All right," said Grace flatly. "I'm here. Show yourself."

The air around Grace curdled. The room grew colder. A female figure took shape in front of her, but Grace could not see her clearly. She was an old woman and she was a young girl. She was a proud queen and a frightened child wringing her hands. She was certain and she was confused. She was brave, and she was cringing back, terrified.

You came.

Grace's mouth had gone dry. "You're not Ingrid," she said stupidly. "Or Bridget."

No. I am sorry. Regret wrapped around Grace like a cool wind.

Grace felt panic rise inside her. "Who are you?"

Memories that were not her own flooded Grace's mind; visions of a man in white and gold holding a golden crown over her head, of sitting in a high throne, looking down on a host of fantastically dressed people who all bowed to her, of running across a broad stretch of grass at the edge of a canal, of watching a young man she knew was her son and thinking desperately that she must save him from his wife.

With the strange visions came a strange name. Medeoan. The ghost who haunted this place was Medeoan.

This was wrong, wrong. Grace felt it in her bones and in her blood. This strange, shifting ghost should not be here. Something bad had happened. "Where is my niece? What happened to her?"

She was tricked and she was tried, but she overcame, and in so doing put herself in even greater danger, although she doesn't know it yet.

"What do you mean?" demanded Grace, even as she took a step away. So much was wrong here, she couldn't begin to comprehend it. She saw bright flickers out of the corners of her eyes, as if the flames that had scorched the wall and heated the stove still burned. She raised her hand to her temple to try to block out the bright illusions. "I don't understand you."

I asked her to take up my shame, and have placed her and my land in danger.

More flames flickered at the corners of Grace's vision. She saw strange glowing shadows about the room—a golden cage, a bird of flame, a dark-haired man with cruel, cruel eyes. Bridget. In the middle of it all stood the ghost, little girl, young bride, old crone, beautiful, mad, regal, pathetic, still in the present and in frantic motion in the glimmering past.

Grace could make no sense of these bizarre bits and pieces. "What have you done to Bridget?" she screamed at the ghost. "What *are* you?"

One who needs. She will come back, but not to me. Not without your help. I must undo what I have done, or I will have no rest.

"Why should I?" Grace backed toward the door. "Why should I care?"

Do not leave me alone in the cold. I must atone. I cannot do that here.

Grace felt regret roll in slow waves from the shifting ghost and shuddered under the onslaught. "Leave me alone."

I cannot.

More images crowded in on the edge of Grace's mind. Shrouded figures laid out in a gilded church. A young woman sitting alone before a blazing fire and wishing desperately for help, for release.

"If Bridget's coming back, you must wait for her," muttered Grace. "She has the sight and the power, as she'd be quick to remind me. I'm just a bitter old woman."

As was I. Bitter. Wronged and wronging. Frightened and terrifying.

"And so?" Grace tried to keep her voice hard and her mind closed, but she was tired after the long trip across the barely-thawed lake. She wanted to be gone, despite her previous determination to solve this mystery. She did not want to face this haunting, this sorrowful voice and the fleeting visions it brought.

The ghost drifted nearer, settling for a moment into its visage as an old woman, straight and proud but with a face heavily lined from anger and the passage of years. *We are alike, you and I. We have blamed but do not take blame. We have acted but say that it is only because we were forced. We abandoned those who trusted us.*

"How dare you!"

The words burst from her, loud and forcefully. But the ghost was undeterred. The shade spoke again, coming nearer yet.

Like and like, you and I. That is why I may speak to you. That is why only you can help me. I have no other bond to this mortal world, and I am fading.

"Fading?" Nothing had prepared her for this. Certainly not her "training" as a medium, nor the dozens of books on spiritualism she read so she could expand her repertoire of patter.

My body is gone, Medeoan told her. *My bones are ash and the ash is scattered. I cannot hold onto myself. Spring wakes the world and the rush of life will overwhelm me. Even in the Land of Death and Spirit I will be dif-fuse, an aimless ghost without bones or heart to bind. I will only be mourned for some self I was in the distant past. It will not be enough.*

Grace knew she should have felt relief at this, but an unaccountable sadness bloomed inside her. The ghost flickered into her shape as a young woman, at once facing Grace, and turning toward Bridget, her arms outstretched and pleading.

I want to help. What comes is my doing, and my wish to undo came too late. I can neither hold nor help if you will not help me.

"I want to be left alone."

You do not want to be left alone. You want not to have turned away at the wrong time, from your sister, from her daughter. So I from my son, and from the true burdens of my birth. But I was old and bitter, older than you and far more crabbed in my heart. My ghosts came to me too late and I turned even from them. That last turning trapped me here to beg and to cry.

"Stop it." Grace pressed her hands against her temples. "You don't need me."

Medeoan was an old woman again, and her regret filled the room. *She is strong, your niece, but what is to come will terrify her. She may re-gain all she has lost, or she may through turning away lose all there is to gain. She will be terrible in her anger, and it will take more than one love to turn her back. I am weak. I cannot see so far. If she cannot be turned, the child will remain alone. Do not leave her. Do not give her more reason for sorrow.*

"The child?" Grace asked weakly.

Help me. Medeoan's need drowned her. *Help me save the child, and my own son and the realm. Help me do what I could not in life.*

Grace pressed her hand to her mouth. She did not want this. She felt the ghost's sorrow, her desperation. The dead woman's memories washed over her yet again. A boy, straight and handsome in fine clothes.

A black-eyed man whispering poison in her ears. Another man with dark gold hair dying beside a golden cage. With a shock, Grace realized she knew him. That man was Avan, Ingrid's lover.

Grace swallowed. She had not known that Avan had died.

"Grace? What the hell's going on?"

Frank. When had Frank come in? He stood in the doorway, the spring winds blowing in behind him. It seemed the Medeoan wavered for a moment, like a reflection rippling in disturbed water.

"I've been waiting for you." Frank stepped forward, letting the door swing shut behind him. He jerked his thumb over his shoulder. "I blew the fog horn twice. Didn't you hear?"

"I . . . Frank . . . no . . . I'm sorry," stammered Grace. Somehow he was harder to see than Medeoan. After all that had passed, he seemed not to belong in her world anymore.

You can choose now. Turn away again, and you will only be as you are. Turn forward, and you can shed the past, shed the sight you do not want, and in the end you will have my silence. I will be gone, expelled when all is over, but I will also be forgiven. Please. Please. I am dead and I am lost, and I need the help only you can give. Please.

To be needed, to be forgiven. Grace bowed her head. Oh, she understood this woman's yearning well. To forgive, to act instead of being acted on.

"Grace, what's the matter? Did you get what you wanted?"

What did Grace want? Only silence? Only her rooms and her trick-eries? She had wanted to help Bridget. She had tried, but it was not enough. Here was her chance, to try again, to show Ingrid that she was good for more than smiles and flirtations, to show Bridget that they were truly family, to show herself that she was not what she feared.

Grace shook. All this lay at the heart of the ghost's offer, but ghosts lied. She'd been touched before, possessed by the need of another. She knew that cold and ice, that unyielding dread and hunger that could never be sated. It had drained her hollow once before. What if this ghost came only to do the same?

Frank touched her shoulder. She looked up at his worried, kind face, but saw it only with difficulty. He didn't know what was happening, had no eyes to see or ears to hear, and she had no voice left to explain.

"Come away, Grace. This is no good for you."

But at the same time, inside her mind she heard Medeoan's fading voice. *Please. Please.*

She wouldn't survive it again. Ingrid would not come running down the sands to save her with a Finnish sorcerer in tow as she had before. This time she'd shrivel and die.

But she'd die trying. That was the coldest comfort, but not so cold as the years that stretched ahead without it.

Grace covered Frank's hand where he held her shoulder. "You're a good man, Frank Bluchard. You deserve far better than I've given you."

"Grace . . ." he began, but she did not let him finish. She turned away from him yet again.

"Very well," she said to the ghost.

For one heartbeat, Grace saw the woman's face clearly. She knew the lines and the eyes that had seen far too much. For one heartbeat, she felt the absolute cold of the ghost's touch. In the next, cold dissolved in the warmth of her flesh and blood, it spread through her, and took unshakable hold. And she saw . . .

She saw the greenish brown waters of a canal slip by the gilded gunwale of her barge.

She saw her hand grip Frank's hard and felt her knees tremble.

She saw her daughter-in-law kneel before her and hated her for it.

She saw the whitewashed fire door that led to the light through a haze of tears.

She saw the Firebird in all its glory soaring through the blue sky and knew it came at her call.

The visions overwhelmed her, robbing her of sense and will. Distantly, Grace felt herself fall. She felt Frank catch her in his strong arms and cradle her close.

"Oh, Grace," she heard him say. "What've you done to yourself?"

It's only for a little while, she tried to tell him. *Only until Bridget comes home.*

Bridget, said the voice of the ghost she carried. *Come home.*

Chapter Six

Lord Daren watched the Firebird through the eye of his mind. A glorious blaze of fire, it streaked through the pale sky of the Land of Death and Spirit, its tail streaming out behind it to light all the Shifting Lands.

It was coming for Isavalta. Daren could feel that. The Firebird screamed its intent before it. Its anger welled out like blood from an open wound.

He should have run. He knew that. He was but the sliver of a spirit here in the shape of a red-tailed hawk, but he had to make a stand. If the Firebird could be turned, or dissuaded before it reached Isavalta, then all would be safe. If there was a way to touch, a way to try . . .

But before Daren even moved his will beyond that thought, the bird twisted its long neck, and regarded his hawk's shape with one burning blue eye.

It did not speak. It did not bother to challenge or warn. It flicked its great wing, and the curtain of flame fell over Daren, all light and color, and bright, blazing pain. Daren screamed with all the strength of his soul, screamed as if he would never stop, and the spell broke, but the pain did not, and he fell, shuddering, onto the stone floor of his chamber.

Chapter Seven

The door to Bridget's room banged open. She shot up in bed, her heart pounding.

"Mistress . . ." came Richikha's startled voice.

"Is she here?" demanded a woman shrilly.

Bridget tossed aside the heavy bedclothes and scrambled from the bed. The stones were cold under her stockinged feet as she hurried around the bed screens.

The room's single window showed that dawn had just begun to light the sky. Richikha and Prathad, both of them up and dressed, blocked the path of a tall woman whose white hair was piled high on her head. Anger tightened her face, making her cheekbones stand out sharply and darkening her blue eyes.

"Good morning, Mistress Urshila," said Bridget, coming forward to join her determined, but outmatched maids. "I did not think . . ."

"Evidently not," snapped the other woman. "You send for the lord sorcerer, you send for the southerner, but you do not send for your teacher. I can only hope this is misguided courtesy on the part of a student determined to be careful of my age and greying head."

Bridget accepted the rebuke. Mistress Urshila Daromiladoch Jarohnevosh had been brought to court, recalled actually, specifically to teach Bridget the art of sorcery. She had been one of the court sorcerers in the early days of Medeoan's reign. She had also been expelled with the others when Valin Kalami came into power as Lord Sorcerer. One of the acts the current emperor and empress had undertaken was to recall all those who still lived and restore to them their titles and positions.

Bridget believed Mistress Urshila to be powerful and learned. She also knew the older woman was of two minds about her assignment. Bridget had balked at the idea of becoming an "apprentice," and this was clearly not a response Mistress Urshila expected or welcomed. But when Sakra had point-blank refused to teach Bridget, saying that as she was going to live in Isavalta she needed to learn Isavalta's magics, Bridget was left with little choice. Mistress Urshila herself was under imperial order and had even less choice.

Despite their uneasy relationship, Bridget acknowledged Urshila to be a thorough, if exacting teacher. She had begun their training by insisting Bridget learn the language of Isavalta by rote.

"But I speak perfectly . . ." Bridget had said.

"You speak the language of Isavalta because of an enchantment," countered Mistress Urshila. "If that enchantment is undone, then what?"

Which, Bridget had to admit, was not something she had considered.

She tried to be a good student. She knew she had a great deal to learn and she did wish to learn. But she was not a child, and she would not be treated, or taught, like one. Her new teacher, however, seemed determined to do exactly that.

Mistress Urshila sat down in the nearest chair, her back straight as a poker. She gestured impatiently to Richikha, who hurried forward with a cup of the smoky, sweet tea favored by Isavaltans as a morning beverage.

"So," Urshila said between sips. "What did the *lokai*'s queen say to you? Exactly."

Bridget smoothed down her overfrilled nightdress. She was not going to be given the time to make herself decent, obviously, but it was no good protesting that fact to Mistress Urshila. She took another chair next to the firepit, accepted a cup of tea from Prathad, and told Mistress Urshila of the Vixen and the Phoenix. Bridget was quite sure her teacher had heard all of that from other sources, or she would not have been so outraged. Then, although it tested Bridget to do so, she told Mistress Urshila of the conversation she and Sakra had held afterward.

Mistress Urshila listened in stony silence. Her tea cooled untouched in its cup.

When Bridget fell silent, Mistress Urshila set the cup carefully down on the table Richikha had placed at hand for the purpose. "No."

Bridget blinked. "I beg your pardon?"

Mistress Urshila sighed in exasperation. "No, you will not cross into the Land of Death and Spirit to return to your home."

Very carefully, Bridget set her teacup down. Her hand had clutched it convulsively, and she feared it might shatter. "But it is the only way I can be certain . . ." she tried.

"Nonetheless," replied Mistress Urshila implacably.

"Because you tell me so?" Bridget heard the warning note in her own voice.

Mistress Urshila nodded once. "Because I tell you so."

Bridget stood. She paced halfway around the firepit before she was able to trust herself enough to turn and say, "You do understand that this is my daughter we are speaking of?"

Urshila also stood. "It is not. It is your power and its use."

Bridget stared at Mistress Urshila. It was not often she had to look up into the eyes of another woman, but Mistress Urshila was taller than her by at least three inches. The weight of three centuries of life had not stooped the sorceress one bit.

Bridget took a deep breath. "Mistress, I did not ask your permission."

"You should have," Mistress Urshila rapped back. "You are apprenticed to me. I say how you may exercise your powers."

Bridget strove to keep a civil tongue. This woman was, after all, doing her duty as she saw it. Bridget could understand that. "If I was a girl of fourteen, perhaps . . ."

"In art you might as well be. You cannot even speak one language of Isavalta, let alone properly study the laws and principles of the power you sling about so carelessly." The sorceress's color deepened as her anger rose again. "You hold conversation with the Vixen—*the Vixen!*—without consulting me. You are ten times a fool and more ignorant yet than that."

"I have dealt with her before . . ."

Mistress Urshila gestured sharply, cutting off Bridget's words. "She has dealt with you, for her own purposes and to her own ends. That is all she ever does. The moment you forget this, or disregard it, you are lost to her games." Urshila planted both fists on her hips. "You cannot even keep that much in your head."

Bridget swayed on her feet. Her temper was coming dangerously close to betraying itself. "Mistress, this is a dangerous time. No one else may be spared to go on this errand. It is not something I can disregard."

Mistress Urshila regarded her sternly for a long moment, but something in her eyes softened. "I understand more than you think I do, Bridget Lederle. You were tossed early and alone into an ocean of dark circumstance. By raw strength and good luck, you won through, and this has been to the benefit of us all. You consult with emperors and you are courted by power and the Vixen herself comes to warn you—not the lord sorcerer, but you—of what is to come. Why should you not stand confident before them all?

"But this is the seduction and this is the danger that we all face no matter how weak our powers. Power attracts. It pulls and it changes. No matter how blessed a sorcerer's sight, power and the closeness of power clouds it. You are very much in danger of going blind."

Bridget stared at her teacher. Did the woman truly not understand? This was not about magic. It had nothing to do with power. It was about *Anna*.

She threw up her hands. "What would you suggest I do then? If my daughter is still alive?"

"If your daughter is alive . . ." Mistress Urshila emphasized the "if" with forced patience. "She will remain so until you learn the laws and rules of the power you wield. You do not seem to realize that as you are, you pose a danger to your child."

"Nonsense," snapped Bridget. How could this woman even think such a thing? She was Anna's *mother*.

"Is it?" Mistress Urshila arched her brows. "How do you know?"

Ludicrous. The woman is attempting to prey on my doubts. "I think I know myself that well," Bridget answered primly.

Mistress Urshila walked up to Bridget until she was mere inches away. Her eyes were wide and grey. "Do you?" she asked softly. "Here, in this place, in this world, in this condition that is so wholly new to you? Do you still know yourself."

Bridget met Urshila's steady, unblinking gaze for as long as she could. But, to her shame, she had to look away at last. She wrapped her arms around herself, but what she was trying to hold in she could not say.

I am still myself. For all the changes around me, I am still myself. That is all that matters.

But she did not say this to Mistress Urshila, who clearly would not have accepted the statement if she had. "Sakra will be walking with me," she said instead, although a small voice in the back of her head reminded her that she did not know if this was true. Sakra had not yet spoken to Ananda.

Mistress Urshila, however, was as ready to dismiss that assurance as she was all the others. "The doubling of your power does not make you safer. It puts you more at risk. It will call things to you that Sakra will not see."

That, at least, Bridget had an answer for. "My vision will keep us in safety. I cannot be deceived by magic."

Urshila bowed her head and pressed the heel of her palm against her brow. She held that pose for a long time. When at last she lifted her gaze, she sighed deeply and said, "In the mortal world, you see through illusion. That is not the same. The Shifting Lands do not produce illusion. Each thing you see there, in each shape it takes, including the clarity of air, is part of the truth of that thing."

Now it was Bridget's turn to be dismissive. "I have walked the Shifting Lands before, I know to keep my wits about me." *I have, after all, found my own way from Wisconsin to Isavalta, or have you forgotten?* She let that challenge stand in her gaze. She remembered too well the strange forests and planes, the beauteous illusions. But she had felt the road with heart and instinct and she had held to it, and come safe again to the shores that had taken her in.

"Because last time nothing happened and no power felt the need of you. But the first time, miss? What happened then?"

Bridget swallowed. The Vixen had taken her then. She had her foxes waylay Bridget because she wanted the healing that Bridget could give. In return, she had enhanced Bridget's second sight.

"She did me no harm," said Bridget, but even she knew that was no argument.

"None that you yet know," countered Urshila. "But it has only been a few months, and here she is again to keep you in her game."

"She came to warn us that the Firebird is seeking revenge!"

"Did she?" replied Urshila calmly. "She came to help us all, did she? And just, incidently, to tell you the one piece of news guaranteed to drive you insane?"

Bridget snorted in disgust, and was embarrassed by the sound. Mistress Urshila did not understand. She could not, and there was no way to explain. "It does not matter why she did it. It is done, and I have to know if it is the truth."

Mistress Urshila shook her head. "Snared so easily and you still declare your blessed sight will keep you safe."

Bridget realized her mouth had gone dry. There was sense in what

Mistress Urshila said, she could hear it, she could understand it, but she could not make herself listen. She stepped away, trying not to catch sight of Richikha or Prathad who were in their usual corner, waiting to be needed, pretending not to hear. What were they thinking? What was she herself thinking? She wrapped her arms tightly around herself. She did not look back at her teacher.

"Sakra says we must go to Wisconsin," she said softly. "He says the only way to be sure of what has happened to Anna is to work a scrying from the graveside."

"You listen to that southerner before you will heed me." The accusation in Urshila's voice was plain.

Bridget bridled. Say what she would of Bridget, this woman would not impugn Sakra. She swung around. "That southerner is a skilled and dedicated sorcerer."

Mistress Urshila's mouth tightened into a smirk. "From a land where the powers are tamed and the gods hold court over decisions of law. Oh, no, miss, that is not eternal Isavalta and he does not know Isavalta's ways."

Bridget rested the tips of her fingers on the table's edge. She tried not to shake. She tried to stop her ears against Mistress Urshila's words and the fears they raised. *Think of Anna. Think of Anna, alive and well and in your arms again. Can anything else really matter? I will find my way. I have done so before and I will do it again.* "I am going," she said flatly.

"Then you are no more my apprentice."

Bridget drew herself up straight. "I will be sorry to lose your services."

For a moment Urshila stared at her, as if she could not believe her ears. "Like that. As if I were a nursery tutor." Bridget opened her mouth, but Mistress Urshila's eyes flashed with such grim and sudden anger, the words died in her throat. "You understand nothing. I pray to Vyshko and Vyshemir that we survive your foolishness."

With that, Mistress Urshila turned on her heel and swept out of the room, letting the door slam shut behind her. The boom of it echoed around the stone chamber, filling Bridget's ears with a sound like an omen as she stood alone, clutching the collar of her nightdress and trying not to be afraid.

Chapter Eight

Mistress Urshila Daromiladoch Jarohnevosh, who three hundred years before had been born under a very different name, stormed down the corridors of Vyshtavos, clenching and unclenching her fists as if she sought to throttle the air around her for not giving way fast enough.

The idiocy of the woman! The stubborn, persistent *idiocy*! How could the gods permit such power and such deadly naivete to exist in one person?

Servants fluttered away on either side of her, giving her the widest berth the hall allowed. It was only when she realized she had no idea where she was going that Urshila slowed her pace and forced herself to think.

What she wanted to do was go directly to the lord sorcerer. He could advise the emperor that the woman Bridget was a danger and should be closely confined until she could be brought under control. Urshila realized her anger was making her puff like a bellows. This would not do. None of this. She drew herself up and collected herself.

The emperor would not listen to the lord sorcerer if he said such things. No one would. Bridget Lederle had saved Isavalta from Kalami and Medeoan. No one would hear what a danger she was.

Least of all Bridget herself.

She was a gift to us from the Vixen. Vyshemir's knife, even the southerners should know not to accept such gifts.

Urshila smoothed her hair back. She had not even taken the time to veil herself decently. Now she must take the time to think. The first course was obvious. If Bridget Lederle was so ruled by the southern sorcerer, she must try there first.

Urshila took her bearings. It had not taken long to accustom herself to the ways of the palace again. She tried not to note that the polished marbles and woods seemed less bright than when she first walked these halls, proud to be called to the service of the old empress. She tried not to look at the slender, pale boy and his Hastinapuran wife and wonder if they understood what strength their station required of them, and if they did, whether they possessed even a portion of that strength.

Medeoan had been mad. Medeoan had banished Urshila from the palace and the imperial cities, but Medeoan at least was strong.

Medeoan was also the one who allowed Bridget Lederle to be brought here in the first place, Urshila reminded herself.

She'd come to the long gallery, with the gilt-framed portraits of the kings and queens who had ruled Isavalta as it grew to take in all the north lands and become an empire. They all looked down on her with severe and dignified eyes. Styles of painting and posing had changed across the centuries, but that stern gaze did not. The largest portrait of all hung over the central hearth. Painted life-sized and full-length, there stood the first empress, Nacherada Banconidoch Taidalavosh. Crowned in gold and sapphires, she stood straight and tall. One strong hand held the golden rod that symbolized the temporal rule of Isavalta, the other clutched the worn shaft of Vyshemir's knife, saying whose spiritual daughter she was.

The artist had gotten her eyes exactly right. Even when they were no more than blue paint on wood, Nacherada's eyes could still make you feel you were being peeled apart and examined for flaws.

Had Mother Nacherada known of Urshila's flaws? Had she seen into Urshila's veins and seen the nature of the blood there? She had never said anything.

Others had. Oh, yes, down the years, others had a great deal to say.

And therefore will you now keep silent? Empress Nacherada seemed to ask. *For thirty years you held your tongue, hoping to be brought back into high service. Now that you are here, will you serve?*

Urshila dropped her gaze and hurried on.

The southerner had been housed as close to the imperial apartments as propriety allowed. No page or guard stood outside his door however, so Urshila had to raise her fist and knock, and wait. Her toe tapped impatiently and she stilled it. She would not make such a show for whatever servant answered her knock.

To her surprise, the door opened to reveal Sakra himself. If he was surprised to see her, he did not show it. He just stood back to give her room to enter.

Urshila stalked into the room, curious in spite of herself. She had never been here before. The Hastinapurans were said to love displays of opulence and sensuality. Nothing of the kind was on display here, however. The place was almost stark. The bed was well covered, but narrow and unscreened. The furnishings were as plain as anything the palace might offer. There were only two real luxuries. The floor was thickly carpeted with woven tapestries, adding warmth and muffling her footfalls, and against the back wall waited a series of shelves filled with scrolls and thick folios. A writing desk had been set up beneath the window overlooking the courtyard. A cracked and flaking vellum scroll, carefully weighted so it remained open, lay ready for copying along with sharpened pens and pots of fresh inks.

Ah, yes. That was something else the southerners were said to love. They wrote everything down, obsessively, so that any might read it. They understood many things, but not, it seemed, the power of secrets.

Remember your manners, Urshila reminded herself. *You did come here seeking help.*

She faced the southerner, folding her hands across her chest and bowing her head, a reverence between equals.

"Sakra *dva* Dhirendra Phanidraela."

The sorcerer bowed in the fashion of his country, with his hands pressed over his eyes. It was said to be a sign of trust and respect, and Urshila supposed this was so. "Mistress Urshila Daromiladoch Jarohnevosh," he said. "How can I help you?"

How indeed? She pushed the wisps of hair that had fallen across her brow back again. "I need to speak with you about Bridget Lederle."

Sakra's eyebrows rose. "How so?" He gestured to one of the straight-backed chairs pulled up by the firepit that was a bright bed of coals.

Urshila did not move. "I don't pretend to understand your ways, Master Sakra, and I do not pretend to like you."

Sakra regarded her in silence for a moment. "I thank you for your honesty, at least," he said at last. He sat in the second chair. The coals gave off waves of heat, making the room uncomfortably stuffy on this pleasant spring morning. Again, he gestured to the other chair.

Urshila still did not sit. She was too agitated. She just gripped the chair back, and tried to keep her temper under control. "You too are a sorcerer, and raised and trained properly as one, as far as the ways of your country allow." Sakra said nothing to that. Urshila took a deep breath. This was ridiculous. This was humiliating. If her apprentice would not obey, she should have simply walked away and made it known the 'prentice was ungovernable. She had done so before. But this was not an ordinary student. She noticed her knuckles turning white where they gripped the chair. "I am asking you to stop Bridget Lederle in her new enterprise. It is dangerous and foolhardy and not just to herself as she seems to believe."

The southerner was silent for another long moment, and Urshila felt her spine stiffening, getting ready for his refusal, which would surely be reasoned and so politely delivered. She would have to go to Lord Daren next.

"You are right," said Sakra.

Urshila was taken aback, and surprised. Her hands slowly released the chair back. "Then you will speak to her?"

Sakra shook his head. "No."

Urshila clamped her teeth down around a shout. "And why not?" she asked with as much calm as she could muster.

Sakra looked down at his hands. Urshila steeled herself, getting ready to unearth the lie he was surely about to weave. "Because," he said, "I believe it is more dangerous for her to remain in such distress."

Which was not the sort of answer she was expecting. Still, it was not acceptable. "That is your affection for her speaking, not your sense."

Now Sakra looked up at her, and his gaze was remarkably steady and open. "It is both." There was an undercurrent of tension to his words, as if saying this were difficult for him. Against her will, Urshila felt herself wondering if this southerner was an honest man after all. "She is badly distressed and distracted. This is a dangerous state for anyone with power. Unless and until the fate of her daughter is known, she will not be able to bring her thoughts and spirits back into some sort of order."

"If she cannot govern herself . . ." began Urshila, but Sakra cut her off quickly.

"Then what?" he asked.

Urshila closed her mouth. *If she cannot govern herself, she should be confined, or returned to this place called Wisconsin, where she is no danger.* But with the little learning she had, was there anyplace the woman would not be a danger? One glance at Sakra told her that this thought had crossed his mind as well.

"You have not spoken so to her," she said slowly.

Sakra seemed to know exactly what she was referring to. "I admit, I have not."

"Will you?"

"I hope I do not have to." Sakra's smile was small, and entirely without levity. "And yes, Mistress Urshila, that is my affection speaking. I am not the first man whose conscience and heart have gone to war."

"No," admitted Urshila. She sighed and rubbed her eyes. "And what if the child is alive, what then?"

"Then I pity those who have secreted her from her mother." A muscle in Sakra's right cheek twitched. Urshila wondered what expression he was holding back. "I hope Bridget's reason can continue to govern her passions well enough while she seeks the child out." He shook his head. "There are still several things about this that she cannot even bring herself to consider, and should any of them be true . . ."

Urshila studied him for a moment, trying to divine what he had not said. "You truly think Kalami stole the child? Why would he do that and then not tell her while he was trying to lure her to Isavalta? The child would have been the most tempting bait."

Again, Sakra turned his gaze from her. For a long moment, he watched the glowing coals with their subtly shifting shades of orange, grey, and white. He was, Urshila realized, deciding how much to tell her. Would he lie? Or just omit an essential truth to protect Bridget?

Slowly, Sakra said, "I think Kalami had other reasons for taking the child."

Urshila narrowed her eyes. Several half-formed notions dropped into place at once. "You think Kalami was the father?"

Sakra shrugged, for the first time betraying faint signs of irritation. "I think Bridget's powers are attractive beyond telling, especially to one so greedy for power. I think he was aware that Bridget's mother was able to conceive under the attentions of a sorcerer of Isavalta. He may have wondered if the same would be true of Bridget, and the idea of a child from three generations of sorcerers was irresistible, especially when he believed he could eventually harness all that power to the purposes of Tuukos."

Urshila held herself still at the mention of the place she still instinctively thought of as Holy Island. "If he was the father, why did she not recognize him when he came to her on Medeoan's errand?"

Sakra's mouth worked back and forth, again deciding what he would say. "I think there were reasons, and I think she would not thank me for speaking of them."

Urshila gave one short, sharp laugh. "Would she thank you for any portion of this conversation?"

"No," he admitted, and looked back to her with a shrewd eye. "But nor would she thank you."

Urshila waved her hand, acknowledging his words as true but wishing them quickly gone. She was tired. Worry was beginning to gnaw more deeply at her bones. If this child Bridget Lederle was determined to seek out *was* the daughter of Valin Kalami, there were implications of blood and power Sakra had no way of understanding. Nor did anyone else in this court.

Implications she had no way to speak of.

"We would be safer if she had never been found," Urshila muttered.

Sakra stood. He was not tall, and he had to lift his chin to look into her eyes, but he was a presence. He had his own certainties. She could feel them radiating from him as she might feel his magic during a working. "Mistress Urshila," he said in tones of careful respect, "Bridget Lederle is not just a power. She is a woman of conscience and sense. She has thrown in her lot with Isavalta, and she will not willingly betray that trust or easily change her loyalties."

He believed it. He was not blind, nor dishonest. He believed what he was saying. What if he was right?

But what if he is wrong? "I hope it is as you say, Master Sakra." She realized her shoulders had slumped and she straightened them. "Thank you for hearing me out."

Sakra inclined his head and made no move to stop her or to have the last word as she left him there.

The door closed behind her. Urshila stood alone in the dim hallway for a moment, trying to sort out the whole of what she had heard, and what she had said. She had seen the true face of Ananda's bound-sorcerer in there, and she had not expected to. He served at his best, that much was clear, but he still served the empress. What if she decided not to serve Isavalta?

And what of this child? This child who might be not just Bridget's child, but Kalami's child? Even with the danger of the Firebird looming over them all, if this child was out in the world, as untutored and unguided as her mother, it would be a threat almost as grave. Perhaps the mother should go out and find her. They would bring her back here, and then at least the threats would be gathered together under one roof, where there were sorcerers who could teach and, if necessary, oppose them.

Urshila bit her lip. *Does anyone on the Holy Island know Valin Kalami had a child?*

She needed to think. She had been away from politics and intrigues for thirty years. Even she could not pretend that was not a significant amount of time. Her mind no longer ran quickly down such channels.

Urshila turned on her heel and strode again down the corridor to the north stairs. She descended them and with nothing more than a glower caused the house guards stationed at the doors to open them for her, letting in the fresh spring breeze.

The day outside was clear, despite the slight chill. The green grass had begun to poke through the mud, bringing with it the first of the snowdrops and crocuses. The fresh air went straight through her, clearing and calming her mind, as it always did.

Careless of her shoes, Urshila wandered down to the canal's edge. The wind prickled her skin and the back of her neck, waking up her thoughts, brushing away the inconsequential. The canal flowed black and sluggish past the banks that were still speckled with the last, stubborn patches of snow.

The cool air settled her thoughts into more reasonable patterns. What was the harm in letting Bridget and the southerner, Sakra, go in search of a child that might not exist? It was a harsh thought, but if they failed, or were lost in the attempt, Isavalta might be better off. If they succeeded and brought the child back, she would be under proper supervision, her powers advisably watched and channeled.

In the meantime, she and Lord Daren could solve the riddle of the

Firebird, which would bring them more prominence in the eyes of the new emperor, and more power at the court to order the doings of its sorcerers as was best.

Urshila sighed sharply and gazed out across the canal. Given a little time it seemed she could indeed still scheme like a courtier.

The work yards stretched out behind Vyshtavos like the pale train of a worn dress. The smells from the tannery and brewery drifted to her on the wind, making her nose twitch. Workmen, bonded to imperial service, came and went along muddy paths, fetching water from the partially thawed canal or dumping slops into the freshly thawed water.

Urshila lifted her hems to step across one of the mucky workmen's paths. As she did, an ancient woman tottering along with remarkable speed under a yoke of slop buckets from the kitchens, the contents of which were still steaming in the damp air.

"And where are you going, Little Daughter?" she croaked in a shrewd but raspy voice. "Does the spring call you out?"

Urshila froze, hems knotted in both hands. The woman who looked up at her with a wrinkled, leather-brown face did not speak low Isavaltan dialect. Instead, she spoke the language of Tuukos.

Urshila swallowed, and made herself answer in Isavaltan. "You mistake me, Honored Mother." She bit her tongue. She should not have used the honorific.

The old woman's eyes sparkled mischievously. She set the noisome buckets down and straightened her bowed back. "I think not, Daughter. You have the True Blood."

She had already given herself away. Urshila licked her lips and glanced up toward the yards. Only the workmen, serving women, and artisans came and went. But who knew who watched from the palace? Still, there was no one close enough to hear. "My blood is old, Mother," she said softly in her native tongue. "My blood does not remember where it is from."

That only earned her a look of mocking surprise. The woman was taller than she had initially seemed. Urshila had the sudden suspicion she made herself smaller to seem more harmless. "Your blood has a poorer memory than your tongue?"

Now it was Urshila's turn to smile. "My blood is far slower." No one was using this path. Others trudged up and down in the distance, up to their ankles in the mud. No one spared them a glance. Not even the soldier who passed by the yard's high fence.

Of course, the fact of Urshila's gaze darting back and forth was not missed by the old woman. She jerked her chin toward Vysthavos's stone walls. "And if they knew up at the palace of this slow blood of yours?"

But she already knew the answer to that as well as Urshila did. Urshila did not bother to suppress her impatient sigh. "Honored Mother, what is it you want?"

The old woman shrugged. "Words, Daughter, words only."

Urshila raised her eyebrows. "What have we had up until now?" *Honored Mother, I am older than you. I have played this sort of game for a very long time. I can wait.*

The old woman squinted up at her, as if attempting to see directly into her mind. Urshila kept her face a studied blank. At last, the old woman gave in. "They say things are changing on the Holy Island," she said softly. Getting to the heart of the matter, she seemed to become cautious as well.

"So I have heard." *This is why you delay and endanger me, Mother? For court gossip?*

"They say the new emperor has given new orders, and that this new Lord Master, this Peshek, is a decent man."

Those in charge of the household might have organized the expulsion of all those of Tuukosov blood from the palace, but at the same time, Emperor Mikkel had sent one of the few Lords Master he could trust absolutely up to the Holy Island to, among other things, lift the ban against speaking the old language, and start bringing the punishments for crimes by those of the old blood more into line with the rest of the empire. "He has and he is," was all she said aloud. She wanted to be on her way. She should have never stopped for this crone. She had too much else to do.

But the old woman was not done with her yet. "Is the emperor sincere?"

Always an excellent question with emperors. "He knows what it is to be in harsh bondage."

Now the old woman looked over her shoulder. They were still out of earshot of the others whose business took them out into the muddy spring. "Will he give the island its freedom?" she asked softly, as if she did not believe their foreign tongue was enough to protect such words from being overheard and understood.

Urshila knew what she should answer. She should attest to the eternity and indivisibility of Isavalta. It was the only answer that could not be interpreted as treasonous. But for a moment, the old woman did not look shrewd, or mischievous , she only looked worried, and a little homesick. Something inside Urshila softened. "I believe he will give it freedom." *And with that we must be content.*

That thought, however, did not seem to occur to her interrogator. "Is that answer the same as what I asked?" She turned the words so they had a cutting edge.

All Urshila could do was laugh. "Trade words with a sorcerer, Mother, and you will come away with a bad bargain."

"What are the words of the lord sorcerer?"

"Many, and few to the point. I must go, Honored Mother." She gathered her hems up again and stepped over the path onto the relatively dry grass on the other side.

"But how far, Daughter," said the old woman to her back, "and where to?"

Urshila knew she should just keep walking and pretend she'd never heard those words or any others this morning. Now was not the time to argue the fate of Tuukos. Despite knowing all this, she turned, she bent close to the old woman, and she whispered, clearly and fiercely, "Mother, listen to me. My mother left Tuukos when I was a child. Do you have any idea how old I am? I'll lay you long odds I remember the year of your birth. And for all that time and more have I been ashamed of the blood in me. Look elsewhere for your liberation. I am *not* Valin Kalami."

There. She'd said it. The man was no savior, failed or otherwise. It was only luck that the emperor did not use what he had done to start up the slaughters again. Luck and, as much as she hated to admit it, the influence of his southern wife.

The old woman pursed her lips and for a moment Urshila thought she was going to spit. Instead she just moved closer, so close Urshila could smell her sour breath. One crabbed hand shot out and gripped her arm tightly. "Such shame. Yet where were you when Kalami threatened Isavalta? You sat quiet in your exile then. If you love Isavalta so much, why did you not challenge the lord sorcerer? No, do not answer me, Daughter." The old woman pushed her away again. "Answer yourself."

With surprising dexterity, the old woman reclaimed her burden and hobbled away. Urshila stared after her with the words "Because I did not wish to die" poised on her lips, but some small, treacherous part of her brain was already wondering if that was the whole of the truth.

Urshila fixed her gaze rigidly ahead. She wanted to turn back and return to the palace, but that would feel too much like retreat. She had come out to walk and think, and walk she would.

Should she say anything of this? How would she do so without giving herself away? Daren had already spent the past few months sniffing about for those of Tuukosov heritage in the work yard and sending them packing.

Which made her wonder how it was that old woman, whose name she had not bothered to ask, remained in service. Perhaps she too wore a mask of name and language. In which case she was a fine one to reproach Urshila.

If the new rulers knew their servants were being turned out without cause, they were doing nothing about it. The new chatelaine was certainly doing nothing. A word in her ear, perhaps . . . ? And then have Daren hear about it and wonder why she cared? She had just gained the palace again after thirty years. Thirty years that should have been as nothing. Sorcerers were patient. They could afford to be. She knew that patience and the virtues of it, but there had been thirty years of isolation and poverty, because no one of name would have her in their household after she had been dismissed from imperial service. Thirty years as a midwife and a caster of horoscopes for milkmaids.

Why had she not worked against Valin Kalami? Why had none of them? Before Medeoan took the throne, there were a dozen sorcerers in the imperial court. After she ascended and took Kalami as her lord sorcerer, not one of them, not a single one lifted a finger to stand against him.

So angry? So frightened? So jealous? So patient?

So ready to let Isavalta fall for the sake of wounded pride?

Perhaps because we saw Isavalta rise and are not afraid to see it fall to the whims of emperors, despite all our oaths of loyalty. She bit her lip. *Perhaps there is something to the way these southerners do things after all.*

Without families, children, or countries, perhaps it is necessary to bind us to some cause other than ourselves.

But even as she thought that, she tasted bitterness like a trace of gall in the back of her throat. Did she want to be chained? To be walled in and imprisoned in a life that was not hers?

Did she want Isavalta or Tuukos? Peace or power?

And how much longer was she willing to wait while emperors rose and fell, taking her fortunes with them?

Damn the woman! There was no time for this. There was a danger hanging over them that would not care who was Isavaltan, who was Kasatani or Stovorish, and who was Tuukosov. That was where her mind should be.

But in trying to turn her thoughts from Tuukos, she found she could think of nothing else, and her frustration just redoubled.

"Mistress Urshila!"

At once startled and relieved, Urshila turned her head. A young boy in imperial blue with a gold sash around his waist splashed through the mud and puddles, barely keeping his feet as he skidded to a halt in front of her.

"What's the matter?" asked Urshila at once. Despite his exercise, the boy was nearly white.

The boy opened his mouth, but he was panting so hard he could not speak. He swallowed hard to clear his throat and tried again. "The lord sorcerer has collapsed!" he gasped. "They found him . . . it was . . . you're wanted. All the sorcerers are wanted."

"Take me to him." Urshila caught up her hems almost to the point of immodesty and followed the page boy, concentrating only on picking her way across mud and slick grass as fast as she could without turning an ankle.

They squelched through the work yard with the guards at the gate giving them no more than a curious glance. They skidded and slipped through the back hallways, leaving dollops of spring behind them. By the time they reached the front of the house, their soles were relatively dry and the boy could run and Urshila could stride close behind.

Lord Daren collapsed? The words rang through her mind again, and again. *What was he trying to do?*

Whatever it was, it must not have worked, or he would have gone straight to the emperor for credit and not bothered with the rest of them.

She had thought the page would take her to Daren's apartments, but instead he led her up the west stairs to the palace's third story, where the minor courtiers and *boyars* were housed, and where the lord sorcerer's new workroom had been created.

It was a long, low chamber running along the northwest wall that had once been a music room. There were still pegs on the walls where instruments had hung and the inlaid floor had a pattern of roses, harps, and lutes. Most of the furnishings had been cleared away to make room for long tables and writing desks. The tables were covered with rich and filigreed artifacts; silver clocks, gold-framed mirrors, bottles of colored glass with swan necks and sealed corks, small chests of sweet-scented woods banded and locked with brass or copper, large oak chests banded with iron.

These were part of Medeoan's legacy to Isavalta. In her isolation, she had collected or commissioned a startling variety of artifacts that were either themselves magical or could be used in the working of spells. Once they had all been locked in one room of the imperial apartments, but now it was the work of the lord sorcerer and his assistants to sort them out, to understand them and to catalogue them for the treasury.

At the far end of the room, under the largest windows, was a single great table spread with a white linen cloth. On it waited fragments of wire, loose jewels, delicate filigree spheres of bronze, gold, and copper that had been dented and twisted. Gears, cogs, and springs lay in tidy rows between bits of ruined art.

This was Lord Daren's personal labor. Once these fragments had been the Portrait of Worlds, the greatest tool of divination ever created. If it had still been whole, the Firebird could never have hidden from them. They would have known at once where Bridget's lost child was, even if she was the tiniest wisp in the Land of Death and Spirit. Medeoan, however, had smashed it before she fled to her doom. Daren had sworn he would repair the Portrait, or duplicate it, if it took a hundred years, as, indeed, it might.

But there was no work in Daren now. He slumped in a heavy chair, his skin a muddy grey and his head hanging to the side as if he lacked the strength to hold it up. His hands twitched and scrabbled at the chair arms, making sounds like mice skittering behind the walls. Korta, the youngest of the recalled sorcerers, stood beside his chair with a wooden goblet in his hands. Red stains on Daren's beard said he had not even been able to drink the wine.

There should have been a dozen there to attend him, but they were only six, counting the lord sorcerer and young Korta. The recall of the old court sorcerers had been proceeding only slowly. Some had vanished, some were believed murdered, but the emperor was insistent that all should be offered their old places before new court sorcerers should be chosen. He might come to regret that stubbornness.

As it was, the court sorcerers were divided, cantankerous, and few in number. There was crabbed, old Luden who had been bribed by Mother Nacherada to forsake his warlord master and serve the imperial throne, and who had stuck by his oath since then. With him stood Sidor, whose grey beard hung down to his waist and who leaned on a walking stick he had carved with a pattern of braids Urshila still had not been able to decipher. Nedu, the only other woman present, was golden and petite. Her head barely came up to Urshila's shoulder. Her delicate appearance disguised a subtle sorceress and it was a common mistake to underestimate her.

If either Bridget or Sakra had been sent for, they were not here yet.

"What happened?" demanded Urshila.

Daren lifted his gaze to look at her, but his eyes were cloudy and unfocused. It was Sidor who answered, gripping his stick so tightly that his hand trembled. "The lord sorcerer has seen the Firebird. It is coming."

Urshila felt herself blanch. "When?"

"Soon," croaked Daren. His bleary eyes rolled to try to take in the whole assemblage. "I tried . . . to stand . . . it scarce looked at me . . ." His breath rattled in his throat.

Urshila had once healed a man whose house had succumbed to fire. He'd inhaled a quantity of smoke, and his breath had sounded as the lord sorcerer's did now. It had been most painful, but Urshila's sympathy refused to rise.

"You tried to stand before the Firebird?" she cried. "Alone? What in Vyshko's name did you think you could do?"

Daren stared at her. So did all the others.

"We should not be casting blame at this time," began proper, petite Nedu. "The lord sorcerer is ill."

"And whose fault is that?" Urshila planted her fists against her hips. "His pride and his need to prove himself in his new position led him to do something the gods themselves would hesitate to do, and look what he has accomplished. We will be without his strength for days."

"What would you have him do?" croaked Luden. His eyes were still bright in his wizened face. How old was he? Twice her age? Three times? "We are vulnerable here."

"We are vulnerable everywhere." Urshila tried to collect herself. This would not do. "We have been scattered to the four winds, our most powerful tools are lost or locked away in chests, for which we do not even have the keys anymore." She glowered at the nearest box locked with silver and magic. "This thing finds us not only unready but jostling each other for pride and position in a brand-new court."

"I ask again, Mistress Urshila, what would you have him, have us, do?" Luden spread his hands. "We are as we are, and this thing comes, whether we like our circumstances or not. Would you have us remake its cage? Excellent. Where is that knowledge please?"

Urshila's mouth hardened into a straight line. Luden's criticism was a fair one, if wholly unwelcome.

"We must destroy it," she heard herself say, as if from a long way off.

The statement was greeted with absolute silence, except for the rasping breath of the lord sorcerer.

"Not enough power . . ." he gasped. "Never be enough . . ."

"There might be, my lord." Urshila straightened her back and met the eyes of her compatriots. "The Vixen has informed Bridget Lederle that the daughter she thought lost is still alive. That daughter is a third-generation sorcerer. With such power as she will possess at our command, we will have enough. Bridget wishes to find her daughter. Let me recommend she be allowed to do so. While she is gone, we can find the knowledge to put the power of that child to use."

Vyshemir help me if I am wrong, she thought as she watched them take in the possibilities. *But, oh, Vyshemir help me if I am right, for I am offering up the life of a child to try to save such a meaningless thing as an empire.*

It had taken a life to cage the Firebird. How much more would it take to destroy it?

Oh, Vyshemir, help us all.

Senja Palo, who had masked herself many years ago with the *murhata* name of Samona, hobbled across the muddy work yard. Each step brought muck oozing up through the loose soles of her shoes, adding to the filth already caked on her feet. She entered the scullery with its blast of heat and stink, and shrugged the yoke off her shoulders. She grabbed up one of the buckets that she'd filled from the canal and lugged it across the kitchen. Preparations for the midday meal were proceeding in their usual frenzy of banging, clattering, thumping, and shouting. No one spared a moment for one old woman with a bucket of water. Let her finish whatever her errand happened to be and give her another when her bucket was empty.

So no one remarked and few even noticed when she took her bucket through the nearest inner door into the dim and narrow corridors that were the world of the lowliest servants of Vyshtavos.

The back corridors were a maze. They actually took up most of the lower story of the palace, allowing the servants to flit back and forth and spend a minimum amount of time where they might actually be seen. Footmen and maids, valets, butlers, and waiting ladies might come into view of the high and the mighty, but old women with buckets . . . not unless absolutely necessary.

The advantage of all these hundreds of yards of corridors, store-rooms, and cramped quarters was that if one wished to hide, one had plenty of choices. There were dozens of storerooms that would only be entered once or twice a year on set days to be aired and inventoried. Once, the illegitimate child of a scullery maid had been discovered living in one of these rooms two years after his mother had died of fever.

One of the smaller, unlocked rooms was a former drying room that was now full of nothing but bales of stained and unfashionable linens. Once they had been put there to be cleaned and mended, but that mending had never occurred and no subsequent mistress of the house had thought to throw them out. Senja set her bucket just inside the threshold,

so she would have some warning if the unthinkable happened and someone besides herself decided to open this door.

With the door shut, the storeroom was pitch-black. In the late afternoon, a few slim shafts of light might squeeze through the ventilation
slits, but that time was hours away. Senja, however, knew her way by
touch. Behind a stack of bales her fingers found the cold skin of a tin
lantern, then found the tinderbox stored inside it along with the whole
tallow candle she had risked much to steal.

It was the work of a few patient moments to make her light. Senja
closed the lantern housing and pushed it back into the deepest shadows
under the shelves so that she had only a few slivers of light to see by, but
no stray glimmer beneath the door would betray her. From under the
nearest bale, she drew out a knotted bundle of canvas. There was no
magic in the knot, only some tricks of tying so she would see if it had
been meddled with. She was not a *murhata* to waste her gifts on trivia.

Those destined for bondage in the weaving shed, in the tannery, the
forge or pottery were all carefully examined by the lord sorcerer to
make sure that they had none of the invisible gifts about them. Not so
the drudges in the scullery, or old women who swept the yards and carried the slops, not even when the lord sorcerer was on the prowl among
the bondsmen to prove his diligence.

While Valin Kalami held the post of lord sorcerer, she had little need
for such precautions as she now took. She had only to keep eyes and ears
open to know that the cause of the Holy Island was being served. Senja
was not even certain Kalami knew she was there, but she had kept her
head down. If she was needed by him, blood and destiny would lead
them to one another.

Senja smiled, remembering the day she had first seen Kalami. He
was striding through the work yard on his way to interview the mistress
of the weaving shed. He was so straight, so confident, already looking as
if he owned the palace. She had smiled then as well, because he reminded
her of other things, yet further back, that she sometimes wondered if she
had dreamed.

He reminded her that there was a time when the sorcerers of the
True Blood had met together openly in the sacred grove on the day the
sun vanished and the day it returned. The bone fires had burned hot and
red, and justice and prophecy had been spoken. The seer had not been

broken then, living cramped, crooked, and half-mad in his cave. He had been tall and proud, the crown carved of antler and ivory on his brow. Senja had knelt before him when her time came, offering up the *viina* she had brewed herself in a bowl of glass as clear as ice that had cost her father three calves and three lambs. With a proud smile, he had accepted the drink and her petition to be tutored in the invisible arts, even though her voice had trembled as she spoke the request. She had felt warm at that smile, as if she were the one who had drunk the *viina*.

Senja closed her eyes for a moment. The glass. The glass had been real too. The most sacred art, combining all the elements, earth, fire, air, water, and metal, and synthesizing them into a form new and indivisible. She remembered the sharp smell of the furnaces, the heat of the blow-pipes, the searing of steam in her lungs, the sparkle and brilliance of the finished creation.

She remembered Isavaltans riding their horses through the *ateljee* and the work of a hundred hands being smashed with a sound like the most fragile of bells. She remembered the blood and the smells of burning flesh as the priests and the sorcerers were pushed into the crucibles and the sound of the *murhata*'s laughter, and their curses as the glass cut the hides of their precious horses, as if that were the Tuukosov's fault.

She remembered her own failing, standing there with the life blood of sorcerers flowing freely, with fire, water, and death, so much death. She remembered raising up her hands with their blood running down her bare arms and crying out every curse she knew, every prayer to bring down the lightning, the darkness, plague, fire, nightmare, and death, death, death.

Nothing had happened, nothing at all. She had been unable to think, unable to draw or shape the power she commanded. The *murhata* had laughed louder, believing her to be only a terrified young woman, and one of them had reached down for her. She was never sure after that just how she had gotten away, but she did and she remained hidden in the woods for the better part of a month. When she finally crept back, cold and starving, the world had changed. The Isavaltans were in control, and the sorcerers of the True Blood were hanging like fruit from the trees.

They called the Tuukosov dogs and whipped them through the streets. They called them worms and made them crawl, and Senja had vowed then to become what they believed she was. They believed she was a dog;

she would live in their home until she found a way to bite. They believed she was a worm; she would dwell in their garden until she could infect its heart.

In the moment when she saw Valin Kalami in the work yard, it seemed to her that time had come. Now there would be more to do than wait and watch and relay what information she could to the seer. Kalami had played the weaknesses of Isavalta's empress like a master musician, and almost, *almost* he had brought it all to the end.

He had fallen, and Senja had thought her heart would finally break when Mikkel took the throne, but now she saw the extent of Kalami's triumph. He had brought all to the brink, and behind the rise of this new *murhata* emperor, all was still in motion. The last push was ready, and Isavalta would fall.

Inside her little bundle lay a stone mortar and pestle, a small packet of herbs gathered in the previous year and now dried almost to dust, another packet of coarse salt, a small but precious sphere of clear glass scarcely two fingers wide, and a short, sharp knife.

She picked up the sphere first. Despite the passage of years, she remembered the heat and the crucible stench of its making. It was called a witch's eye, and if a *murhata* found it and recognized it, she would be hanged from the walls.

She'd smuggled in two of the precious spheres with her when she had first come to Vyshtavos, but the other had been sacrificed for other work.

From her sleeve she drew the kerchief she had lifted from the pocket of the one who called herself Urshila. She laid it across her hand and then laid the witch's eye in it. Reverently, she kissed the sphere's smooth surface to awaken its sight. She breathed across so that it might recognize the presence of its maker. Leaning close to it she whispered, drawing out the magic she'd placed into the eye at its making.

"Open, open and see. Show me the one who owned the cloth where you rest, by the first witch, the Old Witch, by the earth and the fire. Show me."

She closed her eyes and touched the sphere to her right eye. As the glass warmed by her skin touched her eyelid, her private darkness bloomed into fresh light.

Senja recognized the lord sorcerer's workroom right away. There was a mirror there that had known the sands of the Holy Island, that had long ago been shaped and smoothed by careful artisans who understood the craft of fires and of earths. It had been carelessly propped up on a shelf by some seemingly unthinking hand before the lord sorcerer had decided to ban the usual palace servants from his workroom. Her witch's eye could take her easily through that mirror, allowing her to look, and to listen.

All the sorcerers in the court of Isavalta, save for two, were clustered around their lord sorcerer who collapsed in a chair, but their attention was not on him. It was on the one calling herself Urshila.

"Mistress Urshila, that is a cold thought," said Korta, the youngest of them.

She did not look away at that, displaying some courage of conviction after all. "Death is colder."

Luden craned his bent neck so he could look up at her. "I take it you do not mean to inform Mistress Bridget what you intend for her child."

"What we intend." Urshila enunciated each word clearly.

So.

Neda frowned hard, glancing about the room. For a moment, Senja thought her gaze rested on the mirror, but all she said was, "I have heard no one else here agree to this plan."

"There is no plan, only hopes and fears."

The tiny, golden woman spread her hands. "Is this what we are driven to?"

Urshila did not even hesitate. "Yes." Her gaze held steady and she turned it on each of the sorcerers in turn. "If we can find another way, then let us find it, but we may fail, or we may be too few or too weak. In that case, we will need power from wherever we can find it."

Korta did not look at her; instead he studied the depths of the wine cup he held. "Surely Vyshko and Vyshemir will not permit the Firebird to destroy their realm."

It was Sidor who answered, and his voice held the tone of defeat. "They permitted the Firebird to be released."

Luden wagged his ancient head. "I do not like this, but I fear she is right."

Lord Daren gripped the arm of his chair, as if hanging on for grim life. His whole body trembled, and for a moment Senja thought he was going to have a seizure, but he only spoke. "Let . . . it be done."

So.

Senja lowered the witch's eye. There would be more discussion, more planning certainly, and more swearing to secrecy. Things it would be useful to know would be said, but it did not do to spy too long on sorcerers through magic. She had what she most wanted from them. She needed to take the precious time she had left to communicate what she now knew.

Using the witch's eye was tiring, but not as bad as what was to come. Senja tucked the glass sphere away under the bale so that if she was discovered, it, at least, would not be. Then, she took the herbs and the salt and poured them into the mortar. She rolled back her sleeve and laid the knife's edge against her forearm.

The cut was swift and shallow. Glistening blood welled up immediately. She took up the pestle and began to steadily grind down the herbs and salt. The blood flowed from her arm, down her hand and down the pestle into the mortar. Her grinding mixed it well with the salt and the scrape of stone on stone mixed with the scents of the herbs, with the darkness and the blood.

When at last the paste was smooth, Senja dipped two fingers into it and smeared a quantity on her lips, the tang of salt and iron stinging her flesh, adding a bright flash of pain to the weaving.

"Earth to earth, air to air, blood to blood, breath to breath," she murmured, drawing the magic in, pouring the magic out. "Knowing to knowing, Senja to Niku."

Over and again she repeated the chant until she felt as if she had begun to fade. She was lighter than air, she was nothing but thought. She could be anywhere. She could be everywhere.

"Earth to earth, air to air . . ."

Senja. Niku's voice, deep and solid as stone, sounded in her mind. *What news?*

Discipline helped Senja form a single thought. She might otherwise pour her whole mind out to Niku, leaving him with too much information to understand, and leaving her with nothing at all to return to. *The Firebird comes to Isavalta. The sorcerers struggle to find a way to stand against it.*

They will fail. There was no smugness in Niku's tone, only calm certainty.

Urshila herself was less sure. *Perhaps. What do the bones say of Ulla?*

She used Urshila's true birth name. It was important to speak only truths when speaking mind to mind. Lies weakened the link, opened the gates to loose and losing thought.

She is weary and loses touch. We may not depend on her. Not yet. Her role is yet unclear.

Which was as she thought. *Do the bones still speak of Kalami's return?*

Past life, past death. Blood calls him back. It is still part of the song.

I have seen, I think, how it may be.

Niku paused for a single heartbeat, but Senja felt his mind quicken. *Tell me.*

Senja felt her distant body smile with its bloody lips. She carefully fashioned memories of memories, showing Niku the meeting of the sorcerers. The song was true. Father and child would return, and the future would be complete in them. The *murhata* would fall in fire and blood, and Tuukos would have the victory too long denied.

The Holy Island would at last, at *last,* be free.

Chapter Nine

The long, hot day wore away. Mae Shan watched over Tsan Nu as the child slept, tossing and turning in what was surely the rudest bed she had ever known. Mae Shan dozed a few times, but always brought herself sharply awake. There was no one else to take this watch.

At last, the only way she kept awake was by running through the training forms with her spear. The familiar moves, with their emphasis on relaxation and concentration, helped shake the fog from her mind and reinvigorate her blood. It helped too that it was said these forms were given to the first emperor by the gods so he could use them to drive off the forty thousand companies of devils that occupied the land. With real devils in the sky overhead, every little bit must help.

She broke her bouts of training to make sure the boy soldiers rotated their watch in the tower, and to take their reports. Fires were spreading in the city. The clouds of ash and smoke were dense and the streets were filled with people. Mae Shan could hear their voices vibrating through the shutters of the blockhouse, crying, shouting, screaming in their panic. She ordered the windows closed. Fortunately, the mob had not yet thought to storm the garrison for weapons, but that would come. When they realized no word or command was to be had from the Heart of the World, that would surely come.

She looked at the pale child, still fitfully asleep in the officer's bed, and thought of how firmly she had spoken her dreadful prophecy. Did she realize what it meant? Could she, foreigner and child that she was? Mae Shan could barely compass it all. Probably Tsan Nu mostly thought of it in terms of how foolish those around her had been when they failed to heed the words she had spoken two days ago.

Two days ago. Had it only been two days? Two days, and a few hours since she'd last seen Wei Lin.

It was the general custom of the ladies who were not required to attend at the emperor's dinner to spend fine spring evenings out in the garden—reading, playing music, writing, or simply sitting and enjoying the twilight. Technically, as a resident of the women's palace, Mae Shan was allowed to enjoy the Moon Garden, and its companion the Star Garden, whenever she chose, but she and the other bodyguards generally chose not to do so, as many of the ladies considered them coarse. It was simpler to avoid the pampered creatures rather than ignore their jibes. Her exception to this general rule was when she had a moment to catch up with Wei Lin.

Wei Lin was the oldest of the five daughters in Mae Shan's large family. She was also the most beautiful. Their parents had cultivated that beauty carefully, keeping her out of the sun, taking her frequently to the baths and the doctors for cosmetics and treatments to keep her skin soft and her eyes bright. Nor did they neglect her education, sending her to the best girls' school they could afford so she could learn reading, calligraphy, music, dance, and poetry.

Their investment proved itself. When the new emperor came of age it was determined that a new crop of ladies would be needed for the women's palace. The procurers came to the nearby city, instructing all parents who wished to have their daughters evaluated to come to the Temple of Rains. Wei Lin was one of five girls chosen for imperial service. She was sent to the women's palace, given the rank of Shining Lady, a full wardrobe, continuing education, and a stipend of twenty strings of silver a year.

Wei Lin's privilege, however, had not spoiled her. She sent home ten strings of silver every year to the family. She had arranged for their oldest brother to gain a position in the city storehouses as a recorder, and three of their sisters were lady's maids in the palace of the governor general. It was she who ensured that strong, square Mae Shan was admitted to the examinations for the Heart's Own Guard when she turned fifteen.

Mae Shan remembered emerging from the southeast gate of the Moon Garden, blinking in the fading daylight. Breathing the freshening breeze deeply, she strolled around the edges of the wall, moving silently, keeping herself quiet and unnoticed as she had been taught to do.

Some imperial ladies sat here and there among the flowers on low benches and beautifully carved folding chairs. Some read, or played soft tunes on their dulcimers, earning polite applause from their listeners. Others strolled between the artfully planted groves, arm in arm, talking softly among themselves, perhaps exchanging gossip and the news of the day. Possibly, as Mae Shan knew from Wei Lin, exchanging plans for bettering their own positions, or poison words to tear down one of their fellows, or both.

They were a moving portrait of womanly beauty and serenity, just as they were supposed to be, and every one of them was supremely conscious of how they appeared in that portrait. It was the work of their lives.

Wei Lin herself sat between a pair of silver-leafed birch trees, her sky-blue robes making a pleasant picture against their white trunks, a detail she surely had not failed to notice when she settled herself there. A folio of closely written pages lay open on her lap, and she read them with every semblance of great care. A pot of tea and two cups waited on a table beside the low bench where she sat and Mae Shan smiled. They were seldom able to arrange these evening meetings, but as suited one who must be prepared to be called to her own duties at a moment's notice, Wei Lin remained ready for them.

Mae Shan had watched her sister for a moment, studying Wei Lin as she studied her folio. Sometimes Mae Shan wondered that she was not more jealous of this creature who had been so tenderly reared while she had been sent out to the fields to put her broad back and strong hands to "good use." But there it was. Perhaps she had grown accustomed to seeing her sister as a treasured family artifact that must be carefully guarded.

"Good evening, Big Sister," said Mae Shan at last, stepping forward. Her thoughts had threatened to turn toward her sister's safety, which would bring them back to all she had heard that day, and those were things she could not dwell on. Her duty would come on her as it would.

Wei Lin turned and a pretty smile brightened her lotus-pink face. "Mae-Mae!" she cried happily. "Come, sit with me." She patted the bench beside her. "Tell me what you have heard in the secret councils today."

Mae Shan laughed and settled herself beside Wei Lin. "I heard that the Ninth Recorder of the Wharf has been turned into a bird and hung in the Sun Garden for daring to suggest that the Fifth Minister of the Northwest's short wife was actually a boy in disguise."

"Sister!" Wei Lin covered her mouth, her eyes wide in mock horror. "You shock me! Can it be true?"

Mae Shan looked around seriously, as if afraid of listening ears. "I could not say myself, of course," she whispered, bending close, "but I have been told by my lieutenant's sister's cousin that she only goes to the baths at midnight, and then only with mute attendants."

"Oh, but, Sister," Wei Lin laid a hand on her sleeve, looking her in the eyes most seriously, "that is because she goes to meet her lover, the Tenth Undersecretary of the Third Wind."

Mae Shan made her eyebrows shoot up, and Wei Lin nodded solemnly, and they held each other's gazes until they could stand it no longer and burst out laughing.

"Ah, Mae-Mae!" she sighed, dabbing delicately at her eyes. "It is good to see you. Tell me how it truly goes."

While Wei Lin poured the tea and wiped the rims of the cups, Mae Shan told her what she could of the small doings of the barracks, the promises of the new trainees, how Quyen, one of the bodyguards to the Nine Elders, had begun to make moon eyes at her and showed every sign of being about to contemplate writing poetry.

"And you have done nothing to encourage this, of course?" said Wei Lin archly as she handed across the warm teacup.

"Of course not." Mae Shan stuck her chin out. "I'm a soldier. I think of nothing beyond my duty."

"Oh, yes, and Kein never had to transfer to the city guard of Nhi Tao because you were caught with him in the . . ."

"I will dump this tea over your head and spoil your makeup if you finish that sentence, Big Sister," growled Mae Shan.

They had laughed again, and sipped their tea as the daylight dimmed around them, enjoying the simple fact of being together.

But no more. No more.

Tears threatened and Mae Shan blinked hard and cast about for distraction. Dawn was brightening. Mae Shan lifted her eyes to the grey sky smudged with the black cloud that marked the ruin of the Heart of the World. The Moon Garden was a waste of ashes and coals, and where was

Wei Lin? Did her ghost now cry in those cooling ashes? Did it call for her sister to come save her?

Did she understand that Mae Shan could not come? She rubbed her tired eyes. Which led to a new question.

What happens now?

Tsan Nu rolled over again, her wavy hair spreading across her pale cheeks. Mae Shan knew she must decide what to do, but a single thought kept interrupting all the others in her mind.

If no one had been able to save Wei Lin, no one had even tried to save Tsan Nu.

In the Heart, not one guard had hammered on the door. Neither of the maids had rushed in to reach the child. None of the tutors had come to find her. Tsan Nu, a foreign child, a hostage against her father's good behavior and surety of his promises, had been left to burn.

And now invisible devils filled the sky to be fought by invisible ghosts, all presiding over a chaos that was only going to get worse.

She had to get Tsan Nu out of the city, had to take her somewhere safe until order rose from the ash again. That much was clear. But where could they go? The obvious answer was to Isavalta and the child's kin, but that was a journey of weeks, even if they could find a boat to cross the Sea of Azure. If they couldn't, it would become a journey of months across a country that was going to be in anarchy and disarray.

Goddess of Mercy, we would atone if we could, she prayed wearily. *If you would just tell us what we've done. I'd throw myself on my dagger in the last apology if it would help, if I could just know what fault I'd help commit.*

Boots pounded down the stairs from the watchtower. Tsan Nu shot bolt upright, eyes staring in panic.

"It's all right, mistress," said Mae Shan. "I'll see what is making those boys raise such a fuss. You wait here."

She sheathed her knife inside her jacket and strode into the common room.

"They're coming this way!" Trainee Chen was telling his fellows. "What do we do?"

"Who is coming?" demanded Mae Shan.

Chen turned toward her and she saw the boy had gone as white as bone. "The whole world."

Mae Shan hesitated. She should not go so far from Tsan Nu, but she had to ascertain the threat.

"Guard my mistress's door," she ordered Chen, and she ran up the watchtower steps.

Out on the battlements, the air still burned and ash swirled thickly on the wind. The sound of crying had grown into a heartrending wail the size of the whole city. Over the walls, she could count four, five, six fresh fires. That much was bad enough, but then Mae Shan looked down into the streets.

The streets were black with the size of the mob and the thunder of shouts and the weeping of both men and women reached up to Heaven.

God of us all, Chen was right.

No guards, no cryers, no curfew bells ringing over the din.

No order.

Mae Shan swallowed hard. The only way this could be happening was if the Heart was truly destroyed, and if Tsan Nu had again spoken the truth. The emperor was gone. The Nine Elders were gone. They were all burned to ash by the Phoenix and no god or guardian had risen to say this thing was not to be.

Mae Shan felt her knees tremble and gripped the rail running around the watch platform. Despite all, she hadn't believed it possible. She had seen the Phoenix above the flames of the Heart, and she had still believed the Son of Heaven and Earth and the Nine Elders must survive, because without them . . . without them there was no empire. The Red Center that was Hung-Tse was pierced through.

Goddess of Mercy.

She could not even begin to wrap her mind around the enormity of that concept. It was not something to even contemplate and to try left her paralyzed. The portion of her that was only soldier felt panic begin. Where were her orders to come from? What was she to do?

The mob spread. People were coming out of their houses and hearing the rumors and joining the dark mass, to pray, to run, to go mad, because there was nothing else to do. They ran from the spreading fires and from their own fear.

They ran from the end of the world.

She had to get out. Now, while they were still ahead of the mob. It occurred to her that Tsan Nu's presence would slow her down. It occurred to her that there was no one left to know, or care, if she left the girl here to be swept up by the mob. She swallowed. There was no one else left for Tsan Nu, or the three boys either.

Mae Shan ran back down the stairs. She knew about mobs. She had been trained to deal with them, as a soldier though, with other soldiers beside her, not with three raw trainees and a child. Older parts of her mind spoke to her now. The parts that still remembered being a peasant girl in the southern provinces.

The trainees hunched together at the foot of the stairs, waiting to be told what to do, fearing there was no answer.

"We must get out of the city," she told them. "We have a few minutes at best. Never mind your armor. If you have street clothes, get in them. We need food, water, and weapons, but most especially water. Wrap whatever you can in blankets. We will make for the Left Wall and try to get out that way. I'll get the girl."

Trainee Kyun fingered his mole nervously. "But should we not wait for orders? Our superiors will return."

Mae Shan thought about Tsan Nu's sky full of ghosts and devils. "I do not say this lightly, but I do not believe there will be orders. If they could, I think your officers would have returned by now. But, do what you must. If it helps, I order you to come with me."

Chen, who of the three had seen what was coming, snatched a satchel off a peg on the wall and bolted for the kitchen. Kyun looked at Mae Shan, looked at the door, and retreated to the barracks.

Airic, however, drew himself to attention.

"I am a city guard," he said. "It is my duty to stay."

Mae Shan had no time to argue, and was not sure it was her place to do so.

"Keep a fire burning," she said. "Let the smoke be a signal to your officers that someone is still manning this garrison, but keep the door barred and the windows shuttered and do not try to go into the street. If you would serve your city, keep the weapons here out of the hands of the mob. If you do not think you will be able to do that, destroy them."

He bowed in salute to her, his face serious and more than a little scared. In her heart, Mae Shan wished him well, and she hurried into the barracks.

Tsan Nu was up and on the edge of the bed.

"You heard, mistress?" asked Mae Shan. She peered through the slit in the shutters. The street outside was still quiet, but the thunder of the mob was becoming audible.

"Where will we go?" Tsan Nu asked in a small voice.

"First we get safely out of the city." Mae Shan ripped the blanket off the bed. "Then we decide."

"But the devils will be able to catch us if we go outside the walls."

"The mob will take us if we stay inside," replied Mae Shan. "Look out, tell me what you see above."

Tsan Nu clambered up on the bed and peered out the window, craning her neck to get the best view of the sky.

"They are still fighting," she said. "The devils and the Heart's ghosts. I think the devils have a few more banners, but I can't tell. The smoke is very thick."

Listening to her, Mae Shan realized there was only one place to go that might possibly be safe.

"Come, mistress." She held out her hand and Tsan Nu jumped down and took it. The child looked frightened.

"If my father were here, he could walk us to safety," she said. "He is a powerful sorcerer."

"I know, but we cannot wait for him." Mae Shan pulled the girl along gently to the armory. "Fortunately, my mistress is not the only one who has a sorcerer for a relative."

"You?" Tsan Nu looked stunned, and Mae Shan smiled briefly.

Kyun was still in the armory, rolling pikes and knives into blankets. They weren't going to be able to carry all the bundles he had made, but she didn't stop the boy, who looked on the edge of tears. He needed something to do.

Instead, she plucked one of his blankets from the pile and spread it out on the floor. "My uncle, Lien, is also a powerful sorcerer. He will give us shelter in his summer house."

If he's there. Heaven itself doesn't always know where Uncle Lien keeps himself.

"Tsan Nu, there will be bows and quivers of arrows in that cabinet. Bring one of each," Mae Shan said as she pulled a spear and a poleax from their racks and laid them on her own blanket. Tsan Nu trotted over with a bow and a full quiver and laid them beside the other weapons. Mae Shan wrapped them swiftly and discarded the idea of binding them with leather straps in favor of a length of rope hanging from a hook on the wall. Looking poor and as if you had nothing of value to steal was an advantage now. Again she thanked the Goddess of Mercy that she and Tsan Nu were in nightclothes for there was no time to disguise themselves. She tied the girl's nightdress off with an additional length of rope to help disguise the fineness of the fabric. The cloth slippers she had risked them both to get were now on her feet, but they were scuffed and rumpled enough to pass casual inspection without comment.

"Bring two of those bundles," said Mae Shan to Kyun. "We're going now." She slung her own bundle across her shoulders with a knack she remembered from her younger days and took Tsan Nu's hand again. "Chen! Now!" she called as she strode toward the door.

Chen appeared. Two bulging satchels and four sloshing bottles hung on his shoulders, making him look more like a peddler than anything else. Mae Shan relieved him of one bottle and one satchel. She shoved them under her anonymous-looking blanket roll.

"As soon as we get onto the soldier's road, we run," said Mae Shan, leading them up the stairs. "Keep together. If we become separated, we will meet on top of the Hill of Last Rays at sunrise tomorrow. If you cannot get there, do what you can to get to your families. If we meet the mob, do what you must and no more. These are the ones you are sworn to protect."

Sworn to whom? We took our oaths before the gods and the emperor, and the one has killed the other. Mae Shan pushed the thought aside. Like Kyun, only movement kept her mind steady.

"Airic, open the door."

The boy did and Mae Shan ducked through, keeping tight hold of Tsan Nu. She did not look back to make sure the trainees followed.

Like the Heart, the doubled walls of the city created a second tier of roads running above the ordinary streets. The only way to reach them was through garrisons such as these, and when the mob remembered . . . Mae Shan could only hope Airic would find someplace to hide.

The air outside was hot and harsh. Smoke instantly wrung tears from her eyes, and ash settled hot against the backs of her hands. Seven Generations Street ran east-west, with the soldier's road running parallel to it, so they were able to run straight down its length. Chen ran with the back of his hand pressed against his mouth, almost doubled over by his burden. Kyun jogged, his sweat smearing the ash that had already settled on his face. From his wide eyes Mae Shan knew he had noticed the shouts and the crumbling, crashing, tearing sounds getting closer.

Tsan Nu stumbled constantly over the slightly uneven stones because she would not look where she was going. She kept her attention fixed firmly on the sky and the battle her sorcerer's eyes saw there. Mae Shan wanted to tell her to stop that. The reminder that there was something worse happening than fires and mobs tore at what calm she still possessed, but she said nothing. If that battle came to earth, they would need to know that too, if only so they could pray.

At the next corner, they found the mob.

Seven Generations crossed the Street of Winter's Shelter, a place of modest homes and gardens. The street was plugged tight with bodies. Some screamed to be allowed through, some laughed as if insanity had already taken them. Gates had been flung open and household goods were tossed from hand to hand or trampled underfoot. People ran in and out of houses, as if in frantic search for some lost, precious thing. Some leapt and clawed at the walls, trying to reach the soldier's road overhead. First one woman, then a man squeezed free of the surging crowd and raced down the street, the mob spreading out behind them to claim new territory.

Where were they going? What did they think they were doing? Were they just trying to get out, get to the walls, like she and her charges were, or had the realization that the heart had been cut out of Hung-Tse driven them all mad?

Both were probably true, but that truth did her no good right now.

"Don't stop!" Mae Shan pulled Tsan Nu closer and ran on.

The world flashed past; red roofs, dark bodies, white faces, and the constant noise. Here and there, some managed to boost each other onto the soldier's road and run. Mae Shan raised no cry. *Let them think that's what we have done.*

"Something's happening!" cried Tsan Nu all at once. "Some of the demons are breaking away. They're flying toward us!"

Mae Shan scooped Tsan Nu up into her arms and she ran faster. She didn't know what else to do.

I accept my death as ordained. I humbly ask forgiveness for my transgressions. I stand by my duty until my breath is done. I . . .

"They've gone past!" reported Tsan Nu wonderingly. "It's as if they're headed for the gates too."

"Is the girl mad?" cried Kyun. "What is she talking about?"

"Save your breath!" shot back Mae Shan, mostly because she did not wish to waste hers in explanations.

Kyun mopped at his forehead and kept on in silence, but his gaze was more and more drawn down to the streets. Mae Shan glanced down too. If the streets had been full before, they were packed now with people shoved together until there was no room to move. What was happening?

Ahead of them, a group of men pushed a young woman up on their shoulders and she scrambled up onto the soldier's road. They called out to her, but she only turned and ran. Another woman, her baby tied tight to her breast, climbed over heads and shoulders as if wading between stones. Mae Shan strangled a frustrated cry.

"Chen! Kyun!" She pointed to the floundering woman. They stared and for a moment she thought they might disobey, but they ran to the battlement and together reached out, dragging the woman out of the mob's reach. She babbled her thanks, incoherent in her fear and relief, clutching her wailing baby to her. Behind and below her, hands reached up and shrieks for help tore through the air.

Chen and Kyun looked to Mae Shan.

"We need to get ahead of it," she said. "Find out what's happening at the gate." *Where are the other soldiers? What's happened to them?*

And so they ran on. The woman and her baby ran beside them for a ways, but soon fell behind. Mae Shan hoped she did not fall back down into the streets.

"Do you still see those demons, Tsan Nu?" she asked, hoisting the girl a little higher in her arms. Tsan Nu only shook her head. To her surprise, Mae Shan felt no relief.

At last, she was able to see the outer walls and the Left Gate. The outer portals had been flung wide open, but the inner stuck fast. The screams of the mob became a deafening roar as people hammered the ancient iron-bound wood with their bodies, trying desperately to break it open. They pushed each other up to the tops of the walls in an attempt to scramble over, but they slid back down, helpless.

Mae Shan slowed to a stop, appalled. Chen and Kyun stopped beside her, wiping their faces and eyes, and trying not to look down below.

"What is this?" Mae Shan croaked. "Where is the guard?"

Tsan Nu buried her head against Mae Shan's shoulder. "It's the demons. The ones that flew ahead of us."

The screech and roar of the thousands of voices was deafening, more the sound of a storm than of humanity. Mae Shan had to shout to be heard, even by Tsan Nu. "What are they doing?"

"They're holding the gate shut. They're on top of the walls and pushing people back down." Tsan Nu shook in her arms. "They don't want anybody to get out, for when they win."

Mae Shan did nothing but hold Tsan Nu close for a moment. The child should not have to see what she did.

And what about the children down below? The crowd surged back, then forward as they tried to batter the gate open.

"Mistress, is there anything you can do to get the gates open?"

"No! I can't!" But she pressed her face harder against Mae Shan's shoulder and trembled, and Mae Shan remembered her younger brothers making such refusals when they truly meant "I won't."

Swiftly but gently, Mae Shan set Tsan Nu down on her feet and crouched in front of her so the child could easily look her in the eye.

"Is there *anything* you can do, mistress? You must tell me if there is."

Tsan Nu screwed up her fists, her face paper-white with fear. "I can't! The demons are down there! They'll feel it and they'll come get me!"

Mae Shan swallowed. "Tsan Nu, you must do whatever you can. We are the Heart of the World here, you and I. We *must* serve. You are the one with the power to do this, as I have the power to protect you while it is done." She did not say, "And if there are devils on the walls, they may knock us over into the crowd, and then what?" The child was on the verge of panic as it was.

"You can't even see them, how can you fight them?" protested Tsan Nu.

"Because I am a soldier," replied Mae Shan. "Is there something you can do? Can you open the gate as you did the grating?" The noise buffeted her like a physical force. She imagined red-faced demons from the pantomimes standing on top of the walls laughing and jeering at the terrified crowd.

Tsan Nu was silent for a moment. "It's bound in cold iron. I can't break that." Mae Shan's heart sank. "But I can break the beam holding it shut."

"What do you need?"

"Something to write on. Something hard that can break."

Mae Shan looked around helplessly for a moment. Then, she looked to the red tiles on the gatehouse roof. "Trainee Kyun, bring me a roof tile. Immediately."

"But what do I write with?" demanded Tsan Nu as Kyun saluted. "I don't have any ink."

Mae Shan suppressed the urge to shout at the child. She cast her mind about. Then she cried. "Chen, we need ash and embers. Quick!"

To their credit, the trainees moved with speed and without question. Kyun ran to the guardhouse and used the hooked blade of his pole arm to loosen three tiles. From the corners and edges of the battlement, Chen scooped up handfuls of gritty ashes along with flakes and splinters of charred wood. Mae Shan unslung one of the precious water skins and dampened the little pile, mixing the crude, lumpy ink with her hands.

Tsan Nu saw the idea and picked up a splinter. As soon as Kyun returned with the tiles, she thrust the splinter into the black puddle. But something made her look up, and whatever she saw sent a shudder through her.

"You promise you won't let them hurt me?" she asked in a small voice.

In answer, Mae Shan straightened up and pulled her spear from her bundle and held it over her head in a gesture she knew the boys would recognize. "Trainee Kyun, Trainee Chen, form up!"

The boys dropped their bundles, grabbed their long-pole weapons, and pulled themselves to attention behind Tsan Nu.

Mae Shan stood before them all. "Raise hands!" she cried, lifting her free hand up to the height of her shoulders.

These were the exercises every soldier was taught, meditations of motion that held the basic movements of weaponry and hand fighting.

These were the same moves Mae Shan had used to keep herself awake through the long night. With all she had seen and all Tsan Nu said, she was ready to believe the much told tale, that this dance was handed down from the gods themselves so the first emperor could teach the great heroes and they could drive the forty thousand companies of devils back from Hung-Tse and make it into the Sacred Empire. Surely it would hold off a few dozen demons from a tiny girl trying to save what was left of the city.

If nothing else, it would keep them all from being paralyzed by their fear.

Mae Shan moved slowly, breathing, relaxing her muscles, letting soul and spirit flow, concentrating on the precision of each movement, raising the spear, sweep, stab, step to the side, kick, kick again, pivot, stab, step back, circle the spear, switch hands, sweep back, stab again. Concentrate. Don't speed up. Breathe evenly down to the belly. Step, step, stab, sweep aside, pivot, kick, stab again, turn . . .

She caught sight of Tsan Nu, staring openmouthed past her.

"You're not doing magic," she said. "But they're scared. They're jumping up and down and yelling at each other."

Concentrate, concentrate, Mae Shan schooled herself. Turn again, sweep out, raise the spear, stab left, stab right, kick . . .

Whatever was happening in that invisible world, Tsan Nu seemed to gain confidence. She dampened her splinter and began drawing faint grey markings on the glazed tile that Mae Shan could only hope were enough for her art.

Don't think of that. Concentrate. Step back. Breathe.

Tsan Nu began to sing. Her voice was high and clear, a young girl's confident soprano, calling out the spell language of those with the spirit gifts.

Concentrate.

Mae Shan focused on her movements, on the rhythm of her breathing, on the sweep of her spear, its position, that it was level and straight at the correct height for each move. From the corner of her eye, she saw Chen and Kyun fall into closer time with her. Somehow, Tsan Nu's singing made the shrieks of the crowd easier to dismiss, as if the girl were pushing the world back with her clear voice.

A fresh wind brushed ash into Mae Shan's eyes. She blinked hard, but did not allow herself to pause. She stepped forward and slammed down the butt of her spear, as if at a fallen enemy, then swung the spear high and pivoted on one heel to stab behind her, pivoted again, sweeping out above her head.

In front of her, the ashes were dancing.

It was a silhouette of some strange creature, all smeared in ash. It had five horns and huge, clawed hands. Through the hollows where its eyes should have been, she could see the crowd battering hopelessly at the gate, as if the ashy shadow contained them all and laughed at what it saw.

Mae Shan's movement faltered. The ash demon's mouth gaped wider and it danced closer, hopping and spinning madly from one foot to another, in what Mae Shan realized was a parody of her own movements. Oddly, she did not find it in her to be afraid, only affronted at this thing's rudeness.

"Lieutenant . . ." said Kyun, his voice shaking.

"Concentrate!" cried Mae Shan, trying to keep her hands from tightening on her spear. "Keep moving!"

To her relief, Tsan Nu's song did not falter. The ashen demon twirled and swung its arms out, and Mae Shan drew herself back up to attention, and began the sequence once more.

The ash demon's mouth stretched out in fury, and the wind rose again. A cluster of embers blew up from nowhere and brushed Mae Shan's arms. Pain sparkled across her skin. She did not pause. She did not look. The ash demon danced before her in silent rage, but it did not press past her to where Tsan Nu knelt, singing her spell and capturing that song in the words she painted with the char of ruined homes.

Sweat poured down Mae Shan's face, and her sleepless night weighed on her like iron chains. She saw the mob through the swaying, spinning form of the demon before her, heard their screams, heard Chen's and Kyun's breathing grow ragged, even as she heard Tsan Nu's song grow hoarse with effort. They would not last much longer, and what then?

The demon leapt closer, as if sensing the doubt creeping into her thoughts. Keeping just beyond the sweep of Mae Shan's spear, it drew its sword, miming her parry for parry. She could see the blade's keen edge outlined in grey ash and for a moment her breath faltered. The demon threw its head back, its mouth gaping in triumph.

At that same moment, Tsan Nu staggered to her feet, grasping the tile to her chest as if it weighed four hundred pounds. She stumbled to the edge of the wall, raised the tile over her head, and hurled it down.

The ash demon dove after the tile, but it was too late. The red clay hit the stones and burst into a thousand pieces. At that exact moment, the Left Gate swung open and the mob, roaring its relief as it had a moment ago roared its frustration, poured through, spreading out like a flood of water, heading for the hills or the river, wherever they thought they could go for safety.

In front of Mae Shan's eyes, the ash demon scattered on the hot winds. She lowered her spear and wiped the sweat from her face. Tsan Nu stood before the battlements swaying on her feet. Mae Shan reached her just as she began to crumple, catching her thin, limp body and laying her down gently on the stones. She bent her ear to the child's chest and heard her heart beat fast but steady, and felt the rise and fall of her chest. Tsan Nu was alive, and she would stay that way. She was only exhausted beyond her young endurance.

"Rest then, mistress," said Mae Shan, lifting the girl into her arms. "Chen, Kyun, we must be gone."

The boys gaped at her, and she could see that for once they were coming to understand what it truly meant to be a soldier and to serve until you had nothing left to give. *Their parents should be proud,* thought Mae Shan, for they both picked up their burdens and marched after her as she led them down to join the crowd and flee the city without once looking back.

Chapter Ten

Sakra stood outside the door of Ananda's study, trying to rid himself of the childish wish to be elsewhere.

The golden-haired page girl reappeared. "You may enter," she said carefully, as if she were new to her post and still needed to make extra sure she spoke her piece correctly.

Sakra gave the girl a smile he hoped was reassuring as he passed her. How old was she? Nine perhaps? The age of Bridget's daughter.

In the study, Ananda sat at her new-made writing desk, placing the cap on a crystal inkwell. Light streamed in through the tall windows in the solarium that had over the past three months been converted to a study for her private use. The bright sun had topped the walls and the beams slanted through the tiny diamond panes, throwing warmth, gold bars, and tiny rainbows across the floor lined with rushes and the carefully dried petals of last year's roses, raising up a faint, fresh perfume that spoke of the coming of summer.

On the other side of the room, her secretary, Mathura, worked steadily and quietly at his own copying. For the empress there was a great deal to be done. The long, slow dark season of contemplation, reading, and thoughtful conversation began to break up like the ice, opening clear, crooked paths that would turn into wide canals, and the torrent of the Isavaltan summer would soon flow free.

He had lived in the north for six years, but this still felt strange for Sakra. In Hastinapura where the clime ranged from warm to torrid, life proceeded at a steady pace. The only pause came with the first and second rains, and those lasted a total of two months. Snow and cold came only in the high mountains on the border of Hung-Tse. Elsewhere, planting, growing, reaping, and travel, these things were continuous and there was no need to hurry them.

But here, there were but a few short months before the cold came back, and the *rasputitsa* was the time when the whole world began to tense itself for the rush of warmth, green beauty, and dry roads that came with the spring.

For all administrators, it was a time to write letters, to examine old accounts and note down plans for putting into play all the ideas that came in winter's night. For Ananda, it was also the time to write to her parents in Hastinapura and give them all the news, and ask for all the news of family and the Pearl Throne. The ships would be leaving even sooner than the overland messengers. There was no ambassador from Hastinapura in Vysthavos. Medeoan had sent the last one back in disgrace, declaring him a thief and a womanizer, and there had been no chance for a new ambassador to arrive before the harbors froze. So there was only Ananda to tell her father, and the court of the Pearl Throne what had happened here, how Mikkel had come to the throne, and how all was now well.

Or would have been well. Sakra's jaw tightened.

"Imperial Majesty," Sakra said, dropping automatically into the language of their old home as he gave the salute of trust. She touched the back of his head, signaling that she accepted the fealty of his gesture and he could stand straight again. They had only resumed formalities since Mikkel had ascended the throne, and Sakra had been able to return openly to Vyshtavos. Ananda said she missed the casualness their clandestine meetings had enforced, but Sakra insisted. She was empress now, and they would celebrate that truth with all the honor it merited.

Sakra straightened. He hoped she didn't see how tired he was. His skin felt as if it had stretched itself tight across his bones. After Bridget had found her way to sleep, he had done nothing but walk the corridors, trying to understand what he felt, trying to decide for the first time since he was a boy what he wanted.

"Marutha, I require privacy," said Ananda. Marutha had apparently anticipated this, for his ink was capped and he laid a protective sheet of linen over his completed, dried correspondence. He reverenced, and took himself from the room.

"What's wrong, Sakra?" asked Ananda as soon as the door closed. She waved him to a chair. Of course she had seen it. They knew each other well. She looked weary herself, and he wondered what was the matter. He should not be here like this. She did not need any more troubles.

I have looked after this girl, this woman, all of her life. Can she ever truly be less than the thing uppermost in my mind?

"I am only tired, Majesty," he said.

"And you have something difficult to say," prompted Ananda. "What news do you bring me, Sakra?"

He knew her small, slightly apprehensive smile better than any other expression. His parents' faces and the sights of his old home had long since settled into the deeper recesses of memory, but Ananda was ever before him, as it should be.

Yet, all of a sudden he couldn't look at her. He turned his face to the window. Below them spread Vyshtavos's garden, the black and grey trees shedding their winter coverings of snow, and waiting for spring to bring their green robes. The imperial canal was a straight black line between banks patched brown and white like the coat of a mongrel dog.

In his mind's eye, he saw how Bridget looked the night before when she had fallen asleep. Her face had softened, and he saw how she might look in times to come, when the years of loneliness and struggle were put behind her, when she had a life with friends who esteemed her. When she had love.

He remembered how he had been struck when he first saw her. Even when he thought she was Ananda's enemy and therefore his, he found her magnificent. Not just for her beauty, although she was beautiful, nor for her power, which was blinding, but for the sheer strength of self and spirit in her. She would never bow, never bend, but meet her fate proudly.

Even if it broke her. Sakra hung his head. Even if he broke her.

How would it feel to meet Bridget's child? To see her as a mother? How would it be to live beside her, to care for another child as he had cared for Ananda? Could he? Would duty permit?

Did duty allow him room in his heart for anything but duty itself?

I hate this place, he thought suddenly, vehemently toward the thawing garden. *I hate this barbarian wilderness where its people dance through the chaos and don't even realize there is a better way. It gets into the blood and the brain, and makes a new wilderness within. It is this place that has done this to me. I should not be thinking these things. I should not be feeling so for this woman. I am bound to Ananda, and that is my life until hers is over and I am freed, if I am freed, for there will be children and they too will need me.*

Mother Chitrani help me, for I also do not want this wilderness to forsake me.

Without turning around, Sakra told Ananda of his conversation with Bridget the previous night, and of his conversation with Mistress Urshila earlier that morning. He heard no movement from Ananda. She sat still, drinking in his words, most likely trying to understand what in them was so important that he could not even look at her as he spoke. A child, a child thought dead and now alive. Ananda hoped for a child of her own soon. Sakra knew he would never have any. It was one of the prices of being a sorcerer. One, it seemed, of many, many prices.

"Thank you for coming to me with this," said Ananda, her voice tense and breathy beneath the formality of the statement. "I'll now be ready when Bridget comes."

Sakra turned toward her again. "What will you say?" He felt as brittle as glass, and feared for a moment her answer might break him in two.

She looked at him with startled eyes. *Surely you know what I must say?* her expression told him before she could speak. "That such a quest must wait until we know whether we have anything to fear from the Firebird."

Sakra was silent. She was so different from the girl he had shepherded to this wilderness. He wondered if Ananda herself even knew all the changes that had taken root within her. She was a diplomat and negotiator. She could give an order as frostily as any Isavaltan lady and command obedience as readily as her mother the First of All Queens did. She could see what was best for the realm she now ruled, and do what she had to, whether she wanted to or not.

"You do not believe she will take such news well," said Ananda with exaggerated mildness.

He knew the remark was intended to raise the smile. He could not oblige.

"What's the matter, Sakra?" asked Ananda.

What is the matter? Sakra's arms tightened until the individual fibers spasmed beneath the skin. "I am betraying her," he whispered, for there was no shout loud enough to release the anguish in him.

Ananda simply frowned. "How is this betrayal?"

For a moment Sakra was stunned. How could Ananda not understand at once? Surely it was obvious. "She does not know I am speaking with you, and she does not know I have spoken with Mistress Urshila. She does not want others making what she believes is a deeply personal decision."

"But you know it is not," Ananda pointed out. "Nothing that concerns the well-being of Isavalta can be."

The room suddenly seemed too empty. There was too much room. There was nothing to hold the emotion in, no propriety, no witness to help keep feeling contained. For a moment Sakra thought he would overflow with what he was feeling, and he wondered what Ananda would do if he did. It would be as if the birds flew north for winter. He cared for her, he soothed her feelings and solved her problems, saved her life. He served her. She did not serve him.

In the end he could only find words for part of the truth. "I do not want Bridget hurt."

Ananda was trying to understand, he could tell that much from her eyes. She was trying hard to fathom all that he had not said. She did understand he was distressed. "What would you have me do?"

Release me from my bond. Leave me free to be with Bridget. Do not need me anymore. "If you could, Majesty, I would have you take her story at its face when she comes, and let us go."

"Why, Sakra?" she said, but in his mind, he heard her answer the words he had not spoken. *How could you ask such a thing, even in your heart?*

"Because Mistress Urshila is right, and so is Bridget. We must not forget that the Vixen is involved in this, and thwarting her can only make what will be bad worse." *Because I am infected by Isavalta's wilderness. Because I am in love.*

"You believe the Vixen is using Bridget?" *Then you are as false as the* lokai's *queen.*

"I do." *No, Ananda. I swear. I did not look for this. I never wished for release from my bond.*

"Does she realize this?" *Can you even know what such love is? How can you be certain these feelings are true?*

"She does not wish to." *I can't. I can only know they burn as if they were true.*

"And you will let it happen?" *So you would have your oaths broken and abandon me for what might be nothing more than lust after a woman's body and power?*

No. It was not that. He loved Bridget. He loved her smile and the light in her eyes. He loved her wit and her bravery. He loved the way he felt beside her, talking with her, sharing a joke or a fleeting touch. These things were real.

"She is in danger. She denies it. She sees only her child, and that is the Vixen's intent, and for the sake of duty and empire, and . . ." *Heart.* He could not speak the word. Not to Ananda. Not yet. He could barely speak it to himself. "I can only walk beside her into danger."

Walk beside her, to her other world, into the Vixen's trap, because he could not abandon Bridget any more than he could abandon Ananda.

"I will need you here, whatever comes." That was nothing less than the truth too. Lord Daren, the other court sorcerers, they still saw Ananda as a "southerner," as duplicitous as they feared all such were. It was out in the open now, how she had successfully pretended to possess the invisible gifts for the years of Mikkel's enchantment. They looked at such a successful liar and their minds, honed by years of plotting in the court and out of it, walked the paths of suspicion. She needed someone she could trust who understood the world of magics. She needed the one who had been beside her in all other troubles. She would not be safe, or sure, if the Vixen took Sakra away.

Or if Bridget took Sakra away.

He couldn't breathe. His lungs seemed to have shrunken, leaving no breath for speech. "I wish to be here," he managed to whisper. *That is true, that is true, I swear it is.* "But I am afraid for what will happen if I do not walk with Bridget."

"What will happen if you do?"

Sakra shook his head, his gaze wandering back to the window and the melting gardens. "I don't know."

"You are not afraid of what will happen when you are gone?" Ananda tried to speak in a light tone, a gentle tease, but the attempt fell flat and her voice only sounded tremulous.

"You mistake me, Majesty, I am terrified of what will happen."

Ananda was twisting her hands together in her lap. She pulled them apart ruthlessly, laying them on the chair arms. A thousand images ran through Sakra's mind. Ananda looking up from a book in the queen's library and grinning at Sakra, because she'd just read her first sentence. The thin, sprightly girl pouring her heart out to Sakra because she was twelve and getting love letters from someone who would not even sign his name, and she was sure she loved this anonymous someone more than anyone in the world. The touch of Ananda's hand, right before she had to walk down the gangplank and set foot on Isavalta's soil for the first time. All the hurried meetings, the desperate consultations, the hundred deceptions that her life in Isavalta became, and all the time spent, a whole life spent, if not beside her, out there, working for her, protecting her.

"You love her," Ananda said.

"Yes."

Sakra met Ananda's eyes, and saw the deep distress there. For one wild moment he wondered if she was jealous. Had she ever looked on Sakra with that kind of love? No. He was her older brother, her guard and guide. Mikkel was her lover, and Sakra had moved Heaven and Earth to bring Mikkel back to her, and they had both believed her gratitude to be boundless and the need for deceptions over.

But here they were again, in a secret conference, voices hushed, heads bowed, afraid someone might hear what was said between them.

It was her turn to look away. She looked at the letter she had been just beginning. She had written *To My Beloved Father.*

What would come next?

He thought Ananda was probably wondering the same thing. "I never thought of you loving anyone but . . . I never thought of it."

"Neither did I." The words were rueful, but he was surprised to find there was wonder underneath them.

"We knew things must change." Platitudes. At such a time they had more between them than platitudes.

"Yes." Sakra touched her hand, and Ananda stared at him, even though it was a gesture he had made a thousand times before. "But we did not know they would be like this."

She needed him. The set of her face, the dimness of her eyes, her whole being told him as much. She had thought once Mikkel was free, the worst would be over. But there had been no time to adjust, no real time to plan. No time to review and rearrange. The court was still largely the place Medeoan had made it, scheming, selfish, and petty. The lords master all gave their oaths eagerly, but did they all mean to keep them diligently? There was no way to tell, and so few that she could trust.

And Mikkel still shuddered in his nightmares, still struggled with his duties. He needed her and she needed Sakra.

"You've told me the Vixen plays long and complex games," said Ananda, grasping at faint hopes. "Can we wait to make this move?"

"I don't believe we can." He made a decision. If he framed his words carefully, perhaps he could spare them both some pain. "I will be no more than a day or two, depending on how fast we can make the crossing. I don't believe the child can truly be alive. We will go swiftly and come back, and then you will have both Bridget and I to aid in whatever may come."

Outrage burned in Ananda's eyes and Sakra knew he had made a disastrous mistake.

"You don't believe that," she said. "You don't."

Sakra closed his eyes, pained. He lied to her. He had tried to *lie* to her.

"I hope," he said, trying to undo what had just happened. "I hope only. I believe . . ."

Grieved and furious, Ananda blurted out, "Must I order you to stay?"

"You may order me to stay." There was nothing but resignation in the words. He knew what he had done, and he accepted the consequences. "I am your servant."

The last word stung. They had never used that word between them. But then, they had never lied to each other either.

Ananda stood. She turned away and faced her writing desk. She stared down at the creamy paper and the drying ink.

" 'To My Beloved Father,' " she read. "I've been trying to decide what to write next. Perhaps 'To My Beloved Father, the son of Samudra, who came to glory wresting the last of our lands from the *Huni,* whose brother let the sorcerer Yamuna talk him into trying to steal the empire of Isavalta and so condemned me to life as a peace offering.' "

Sakra had stood beside her as her father had spoken to her on the deck of the ship sailing for Isavalta. *Remember, Daughter,* he'd said, *when you are empress, in the end it is the realm in your care that matters. All other considerations must be set aside.* All *other considerations.*

All other considerations. Bridget, forlorn, might become a danger. The Vixen might be playing a game. The Firebird might be coming to burn the world down. Sakra might leave her forever. Which was worst?

"Or perhaps, 'To My Beloved Father, today I sealed the fate of Isavalta.'" She crumpled the paper up fiercely.

"I cannot let you go, Sakra," she said without looking up. "Not yet. We are both thinking of my father's words, I know we are. I must be empress. You know this. I must look to Isavalta first and Isavalta needs you and Bridget." A spark of hope shimmered inside her, enabling her to turn. "Perhaps this day will bring other answers."

Sakra gave her the salute of trust, and kept his silence. She touched his head, as mistress to servant, giving him leave to stand, and to depart.

Once in the corridor, Sakra got himself as quickly out of sight of the pages and guards as he could. He hid himself in a small coffee room that was empty of any other people. He could not let anyone see him bow his head into his hand. He could not let anyone see him clench his fist as he tried to bring himself back under control. He could not let any see the single tear of sorrow and anger trickle from the corner of his eye.

Ananda must be empress, and I must serve. Oh, Mothers All, Bridget, I'm sorry.

It was dark when the Firebird returned to Isavalta.

It shot overhead, faint and silent, little more than a piece of stardust in the spring night. In its wake, all other lights flickered, and died, their fuel going so instantly cold that not even the smoke remained.

In the palace of Vyshtavos, the coals in the great ovens immediately fell dark, the coals under their nightly blankets of ash in the hearths and firepits became silent and still. The bed warmers, the braziers, the lamps burning late and early in the apartments of the sorcerers and scholars, all winked out. The candles and braziers tended all night by a special pair of footmen in the imperial apartments were snuffed out as quickly as if they had been doused in water.

Mikkel Medeoanasyn Edemskoivin, the emperor of Isavalta, started awake with a wordless shout. Over the thunder of his heartbeat, he heard the sound of the servants scrambling, but the room remained dark. The mattress and blankets shifted. Hands touched him, and for a moment he stiffened, until he recognized the hand as Ananda's.

"What's happened?" he whispered before he remembered who and where he was. "What's happened!" he shouted so the servants could hear.

"Forgiveness, Majesty," called Barta, Mikkel's chief waiting gentleman. "There will be light in a moment."

Out of the dark came shuffling, mumbles, clanks, and the crack of some heavy thing against the stone floor, but the promised light did not come. There only came more noises of men moving back and forth, blind and trying not to stumble.

Ananda's fine hand slipped under his and Mikkel closed his fingers around hers gratefully. What was kept a secret in this chamber was that the emperor of Isavalta, Vyshko's heir, was afraid of the dark.

The binding his mother had laid on his mind had dimmed his sight. For a time he could not then measure, but now knew was three solid years, he had wandered in a world that faded from twilight to darkness, his mind thick and murky. There was no time, no light, no joy, only an endless dreariness, a haunting need that he could no longer understand, and a name. Ananda. His wife who shivered beside him now.

Rallying himself, Mikkel groped for the edge of the coverlet with his free hand and pulled it up around their shoulders. The clamor of the servants failed to fill up the silence and Mikkel's ears began to ring.

Did Ananda feel his skin begin to prickle?

"What can be taking so long?" she muttered with simple, everyday annoyance. Nothing portentous, nothing special. An unremarkable grumble. He wished he could see her. Her scent was sharp, her touch warm, familiar, and welcome, but the darkness was thick, and he imagined he felt it trying to seep into his skin like water and reach through to his soul.

He shivered and tried to slow his breathing.

Ananda urged him to be patient with himself. Bound for three years as he was, it was not something he could shake off in a matter of days. Sometimes, though, he thought he saw disappointment in her eyes as she said it. There was no time for such patience. He was emperor now. His mother was dead a world away and there was no one but him to take the praise or the blame for what happened to the realm of Vyshko and Vyshemir.

"Open a window," Barta ordered.

"What?" Unable to sit still any longer, Mikkel scrambled from the bed, pushing his way through unseen velvet curtains that fell heavy and smooth past his shoulders. The sound of Ananda followed behind him.

He moved as quickly as he dared in order to remind himself that he *could* move quickly, that this darkness was an external thing. His out-stretched hands found the edge of the carved bed screens and he was able to pass them without knocking them over. Beyond the screens, Huras had drawn back the tapestry curtains on the two arched windows that overlooked the courtyard. The faint silver light of the quarter moon pro-vided just enough illumination for Mikkel to see the shapes of his serv-ing men. One crouched beside the firepit with a long poker, stirring frantically at the ashes and coughing as they swirled up around him. An-other bent over a table, struggling with a tinderbox. The tiny "ching-ching" of flint and steel sounded between his breathy curses. Another stood before the window, fingering a candle's wick, trying to tell if it was long enough, or if it had drowned in its wax.

"What is the matter here?" he demanded, and all the men froze in place, comic in their odd poses. "Why is there no light?"

Mikkel had to squint to see that it was Barta who pulled himself up-right from his work with the tinderbox and reverenced. "I regret . . . I do not know, Majesty. We are trying, but the tinder will not catch."

Ananda was behind him. "Fetch a light from the kitchen fires," she said. "I'll wake my ladies." She picked her way to the connecting door that led to her private apartments.

Huras reverenced to the empress's retreating back and put action to orders. Mikkel heard the rumble of his voice as he reported to the guards on duty outside. What was he saying to them? What was going on?

Standing there without any fire and without a proper robe he felt the cold begin to rest heavily against his skin. He rubbed his arms, staring hard around himself, as if trying to let as much light into his eyes as pos-sible. It was only cold. It was only the darkness of a night during the *rasputitsa*. Barta saw him rubbing his arms and abandoned the seemingly futile work with the tinderbox to catch up a night robe from its stand and hold it up for Mikkel who gratefully allowed himself to be wrapped in its fur-lined warmth.

His eyes had begun to adjust to the darkness, but even so he would have had no trouble picking out Ananda's silhouette among the men as she came hurrying back. "The fire has died in my rooms as well, and nothing can be made to kindle."

Magic. This was magic. Mikkel knew the touch of it better than any. But what was being done and how? And who was it meant for?

Is Mother not done with me yet? The thought rooted him to the ground with fear. It was too dark and too cold to think safely of Mother. It was too hard to remember that day must come soon, with sunlight and warmth, and that what he felt was only the curl of a draft around his neck, not a thread of magic reaching out to capture his mind and drag it forever into the darkness.

Ananda gripped his arm, breaking Mikkel out of his blackening spiral of thought. Did she see his paralysis despite the dark, or did she just know? "Someone send for the lord sorcerer," she snapped in a peremptory tone that was unusual for her.

The words had barely been spoken when a knock sounded on the door. Mikkel shook himself and covered Ananda's hand, trying to let her know by touch he would be all right.

"Come," he croaked.

The door opened and two men, little more than blurs of motion in the darkness, entered. The moon was sinking toward the rooftop and what little light it provided would soon be gone.

"Imperial Majesties," said the straighter of the pair. It was not the lord sorcerer. It was Master Sidor, the first of the sorcerers to return at his command, the first to take the loyal oath. "I am sorry we were not here before, but there is no light in the halls . . ."

Of course, the interior of the palace would be pitch-black. No wonder Huras had not yet returned. "Is there any light left in the palace?"

The second man, whose crooked shape and reedy voice identified him as Master Luden, said, "Nothing will light. None of the candles, the fires in the hearths. The flint and steel will not even strike a spark." He nodded toward the table where Barta had been trying so unsuccessfully to light the lamp. "As your men have discovered."

Darkness everywhere, no way to see out of it, no end. No. "Where is the lord sorcerer?"

The man's breath wheezed in and out several times before he was able to answer. "He is ill, sir, from his efforts in trying to find the Fire-bird. Sir, he thinks it is come."

"What?" Ananda spoke the question before Mikkel could.

It was Luden who answered. Was he leaning on Sidor's arm, or was it the other way around? The moonlight was fading, and it was too hard to see. "The Firebird is flame incarnate. It can spread fire, or it can . . . remove it."

No fire? It was as if the man had said there could be no air. Fire was warmth, light, and food. It was the forge, the crucible, the cauldron. In winter it was life itself.

"How far will it have gone?" From the sound of Ananda's voice, Mikkel knew she had gone pale. It was dark enough now that even she was only a shadow among the shadows.

Cloth rustled. Luden made an attempt to straighten himself up. "It could cross the empire in a night."

No fire, anywhere in the empire. Spring had barely begun in the far north. They could still freeze to death. Which would be faster than star-vation, which would also come into their homes or on the road as they fled . . . and where would they go? To Vyshtavos. To their emperor. They would come to him to beg for deliverance from this magic that af-flicted them.

An image rose suddenly in front of him, of his mother's false smile as she held up the silver girdle saying it would help him please his new bride . . .

Then blindness. Blindness of the eyes and blindness of the mind. Cold, like this, settling ever deeper, and not enough thought left to com-prehend what was wrong.

A pain ran up his arm, clearing the memories from his mind. Aware of himself again, Mikkel uncurled the fist that he had smashed against a tabletop. Ananda, startled, had let go of him. He stretched out his hand to her again, or rather where he thought she was. The moonlight was down to a single silver shaft lighting up nothing but a strip of stone floor and the dead ashes of the firepit. His fingers did not find her and he could not bring himself to wave his hand about like a blind man looking for his stick.

"Why are we afflicted with this curse of magic?" he said, rubbing his forehead with the hand that had sought Ananda. "Why did Vyshko and Vyshemir decide of all things this would remain with us?"

But Ananda only shook her head. "I don't know, my husband."

"Perhaps the lord sorcerer could find the answer in the Red Library." He glanced toward the men who had come because the first among them had been struck down so hard he could not come to his emperor. All others would come here, and they would need to be properly met. There was no one else to do this thing. The thought was a lonely one, but at the same time, Mikkel found to his surprise there was a stark comfort in it. This responsibility was his, and no one could, or would, take it from him.

Mikkel dragged his wits together. "I'm sorry, Master Luden, Master Sidor. You and the others must find an answer. You must defeat this thing or destroy it, somehow."

"Yes, Imperial Majesty," said Sidor with proper feeling, although Mikkel had surely not said anything the sorcerer didn't know. "We will begin searching as soon as it is light."

"We must get ready as soon as it's light as well," Mikkel went on, speaking mostly to Ananda now. *For it will be light. It will be.* "People will be coming here. We'll need . . ." *Vyshko's pike, need what?* "Shelter, blankets, bread."

"Yes," agreed Ananda. Her voice was close. He reached out. This time his hand found hers and their fingers locked together. "We need to know how far it's gone," she was saying. "Send out some of the house guard to try to get ahead of it. If there are fugitives, they can be set on the road to where the Firebird hasn't reached yet."

She would think of that. She'd told him of the floods in her country, of the plagues and droughts that sometimes came when the rains did not, and of how the great masses of people would take to the roads.

When the rains did not come, when the gods failed and the sorcerers failed and they were all that was left.

"If a limit to this . . . loss of fire is found, Your Majesties may wish to consider moving the household . . ." began Luden.

"No," snapped Mikkel. He would not flee. Whatever came, he would face it here, even if no one else did. "I will not go nor will any in this household."

He would never be consigned to the shadows again. No one else would be permitted to flee in a crisis. Especially not the sorcerers. It was good to bring them back, to show how he meant to undo all of his mother's madness, but this time they would not be permitted to leave without a backward glance, without a thought.

Mikkel swallowed. He must curb this anger. It blackened his mind as even his mother's spells had failed to do.

"Go, Luden, Sidor," he said, his voice hoarse from his effort to control it. "Find an answer and quickly."

"Yes, Imperial Majesty." Sidor reverenced, but Luden held his ground.

"There is one other point, Majesties." Luden's voice was thin, but strong.

"Yes?" The moonlight must have shown Ananda how Mikkel's jaw shook, so she quickly answered for him.

"Bridget Lederle has requested permission to seek her daughter beyond the boundaries of the world."

The auburn-haired woman had come to stand before them that morning with Sakra at her side, telling a portion of her encounter with the Vixen she had held back. She had apologized for it. She said she had not understood, at least not fully, what it meant. She asked to be allowed to return to the home of her birth, to find out by magic or any other means at her disposal whether her child might still be alive.

She had spoken calmly, almost as if she had rehearsed the words, but Mikkel had seen the sheen of desperation in her eyes. This was a mother who loved her child. This was a mother who would sacrifice for that child, not use it to further her own ends.

He had meant to make closer inquiry into the matter, what would she need for her travels, how long might she be gone when every hand might be needed to help Isavalta, but to his surprise, Ananda had interrupted.

"The ambassador from Hung-Tse waits on you, Husband Imperial," she said. "Shall I tell him to continue to wait, or may we pray Mistress Bridget have patience and we will let her know our mind as soon as may be?"

He had understood the look in her eyes. She also wanted to make an additional inquiry, but out of Bridget's range of hearing. The woman was, after all, a sorcerer and with magic came . . . he did not want to think duplicity. Not all sorcerers were as his mother was. Surely not. This Bridget Lederle had saved his life. Surely she was a different type of sorcerer, and parent.

But he had nodded, and let Ananda make their excuses to Bridget who had gone away dissatisfied, but she had gone. Ananda had not spoken of her again during the whole long day that primarily involved careful dancing with Hung-Tse's ambassador to determine what, if anything, he had heard from the Heart of the World of late regarding their emperor's plans for future relations with Vysthavos and Isavalta. There had been no answers there either.

Did this remark of Luden's bear any relation as to why Ananda had wanted to delay giving Bridget Lederle permission for her quest?

Given what they had just been told, it was fortunate she had orchestrated that delay.

"Surely her eyes are needed here," said Mikkel, aware of the irony of speaking of sight in the deepening darkness. "She will understand she must have a safe home to bring the child to, should it still be living."

Luden's shadow dipped. A reverence? It was impossible to tell. Mikkel fought down the fear that thickened with his blindness.

"It is our belief she should be permitted to go at once," said Luden. The darkness seemed to make his voice higher and more querulous.

Ananda moved a little closer to Mikkel. Her hand brushed his, and it was cold. She also feared this darkness, this air that smelled of lingering winter, and lacked the ever-present scents of charcoal, smoke, and wood. "Why?" she asked.

"The child may be . . . useful in this time of danger," said Sidor, his voice rougher than it should have been. "Her parentage would make her a source of great power."

Mikkel's frown pulled his mouth and brow tight, although by now not even Ananda would have been able to see the expression. "You think the child may be of use?" he asked, and he heard the danger underneath the words.

There was a pause that might have been for Luden to nod, or just to collect his breath for more speech. "Even more so than the mother, if the worst happens and our efforts prove futile." The words were dry. He might have been speaking of the prospects for rain in the coming spring.

Discussing making use of a child. For without that child everyone might die, the empire might collapse.

Had such thoughts gone through his mother's head when she decided to make use of him?

Ananda moved closer, her warmth touching his skin. "The child is a sorcerer," she murmured, her voice heavy with resignation. "The gods gave us them for our use, our protection, and our blessing. It is their duty to serve."

For a moment, Mikkel could not believe what he was hearing. He looked toward her automatically, and saw only shadow. "That is different." He strove to keep his voice low, so the sorcerers would not hear them in disagreement, or at least not hear the nature of the disagreement. "This child is not bound to us."

"Her mother has taken the loyalty oath, has she not?" There was something hard under Ananda's words, as if she were forcing them out. *Ananda?* he wanted to say. *Is this truly you speaking to me?* "That makes the child subject to us."

"But still a child."

"Yes, and I am sorry it is so."

Mikkel swallowed. What to do? What must he do? It might not come to the worst. The child might not have to be . . . used, whatever the sorcerers meant by that. Power could be transferred between them, he knew. Was that what they meant to do? And if he was truly emperor, could he ignore a resource or an action that might save his empire?

We could die if the fires are not rekindled. I don't care for me, I walked around dead for so many years, I'll probably feel at home when the Grandfather comes for me, but Isavalta could die from this. This place she did not trust to my hands. This empire she was determined to take to the grave with her. All these people who were waiting for me to wake up, who must wonder now couldn't he have fought harder? Couldn't he have tried? It's my duty to use whatever means I must to save them.

"Yes," he said, and the word dropped from his lips like a stone. "If the child lives, let its mother find it and bring it here."

"Yes, Imperial Majesty," said Luden.

"Yes, Imperial Majesty," said Sidor.

The darkness was complete now. There was only the sound of old men's footsteps shuffling, trying not to stumble, of cloth dragging slowly on stone, of fingertips brushing this surface and that until the faint creak of metal, wood scraping stone and a wafting of cold, wood-scented air that told that the door had been found, and opened, and closed again.

Silence in the darkness, except for the breathing of a few frightened souls.

"Husband Imperial," said Ananda, mindful of the servants out there in the blackness that was his private room. "There is nothing that can be done until the light returns. It is useless us standing here until night's cold settles into our blood. If it is your wish, let us return to bed to wait for dawn, for I doubt sleep will come again to any of us."

"Yes," said Mikkel, although he was not sure which statement exactly he was agreeing to. "Take to bed, all of you, until the light comes. We must all be ready to work, and work quickly."

For it will return. I waited in darkness for three years, I can wait a few hours longer. This is different. This time I am not trapped. This time I can make myself heard, and I will.

Chapter Eleven

Bridget was in the Red Library when the light flickered and went out.

The day itself had been spent trying to get answers and audiences. Not a single court sorcerer had found a moment to spare for her. All of them were engaged in the hunt for the Firebird. She had spent some time in her rooms attempting to apply the arts Mistress Urshila had tried to teach her to induce a vision to come, but all she had induced was a headache. Sakra said even he had not been able to get in to see the empress, who had been closeted with the emperor and the ambassador from Hung-Tse. Mistress Urshila had sequestered herself with the other court sorcerers, none of whom would give Bridget any kind of straight answer when she asked them what was happening. Where Sakra was now, she didn't know, and although it felt cowardly, she did not seek him out. As much as she wanted answers, she wanted to be alone to think and to plan her course of action.

She wanted to leave, now, this second. She wanted to pack a bundle and walk away, the way she had walked here. Surely, Mistress Urshila exaggerated the dangers. What importance was Bridget to anyone? Today had shown that not even this one grand household held her in serious esteem, for all they had spoken so many pretty words to her recently.

She did, however, recognize that to walk away without permission was to burn her bridges behind her. She would not be easily able to come back to Isavalta, and if she did find Anna, then what? She could not go back to Bayfield where she would be penniless and without employment. Here she had a house she could bring Anna to, if it was not quite a home yet. Here, she hoped, was a life she could live openly and without censure.

As the empress evidently had no need of her services, and there was a limit to the amount of pacing she could do without driving herself completely to distraction, Bridget took herself to the Red Library. Named for the red marble pillars that served as its ornamentation, the Red Library was the imperial collection of texts on magic. There had to be something in there on scrying for the living, or the dead. Perhaps she did not have to try to get back to Bayfield at all. Perhaps there was a way to be sure without leaving Isavalta.

So, Bridget hunched over what she thought might be likely tomes and scrolls, painfully spelling out the words one letter at a time, trying to remember the tenses of the various verbs, and wishing to heaven that she had a dictionary. Richikha brought her supper, and later Prathad brought a candle and a brazier.

She had hoped to exhaust herself eventually, but although her eyes burned and her fingers felt as dry as the parchment pages they turned, Bridget felt as awake as ever. Nervous energy drove away all possibility of sleep, even though she noted the moon making its way up the star-filled dome of the sky, and then back down again.

Then the candle went out as suddenly as if an invisible snuffer had been clapped over the flame. In the darkness, Bridget's eyes automatically strained to see, and she saw . . .

A black-haired woman kneeling before an old man, trying in vain to stanch the blood flowing from a wound in his belly.

The Firebird sitting on the crooked branch of a dead tree, with the Vixen crouched down below, just beyond the reach of the trailing flames of its wings.

An ancient man in a cave with walls so slick it appeared as if they were perspiring. He wore nothing but a kilt of hides with the hair still on. He hunched his crooked back over a stone mortar and pestle, grinding down something that steamed in the flickering orange light of his fire.

The old man lifted his head. He looked directly at Bridget, and he grinned.

Bridget started, but the vision did not break. Instead the man beckoned with one hand, pointing at his mortar with one grimy finger.

This should not be happening. The palace is protected from magics. How can this be happening?

Her sight drew closer to the ancient man, whose skin was as slick and shining as the cave walls. Her vision showed her the mortar was filled with dank water, swirling with some dark liquid that might have been ink or might have been blood. At the very bottom, she saw a piece of pale, scraped hide. The vision pulled her in, so it seemed she leaned right over the bowl, seeing the dark swirl in the rippling water and the white hide . . . and words. Words in no language she could read, but that she nonetheless understood.

You will not find your daughter.

Bridget felt her body jerk back, felt her head lift up, but her vision was held fast. She could see nothing but the bowl and its missive.

"Who are you?" she heard herself demand, although she understood no sound could be imparted through such a forced vision as this.

But it seemed she was wrong about that as well, because the ancient man stabbed his finger into the mortar, swirling the water and ink (just ink, though for such magic as this blood was spilled somewhere), and the words changed.

I am a seer, like you.

"What do you know of me?"

The old man's finger stirred the water again. *I know you will not find your daughter. She is not in the compasses of the world where you walk.*

Bridget's throat closed. She ground her teeth together. What did he mean, this . . . seer, whoever and whatever he was? Did he mean Anna was truly dead? That her shade walked the Land of Death and Spirit? Or did he mean she was still in the world of her birth somehow?

"Who *are* you?" she demanded a second time.

The one who can find your daughter. The one who can call her back from where she has gone.

Bridget's fists and eyes squeezed shut. But the words stayed before her mind's eye. "No!" she shouted. "No! I will not hear this!"

The water swirled, the gnarled finger pointed, the words changed. *Your aid is all that is required. You cannot find her alone. I can call her back for you.*

"No!" screamed Bridget at the top of her lungs, and she lurched to her feet, reaching down into the seat of her will. "You will leave me alone!"

Then, there was only darkness and the echo of her own voice ringing in her ears.

"Mistress Bridget?" called a faint voice from off to her right. "Are you all right?"

Bridget's hand flew to her freshly raw throat. What had happened? What had been done to her?

Why was it every stranger, every power seemed to know about Anna? What could Anna possibly matter to anyone but her? She was a babe in arms. She was nothing yet. She was everything.

"Mistress Bridget?"

The anxious voice was coming from outside the door. Her candle and brazier had gone completely dead and there was nothing left but the faintest moonlight to show her the outline of the table and books before her.

"I'm all right!" She called out the lie with as much conviction as she could manage.

All right, except that I am in the dark without means of making a light and I am being bribed with the life of my nine-years-gone daughter by a filthy sorcerer who wants God knows what from me.

What is happening? And what about the other things I saw? The aftermath of attempted murder? The Firebird, and the Vixen. They had the feel of true visions that came of her own second sight.

The Firebird, and the Vixen.

She came to warn us that the Firebird is seeking revenge! she heard her own voice say from memory.

She came to help us all, did she? And just, incidently, to tell you the one piece of news guaranteed to drive you insane?

God Almighty, what if Urshila was right?

Bridget smoothed down the skirts of her robe. Her eyes had adjusted to the darkness and she could see her way to the door. Standing here in the dark would accomplish nothing, and motion would be easier than thought. She reached gingerly for the edge of the brazier, but found it had gone stone cold.

How long did that . . . seer hold me for? Forced visions could bend time. She squinted at the moon, which still showed a full inch of itself above the roofs. She could not have been . . . gone for that long. The brazier should at least have been warm.

Foreboding leapt into the forefront of her mind. Bridget quickly rounded the table and opened the door onto the blackened corridor. To her surprise, voices called out, faint but clear.

"Where is that girl?"

"What's happening? Why can't you make a light?"

"I need a light! A light!"

It's started. Fear sent Bridget's blood surging. *It's come.*

When she had first seen the Firebird in the golden cage woven by the Dowager Medeoan and Bridget's own father, Avanasy, its presence had opened her second sight, and she had seen what it could do. She had seen it burn cities by bringing too much fire, but she had also seen it freeze them, by taking the fire away.

No wonder the brazier was so cold, she thought dazedly as the calls and cries of a small city's worth of people suddenly found themselves lost in their own home.

Then, a steady, martial voice cut across the rising babble. "Their Majesties Imperial bid you keep to your rooms until daylight." It was Commander Chadek, head of the house guard, out in the night although his rank meant he served his turn during the daylight hours.

Oh, yes, it had started, and the panic would only spread from here, despite Chadek's best efforts, and there was reason for panic. Slowly, like water welling up through the loose seam of a boat, what it meant that there was no fire and no means of making one in this great palace began to sink into her. Bridget lived with fire, worked with it. When she was a lighthouse keeper every night she lit the four-wicked lamp in her tower. If the light went out, it could spell doom for an entire ship. She had certainly lived through more than one winter where the lack of a fire could mean far worse than discomfort, and how would any food be cooked?

And now that it has come, who will let you go haring off on your own errands? Bridget stopped in her tracks. No. Her fists curled up. This was not some simple errand. She could not start to think like that. This was life and death, as much as any other disaster.

Life and death of one or two, against that of hundreds, perhaps thousands. Her life until recently had been devoted to the cause of saving other lives. If she left now, she was turning her back on the only meaning all those empty years had.

But those hundreds and thousands have hundreds of others to care for them. Anna has no one but me.

You cannot find her alone. I can call her back for you.

Bridget hardened her mind against the memory of the stranger's words. She swayed on her feet. God Almighty, she was tired. How long until sunrise? How long until she could move again?

"Who's there?" demanded Captain Chadek. His voice was near. She'd been so sunken in her own thoughts, she hadn't even heard the footsteps.

"Bridget Lederle, Commander," she croaked. Her throat had gone dry and her tongue felt swollen in her mouth. "I was in the Red Library."

"Mistress Bridget, all are instructed to return to their rooms."

Bridget's eyes could not stop from straining in the corridor's darkness. There was not even any moonlight from the library windows. She could just make out the commander's straight shadow. "I am embarrassed to admit it, Commander, but I don't think I can find my room from here."

"Then I will escort you. Over-Lieutenant, continue the rounds. Do not lose the under-sergeant." Bridget was sure he had meant that last as a joke, but there was honest worry under the words.

"Sir," said a pair of strange voices. Boots tramped against wood and the breeze of motion passed Bridget by.

"If you will permit me, mistress." The commander's hand found her arm and he took hold of her as if they were a couple courting, steering her down the corridor opposite from the way his men had gone.

His pace was measured, but in the dark it felt fast. Bridget tried not to clamp her hand around his arm and trusted he would not deliberately lead her into any doorways. Her feet moved reluctantly, trying to feel their way, now stumbling over nothing, now hurrying to catch up with Chadek.

"How is it you can find your way so well?" she asked.

"Years of drill, mistress," came the reply. "We are told we must all know Vyshtavos blind. This is our chance to prove it."

"Has anyone said what's happened?"

"Not to me, mistress."

And you would not ask. You know your place, as you know these corridors.

They turned and walked, and turned again. Bridget had walked these halls almost every day since she came, but she still felt completely lost.

"Here, mistress. On the left. Instruct your people that they should remain behind doors with you until daylight."

"Yes, Commander." Bridget reached out and felt the grain of the wooden door. After a small amount of fumbling she found the handle. She turned it, and the door swung open. At that sound, Commander Chadek's boot heels clacked against the floor as he turned back to his rounds.

"Prathad? Richikha?" Bridget shuffled into the room. Without Chadek to set the pace, her feet grew timid.

"Mistress?" answered Richikha. "Are you there?"

"I do seem to be," said Bridget tartly, but she quickly regretted the words. "Yes, Richikha, I am. Prathad?" Bridget moved forward a few cautious steps and let the door swing softly shut behind her.

"I am here, mistress." The older woman's voice was accompanied by the rustle of cloth and the scrape of wood on stone. "Is it known what is happening?"

Bridget hesitated, then set her jaw. These two were her people. She was responsible for them. "The Firebird has come."

Sharp intakes of breath, one to the left, one to the right, and again the rustle of cloth.

"What does it want?" asked Richikha.

But it was Sakra's voice that came in answer. "Payment for thirty years."

Bridget turned reflexively, although she could see nothing but darkness. "Has there been any new word?" *And how did you find your way here?*

"Very little." Footsteps came closer, a hint of human warmth touched her skin. "The lord sorcerer tried to stop its coming, and failed. Now all are seeking a way to destroy it, or at least cage it again." His voice darkened as he spoke. He did not approve of something that was happening. Before Bridget could question him further he said, "But our quest is different."

"Sakra . . ." she began. *What am I to do? I can't think straight knowing Anna might be out there . . .*

"I have just come from Master Luden. You and I are to travel at once to find the truth about your daughter and return as quickly as may be."

Bridget felt as if there were no air left in the room. "It's agreed? But . . . how?"

"I spoke with the empress." His voice was still tight. Something uncomfortable had passed between them. That thought only flitted through Bridget's mind.

Anna. They were going to find Anna. Anna.

Questions, too unformed yet for her mind to put into words, rose like mist. She brushed them aside. There was no question that could matter now.

Anna.

Bridget pressed her hands against her belly, trying to slow her breathing. Nothing would be helped or hurried if she fainted.

"Dawn is coming," said Sakra softly. "There will soon be light to see by."

Bridget waved, forgetting Sakra could not see the gesture. "We do not need to wait for dawn."

"Your confidence is flattering," he said in the dry tone he used when making a joke. "But even I must be able to see to work a spell of crossing."

"But I can see well enough to get us where we need to go." She reached out, found his hand, and clasped it. "Come."

Anna. Anna, if you are yet living, I will find you. She wanted to shout those words, she wanted the whole world, all the worlds to know that if they had hidden her daughter, she would be found, and those who had taken her . . . a blaze of anger beyond words shot through Bridget's mind.

She found the door, she found the handle, she opened it onto the corridor. She closed her left eye, and it made no difference in the depth of the darkness.

Snared so easily and you still declare your blessed sight will keep you safe.

The one who can find your daughter. The one who can call her back from where she has gone.

None of those voices mattered. Nothing mattered except the way forward. Bridget steeled her mind. She reached within, and she reached without. Holding Sakra's hand tightly, she began to walk, rapid, confident, loud footsteps, and to the rhythm of their steps, and the rhythm of heart and breath and hope, she raised her magic, and with her true-seeing eye she looked, and she saw . . .

She saw the world was a veil, rippling, translucent, only patterns on patterns.

She saw the path, darker than even the blackness of the corridor, a shimmering of shadow.

She saw that beyond the veil the world had become shone a pale green light.

Bridget set her feet on the path to the Land of Death and Spirit, and she began to run.

To Sakra, the living world melted away as simply as spun sugar in the rain. Darkness faded into the perpetual emerald that was both daylight and moonglow in the Silent Lands. His eyes, adjusted to the dark, flinched and squinted, their nascent tears making fantastic shapes of the changing world around him.

He could scarce breathe. Never had he made this transition so quickly. He had not realized such a feat was possible, even for Bridget. She had done no more than run. She had woven no pattern, spoken no words. She had simply seen the way, and followed it.

Mothers All, she has no gauge of her own strength. How much have we underestimated her?

His blurred vision cleared and the Land of Death and Spirit put on one of its many masks for him. He had expected the evergreen forest he had known before, but instead they walked a well-trodden path through green, grassy hills. Not a tree was to be seen in any direction, only a rolling ocean of knee-high grass waving in the silent wind beneath the sunless sky. Sakra wanted to shrink in on himself. He felt exposed. Anything might see them here. Better to leave the path, to pull Bridget with him, rather than wait here for whatever power might happen by . . .

Sakra caught his runaway thoughts and forced them back into order. He'd had no time to compose himself before leaving the living world, but his training did not desert him. To leave the path they now walked would be to lose themselves in the endless illusions of the Silent Lands. He concentrated on the feel of Bridget's hand around his. Her skin was warm with her excitement and effort. The calluses of her former life had not yet begun to fade. This touch was real. This touch, and the memories he carried in his mind. These things he could trust here. There was nothing else.

Bridget forged ahead with her long, swinging stride. Did she still have only one eye open? The path was too narrow for them to walk side by side so he could not tell.

"What do you see?" he asked, unable to restrain his curiosity.

"Birch trees," she said shortly. It was always difficult to breathe here, but she did not slow down. "Thorn, and wild apple. Ridiculous. Shouldn't be growing together like this." Her palm began to grow clammy. "I feel like I should know this place, but I can't remember . . ."

"Do you see the river?" There was only one river in the Shifting Lands. It was entrance to this place, and it was egress. It encompassed all the living worlds.

"Ahead. It sparkles in the light."

Sakra resisted the urge to look. He concentrated on calming his mind. Strong desires had bad effects here. They could call down the dangerous, or the simply mischievous. There were so many powers here, so many of them unknown, and so many with uses for beating hearts and the breath of life.

It was dangerous enough that Bridget's heart yearning for her daughter was surely crying out loud for all such things to hear.

The world changed. The hills and knolls faded to a whiteness that reshaped itself into a lacework of ivory and ebony. Slowly, Sakra recognized the corridors of the Palace of the Pearl Throne with their gilding, polished coral and bas reliefs of the Mothers, and their symbols worked over and again. Eyes watched him from behind cunning screens. This was the women's wing, but the corridors had no end, only shadows flickering in the adjoining corridors, drawing his eye, vying for his attention, only the sensation of hidden eyes watching, judging, silently laughing . . .

Silent. No sound. You should hear the soles of your boots on the floor. You are not home. Pay attention.

He locked his gaze on the auburn waves of Bridget's hair. She'd had no chance to bind it up for the night and it flowed freely down her shoulders without veil or pin to hinder it. He'd wondered how it would feel to run his hands through her hair, to feel the soft skin of her neck underneath, to hear her sigh as she touched him.

Stop, stop, he warned himself. *Memories. Memories only, not dreams, not desires. There lies the danger.*

But the world had already changed again. Now he saw the forest, a hundred different kinds of flora all jumbled together and tangled by gnarled thorns and bitter green apple trees.

Bridget's stride broke for one bare instant. She did not wait for him to ask what she saw.

"Something's coming, through the grass . . ."

Grass? What place did she see into now?

Then, he saw the bracken swaying violently, and although he turned his eyes back to Bridget, a sudden flash of motion jerked them away again to see a brown blur streak soundlessly from a screen of fern.

A rabbit, earth-brown with a white star of a tail, flung itself exhausted at Bridget's feet. Blood ran down its flanks where claws had mauled it.

It was not alone. It seemed a red river flowed after it, silent, as everything in this place must be. In an eyeblink, the river resolved itself into a pack of hunting hounds with blind eyes, their jaws open and their teeth glinting in the pale light.

Bridget let go of Sakra's hand, scooped the wounded rabbit into her arms.

"No!" Sakra reached for her, but it was too late. Quicker than thought, the dogs surrounded her, their white eyes shining like their bared teeth and Sakra found himself on the other side of a fence of bloodred bodies although he had felt nothing brush him aside.

Then two of the dogs lengthened. They reared up onto their hind legs and changed. Their paws grew fingers and skin appeared as the fur pulled itself away. A pair of naked men stood before Bridget with the hounds at their heels.

"Pretty mistress," said one in a low, deep voice. "Give us our prey."

"Pretty mistress," said the other. "That is ours by gift and law, mistress. Give us it."

"Take care," said Sakra. She felt a mile away from him. The dogs all bared their teeth, lean and hungry beyond anything a living creature could be. "Look hard. What do you really see?" He wanted to call her name, to bring her mind fully to him, but he did not dare with all these ears. A hundred possible spells tugged at his mind. *Just do this,* his own power whispered. *Free your magics, save her.*

Lose us both.

"I see a rabbit," said Bridget. "I see hounds. I see two men." She squared her shoulders. "If this is yours by so strong a claim," she said to the men, "why do you not take it from me?"

The first of the men, the one with grey hair, walked forward. He reached for the rabbit with long fingers. The rabbit squealed and kicked hard as it tried to burrow deeper into Bridget's arms. The blow made her shudder, but she held on. The grey-haired man's hand stopped a full inch from the rabbit, and he let it fall.

It must be true, if she sees it. Her vision is true sight, granted by the Vixen. It cannot be fooled.

Except perhaps by the Vixen.

Sakra's head spun. Images piled up on top of one another. He was in the tangled woods, in the evergreen forest, in the meadows, in the gardens of Vyshtavos. Only Bridget and the hungry red hounds remained steady.

"Pretty mistress," said Grey Hair again. "This does not concern you. Because you can do this thing does not mean you are free to do this thing. Give us our prey and get you gone."

"Give it to them," Sakra heard himself say, so dizzy now he could barely keep his feet. "Whatever this is, it is no game of ours."

But Bridget held her ground as the world swam around her. "It is yours to take if you can."

Grey Hair drew his lips back in a sneer. "Oh, clever, oh, caring, oh, mother of hearts and worlds. You say you would claim and protect this thing in your arms?"

"As you see."

"How much may you now keep safe." Grey Hair sat back on his haunches and was a dog again, and the pack slipped back among the trees, and was gone.

The world steadied again, and there were the familiar evergreens, and the gravel bank, and thank the Seven Mothers, the river, shallow and brown, sparkling over rounded pebbles.

Bridget was right beside him again, with the wounded rabbit cradled in her arms. The creature, whatever it truly was, did not seem inclined toward gratitude. Instead, it shook itself and shoved against her forearm with its powerful hind legs. Startled, her hands flew open. The rabbit leapt to the ground and sped away, leaving dark droplets of blood scattered behind it. Biting her lip, Bridget watched it go.

"You are going to say I should not have done that," she murmured.

Not I, he thought, a little sadly. *You know it already.* "We don't know what it was you saved."

Bridget lifted her chin, a gesture she made when she was trying to convince herself of something. "It owes me a debt, now, whatever it was. I saved its life. I can call in the favor later, if it tries to work mischief."

"Yes, that may be done," agreed Sakra slowly.

"You told me once that the laws of magic are the laws of debt and doing." Her gaze stayed on the path the fleeing rabbit had taken. What did she see there? What did she try to see?

"This is true. There may be good yet in what you have done. But we cannot stay any longer."

Bridget shook herself as the rabbit had. "No, you're right. We're almost there." She took his hand again, as if nothing had happened, and led him down the gravel bank, and all the while, Sakra struggled not to look back.

He did not see a pair of great, yellow eyes watching them as they hurried away, nor did he see the sleek, black body that slipped away into the forest, padding off toward its home.

The cat moved delicately between the trees, ignoring the flashes of movement that flickered between the branches and the huge trunks. Occasionally, another pair of eyes gleamed in the darkness, but none approached the cat. All knew its mistress. None would dare raise the mistress's anger by interfering with the progress of her servant.

A faint path emerged from the floor of the thinning forest. The cat followed it lightly, padding steadily, pausing to clean its fur and then bounding forward to hurry on. Gradually, the evergreens gave way to maples, oaks, and ash, which in turn gave way to birches. The cat passed underneath the branches of one decrepit tree, and those limbs lifted themselves to allow it free passage. Ahead of the cat appeared a rickety fence that looked to have once been made of wood, but it had long since been propped up and mended with bleached bones. Two great, black mastiffs flanked the sagging gate, sitting with heads and ears erect, watching the path. Their gazes did not flicker as the cat leapt onto the gatepost and then jumped down into the rutted yard.

Beyond the gate waited the house Ishbushka, turning on its scarred and scaled legs, its great talons gouging the dirt beneath it with each movement. The cat stopped before the nightmare house and sat upright, its tail curled around its legs. The house ceased its restless turning and knelt. The cat disdained the worm-eaten stairs and splintered door. It leapt onto the sill of the open window and ducked inside.

Like the guardian fence, the interior of Ishbushka was framed in bone. Bones curved overhead and gleamed on all sides, holding up the roof and crumbling walls in place of timbers. Human skulls were stacked to make the fireplace and chimney. The bones and skulls of animals hung from the roof beams, left to dry as herbs or onions would have been in a more homely house. Beneath the bones waited a great loom made of grey and ancient ivory and strung with sinew. An old woman wrapped in a tattered black robe sat at the grisly loom, working away with a shuttle made of a jawbone. She did not look up as the cat sauntered over to the hearth.

"What did you see?" asked the witch. The treadles clicked and clacked as she worked, shuttling the jawbone back and forth and back again.

"I saw the Vixen's favorite daughter take the Vixen's favorite prey." The cat sprawled in front of the fire, stretching its belly out to catch the warmth of the flames. "I do not think she knows what she has done."

"No." The witch sprawled her bony hands across the pattern she wove, touching it gently here and there. "She cannot bring herself to doubt her eyes, although she has been warned."

"So." The cat twitched its whiskers.

"So." The Old Witch grinned, displaying all her iron teeth. "The Vixen began this game of daughters. We shall see how she likes this new player."

The rabbit ran through the trees. It skimmed the ground between its great bounds, speeding along like flight or flame. All it truly knew was that its pursuers were no longer there, waiting for its exhaustion so they could bring it down. It was free.

Free, free! The word beat in its mind like the heart that had once beat in its breast.

In the manner of things in that land, the rabbit shifted and changed, and it was no longer a beast, but a black-haired man, naked as a babe.

Valin Kalami huddled exhausted in the shallows of the thousand-named river that ran through the Land of Death and Spirit. Its one true name was Life. Life flowed in its brown waters, life and all the worlds there were, but he could not even manage to wet his skin with it. He must have died, somewhere, sometime. How strange not to know when he had died. But it must be so, because otherwise he could have walked the river and found his life again. If he had been alive still, he would not have heard the voices. Mumbling, whispering, whimpering, wailing, the thousands of voices of the Shifting Lands engulfed him. They were the voices of ghosts, powers, demons, memories, lost souls, the fae and the fearful. They were voices of the place itself that swaddled all the worlds there were, that would disgorge them as they were born and absorb them as they died.

He could not remember when he had begun to hear the voices. All he knew was that they had become his constant companions in his endless flight, and that they threatened, mocked, cajoled, and distracted as he ran. For all he knew, they even now led the Vixen and her sons back to him. Terror lanced through him at the thought of that terrible hunt, of the gleaming, joyful eyes and the yellow teeth that sank deep into his neck and tossed him high to break back, and let him be still only long enough for panic to grow greater than pain so he would try to run again with all the voices laughing around him. They would find him again, had already found him again, it mattered little. There was no single current of time for the dead as there was for the living. The Vixen had, would, did, find him and she renewed the chase, and there was no power that could protect him from her.

Kalami lifted his head. No power, perhaps, but one.

As a living man he would not have considered this, but he was a shade now and had only eternity surrounding him. At least this slavery—if slavery it became—would be his choice, and he had turned such slavery to his advantage before.

Steeling his nerve, Kalami focused all his will on a single name and as he had so many times before, he began to run.

Chapter Twelve

The road out of T'ien was hot, dusty, and crowded. People overflowed the track, jostling each other with elbows and handcarts. Some cried as they went, others hurried by in stunned silence, unable to believe that behind them the Heart of the World was being burned hollow.

Mae Shan led Chen and Kyun off the road and into the high green hills as soon as she could. She carried Tsan Nu against her chest. Despite the noise and the motion, the girl did not wake, or even stir. They were not by any means the only ones who fled across the countryside, but the open ground was nothing like as crowded as the road they left behind.

At sunset, Mae Shan called a halt. She laid Tsan Nu on the cool grass under a linden tree. Chen and Kyun collapsed unceremoniously beside them, but Mae Shan let that pass. The touch of the grass seemed to revive Tsan Nu somewhat and her eyes fluttered open. Mae Shan uncapped one of the water bottles and dribbled some into the child's mouth. She drank it neatly enough, and Mae Shan gave her some more, glancing up to signal the trainees that they could take their share as well. They did not hesitate, but uncorked one of the bottles and drank greedily.

Tsan Nu focused her eyes briefly on Mae Shan. Her mouth moved as if to smile or speak, but she drifted back into sleep before she could do either. However, Mae Shan was sure she saw recognition in Tsan Nu's brief glance, and was reassured.

Under Mae Shan's direction, Kyun lit a small fire. She chose not to notice how his hands shook as he started the small blaze. Her own were not as steady as they should have been for this most mundane of tasks. Chen cooked a measure of rice porridge in the pot he had had the foresight to bring. They ate in silence with Mae Shan spooning some of the porridge into Tsan Nu. The child swallowed, but did not wake.

Darkness settled close around them, allowing them to see other small campfires like distant candles dotting the hillsides. The sound of motion, voices, creaking axles, and feet on hard dirt drifted continuously up from the road, but the world still seemed too quiet, and the scent of burning still tainted the wind.

Mae Shan set the watches, and took the first one herself. The night passed slowly, divided into times of waking and times of sleeping with one arm draped across Tsan Nu, but the sounds of motion and the scent of burning remained constant.

In the morning they ate the remaining porridge cold and drank sparingly of their water. Tsan Nu still did not wake, but her breathing had slowed and deepened, and her color was better. Mae Shan shared out her burdens, except for her bow and arrows, to the trainees and slung Tsan Nu into her arms.

Then they walked on.

The hills around Tien were heavily terraced for the growing of rice and fruit. Mae Shan tried to make sure their passage disturbed as little as possible and forbid Chen and Kyun from raiding the orchards they passed, even when it was clear that the house had been thrown open and the occupants fled. It was also clear from the scuffs and the gouges in the paddies and the dirt, and the cores and seeds on the ground, that others had not been so scrupulous. Chen's face went hard, but he obeyed. Quiet warning stirred in the back of Mae Shan's mind, and as she led them on that day, she often glanced back, and more often than not she saw the two trainees whispering to each other. The warning grew stronger.

They spent their second night in such an abandoned house, because the woods were growing more crowded with people on the move and Mae Shan did not wish to risk another night with nothing at their backs. Tsan Nu was able to sit up then and take a little water and some dried fish with her rice porridge, although she nodded off again with her bowl halfway to her mouth.

On the third day Tsan Nu was able to walk a short distance on her own. They settled in another farmhouse, this one a little less ransacked than the first. Chen found a full cellar with salt fish and bread still good. By now their own supplies were all but gone, so she permitted him to take enough for another three days. In the empty bedroom, she opened her private purse and tucked one of her few coins under the mattress where hopefully the owners of the house would find it upon their return.

Not to do so would be theft and a direct breaking of her oaths as a soldier of the Heart. It was by small derelictions that the greater came into being, said her trainer, and she believed it. She had to. It was all she had at the moment.

But it did raise the question of what to do with the trainees. Mae Shan stared at the faint coals they'd carefully banked in the cottage hearth. They were growing discontent with her insistence on maintaining discipline. The last thing she needed at this time was a confrontation with the boys, a confrontation she was sure to lose, because they were realizing they had few reasons left to obey her.

She picked herself up and stood in the scarred and splintered threshold of the farmhouse door. In the red dawn, she took in the lay of the land. Then she sat down and counted four of the six remaining coins out of her purse.

Coins in hand, she stepped around Tsan Nu, and shook the trainees awake where they slept in the workroom by the back door. As they blinked their eyes open, she gestured to them to keep silent. Their faces were sullen and sleepy as she led them outside. The wind was freshening, but there was scarcely any ash in it this morning, and Mae Shan felt the relief of just being able to breathe.

She pointed between two terraced hills to the northwest. The mountains rose blue and misty in the distance behind them.

"Over those hills is the town of Nhi Tao. It's no more than half a day's good march. The captain of the city guard there is named Kein. Give him my name and tell him I sent you to shore up his garrison." Kein would understand she truly sent the boys to him for safekeeping. He had always understood what she truly meant. For a moment, Mae Shan imagined collapsing into his arms and being cradled like a child while she wept for all she had seen. Perhaps one day.

She held out two coins each to Chen and Kyun. "This is all I have to give you, apart from my thanks for your aid to my mistress."

The trainees stared at one another, and then slowly accepted the coins.

"Are you certain, Lieutenant?" said Chen, tucking his meager pay into his sleeve. "We are ready to accompany you the rest of your way."

Mae Shan would have found that statement more convincing if he had not taken the coins first, but still, it was a show of courage.

"My mistress's way takes us to the barbarian lands, and I do not know how long we may be gone. Hung-Tse will need all her sons, and most especially her soldiers in the coming days. I cannot take you away from her." She gave them a brief smile that she did not feel. "Get your gear and go. Remember, the man you want is Kein."

Chen looked at Kyun, who nodded. The boys snapped to attention, folded their hands in front of them in formal salute, and bowed crisply to her. She bowed in return and they went back inside to collect their things. Mae Shan made a circuit of the house, assuring herself that no one still on the road was coming too close to "their" house, and that no one was watching what was happening here.

She went back in the front door and sat beside sleeping Tsan Nu with her back toward the hearth and her face toward the door. She twisted her sigil ring on her finger and tried hard not to feel she had just cut her last tie to the Heart of the World.

I will return. I will, and I will find my family and I will help rebuild, and Wei Lin will have a spirit tablet in the temple of the Goddess of Mercy and a monk to say all the proper prayers.

She repeated that thought to herself until she found the strength to believe it.

When Tsan Nu woke, she was well enough to be unhappy. She hunched in front of the fire, staring hungrily at the porridge Mae Shan cooked with some of the salt fish from the cellar.

"How much farther, Mae Shan?"

Mae Shan considered. "A day's walk, maybe two." They had to by-pass Nhi Tao and head downhill to the river.

"Couldn't someone give us a ride in a cart?"

"Not over these hills, mistress."

"We need my father. He'd find a way to take us there in a heartbeat."

"I have no doubt, mistress. Unfortunately, we cannot bring him by wishing . . ." But before Mae Shan finished the sentence, she straightened up, remembering who she was talking to. "Can you, mistress?"

"He gave me a spell," said Tsan Nu. "He said that I was to use it if things went badly for me in the Heart of the World."

And they were not going badly enough before this? Mae Shan wondered incredulously at the logic of the child. She would not think to call her father while she was escaping from a burning city, but would to escape a pair of sore feet?

Tsan Nu's father was a powerful sorcerer. How quickly could he cross the Silent Lands to come to her? To take her safe away to the northlands and let Mae Shan look after herself? She would be released from her oath then, having fulfilled her assigned duty. She could make her way across country, find her parents and her siblings and help them through what was to come.

"Are you sure you can do this, mistress?" she asked warily. "You are still weak from your last working."

In answer, Tsan Nu pulled off her slipper, one of the pair she had risked the fire to retrieve. Now Mae Shan could see a small tear in the lining. Tsan Nu stuck two fingers into the tear and pulled out a circle of braided cloth, black, green, blue, and red.

Tsan Nu held up the amulet for her guard's inspection. "This is different than before," she assured Mae Shan. "My father did the working already, I just have to set it into motion. It will take very little magic from me."

Mae Shan swallowed, unlooked-for hope forming inside her. "Then work your spell, mistress, I will keep watch."

"I will need a bowl of water."

Mae Shan wiped the cooking pot clean, filled it from one of the water bottles, and set it before Tsan Nu. The child held up the braided circle, and started to work at the knot that held its complex weaving closed. As she did, she began to speak, but the words sounded strange. They were not the singsong of the spell tongue she had used before. These words were harsh and clipped. They had the rhythm of the drum rather than the zither. Mae Shan realized she must be speaking one of the northern tongues to work this northern spell.

Mae Shan turned her attention to the house door. *Come for your daughter, Master Kalami, I pray you,* she entreated silently. *Let me give over the care of your family so I may go aid in the care of mine.*

Kalami ran through the Shifting Lands for a long time, for a short time, for no time at all. He held tight to the name he sought as he ran through the thick forest of evergreen trees, his footsteps rustling and crackling on the carpet of needles underfoot. The trees whispered and creaked as their branches lifted to move themselves from his passage. Eyes watched him, he knew that, but he was permitted to pass, so they were not the Vixen's eyes and that was all that mattered.

He caught sight of a birch tree, stark, white, and incongruous among the pines. Then there was another, then a grove of them, and hope leapt in him and sped his feet and tightened his thoughts. He was near.

A small stream trickled across his path. He vaulted over it. An ancient birch, craggy from the weight of its years, raised its branches, whipping them back and forth, into his eyes, against his back. But Kalami had known far worse pain and greater fear than this, and although he slowed his pace, he did not stop.

Beyond the birch waited a fence. Human bones tied with leather and sinews had been used to shore up the wooden staves. Kalami had thought now that he was dead such a sight could have no terror for him, but as he approached the fence, he found he had been wrong, and he trembled. And the fence was nothing compared to what walked in the dirt yard beyond it. The house Ishbushka turned slowly on great, taloned legs. He had stood here before, but now he heard the grating as its claws scraped the ground, the screech as they scraped against stone, its muscle creaking like timber. The obscene dwelling measured its restless pace by its fearful mistress's will, allowing her to see all the worlds from its windows if she so wished.

A sagging gate hung between two fence posts. It was shut tight, and Kalami reached out tentatively to push it open. But before he could touch it, a black blur leapt up onto the right-hand gatepost. He started backward, and then realized it was nothing more or less than a black cat with a white blaze on its chest. The creature regarded him steadily and with intelligent recognition in its eyes. Kalami was not surprised. He had met this cat before. What did surprise him was the wave of cold he felt wash over him. It came from the animal's bright gaze, from the bones of the fence, from Ishbushka itself. How could cold touch him as he was? But it did, that cold turned his mind thick and heavy.

Drawing his composure together, he reverenced politely in the courtly Isavaltan style.

"And what brings the great sorcerer of Tuukos to this house?" the cat inquired.

"I am come to seek an audience with your mistress," Kalami said as he straightened.

The cat tucked all four of its legs up under itself, settling comfortably onto the post. "Why should she grant such an audience?"

"I have power I would place in her service."

"You are dead," said the cat flatly, twitching its tail. Cold emanated from its voice, from the whole of its being. "You are nothing beyond the boundaries of this place. If you had power she wanted, she would have taken it by now."

The cold and the paralysis it brought threatened to overwhelm Kalami. He had one last cast.

"The Vixen claims me for her own. Perhaps that fact would be of interest."

"Ah!" The cat's yellow eyes gleamed and the cold subsided just a little. Kalami felt his mind clear again. "Now you have said it. Now you understand your place." The cat stretched out its hind leg and began washing it lazily. "If you step through the gate, she will grant you audience." The cat stopped washing and regarded him again, this time with hunger in its eyes. "And perhaps more than that."

The gate opened with a long shriek. Beyond it waited two huge, black mastiffs, their eyes as awake and intelligent as the cat's. Cold and weak, Kalami went through. As he crossed the line of the bone fence, the voices that were the constant background of his journey fell silent. Kalami felt light, alone, and small, as if he were a moth or a feather and that any wind might blow him away. Ahead of him waited Baba Yaga's fearful dwelling. The dogs stalked beside him, their ears alert, but for what he did not know. One scratched at the dirt. In response, Ishbushka knelt, and its door hissed as it fell open. Still escorted by the mastiffs, Kalami mounted the steps that creaked and groaned underneath him, although he could not feel the touch of the boards.

Inside Ishbushka's single room, built of bone and hung with bone, Baba Yaga worked at her loom. A bright fire burned in her hearth of skulls. The flicker of the flame drew his gaze and for a moment he saw in there a palace with a golden tower at its center. Saffron walls protected its lovely gardens and wide stone court. Voices rose whispering from the flames, and Kalami drew back. The Heart of the World gleamed in Baba Yaga's hearth, and in a moment it was gone.

"So," said the Old Witch, looking up from her work with black eyes that glittered in the firelight. "You would come to me?"

Kalami tried to pull his wits together. He had faced Baba Yaga in life. He knew her ways. He was still a sorcerer. He still had his powers and his learning.

"I do, mistress. I am . . ."

"Would I have admitted you, little spirit, if I did not know you?" Her bone-thin finger traced the pattern of her macabre weaving. "You are Valin Kalami. You were trapped by the Vixen while you were yet living, and now you come to me."

"Because it is only you who are great enough to shelter me from her." Kalami reverenced deeply. "You are the only one she cannot deceive."

"You seek to flatter me," said Baba Yaga. "You will not do so by speaking such simple truths."

"I seek shelter," said Kalami. "In return I offer my service."

"You are dead," said the Old Witch bluntly. "You have no service to offer, only self."

Kalami thought of the *lokai,* of the horror of the hunt, and of knowing that he would be caught, and wrenched in two, set to run and caught again. "Then I offer myself."

Baba Yaga's cold eyes gleamed and she clacked her iron teeth. "I am not as your other mistress, and this is not as your life. You seek to barter, and think you may yet escape any bargain that you make. You are a fool, little ghost, without blessing or true understanding."

Kalami felt how small he was, how light and fragile, as if he were only a dream, or a memory, which, in truth, he was. He could drift away and be caught on a thorn like a cobweb.

But Baba Yaga laid her finger again on her cloth of sinews and hair and bared her teeth at what she saw there.

"Your daughter calls you."

Kalami started. He thought to say the child's name, and but held his peace.

Baba Yaga's gaze warmed slightly with something like approval. "She calls her father for succor, for the Heart of the World has burned down."

She was using the amulet he left her. He should feel it, tugging at his mind, opening his inward senses. But he felt nothing at all. He was beyond all such bindings.

Baba Yaga considered for a moment. Kalami sensed the currents of the room shift and slip, as if the world around him was being woven. He glanced at the fire and again saw the Heart of the World in its depths. A seer had once told him that all fallen things belong to the Old Witch. He had not known until now what that truly meant.

"You will answer your daughter," Baba Yaga said. "I will permit it."

"Thank you, mistress." Anna, Tsan Nu, the daughter of his blood, his sorcerous child. There were ties between the two of them that might save him yet. It was strange that he had not thought of her before. Truly he was not what he had been. Not yet.

Again the witch clacked her iron teeth. "You should give thanks to Bridget Lederle for this. Without her intervention, even the call of blood could not have reached you.

"Return to the river, speak with your child. Do this and you will find the shelter you seek, but do not forget the words you have spoken here."

Kalami wanted to say "I never could," but he found he feared the response, so instead he reverenced and moved toward the door. The dogs stood aside to let him pass. He traveled down Ishbushka's rickety steps, across the yard and to the bone fence. He passed through the gate under the watchful eyes of the cat, and became at once immersed in the ocean of noise. The birch drew back its branches for him, revealing the brown river that had been so far away before he entered Ishbushka.

Kalami stared out at the surface of the rushing water, hearing in its chatter and song all the noise of life and wondering when it was he had died. Anger ran through him as strong as the current of the river before him. He did not know what to do, what he was or what he would become, and his ignorance infuriated him.

He also did not know what would happen next.

Then, the water roiled, the murmur of the water and the roar of the voices around him faded, and he heard one clear word.

"Father."

Tsan Nu stared into the pot of water. It was so hard and so long. She had never felt her magics reach so far. She had told Mae Shan this working would take little effort from her, but that was not the entire truth. This particular amulet's spell would use her own magic, drawing it out until it touched her father, as easily as if she reached out her hand to him.

Or so it should have been. But now she felt stretched so thin it became painful. It was as if she crossed whole worlds instead of a single country. Every noise around her seemed unbearably loud. Even the sound of Mae Shan's breathing grated against her eardrums. Then, faintly and from far away, she heard her father's voice. It echoed up from the cooking pot, weakened by distance and effort.

Anna?

Relief gushed through her, so strong it almost broke her concentration. Only Father called her Anna. It was her birth name, and he had told her she should not speak it in the Heart, especially not before the Nine Elders, lest they use it and her horoscope against her. She closed her eyes and forced herself to focus. "Father, I need you."

I know. Anna. He sounded sad. *The Heart of the World is gone.*

That jolted Anna. It had not occurred to her that he might have known. "Where are you, Father? Why didn't you come for me?"

Anna, you must be strong, my child. I have died. Anna. I am speaking from the Shifting Lands.

Anna's eyes flew open and she stated at the shimmering water before her. She couldn't understand. She felt as if she had stepped outside herself and this was someone else. Father had never been with her, not since she was a tiny child, but he had always been there in the background. He had been in letters and in the amulet she hid in her shoe. That he had gone on, that he would soon fade into the Shifting Lands, and she didn't know, hadn't felt . . . that he wouldn't be there, ever again . . . that he wasn't truly there now . . .

"I wanted to reach you before," she said, trying to find a way to understand how she could have not known. "But the fire was too bad. Mae Shan wouldn't let us stop."

Your Mae Shan was right.

"I should have drawn your horoscope. Then we would have known and I could have saved you and then you could have saved me."

Father was silent for a long moment, and Tsan Nu wondered if he felt as sad as she did. *Where are you going, Anna?* he finally asked. *I cannot see.*

"Mae Shan is taking me to her family. We were going to wait there for you. Mae Shan says it will be very bad in Hung-Tse. She says the

Phoenix is angry with everyone. I tried to tell the Nine Elders that." She wanted him to know she had done her best, as he always told her she should do, that she had listened to him, and to her teachers.

Father's voice grew soothing. *You are both right. The Phoenix is very angry, and you must leave Hung-Tse.*

"How?" Tsan Nu felt the fear growing close around her again. "Master Liaozhai hasn't taught me to walk the Shifting Lands yet, and Mae Shan only knows Hung-Tse. Will the dowager help us?" Father had often spoken of the dowager empress and how much she depended on him.

The dowager is gone as well, Anna. There is no one in Isavalta who can help you now. There was an undercurrent to his voice turning it tight and brittle. Was he angry? She couldn't tell.

"What should I do?" Her voice came out very small.

Anna, I want to help you, my daughter, but I need your help to do so.

Hope slipped between her and her fear. "Just tell me how, Father."

Father spoke carefully, as he did when he was trying to make absolutely sure she understood. Tsan Nu strained to hear every word.

We are bound by blood, Anna. If you open your heart to me, the spirit that I am can enter into it and from there I will be able to guide you and help you return to Tuukos, where you have other family.

Tsan Nu hesitated. "Master Liaozhai said it is wrong to bring ghosts from the Silent Lands to the waking world. He says it disrupts the flow of the elements."

Master Liaozhai is right, but we have no choice. I cannot come to you any other way.

Tsan Nu felt Mae Shan tensing. Did she hear what Father was saying, or was that for Tsan Nu alone? She couldn't tell if the voice was only in her head. Tsan Nu itched to look up, to say something to reassure her bodyguard, but knew if she did the spell would break, and she and Mae Shan would be alone again.

"All right, but I don't know what to do."

It is very simple, Daughter. You need only reach into your magics, and want me with you.

Tsan Nu swallowed. In the back of her mind, Master Liaozhai frowned at her and spoke the Words of Harmony, "Let the current teach you of the river, let the direction of the wind teach you of the sky," but she also knew if she did not do this thing, she would be alone, and Father would be gone forever.

Tsan Nu concentrated. She reached as deeply into herself as she could, and she wanted. She wanted so hard she shook with wanting. She thought hard of her father, how he looked, how he sounded; she tried to remember every letter he'd ever sent to her, every time she had ever seen him, and she wanted.

She felt her heart open wide. It was strange and frightening, and painful at first, and Tsan Nu gasped. In the next breath, though, the pain was gone and she felt warm and safe, as she had when she had been smaller and taken her father by the hand to show him her pool in the Star Garden. They had shared secrets that day, and in other days that came after. This felt like that, like a great, exciting secret to carry inside her, to make her strong and clever because she knew something no one else did.

Close the gate now, Anna, said Father's voice from deep in her heart. *It is not good to leave the doors open to the Land of Death and Spirit. Something unwanted may follow. Be still and I will help you.*

Excited, as if she were learning a whole new working, Anna stilled herself and held her breath.

The world grew distant. Her senses, which her working had sharpened, turned dull. It was not an uncomfortable or a frightening thing, though, because at the same time she felt Father, warm and pleased in her heart. He lifted her head and slipped her hands into the pot she had used as a gazing bowl, scooping up a handful of water and pouring it out onto the earthen floor. The hard-packed ground drank up the water and Tsan Nu felt the spell dissolve from around her, but her heart was still full where Father waited for her and she smiled.

"Did it work?" asked Mae Shan, her voice tight with strain. "Will he come?"

"He is here," announced Tsan Nu. "Safe in my heart. All will be well now."

Mae Shan's face shifted back and forth, as if she were not certain what to think. "Mistress, I'm only a soldier," she said, speaking carefully. "I don't understand this. Is your father a ghost?"

"He died," said Tsan Nu simply. "But he is with me now."

She fears you are possessed, said Father from her heart. *Say to her that this is a matter between sorcerers and that unlike those untouched by magic we may touch, like to like, without such fears.*

Master Liaozhai had never said such a thing, but it might be they had not reached that lesson yet. Tsan Nu repeated Father's words to Mae Shan. Her frown smoothed out, but she did not look completely reassured.

"Do you feel well enough to go on, mistress?"

To her surprise, Tsan Nu did. She jumped up to her feet, feeling as if she had just had a long rest and it was the first thing on a summer's morning. Everything was bright and golden, and all would be right.

Mae Shan's face shifted again, as if she were holding something back with difficulty. "I'll pack our things, then."

Tsan Nu turned to help by picking up the pot and taking it to the door to empty properly outside.

"I don't think Mae Shan is pleased," she whispered to Father.

She is concerned about your well-being, said Father. *That is a proper thing for a guard. We will watch her closely so we can find ways to help her better understand what is happening.*

"Yes, Father." Tsan Nu shook the last drops from the pot. "I'm glad you're with me."

So am I, Anna. So am I.

You should not be doing this alone, Mistress Urshila told herself.

She stood in her own small workroom. It was a very different place from Daren's. This was a place of pots and paints, of wet clays packed in damp straws, of colored earths, paints, inks, and colored stones. Sharp knives, their delicate blades protected by corks, waited in neat rows beside smooth plaques of precious, sweet-smelling woods brought from across the empire, and stored in the treasury since the last time she had set foot in Vyshtavos.

Urshila was, of course, familiar with many ways of shaping her magics, of the easy arts of thread and weaving, of the more difficult workings of air, or dance, of the perilous uses of blood, but she preferred slower, more careful weavings when she could use them. There was pride in a weaving shaped with precision over long, careful hours that would do its work subtly and last across the years. Carved in wood, baked in clay, set in stone, such magics were truly wondrous things.

Refurnishing this place had been a homecoming, but standing here now her agitation only increased.

You should not be doing this alone.

And what should I do? Distract and divide the others? With the Firebird bringing cold vengeance down on Isavalta, am I to raise the specter of Valin Kalami? And how do I explain this intuition of mine?

You see, Lord Daren, I ran into an old Tuukosov scullery woman and she mentioned to me . . .

Why would a Tuukosov mention anything to you?

You see . . .

Urshila set her hands on her hips. No. It would not do.

The truth was that she wanted to be sure of her decision. She needed to prove to herself that her loyalties did lie with Isavalta, not with Tuukos. That she did what she did of her own free will, because the only other choice was Tuukos, where her Isavaltan blood had made her suspect, where her older brother had been hanged on suspicion of running messages for rebels, and not one of their neighbors, not even the secret sorcerer who said he would take her to 'prentice once she turned ten, did anything at all to stop it.

She would have to hide half of herself for the rest of her days no matter what choice she made, and she had been Isavaltan much longer than she had been Tuukosov.

But her encounter with the old woman yesterday had set her thinking, even as the world went dark around her. She had thought of Tuukos and the unrest of the distant island, the contempt in which its people were held within Isavalta, and the means they had used to try to exact their revenge, or their freedom, whichever they could achieve. One such partisan had been Valin Kalami, and he had nearly succeeded with intrigues that were as carefully laid out as any spell could ever be.

But he had failed in the end, and he had vanished, as had the Firebird. Now the Firebird was back. Where was Valin Kalami? The scullery woman had spoken of him. Given the course of the conversation it was natural enough, but did she know something Urshila did not? No one had witnessed his death, not even Bridget Lederle, who had seen the dowager perish. Kalami had escaped into the Land of Death and Spirit, she said, weak but alive. What had happened to him after that? If he was dead, it was of no matter, but if he was not . . .

If he was not, and the old woman was not alone . . .

Urshila did not want to waste time searching for Kalami. The world was vast, and the Land of Death and Spirit was without limit. She was needed elsewhere, and she could not waste her strength on this, if waste it was.

What was needed was a forbidding.

After a certain amount of wrangling, she had convinced the mistress of the house to yield up the key to the room that had belonged to Valin Kalami. It hung from her own small keyring now. Urshila surveyed her stocks and set to work.

She laid the key on her worktable and opened a pot of red paint. Water from a jug freshened the pigment. She also laid out a lump of red clay brought from the far north, her sharpest, most slender knife, and a small silver box with an exquisitely delicate lock and key that were a gift from a jeweler whose wife Urshila had delivered of twins.

She selected a delicate brush of seal hair. With the skill of a hundred years of practice, she painted the letters of Valin Kalami's name along the barrel of the key, blowing on them gently to dry them, and to add her breath to the paint. As delicately, as precisely as she painted the name, Mistress Urshila began to draw her magics up and in.

"I make my wish, as I have made my wish before, and as my wish before was answered so shall my wish be answered now." She breathed the words once, and again and again as the paint hardened on the shaft of the key. Then she took up the key and pressed it into the clay.

"I have found the bones of Valin Kalami. I have found the heart of Valin Kalami. I have found the name of Valin Kalami and I encase the whole that is Valin Kalami in my clay." She folded the cool clay over the key, pressing it down and sealing it completely. She spat once, working the fluid into the clay and saying the words again. Then she sprinkled salt, and folded the clay again. "I have found the bones of Valin Kalami . . ."

She smoothed the clay into a neat oval and selected her knife. Her magics moved as easy as breathing, permeating the working, flowing through her hands and mind, allowing her to make the delicate cuts into the clay, weaving the letters of the spell and Kalami's name together on the soft red surface. She must not cut too deep, for that would reveal the metal of the key and ruin the shaping. She must not pour out too much power, for that would flood the shaping with more than it could hold, and again the working would shatter.

When the carving was done, she lifted the clay and set it into the box.

"As the key is encased in clay and does not move, so shall Valin Kalami be unable to move in Isavalta. As the box is closed and locked around the clay"—Urshila closed the box lid and turned the tiny key—"so is Isavalta closed and locked to Valin Kalami. As the lock is invisible to the key hidden in the clay, so shall the borders of Isavalta be invisible to Valin Kalami." She laid both hands on the box. "This is my word, and my word is firm. This is my word, and my word is firm!"

The working absorbed the last of her magics. Urshila expelled a long breath and slowly brought herself back from the working. Perspiration beaded her brow and moistened her hands. She wiped both on a clean cloth. Tired but satisfied, she placed the box in one of her storage chests and closed the lid. The key she slipped onto her ring. She would destroy it later when the forges were relit, after she had a chance to bake the clay to set the working more permanently. But for now, at least, she had done what could be done. If Kalami was not in Isavalta, he could not now enter its borders. If he was already here, he could not move freely or easily.

Later, she could let it be known what she had done.

Smiling to herself, Urshila left her room to make her way down the dim corridor to the Red Library where the others were already at work searching for the lore that would help them defeat the Firebird, or at least turn it aside. No such simple forbidding could stop an immortal creature. She doubted the clay would even seal if she tried it, even if one could find the name that would compel the Firebird's essence.

Deep in the bowels of Isavalta's cellars, Senja lifted her head, and frowned.

The Firebird perched in the dead tree. Beneath it, the branch was scorched and blackened and would not hold for long. Its tail hung down behind it, scattering sparks onto the damp forest floor. Under the usual circumstances, a new blaze would have already started, but these were not the usual circumstances.

The Vixen watched the fabulous bird for a while. She noted how it stared at the roofs of the village it had just overflown. She wondered if it was making sure of its work. She saw well how no smoke rose from any of the chimneys, although night was falling and despite it being summer, the air grew chill.

Having seen enough, she trotted from her hiding place to the base of the tree.

"Have you grown tired of smoking ruins then?" she inquired, sitting back on her haunches and blinking up at the Firebird.

"They imprisoned me because they sought the protection of my fire," it replied. "No hero came to free me, no sorcerer bargained for my release. They all feared the loss of the fire. So I remove it from them now."

The Vixen cocked her head, looking down at the village. She could hear the frightened whispers, the crying of children already growing cold and hungry. "You could have flown ahead to winter and done this then. It would have all been over much more quickly that way."

"I do not wish it to be over quickly," replied the Firebird. "My torment lasted thirty years. My tormentors should have some taste of what that is like."

The Vixen shook her head and clicked her tongue. "A taste of thirty years but no taste of bread, no soup, and no warmth. Surely a fitting punishment for those who had no idea of your plight."

The Firebird glowered down at her. "What do you care? Your children have sported in ruins before this."

"Everyone will keep bringing that up." The Vixen sighed. "But if all the children of men are dead, with whom will my children play? And who will yours protect?"

She did not wait for the Firebird's answer, but instead slipped quickly and silently into her own lands.

There was much to do.

The Vixen pulled the Shifting Lands around her like a well-worn cloak and let them settle into shape so that they became green, grassy hills, each topped with a single thorn tree. She herself took on one of her human forms—a woman with pale skin and flame-colored hair dressed in a simple robe of grey fur belted with a braid of fox's hair. Her green eyes became mere slits as she watched for the Old Witch.

For those with ears to hear, a great rumbling and grinding filled the thin air. The Vixen schooled her face into an angry frown.

"Come here," she ordered through teeth that were still sharp despite her human shape. "Stand before me."

And Baba Yaga was there, hunched in her mortar, clutching her stained and battered pestle, her lips pulled back so her black iron teeth showed. She was as crooked as the Vixen was straight, as thin as the other was full, the colors of night, bone, iron, and blood.

"What would you of me?"

The Vixen stalked up to the Old Witch. "You have stolen what is mine, and then you have the gall to cross my lands."

Baba Yaga planted her pestle firmly on the green grass. Her leer became a death's-head grin. "Stole? I would say you lost him."

The Vixen took one step nearer, now close enough to touch the other, if she chose. The Old Witch did not flinch or pull back.

"The man Valin Kalami is my lawful prey. I will have him back."

"Will you?" Baba Yaga clacked her teeth. They too were stained and battered, like the pestle that she leaned on. "You make a great noise over a trifle for one whose mortal lands are about to fall to me."

The Vixen snorted and waved the words away. "The place men call Isavalta? What do I care for the shape of Isavalta? The empire falls and you have it, but the new lands are still my place to play and all my children's. The man Valin Kalami is another matter. He is mine, and I will have him back."

The Old Witch shrugged her bony shoulders. "I stole nothing. Your sons lost their quarry. Perhaps they grew bored, as they are known to do, and found other game. The man eluded them, and came to me."

"It was you who allowed Bridget Lederle to cross his path." The Vixen's hands curled into claws. "It was you who prevented her from using the sight I gave her."

At these words, the foxes appeared. They rose from the tops of the hills. They emerged from behind the thorn trees, and from out of the meadow grass. They were red, brown, grey, and white. They were tiny kits and the size of cart horses, and every one of them had the Vixen's green eyes, and sharp, yellow teeth, and every one of them stared at the Old Witch, ears alert, tails twitching, bodies tensed and ready.

The witch surveyed the Vixen's children, with eyes as calm and expressionless as a bird's.

"You will not send your sons for me," she said, but the Vixen noted how her hands clenched more tightly around her filthy pestle. "You will not start open war over this thing. It is not your way."

The Vixen's own eyes gleamed. "Are you so sure you know all my ways, Baba Yaga? Are you so very sure?"

"I know enough." The Old Witch grinned. "I know your game was interrupted, and I know you cannot prove I played any part in it, or you would not have bothered with this show. The man came to me freely, and I will keep what is mine."

"You will try," said the Vixen, her voice soft as summer mist and sharp as a sword's edge.

Baba Yaga only grinned. She snapped her teeth once at the mass of the *lokai,* and one of the kits yipped in fear. The witch grinned more fiercely. She thumped her pestle once on the green grass, and was gone, leaving behind nothing but a smear of blood on the crushed greenery and the thunder of her passage.

The Vixen, whose eyes saw far in her own country, watched Baba Yaga receding into the distance.

"Very good," she said to herself. "Yes. That was very good indeed."

Chapter Thirteen

It was night in Bayfield when Bridget and Sakra emerged. A full moon turned the cobbled streets to silver. It had only been a matter of months since she had last walked here, but already the place seemed strange to Bridget. The wood and stone houses were too square and plain, but the sparkle of moonlight on so many glazed windows was like a second field of stars. The black lake behind them stretched out flat as a pond until it merged with the night sky.

They had reentered the living world halfway up Bayfield's long bluff. The air smelled green despite the cold, and the lake appeared free of ice as far as she could tell, so it must be spring. The moon was well up, which made her think it was about midnight, or a bit after. Surely, a propitious time to be walking between worlds.

Sakra also gazed at the town spilling down the bluff.

"And this was your home?" he asked.

"No. I lived out on an island." Bridget nodded toward the darkly shining lake. "You can't see it from here."

"A shame. I would have liked to have known that place."

Bridget tried to picture Sakra in the lighthouse, perhaps sitting in the winter kitchen, stretching out his long legs under the table while she served coffee. It was not an image that came easily.

But that house was not hers anymore. The lake had thawed. Boats waited in the harbor, not just the fishing boats, but the big steamers come across from Buffalo for timber, or up from Chicago to deliver finished goods. The lighthouse would be lit, and someone else was the keeper now. Perhaps some man with a family of his own, husband and wife sleeping together in the room that had once been Bridget's. She shivered. It felt strange. She had walked out of that house and closed the door behind her, but she had not felt how finally she had given away her place in this world, until now.

"Perhaps another day. We shouldn't linger about." Bridget turned away from the lake and the hollow feeling inside her. "If I'm recognized, there will be . . . questions." *Especially in these clothes.* She looked down at her dress of Isavaltan velvet trimmed with fur and sashed with silk and lace.

"Especially if you are seen in the company of a strange man," added Sakra, matter-of-factly.

"I'm afraid so, yes."

"Well then, for the sake of your reputation, let us hurry."

She could not help but smile at his dry tone, even as she turned up the street toward the cemetery. She felt strangely glad Sakra could make jokes. He was worried about what had happened in the Shifting Lands. She was also worried, despite her confident words. She had acted on instinct, but now she heard Mistress Urshila's warning in the back of her mind. The woman was right, in so many ways. Bridget didn't know what she was doing. What if she had jeopardized their chances of returning to Isavalta? What if it turned out Anna were a prisoner there? What if Kalami had taken her, not just . . . killed her.

Bridget lengthened her stride.

The full silver moon lit their way. The clear sky meant it was cold, almost as cold as it had been in Isavalta, and her breath steamed white as she led Sakra from the street to the gravel path that ran between Bayfield's two cemeteries.

Nothing in the graveyard had changed. Bridget wasn't sure why she felt it should have. All the monuments stood just as they always had, pale grey above the darker silver of the frosted grass. The tree line was nothing but a series of shadows, some still and some in motion from the stiff breeze that blew off the lake and rattled the branches. The great oak, black and solid, stood sentry over the three stones; one for Mama, one for Papa, and the last one, the smallest one.

Bridget's heart constricted as she laid her hand on that stone.

I'm here, dearest. She remembered how she had said that, waking exhausted in the middle of the night to reach into Anna's cradle. *Mama's here.*

Conflicting emotions twisted inside her heart. She wanted the truth, she needed it as she needed air in her lungs, but at the same time she wanted nothing so much as to hike up her skirts and run away.

"I don't . . . I should . . ." Bridget bit her lip, and tried again. "What do we . . ."

Before she could complete the question, a long beam of pale light touched the grave. Bridget turned, startled, and saw a silhouette in fluttering skirts.

"She's not there."

Sakra stepped forward, ready to get between Bridget and the silhouette, but Bridget laid a hand on his arm.

"Aunt Grace?"

Grace moved out of the shadow of a granite obelisk. Bridget stared at her aunt for a long moment. She had lost weight since Bridget had last seen her. Her face had gone from round to gaunt. Instead of her usual carefully calculated collection of gaudy gypsy garments, she looked like a ragamuffin. A torn skirt of pale silk covered a dark work skirt. Tattered lace shawls that could have done nothing to keep out the spring chill had been tossed carelessly over her shoulders. One already lay puddled at her feet. A bangle dangled from her right ear but had no mate on her left. Her frizzled hair was a cloud around her head, unrestrained by shawl, hat, or pin.

"Not there. She's not there," and then, incredibly, she added in Isavaltan. "But you've come. I've been waiting so long. The cage won't hold a second time. She said that. He told me that."

Bridget could only stare open-mouthed at her aunt. "What . . ." she stammered.

Grace drew herself up, tall and imperious and suddenly familiar, but not as herself. "This isn't the one I expected," she said, still in Isavaltan. "Who is this?"

"This is Sakra," said Bridget, unsure what to add. *My beau? My suitor?* Her head was spinning so fast the idea of making polite introductions seemed quite ludicrous. "My friend."

"Bridget . . . ?" said Sakra softly.

"I don't know. This is my Aunt Grace, but . . ."

"Aunt Grace," Aunt Grace cut her off in English, dwindling back to her dowdy self and clutching at her lacy shawls. "Yes. I am Aunt Grace."

"I am honored to meet Bridget's aunt." Sakra gave the salute of trust. Grace looked him up and down, although dark as it was she could not have seen very much. "He seems more polite than the one you ran off with," she remarked.

Bridget let that pass, and hoped Sakra would be able to as well. At the moment it was hardly anything. "Aunt Grace, what's happened to you? How . . . ?"

Grace sighed. "You came back to find out if she was in her grave. Well, she's not." Grace swayed on her feet, her head whipping left to right, as if she were hearing something she couldn't see. "No, no." The words were again Isavaltan. "Not yet, I told you, the time is not yet."

"Is it possible your aunt followed you through the Shifting Lands?" asked Sakra. "That she has been affected by your family's magic?"

"I swear I don't know." Of all the things that might have come upon their return, Aunt Grace speaking Isavaltan had not even entered her imagination.

"I hear it," Grace said sadly. "I hear it all the time. It is trapped but it never leaves me alone." With those mournful words, Grace crumpled slowly to her knees.

Bridget and Sakra lunged forward to catch her before she toppled onto the grass. At the same time, another voice cried, "Grace!"

A new figure raced out of the darkness, a burly man in a peacoat who knelt at once beside Bridget's aunt.

"Grace, my God, I've been looking all over for you." He squinted up at Bridget and Sakra. "Who the hell . . ." he began, and then he drew back. "Miss Bridget?"

Now Bridget recognized him. This was Francis Bluchard, who ran the tug from Eastbay to Bayfield.

Frank Bluchard looking all over for Aunt Grace? Bridget was momentarily and ludicrously scandalized, but something akin to reason rapidly reasserted itself.

"Frank, what's been going on?" Bridget tried to keep the growing hysteria she was feeling out of her voice. Here was Aunt Grace collapsed at the edge of Anna's grave, saying she was not at rest in it . . . what on earth had she been *doing?*

"I should be askin' you," Frank shot back and for a moment Bridget wasn't sure whether he was answering the question she'd spoken aloud or the one she'd only thought. "Who's that?" His eyes narrowed suspiciously at Sakra.

"His name is Sakra. Frank . . ."

"This the one you ran off with?"

Bridget ignored that. Between them, Aunt Grace was staring at the ground, apparently oblivious to any of them, muttering in Isavaltan, "I tried, I tried, I tried, but they used, they used, they used . . ."

"Is there someplace we can take her?" asked Bridget.

Frank frowned stubbornly, but soon relented. "Back to her place. Come on now, Grace." With surprising gentleness, Frank raised Grace to her feet.

"Used, used, used," Grace muttered angrily, but then she looked up at Frank's eyes, and seemed to snap back to herself. "I can manage this much, thank you," she said, drawing herself up. Gathering her useless shawls about her shoulders she started toward the road. "Come with me if you want to find your answers," she said over her shoulder to Bridget and Sakra.

Bridget in turn looked at Frank. "What's happened to her?" she whispered. She did not know what Aunt Grace would do if she heard them talking about her.

"I don't know. She's been this way for about a week, since we went back to the lighthouse to clear out some of your things, like she said you asked her to." The accusation in Frank's voice was clear. "Sometimes she's gabbling away in her own language, and then all of a sudden she knows more about what's what than I do."

Bridget swallowed to keep from stuttering out the first six thoughts that jumped into her mind. "I didn't ask her to do any such thing."

"Yeah, I thought the story was pretty thin." Frank didn't look toward Bridget as he spoke, but kept his attention firmly on Grace's rigid back. "But she'd heard you'd gone, and about the fire, and she asked me to take her out there. I left her there, didn't see no harm, and went round to East-bay. When I came back for her, she was like . . . this."

"No," said Grace firmly, without turning around. "No more talk out here!"

"Why . . ." began Bridget.

"Because I say so!" Grace answered furiously. "And for once, one of you is going to do what I say!"

Bridget shut her mouth, and somewhat to her embarrassment, shrank back nearer to Sakra. What had happened here? What was going on?

Had she left something undone at the light? It seemed Aunt Grace must have been touched by Isavalta and what had happened there, but how?

Fortunately, Aunt Grace also decided to hold her tongue. They headed down into Bayfield with its straight, quiet streets. A few stray sounds floated up from the bars by the port, or down from the woods atop the bluff. All the houses were dark. There was no one to see, but Bridget still felt furtive. She had said good-bye to this place, to these people. She did not want to be here again.

In front of the apothecary window, Grace stopped in her tracks. She stared at the bottles of medicines and notions in the glittering in the window.

"It's not the right time," she said in Isavaltan. "These should have all been put away."

"Now, Grace." Frank stepped up quickly to take her elbow, as he obviously had many times before. "We talked about this. This way, girl."

"But these should all have been put away," Grace said, on the verge of tears. "That night is over with. It didn't happen. It didn't have to happen."

"Nice and easy now." Frank pushed open the narrow door that led to an equally narrow set of stairs to Grace's apartment over the apothecary. Grace let herself be led docilely, until they entered the flat. The sight of her own rooms seemed to shake off her melancholy. Without even a glance at Frank, she busied herself with lighting the lamps and poking up the fire in the stove. The windows, Bridget noted, were tightly shuttered. No light would show through to the street.

While Frank watched Grace, ready to intercede in case she was careless with the fire, Sakra looked about him with interest. He took in the lamps with their fringed shades, the wood-framed photographs covering the flocked wallpaper, the shelves crammed with china knickknacks, the hard, slick horsehair furniture and the worn rug. Bridget felt the sudden urge to assure him that she had kept a very different sort of house. She herself saw the dust, the pictures hanging askew, the shawl dropped carelessly by the beaded curtain that led to Aunt Grace's bedroom. The black stocking draped over the back of the sofa. She smelled the faint odor of refuse left indoors too long.

"Has she been . . . able . . ."

Frank seemed to know what she was driving at. "Her rent's paid to the end of the month." *By you, I'm sure,* thought Bridget as she watched his jaw grind back and forth. "But I don't know what I'm going to do. The harbor's all clear now, and I've got a living to earn."

Which would keep him out on the lake two or three days at a time, depending on where he was running out to.

At last Grace seemed satisfied with the level of light in the room. Indeed, Bridget thought it was overly bright. On one previous visit here, Aunt Grace kept the parlor dim so as not to "interfere with the vibrations." The faded, ill-cared-for furnishings looked even more battered in full light. Grace turned to the row of pegs by the door and began unwrapping her shawls, hanging the worn lace up fussily. "Thank you, Frank. You can go now."

"All right, Grace, if you say so." Frank glanced sideways at Bridget, a look that clearly said, *I will be back to talk to you.*

Bridget nodded, trying to convey, *we will take care of her,* in return. She hoped she was not telling a silent lie. "Thank you."

"Yep." Frank nodded, gave Sakra another disapproving glower, and left them there, although Bridget suspected he had second thoughts about doing so. Bridget found she didn't blame him in the least.

As the door shut, Grace gripped a coat peg as if that were all that was keeping her from falling over. Now Bridget saw the shadows under her eyes, deep black smudges that could only have come from whole nights without sleep. In the next heartbeat, Grace had pulled herself upright, and assumed the haughty stance that reminded Bridget of someone, but for the life of her she could not tell who.

But Sakra, it seemed, could. "Grand Majesty," he whispered.

His words staggered Bridget. *"Medeoan?"*

Grace turned to them, looking down her bulbous nose, and Bridget saw it. In the bright light, without the tricks of shadow and moonlight, she saw the faint reflection of the dowager empress laid over her aunt's pale, tired visage. But in the space of a breath, that reflection was gone, and Grace was simply Grace again.

"Medeoan is here," she whispered, as if afraid someone else might hear. The sound of that name coming from her aunt's mouth spun Bridget's world around yet again.

"Of your courtesy, mistress," said Sakra. "Will you tell us how this came to be, since the one who wore that name is dead."

"I know." Grace crossed the room to the wing-backed chair and dropped into it. It seemed to be a reflexive motion. "Her ghost was trapped at the lighthouse."

Bridget's knees gave way and she sat down abruptly on the horsehair settee. It was obviously no good to protest that Aunt Grace did not, could not possibly know anything of this, but that was what she very much wanted to do.

"She died at the lighthouse," said Sakra gravely. "It would be so."

"But surely as empress, she was bound to Isavalta," said Bridget. "She should be able to cross back." It was wrong to be speaking of such things here, in these shabby, showy, decidedly unmagical surroundings.

"Perhaps not, she held the reign falsely for many years."

"Hold your tongue, Southerner," snapped Aunt Grace and Bridget saw Medeoan looking out from her pale eyes. "It was not you I sent for."

Sakra fell silent at once, and Grace pressed her hand against her forehead. "She's here. She won't be quiet. I shouldn't have listened. I should have . . ." She squeezed her eyes closed. "It's too late now. Far too late."

Slowly, Bridget reached out and took her aunt's hand from her brow and held on to it. It felt strange. She had never made such an intimate gesture to Grace before, and had never foreseen a day when she would want to, but she was the only one who could offer the comfort the older woman so obviously needed now.

"Aunt Grace." Bridget spoke her name firmly, hoping to ground her in the here and now. "Tell me what happened."

Bridget listened in dazed silence as Grace related her story, from hearing the voice during one of her fake seances, to convincing Frank to take her to the lighthouse, to Medeoan talking her into . . . what?

"I thought I was only bringing her back with me." Grace tightened her grip on Bridget's hand. "Freeing her from the lighthouse. But she has not left me. She comes into my dreams when I am asleep. She comes in the day when I try to see my clients. She's living her life over, in my mind. She wants you, but she couldn't reach you, so she drives me to distraction, and plays out all her regrets over, and over, when she's not asking for you."

"But . . ." Bridget swallowed. This was no good. She could not go through this entire interview stammering like a schoolgirl. Aunt Grace was no fraud. She could do as she said, had done as she said. Accept that. Move on. "What is it she says she wants?"

"A chance to redeem herself apparently." Grace pulled her hand out of Bridget's and laid it in her lap, gazing down at her fingernails. "She says her land, this Isavalta of yours, is in grave danger and she wants to help. And I don't care about any of this," she added dully. "Just tell me you'll do what she wants and take her away."

Bridget opened her mouth and shut it again. Take away the ghost of Medeoan, the sad, insane, grasping dowager empress who had caused Bridget to travel to Isavalta in the first place? The idea that the woman was here, now, listening in the back of her aunt's mind left her chilled.

"It is a complex matter, mistress," said Sakra. "In life, the Dowager Empress Medeoan was dangerous and vindictive. It may be she is still so in the Land of Death and Spirit."

Grace closed her eyes. "I don't care what you *do* with her, just get her away from me."

"You may be sure we will not leave you in distress." Sakra glanced at Bridget as he spoke.

"No. No, of course not," Bridget said hastily. Her grievances against Aunt Grace were old and long-standing, but not enough to leave her haunted by Medeoan.

Or could it be a ruse? Could she and Medeoan's ghost be working together? Why? What would the dowager's shade have to offer her? Bridget bit her lip. After all this time, it was so hard to trust Aunt Grace.

Almost as if Bridget had spoken aloud, Grace lifted her head. Her eyes were full of Medeoan, and Medeoan's anger.

"Do you think I would believe you care?" spat Aunt Grace, and the ghost within her. "You did not come back because you care about me! You did not come back because you knew your work was unfinished and you knew the fate I had been condemned to! Oh, no, you came back for your child! Would you see your child? Would you? Then you shall!"

Grace blundered to her feet, her shoulders hunched, her head thrust forward like a crow in the cold. She blundered forward blindly, tripping over rugs, barking her shins against a chair.

"Aunt Grace!" Bridget leapt after her, a split second before Sakra. Grace tore the fringed shawl off the the blue glass sphere she used as a "gazing crystal," and slapped both hands hard against it. Bridget closed her hand around Grace's wrist, and . . .

And she saw.

She saw herself, as a young woman, hardly more than a girl. Despite the darkness surrounding this young self, she instantly recognized her old room in the keeper's quarters of the Sand Island lighthouse. Young Bridget lay awake, looking hungrily toward the window, watching the moon rise over the lake. Bridget knew which night this was. She could feel the anticipation of her younger self.

The young Bridget judged the time was right. She rose, tall and slender in her substantial white nightgown, and pulled on her shoes. She paused a moment to check her face in her mother's silver hand mirror, to pinch a blush into her cheeks and make sure her braided hair hung dramatically over her right shoulder. She took up a long shawl against the cold rather than her normal oilskin coat, but did not bother with candle or lamp. Carefully, she tiptoed down the spiral, wrought-iron staircase, pausing fearfully at an imagined stirring, and crossing her fingers that the weather would remain fair, and that the light had enough oil to get through for at least the next hour.

Outside, thick clouds scudded across the dark sky, lending the half moon a Halloween look. Bridget needed no more light than that to hurry down the stairs that led to the boathouse and the jetty, and the hollow underneath the cliff that could not be seen from the lighthouse.

No, no, stop. Don't, thought Bridget, but whether it was to her younger self, or the vision that unfolded she didn't know.

He came forward, but did not quite leave the shadows. Young Bridget saw the sweep of black hair, the shape of the strong face and body, and knew him to be Asa, the fisherman who had courted and won her to this meeting. Older Bridget looked close and saw and felt a stab at her heart like a knife.

Beneath the facade of Asa waited Valin Kalami. The sorcerer who had brought her to Isavalta with flattering lies, the man who would have murdered her to suit his own ends, he was the one who embraced her younger self. It was his mouth she kissed with heedless passion as he pressed hard against her, already lowering her to the ground.

Why? Why!

But she knew the answer. For the power. She was powerful, she knew that, and Sakra and Mistress Urshila had tried so many times to tell her that raw power was a lure to a sorcerous soul.

Anna, her innocent Anna, was Valin Kalami's child. A sob broke from Bridget's throat and she tried to tear herself free.

"No!" commanded Aunt Grace in a deep voice, quite unlike her own. "See the man. You cannot refuse now to see."

Aunt Grace's hand clamped around Bridget's like an iron band and Bridget knew that even if she closed her body's eyes, her mind's eyes would still see what played out before her.

Night again. A different night, because now the moon was no more than a thumbnail sliver in the clear sky. Again the keeper's quarters, but this time the front room, Kalami, not bothering to disguise himself as Asa this time, slipped through the front door. He carried something wrapped in a blanket under his arm. He concealed himself in the thickest shadows to wait but he did not have to wait long. Footsteps rang on the iron stairs, two people going up to the light, then silence.

Kalami smiled in the darkness. With infinite care, he opened the whitewashed fire door that separated the quarters from the tower stairs. Cautiously he stole upward, one soft step at a time.

This would be the dangerous part. There was no place to hide on those stairs. But no other door opened, and no footsteps descended. Kalami reached the second stairs and stole through the door. He crept to Bridget's room, to the cradle, and the sleeping child that lay there.

Bridget felt a tear trickle down her cheek, but she could not move. She could not do anything but watch.

Kalami laid his burden on the bed and unwrapped it. At first, all Bridget saw was a bundle of twigs and dried flowers. Then she saw Anna, lying unnaturally still on the bed. Slowly, patiently, Kalami lifted the true child and cradled her in the crook of his arm. He dropped the counterfeit in her place, so it fell, arms and legs akimbo, eyes staring dull and dead at the ceiling.

Death would be better than watching any more.

Kalami wrapped sleeping Anna up tenderly in the blanket and hurried down the stairs.

It wasn't until he was out of the house that the baby woke and began to cry, and by then, Bridget knew, her younger self would hear nothing, because by then she had found the counterfeit, and her own cries drowned out all other sound in her ears.

And the vision faded, and once again Bridget faced the distorted reflection of Aunt Grace's parlor in the side of her blue glass ball. Her cheeks were soaked with tears and her ears rang. She jerked her hands free of Grace's grip and pressed her palms against her eyes, shuddering.

Oh, God. Oh, God. Oh, God.

She heard Sakra murmur something, and a chair scraped and cloth rustled. Then, Sakra's familiar touch rested on her shoulder, but Bridget swatted it away, retreating to the windows before she was aware she had moved.

She felt filthy. She felt robbed. There had been only a few moments of that night she could think of without guilt or regret, and they were now gone. Kalami. Not Asa, with his laughing eyes and teasing ways who seduced a lonesome young woman, but Kalami who had lied to her and attempted to own her. He was the one who had given and then taken her daughter.

If he ever came within her reach again, she'd strangle him with her bare hands. If he was dead in the Shifting Lands, she'd hunt his ghost down and tear it to shreds.

"You never cared for me, despite your blood, so I can only hope I have helped give you something you can care for." Aunt Grace's words were crabbed and full of mockery. Bridget whirled around and saw only Medeoan, aged and angry.

"You witch!" she shouted, grabbing Medeoan by the shoulders and shaking her hard. "I should have killed you myself for what you did to me! Where is she? Where is my daughter?"

"Bridget, stop! I know where she is!"

Sakra pulled her back and Bridget blinked, and the image before her shrank in on itself and became Grace again.

"I'm sorry," she whispered. "I tried, I tried. I'm sorry."

Bridget backed away, gripping the collar of her shirt so tightly the buttons strained. Anger, pity, confusion, and a hundred other feelings swept through her. She couldn't stand to look at Grace anymore, not for another second. She knew herself to be as close to losing her mind as her aunt seemed to be. It was too much, being in this place. Fifteen years of pent-up frustration at Grace who had stood aside and done nothing boiled inside her, mixing with her fresher fury at a woman who had done far, far too much.

She faced Sakra instead. "How could . . . how could you know where Anna is?"

"The day I first saw you, I had just received news from my friend

Captain Nisula that he had seen in the women's palace of the Heart of the World a young girl with black hair and tan skin who was said to be the daughter of Valin Kalami. She was being held there as guest-hostage against his good behavior while he and the Hung-Tse planned the overthrow of Isavalta. That may very well be your Anna."

The Heart of the World? She knew about the empire on Isavalta's southern border from her studies with Mistress Urshila and her talks with Sakra. Urshila acknowledged it to be a place of learning and sophistication, but called its people treacherous. Sakra, speaking privately, said he had once believed it more civilized and comprehensible than Isavalta. It was certainly much older.

This was where Anna was? A hostage? The image of a little girl who was her baby in chains was almost more than she could bear.

Sakra covered her hands with his. "She was being well treated, Bridget. I swear. Despite what Mistress Urshila will have told you, they are an honorable people there."

"Oh, yes," sneered Medeoan's voice behind her. "So honorable they sponsored Valin Kalami to betray me."

Bridget felt something vital inside her snap in two. In a single instant, her blood turned to ice in her veins. One step at a time, she turned around. Medeoan stood before her in the translucent shell of Aunt Grace whose green eyes were terrified as they looked at Bridget.

"Get out, Medeoan," Bridget said. She reached inside, she reached outside, she felt the magic in her, distant but she could touch it. It was hers, this place was hers, and she would not be jeered at by this dead woman who had ruined Bridget's life before she even drew breath. "You're dead and gone! You're nothing! Get out!"

All unshaped, the magic swirled around her, a cold wind that somehow seemed to blow away breath itself. "Get out! Get out!"

"Stop!" Sakra ducked between them and brought both hands down hard on Bridget's shoulders. "Bridget Loftfield Lederle, stop this!"

Awash in her own magic, Bridget barely heard him. She would do this thing. From memory she heard Aunt Grace's own words. *For once, one of you will do what I say!* Medeoan would no longer be permitted to interfere with her, or with her family.

Aunt Grace, Medeoan shining through her very skin, raised her hands, seeking to divert the invisible current of Bridget's power, but she was too late. The outpouring of strength brushed the gesture aside. Soon, her power would fill the room, flood every crevice and cranny. Her power, her strength, would encompass everything, and everything would bend before her will.

That understanding sent a shock of exhilaration before Bridget, and she stretched farther, throwing open the gates within her, dragging in the power around her. The walls shook. The countless china knickknacks rang like chimes as they rattled against each other, crashing one by one to the floor as the glass in the picture frames above them cracked and snapped, dagger-sharp pieces dropping like ice on top of the fragmented porcelain. A chair shuddered, dancing across the floor as if pushed by drunken hands. The gazing crystal rocked heavily on its stand, thumping back and forth, a bass note under all the fragile ringing destruction.

Destruction, all the world changing shape, magic pouring forth like breath, like blood from her veins. And it was glorious. She could break apart the whole world, shatter it into pieces and remake it the way it should be, with Medeoan gone to Hell itself if she so chose and Anna beside her. All things were within her compass, and no one was going to determine their shape but her. *No one.*

The window frames creaked as the glass within them shuddered. Aunt Grace screamed again, and a thin trickle of blood ran down her forehead. Good. Good. Break her apart, let the ghost out and seal her tight again . . .

Slowly, beneath the ringing, cracking, screaming, swirling, breathing, bleeding that was all her own, Bridget became aware of words. Steady, careful words, words of peace, words of stillness. Deep words that sought to bind up the glory of her power, that meant to unmake her remaking.

That meant to stop her.

Bridget's power poured out fast, and faster yet, but now there was a dam between her flood and the world. She could see nothing but obstruction and wrong shaping, nothing of her, nothing but what she would, could, must make. Must break the dam of words first, then the whole of the world, must break, must, must must . . .

But the wall of words grew thicker, and stronger, and Bridget realized it was binding up her own power. The more she poured out, the stronger it became. She was fighting herself, and she would not break. A new scream sounded, torn from her own throat as the wall surrounded her, and the power rose around her like water in a well, ready to drown her utterly, but she could not stop, not even as the walls pressed closer and her hands lashed out to beat off a force that was not solid, barely real, but so strong, strong as blood, as water, as waves in a gale, sweeping her off her feet and covering her over until she could not breathe and all the world went away.

Sometime later, Bridget woke to a blinding headache and the realization that she was a mess. Sweat soaked her clothes, and bile stained the front of her shirt. Its bitterness filled her parched mouth.

She lifted her head, deeply, completely ashamed of herself. Sakra knelt before her, straight-backed, his long face calm but his eyes wary. Dark blotches showed on his skin, like the beginnings of bruises, on his cheek and around his eye.

Beside him, huddled on her knees, was Aunt Grace. A thread of blood traced a ragged, red line down her utterly white cheek, but her terrified eyes were all her own.

"Don't, please, no more," begged Grace so pitifully that Bridget's empty stomach curdled. "She can't help it. She tries, but death is the last change, and she is only what she was when she died and when she died she was so torn. Don't." She wagged her head slowly back and forth. "Help us. Help me."

Bridget moved her lips, but not a single word came to her. She managed to push herself up onto her hands, but it was Sakra who wrapped his arm around her shoulders. "Yes. We will help you. But you must rest now. Come."

He raised Grace up. Supporting her weight, he walked with her, brushing past the beaded curtain with his shoulder. He would have had no hard time guessing what that curtain covered. Bridget heard the whisper of heavy cloth and the creak of a bed's frame and springs. Trembling, Bridget pulled herself up onto the settee. The horsehair pricked her palms like so many tiny pins. She tried to sort out what had happened. She remembered the sounds of shattering glass and breaking porcelain, but as she looked around her, she saw all the photos whole in their frames, and the little knickknacks standing in their usual jumble.

Had none of it happened? Or was this Sakra's work?

Sakra reappeared from behind the curtain. One look at his exhausted eyes and Bridget knew which of those things was true. Sakra had stopped her torrent, and healed her damage, and it had cost him heavily to do so.

"Your aunt sleeps," he reported.

Sakra walked past her to the windows. He found the trick of the sash and the shutters and threw them both open, letting in a rush of cold spring air. For a time, he did nothing but stand there and breathe deeply, grounding himself, bringing order back to his mind.

"Is she hurt?" asked Bridget softly, remembering the blood. "Does she need attention?"

"No."

Bridget's fingers knotted in her stained skirt. It was an old gesture, one she had strived to rid herself of in that place where she was more likely to be wearing linens and brocades rather than plain, starched work clothes.

"This is what they were all afraid of. This . . . explosion."

"Yes."

She could only see his profile from where she was. The dark blotch of a bruise darkened his temple. *Turn around. Look at me.*

Forgive me.

Sakra did not turn. He watched the night through the window, drinking in deep draughts of air that smelled of clean water and returning green.

Bridget's fingers wove themselves together. Sakra had been a source of strength and reassurance to her almost since she'd met him, and now she wanted to be anywhere but next to him. "Were you afraid too?"

"Yes."

"And that's why you came." She spoke the words as a statement, not a question.

"Yes."

"Why didn't you tell me?"

Under the bruise, a muscle twitched. "I am not your teacher, Bridget. She did tell you, and you did not listen."

"If you had told me . . ."

"You still would not have listened." He threw back his head, looking to Heaven for strength or patience. "I have never known anyone who longed so much for place, for purpose, but when those ties you want so desperately bind you, you fight like a tiger to be free, and look surprised when those around you are hurt!" At last, Sakra granted her wish, and he looked at her, but there was no forgiveness in the gesture, instead there were bruised eyes full of bewilderment, and hurt, of his body and of his spirit. "You want change, but do not want yourself to change or be changed. You want to be given obedience without giving any in return. Mothers All! How can you have reached such an age and not realized the living world does not work in this fashion!"

His words might have jolted Bridget to her feet, but her knees were too weak to support her. Rage thrummed dangerously through her mind, and the memory of how strong she could truly be set her fingertips twitching, but she also heard the memory of breaking glass and saw afresh the heavy bruises on Sakra's face.

She had been warned, time and again, by Mistress Urshila, and she had dismissed those warnings. She had taken an oath of loyalty to the emperor and empress, and she had dismissed that as well.

She thought about her years at the lighthouse. Was there ever anyone more mistress of their domain than she? Nothing to do days and nights but keep her house, read her books, tend the light, and be alone with her memories. She had no one to answer to but the lighthouse board, and as long as the lamp stayed lit, and the inspector they sent out ever few years could see that regulations were being followed, they left her alone.

She had always thought of herself as a prisoner, but there had been a kind of freedom to her life. The freedom that came of having nothing outside oneself to hold on to.

That was what she had truly given up when she returned to Isavalta, and she had done so without realizing it.

Sakra was again looking out the window across the dark and sleeping expanse of Bayfield.

"You must decide," he said. "Now. Do you accept a life that binds you to others, or do you return to your light and your freedom?" His face was rigid. There were so many things she knew he would not say. He would not say, "Do you care for me?" He would not say, "What of your daughter?" He would not say, "I cannot let you return to Isavalta as you are. You may lose control again."

But I want to come back. I want my past, my daughter, my love. I don't want to be lonely and lost anymore.

But could she? After all her years alone, *could* she throw herself into such a life? She had made a very poor job of it so far.

She could go back, turn away. Stay here. If she couldn't go back to the light, there was surely somewhere she could go, to be alone, to be free.

Amid the surging jumble of thoughts, two things were very clear. If she stayed here, she would still be aware every moment of the untutored, uncontrolled power she carried within her, and she would know she had turned her back on Anna. Neither thing would ever leave her free again.

"I cannot do this alone," she said, her voice hoarse with more emotions than she could name. "I cannot be alone anymore, and I do not want to be alone anymore." Slowly, she unwound her fingers from each other and laid her long, work-worn hands on her knees. "I do not know what to do. I'm only certain of what must be done. I must help Aunt Grace. I must find Anna. Even if . . . even if she were not my daughter, she is a child trapped by disaster, and should be helped."

Slowly Sakra nodded. "I can help with these things, if you permit. But we do not have much time. I feel there is more happening here than our immediate concerns. The dead are not lightly involved in the affairs of the living."

"I don't understand. Medeoan involved herself."

"There is very little the dead can do if they are not permitted to. There is great freedom in death, and there is no freedom at all."

Bridget wanted to say that was nonsense, but bit the words back and tried to think of what she knew instead. She remembered her mother's ghost, coming to her on the night of the solstice in Vyshtavos, speaking of this meeting being permitted, by time, by Vyshko and Vyshemir. Even the dead had choices and limitations. Even the dead could be used.

"Permitted by whom? Or by what?"

"I don't know," said Sakra. "But I'm afraid we will find out before all this is over." The distant look of contemplation came into his autumn eyes. "I do know we would have had to come to this place, whether to find your daughter or not."

"Why?"

"Because knowledge comes in the abandoned places," he said, bringing himself back to the here and now to face her, his bruised face looking as tired as she felt, but his voice calm and even refreshed. "Because Medeoan knows how to cage the Firebird."

Chapter Fourteen

The cook grimaced as he slurped a ladleful of Urshila's soup. "It's cold."

"Yes, but at least it's cooked." Urshila poured the remainder of the broth back into the crockery pot, and into her hand dropped the round stone that had been part of her spell to turn the water, bones, and raw vegetables into soup.

After a whole day's trying, no spell had been able to raise the smallest spark. Hearth and oven remained cold and dead. The inner corridors of the palace were as dark as if the sun had never risen. Tannery, forge, and brewery were silent, and for once the work yard smelled of nothing but dust and the blowing wind.

Despite the house guard that was sent out at first light to both cry and gather the news, to urge calm and that people stay in their homes, the first of the townsfolk showed up at the gates just a few hours after sunrise. It had been the emperor's inspired idea to send Bakhar, the keeper of the emperor's god house, out to meet them and see that the gates were opened. Prayers to Vyshko and Vyshemir had been sung all morning, with the new arrivals joining in and replacing the tired voices. Whether the gods were listening or not, Urshila was not prepared to say, but it kept the people calm until the palace could make shift to feed and shelter those who would not, or could not, return home.

Like the other court sorcerers, Urshila had gone to the Red Library as soon as it was light, and with the others she had searched scroll, book, and memory for the lore of the Firebird, and the spells of bringing and controlling fire itself. But despite her work with Bridget, the habits of study were returning only slowly to Urshila, and as the sun passed noon and began to descend toward the horizon, she found herself cramped, angry, and more than a little frightened that there was so little of use in this great storehouse of knowledge.

It was of no help that the lord sorcerer was obviously dying. Daren had ordered a couch to be brought into the library so he could lie down and whisper orders to his two apprentices. The boys scurried this way and that to find the books Daren wanted. His skin was the color of ash and his eyes looked nearly blind. The boys had to hold up the books for he lacked the strength to raise his hands. Urshila was not even certain he could read them anymore.

Not one of the sorcerers said a word. They just read and consulted and murmured one to another as if nothing were happening. Daren had declared no one was to waste time and strength healing him, and that was that, and all obeyed, including Urshila.

Urshila tried very hard not to see Isavalta itself in his clouded eyes.

So, rather than loose her temper onto her colleagues and the dying man, she had retreated to the kitchens to see if there was anything she could do to help with the food. There was not enough bread, butter, cheese, or salt meat to keep the palace and those seeking its shelter fed for two days, never mind if their plight stretched out into weeks.

So, she had resurrected an ancient spell, one of the first her own master had taught her as being both extremely useful and very impressive should she, as many sorcerers did, ever have to take to the road and earn her keep in a strange holding or village. But while the soup was flavorful and the vegetables in an edible state, it seemed the Firebird would not even permit a single kettle full of warmth in its new domain.

But at least she had done something. There was soup to feed the hungry, and bread to eke out the palace's supplies, and she had gotten away from the books, the Isavaltan books that were full of rules and instructions as to what was allowed, and what was blasphemous, and what was even worse, what was Tuukosov.

"There exists the theory that history or sacrifice can permeate a place and cause it to be more favorable to one element or another," she had read, in the middle of a treatise on the symbols and sympathies that could be used to raise fire from earth, metal, or air. "But this is to be despised as the bloody art of the Tuukosov, and should you encounter any such who work from this theory you may know them to be untrue and place them suspect before the magistrates and *boyars*."

It did not surprise her. She had long known the books and scrolls were full of such. The gods all knew how each quarter day she had to listen to how Vyshko and Vyshemir saved the city of Isavalta from the foul Tuukosov invaders. But she paid that little attention, having set Tuukos aside a long time ago. This passage would not have even made her blink had it not been for her meeting with the ancient scullery woman yesterday. After that her thoughts had started traveling down old paths, pushed farther and faster by the growing fear that they would find nothing in the Red Library to defeat, delay, or appease the Firebird, even if they had all the power to be summoned by Bridget Lederle and her mythical daughter.

But there were other magics, older magics, older ways of knowing and other guardians to ask. But if she suggested any of them, she would be revealed. After that, even if she was not exiled or jailed, not one of those now closeted in the Red Library would hear a single thing she had to say.

Why am I even thinking of this? It's useless. Turning back to the old ways of Tuukos never saved one life. There is power and knowledge enough here. We will find what we need. I have made my choice. I will stand by it.

The cook gestured to one of his assistants who picked up the clay vessel and emptied it into the great iron kettle that would hold the needed amount, but being iron, resisted her workings.

"That should do for now, such as it is," said Cook. "Thank you, mistress." His reverence was perfunctory, and he turned to order his lounging assistants into motion. Two of them caught up the great kettle and struggled to carry it through the kitchen behind him without sloshing soup over the rim. For the moment when Cook passed, there was a vigorous banging of pots and scraping of vegetables. It all faded away when the door closed behind him.

Momentarily ignored, Urshila let herself sigh with relief. Her head was beginning to ache from repeating the same working a dozen times. Vyshemir grant they would have their answer soon, or her aching head would be the least of their worries.

"I thought sorcerers were able to conjure fantastic banquets from thin air."

The voice was so close beside her, Urshila nearly jumped out of her skin. When she was able to look around again, she saw the ancient scullery woman, a bucket in one hand, a worn scrubbing brush in the other. Her eyes twinkled shrewdly as she cocked her head toward Urshila.

Tired as she was, Urshila was not certain whether she wanted to laugh, or just turn away at once. "Without the tools for it, Honored Mother, I am as likely to be able to conjure down the moon." But that was a thought. The treasury held tools of magic locked in its depths. There might be one of the fabled cloths or staffs down there that could produce such a banquet. She must ask the lord sorcerer . . . if he could still speak.

She should get back to the library. She was wasting her time here, but she did not move.

"My daughter has forgiven me for importuning her earlier, ha?" The old woman squinted up at her.

Urshila shrugged. "We are all in this together now, Honored Mother. We will each grow as cold and hungry as the others." The unease in the kitchen was palpable. The servants were chatting and laughing as they idled by the great worktables, as if this were an unexpected holiday. But voices and laughter were brittle, and there were too many sideways glances and hunched shoulders. A fundamental thing had gone wrong with the working of the world. No one could help but wonder what could come next, when not even one of the court sorcerers could bring them warmth.

"None of the other fine sorcerers is willing to come down so far as to worry about feeding us all?" The old woman spoke softly, and she spoke in Tuukosov.

"No other so impatient as I," answered Urshila in Isavaltan. "But I have done what I can and must get back to the library."

"Done what you can?" said the woman before Urshila could finish turning away. "Are you sure? All that you can, Ulla?"

The last word froze Urshila where she stood. Only slowly was she able to force herself back into motion, and set down her heel, turn her torso, lower her chin to fully face the ancient woman again.

"How did you learn that name?"

The woman smiled. "I see farther than most." She swung the cloudy bucket of water toward Urshila, and Urshila looked automatically down into its depths, and glimpsed the tiny sphere of glass that rolled across the bottom.

A witch's eye?

Impossible. It could not be. That would mean this old woman was . . .

The servant gave Urshila a gap-toothed grin. "It is most likely, Daughter, that *I* am the one who remembers the year of *your* birth."

A thousand questions swarmed up in Urshila's mind: *How did you get here? What are you doing here? Who are you?*

But the ancient sorceress did not wait for her to voice any of them. "Would you save your precious Isavalta? Come with me."

Urshila had only a heartbeat to make her decision. The woman was already toting her bucket down the narrow servant's hallway, striding confidently into the pitch-blackness. In another moment, Urshila would not be able to see her at all.

Urshila snatched up her hems and followed the ancient sorceress into the shadows.

Within a few strides, Urshila's only guides were the slap of the sorceress's shoes on the flagstones and the rough stone and plaster of the walls under her outstretched fingertips. The darkness quickly took her sense of time, and the turns of the hall her sense of direction. The suspicion rose in her that the old woman was deliberately trying to disorient her.

I should have thought of that earlier.

Up ahead, the footsteps slowed and stopped. Urshila did the same. A door scraped open and a dim shaft of light fell across the grey flagstones. On the other side was some old drying room, or perhaps a cool room. Right now it seemed to be used for nothing but storage. Anonymous bales were stacked on all sides. Venting slits up near its ceiling let in a few grey and dusty sunbeams.

The woman set down the bucket and began shuffling through the bales, raising dust and the smell of ancient cloth. Urshila finally remembered she had a tongue.

"How am I to call you?"

"I am Senja Palo. The *murhata* know me as Semona."

Murhata. There was a word she had not heard in many a year. It meant "murderer," and was the Tuukosov way of referring to the Isavaltans, when none of them were listening, at any rate.

"Honored Mother, you spoke just now of saving the *murhata*." The word felt strange on her tongue, and brought back memories long buried. Memories of armed men in the darkness, of a young man pleading for his life, of the creak of the gallows tree as the bodies twisted in the winter wind. Of the ones who stood and stared and did nothing, nothing at all.

Of her father, with his dark eyes and face like stone. Of her mother shaking her and saying, *Do you want to die like your brother? Clinging to the old life and the blood magics bleeds them white, and they can't even see it!*

Them. Was that the first time mother had referred to the Tuukosov as "them"? It was the first time Urshila remembered.

"What voice do you hear?"

Urshila shook her head. Senja had straightened up and was staring right at her.

"Honored Mother." Urshila shook her head. "Time is precious. What is it you have to tell me?"

"Not yet, Little Daughter."

Urshila thought of the cold kitchen, the silent work yard, the growing crowd at the gates, Daren coughing out his life in the Red Library, and the coming night with its cold. "Vyshko's pike," she swore exasperatedly. "Yes, Honored Mother. Here, and now."

Senja wagged her head in regret that might have been real or only feigned. Urshila could not tell.

"You speak the name of the *murhata*'s high god," she said, sitting heavily down on one of the bales. "Have you ever heard the true story of their Vyshko and Vyshemir? Did your mother ever tell you?"

So there are limits to your knowledge after all. Urshila folded her arms. "Contrary to the normal way of these things, Honored Mother, my mother was the Isavaltan, not my father. She fell in love. She gave up everything she had and everything she was to marry him. She tried very hard to be a good Tuukosov, but she was still despised, and the fact that her children were only half-breeds kept any of the True Blood from aiding us when my brother was condemned to be hanged."

Her reward for her bluntness was to see surprise in Senja's wrinkled face, and sadness as well. Urshila's mouth pressed into a thin smile.

"The *murhata* hanged your brother, and it is the Tuukosov you hate?"

"The Tuukosov were our neighbors and family. The *murhata* were as much our overseers as anyone else's." She let that truth shimmer in her eyes and watched it take Senja aback. "So tell me, Honored Mother. Tell me the truth of Vyshko and Vyshemir. Tell me what it truly is to be from the Holy Island."

Now Senja's face had sunken deeply in on itself and her shoulders hunched farther down. She seemed to be feeling every one of her long years. For a moment, Urshila thought she might already have won, that the old woman would surrender in the face of the evidence.

She did not, but nor did she look at Urshila as she spoke.

"It began when raiders from Gesilo attacked the Holy Island. They burned and they plundered, and they carried off twenty sons and daughters from the clans to . . . discourage revenge.

"The Gesilan raiders fled to Isavalta, which was then only a single city on the banks of a river. For the right to ransom the captives, the Isavaltans granted them shelter.

"The clan heads met and it was decided that Isavalta could not be attempted at the time, and although the mothers tore out their hair and howled, it was decided to pay the ransom and negotiate their children's release, though it might take years.

"It did take years, but eventually all the captives were returned but one; a girl named Virve. Her captor conceived a love for her, and also conceived two children by her. These were Vyshko and Vyshemir. He would not part with Virve, or her children, no matter what the offered price.

"But Virve had told her children the truth of their blood, and when it became evident to her that they were both sorcerers, she hid this truth from her captor. She had the children taught in deepest secret so that one day they might be able to free her, and themselves.

"At last, the Tuukosov saw there was no way to free Virve but war. They brought the long boats down the river and laid siege to the city. Their only demand was the return of those of their own blood.

"But in the halls of Isavalta it was decided that they would pretend to give in to this demand, and then when the Tuukosov guard was down, they would all be put to the sword and the boats manned with Isavaltan sailors who would return to the Holy Island and wreak havoc for the temerity shown by those who would not abandon their own.

"This evil policy was overheard by Vyshko and Vyshemir and brother and sister conceived a plan. None know how, but Vyshemir escaped from her father and made her way out to the boats. She told the clan heads what the Isavaltans had planned, and then what she and Vyshemir had planned in response, and that it would cost three lives: hers, her brother's, and one other. Vivre's father offered his life up to make their working possible.

"The rest of the tale is as it is told by the Isavaltans. Vyshemir created the great sea, Vyshko the walls, but they did it to protect Tuukosov from the *murhata,* not the other way around, and their work held for five hundred years.

"That is the truth of the *murhata*." Anger heated Senja's voice. She met Urshila's eyes, and Urshila saw utter certainty there. "Even their gods are nothing but stolen, misunderstood images. They stole their empire from other, weaker neighbors, they stole their history and their magic. They stole half of yourself from you. They, not we, stole your brother's life. They made your mother afraid to stand by her heart and condemned you to a servant's life waiting on their pleasure.

"You could choose to help punish those thieves. You could make a new choice, here and now. There is time yet, Daughter, for you to use your skills justly and make whole your wounded past."

Urshila's world tipped. The force of Senja's sincerity pushed away her own certainties. Her speech in the old tongue was a reminder of home, when home was small and close and warm and filled with smiles and the safety of family. It made her life and schemes as a courtier seem brittle by comparison.

Her arms were still folded, and now she gripped her elbows tightly, hugging herself to herself. She had come here with one mind, but now she was split in two, cloven again into Tuukosov and Isavaltan, each side drenched in their blood hatred for the other.

She thought of her brother's body twisting in the warm summer wind on a day when there would be no night except in her mother's heart.

She thought of the members of her father's clan standing mute as the soldiers hauled on the rope.

She thought of the ones she had seen in the streets of Biradost and other towns, the ones with dark hair and dark eyes, kicked and cuffed and forbidden to enter where "decent" folk might walk freely.

She thought of the dowager empress, with her angry, terrified eyes, ordering Urshila's expulsion, condemning her to thirty years of poverty for no reason that existed outside her own mind.

Then she thought of something else. She thought of Bridget Lederle sitting before the Council of Lords.

"It was Kalami who convinced her to finally kill Mikkel," Bridget had said, her voice thick with sorrow and sickness. "They could blame his death on Ananda, and that way they'd be able to get rid of her without risking war."

It was Kalami who convinced Medeoan to kill Mikkel, her son. He had convinced a mother, a woman whom he had helped drive mad, to kill her own child.

Was there any act, any blood price high enough to transform such a thing into justice?

Urshila lowered her arms, smoothing down her dress. "Honored Mother," she said, "you implied you had news that could save Isavalta. Will you give me that freely, or do I have to go to the lord sorcerer and make confession of all our secrets?"

The hope, the certainty, that radiated from Senja dampened. "Then that is the only reason you came?"

Urshila's mouth tightened into a mirthless smile. "Honored Mother, what other reason could there be?"

Senja sighed again and ran a hand through her hair, looking very old indeed. She had probably known one too many defeats in her life. Urshila was sorry to give her another, but she could not and would not justify what had been done in Tuukos's name.

"Very well," said Senja. "If that is all you will do, it will have to be enough. Come here and look." She pointed at the bucket and the witch's eye.

Urshila leaned over and saw the glass sphere shining at the bottom of the clouded liquid. She cleared her mind, ready to see what the eye might show. Quick as a fish, Senja's hand darted into the water and splashed a great handful into Urshila's face.

Sputtering, Urshila reeled back. For a moment, she just stood there, blinking hard and shocked at the cold and the stench of the water.

But blinking did not clear her sight, and her arms went cold even as she reached up to try to wipe the water away. The dim room swam before her eyes, and her mind began to reel.

Poison, she thought. *Magic.*

Her hands had gone numb. She could not feel them work her fingers to make a warding sign. She could see nothing but a blur of grey. The cold crept down into her throat, cutting off voice, breath, and strength.

She felt her knees buckle, felt her knees hit the floor, then her shoulder. Then there was nothing more.

Senja watched Urshila crumble into a heap on the grimy stone floor. She wiped her hand dry on an ancient, yellow cloth, then laid that cloth aside so she would remember not to touch it.

Slowly, for her old bones were heavy with regret, she crouched down beside the woman who had once been Ulla. She could still hear her breathing, rasping and shallow.

"What did you think I would do?" she asked. "What did you think I would have to do? I knew what you had done. There was no time to search your rooms for the working. Your death will break it. I tried, Ulla, you cannot say I didn't try. If you'd been willing to help us, you could have lived. I am sorry, Daughter."

Urshila, Ulla, tried to stir, but she was too weak. Senja felt the Grandfather's silent presence in the room, and stood.

"We must have Kalami back, you see," she said, to the dying woman, to the Grandfather, to the regret in her heart that she had not been able to make Ulla understand. "He brings the daughter, and the daughter is the surety of the mother. We will finish the work Kalami began. Bridget Lederle will give us the Firebird and all its power, for what would she not do to reclaim her lost child?"

Chapter Fifteen

Daren, lord sorcerer of Isavalta, lay on a couch in his workroom, struggling to breathe. The action took all his concentration, robbed all other thought of meaning, and made any other movement impossible. He was aware that others moved around him. Occasionally they spoke, but their words were increasingly difficult to understand. Nor could he understand why they kept the room so dark, and so cold.

No. Wait. That was why he was here instead of his own bed. The dark. The cold.

The Firebird.

"Lord Daren?"

He had fallen into vision and from there into dream so many times he seldom knew where his mind was anymore. The present stepped carefully around him, occasionally whispering in his ear. But when he tried to answer, it was from under the weight of his pain and he found it nearly impossible to understand what he was saying.

"No. I will try. He would want to know. Lord Daren?"

Whose voice? Urshila? No. This was Korta. He had not heard Urshila speak in . . . a long time.

Why should he think of her now? Had he dreamed? A dream of a gull rising up from the cellars of the palace, and soaring into the night, like the Firebird, was it the Firebird? Was it just a dream and a memory of his vision that caused him so much pain?

"Lord Daren, Mistress Urshila is dead."

Dead? Urshila dead? No, she was the gull rising up to meet the Firebird, watched by Valin Kalami.

Who was dead. Who was dead? Urshila was dead. Kalami was dead. Why was Kalami watching Urshila?

"They found her with a witch's eye in her hand. She drowned herself. She was Tuukosov."

You didn't know that? No. Of course not. It was not discussed. Did Urshila even know Daren himself knew?

"She betrayed us, Lord Daren."

No. This is wrong. Wrong.

"We think she was trying to finish what Valin Kalami started. She might have managed to bring the Firebird back here. We are searching her rooms now to find what working might have made the summons so we can construct the banishment."

No. That is not right. It was Medeoan who brought this on us. It was we who brought it on ourselves. What we did and what we permitted to be done. If we do not understand that, we will never rid ourselves of this darkness.

The pain was so heavy. His body was unmarked, he knew. This pain was on his soul, on his mind that had seen the Firebird pass overhead and been seared by its fire. But they were wrong. Urshila did not do this thing. He had to tell them that. He had to find mouth, find breath and speak.

"Rest yourself, Lord Daren." Hands on his shoulders, pressing him back, adding their weight to the weight of the pain.

"No."

Whose voice was that? Was that straggling whisper his voice?

"Lord Daren?"

Eyes. I have eyes to see the world. I will find my eyes.

It hurt. He was so tired. Dreams dragged at him. But for a moment, he focused his will, and he opened his eyes.

Korta leaned over him, his face creased with concern. Beyond him, Daren could just see ancient Luden, books piled around him in crooked stacks.

Where were Sidor and Nedu? Oh, yes. They were searching Urshila's room for what wasn't there.

Never mind. No time to think on them. "Urshila." His voice grated in his throat. Pain made his mind's eye see red.

"We none of us knew." Luden hobbled closer. He seemed smaller than he had and more deeply hunched. What new weight was he carrying? "Rest yourself, Daren. She can do no more than she has. We will unearth her plan and unravel it."

No! He wanted to shout and pound his fist. But all his anger gave him only enough strength to say, "Not Urshila. Not her plan."

Korta licked his lips. "She's Tuukosov, Lord Daren," he said gently, as if reminding a child of a forgotten promise. "She did this and killed herself before we could discover her and make her talk."

Did they believe Urshila was that much of a fool? Vyshko and Vyshemir look down with mercy. They did. Because she was Tuukosov and Kalami was Tuukosov.

And because she was Tuukosov, they would not try to discover who had truly killed her and why.

"A seeing," Daren croaked. "Did you . . ." *It hurt. It hurts. I must speak.* ". . . work a seeing?"

"There was no need, Daren." Luden. Daren heard feet shuffling across the floor, and Luden's face came into view, sinking close enough that even Daren's tear-clouded eyes could make him out clearly. "It was all before us. I too am stunned, but it brings us that much closer to the answers we need."

No! Disbelief robbed him of his strength ebbing for a moment and he had to close his eyes. A hand, it must have been Korta's, laid itself upon his brow.

"He's failing," Korta whispered.

"Yes," agreed Luden. What lay behind that neutral tone? Anger overrode his pain for just a moment. Did Luden think to become lord sorcerer once the Grandfather had taken Daren to the Land of Death and Spirit? So be it, but while Daren breathed he was still lord sorcerer. He could still command. He would.

Daren forced his eyelids back. "Work a seeing, Korta. Find . . ." Fresh pain lanced through his lungs as he spoke. "Find what happened to her."

Then, Daren saw the flash in Luden's ancient eyes, and knew he had made a mistake. It was Luden he should have spoken to, not the boy. Luden would take it as an insult.

Ah, Vyshko and Vyshemir, even now the games of power must be played. Why have we been made thus?

Luden straightened, his face becoming nothing but a white haze. "The lord sorcerer is tired from his affliction. He does not truly understand the facts. You will continue with your work, Korta."

"But, Master . . ."

He could not even see Luden anymore, but the old sorcerer's words fell heavily against his ears. "We cannot work a seeing without fire, Korta. Were the lord sorcerer well, he would remember this. Come, now. We must be ready when Master Sidor and Mistress Nedu find the Tuukosov's summoning."

No fire. Had he the strength, ~~Luden~~ Daren would have cursed gods and Firebird both. The summoning of a true vision required all the elements. Without fire there was no stability to the working, no clarity. His blood and soul burned with pain that was dragging away his life by inches, but there was not one true flame to be summoned.

Or was there? Daren's frame shuddered. He had been touched by the Firebird. He burned within. Could he summon the fire of his pain? Could that ephemeral flame be used to bring the vision of what had happened to Urshila, and what was happening to Isavalta?

If it can be done, it will be the last thing I do.

It would leave Luden in charge, blind, power-hungry Luden to shape a little court of his own with Korta and Nedu helpless against him and Sidor perhaps his willing partner. Daren might not die. He might recover yet. Even Medeoan had not been able to finish him off. He was not ready to meet the Grandfather yet.

Or I might die anyway, traitor to my oath to serve, and to my land that gave me life.

Daren made his decision. It did not lessen the pain, but knowledge that pain would soon end made it easier to bear. He mustered his hoarded strength, and sat up.

"Lord!" cried Korta.

Daren did not waste his breath answering. He heaved his legs, as heavy and unresponsive as clay, over the side of the couch. The pain lanced through them a moment later, but at least it let him feel his knees and his feet. Clamping his teeth down on his tongue to keep from screaming, Daren stood.

"Lord Sorcerer, you cannot . . ." That was Luden. Daren ignored him. He knew what he needed. One agonizing step at a time he lurched down the length of the room toward the table that was set apart from all the others, the table covered with delicate wires and gears and gems wrapped in wires of copper and bronze. The ruin of the Portrait of

Worlds lay before him. It filled the whole world. It was all that he needed.

It seemed Korta guessed what he was about. "My lord, the Portrait is broken."

So am I. He stood before the table, swaying back and forth, trying to see how he might do what must be done.

"Daren, do not do this." Luden again. Was that true concern in his voice? Daren could not turn his head to see the other man's face. He could only stare at the collection of delicate components in front of him, all neatly laid out on their squares of white and blue silk. The work of a century, and more, bent and broken and scattered.

He reached out a shaking hand and grasped one of the tiny sapphires. What it had once been, he did not know, but now it would serve for the palace. The sapphire was the imperial gem. Next, he pulled one of the silk squares toward him. The wires and gears that covered it tinkled delicately as they jumbled together.

"I have come to the wild place," he whispered. "I have stood before the broken mirror and I have called it by its name." Each movement seared him. His hands were so weak, the silk slid through them even as he tried to gather it up, to tie the knots, to begin the weaving. "I have called it the Portrait of Worlds, I have called the creator by his name, Tsepir Senoisyn Vinnetsavin, child of Vyshko and Vyshemir." Cold swept through him. The walls seemed to grow close, listening with their suffocating stones.

No. Not now. He must not be cold. He must be fire. He must burn.

Daren reached within himself, he reached out. He forced his hands to move, to clutch the silk, to begin the knot. He coughed for breath, for air. He spat, for water. Metal and gems waited within the silk, that would do for earth. With fire, the whole world would be with him, and he could weave all together.

On the table beside the pieces of the shattered portrait lay the tools Daren had used to begin his painstaking repairs, the long pins of silver and gold, the tiny hammers, the snips, and the pliers, all made of the finest brass and copper. Steel, that child of iron, could not be used to mend or make a tool of magic.

Daren picked up one of the silver pins. It was the length of his middle finger and as thick as a piece of coarse twine.

"My lord!" cried Korta and Daren's concentration faltered. He heard the slap of skin against skin and knew what had happened. Luden had seized the boy's hand, had held Korta back.

Perhaps I misjudge. It didn't matter. He must not falter. He must reach inside, he must reach outside, he must gather all the world into himself and his weaving. There must be earth and air and water.

And fire.

Daren drove the silver pin into his hand.

The pain exploded inside him, making him see stars and flames. The blood ran hot down his wrist and Daren pressed his hand hard against his silken bundle and the uncompleted knot.

Hands moved against his hand. The whisper of silk crossed his skin. Korta? No. Luden. Tying the knot, binding his hand to the broken portrait. Finishing the working.

"I make the mirror whole again. I see the picture unbroken again. I see the fate of Urshila . . ." No. No. It cannot be that name. It must be the other. "I see the fate of Ulla Raadhar." Beside him Luden started. *Yes, I knew. I know. I permitted her to remain, for I also knew where her loyalty lay.* Pain wracked him, robbing him of words and breath. He must not break. He must be whole. "I see her death and how it was accomplished."

"This is my word . . ." Daren gripped the edge of the table with his one free hand. The feeling was leaving his hands. The fire was dying. The floor rocked beneath him. "My word is firm. This is my word and my word is firm!"

Before him the sapphire shone and sparkled. It glimmered like a tear-filled eye, and like an eye Daren could see the reflection in it. In that reflection he saw Urshila, Ulla, Urshila, and a bent, ancient woman in drudge's clothes. He saw the witch's eye, the bucket of water, how the old woman tricked Urshila near the water, and how Urshila died. He saw that same old woman bundle the corpse into a length of half-rotted cloth and coax another drudge to help her carry it out to the canal, and heave it in.

And with that seeing, he slipped to the floor before the others could catch him. He was nothing but pain now. The connection between flesh and spirit was dissolving, burned away by the fire he had set free.

"Did you see?" he whispered, barely able to hear his own voice for the roaring of the pain in his mind. "Did you?"

"Yes, Daren." Luden took his hand. "It was enough. You can go now."

And the lord sorcerer of Isavalta closed his eyes and gave himself over to the fire.

Sakra insisted he and Bridget try to snatch a few hour's sleep. They put out all but one lamp and Bridget curled herself up on the horsehair sofa, trying to ignore how it itched. Used to sleeping wherever he could find a place, Sakra stretched out on the carpet in front of the stove.

Taking advantage of the dim light, Bridget watched him, taking in afresh the length and shape of his body. Her mind, tired of dwelling on fear and disaster, to her surprise began wandering in directions she had scarcely dared admit to herself she had traveled before. All things considered, it was late in the day for maidenly modesty, but as grim, as uncertain as things stood with them now, such ideas were hardly appropriate, or timely. She had much to prove, to herself and to him, to show that her words were not just desperation. It would take time, and given what waited in Isavalta for their return, God Almighty, given what waited in this flat with them now, that time might not be hers.

But if it was . . . surely it was permissible to dream of what might be, of his hand touching hers more than fleetingly, of drawing her fingers down his face, and his throat, of what love might be when it was more than a flash point on a night in summer, of when it was slow and gentle, and not a lie but a true thing.

Sakra was propped up on one elbow, and staring at her. The realization shook Bridget from her reverie and raised a hot blush in her cheeks.

What must he think of me now? Everything she was thinking must have shown in her face. Lord, would she never stop making a fool of herself?

But nothing in Sakra's expression said he thought her a fool. Instead, his eyes were as full of wishes as her own must have been; wishes for freedom, for knowledge, for permission, for love, and for the time to make all those wishes come true, oh, especially for time.

She thought he was about to speak, but instead, the air was broken by the unmistakable retching sound of someone struggling for air.

Bridget was on her feet and through the doorway to Aunt Grace's room in an instant. Sakra followed close behind, carrying the lamp.

Aunt Grace lay on her narrow bed, whooping, and choking in a terrifying battle for breath. The fight arched her back like a bow, half lifting her up and then slamming her down again so the bed springs creaked and rang and the whole frame rattled from her struggles.

"My God." Bridget ran to her aunt's side. She grasped Grace, pulling her close to try to still the frantic straining. Grace's eyes were wide with fear and strain. She coughed with a noise like a dog barking, but her throat did not clear.

"Fading," she gasped, her whole body bucking against Bridget's as every muscle in her strained to force her lungs into motion. "Fading!"

"What?" Bridget wasn't sure who she was asking the question of. She tried to turn Aunt Grace's face toward her, but her aunt fought the gesture, swinging her head wildly back and forth.

"She!"

Bridget managed to capture her aunt's chin and turn her face toward the light. Grace was seized with a consumptive wheezing and her lips were tinged a dangerous shade of blue. Was she choking? She was not acting like it. What was happening? "Medeoan," said Sakra. "Medeoan is fading."

"What?" asked Bridget again. She forced Aunt Grace's legs up, and bent her down so her head was between her knees. "Breathe, Aunt," she ordered, rubbing Grace's back frantically, trying to help her muscles to loosen, to work more normally. "Don't try to talk. Breathe."

Sakra tried to take Aunt Grace's wrist and look for a pulse, but she flailed out at him.

"No! Not him!" If there were more words, they were broken apart by another spasm of barking coughs that shuddered right through Bridget.

Sakra stood back, his face grave to the point of fear. "The ghost, it has possession of her body. Its essence is dissipating, it will soon be gone. It is using Grace's life to keep itself here."

Blood speckled the coverlet. Grace's hands had gone ice cold. She could not tolerate this much longer. "What can we do?"

Sakra looked away quickly and looked back again. His bruises seemed to deepen. "Can you see Medeoan at all?"

"Aunt Grace, look at me. Look at me." Bridget tipped her aunt's straining, terrified face up. Grace choked as she tried to swallow and Bridget trembled, but she concentrated, and she looked deep.

"Barely. She is still there."

"You will have to reach for her, Bridget. You can see her and follow where she goes and convince her to let your aunt go."

Bridget felt her own bone-deep weariness. She had spent herself into delirium and then into unconsciousness barely an hour ago. She quailed at the thought of having to draw on that part of herself again, but there was no choice. Grace huddled against her now, limp as a child, panting raggedly. "How?"

"I will send you." He saw the question in her eyes, but did not wait for her to voice it. "For many years Medeoan believed you would help her. She never believed so about me, and will not be able to now."

Aunt Grace's spasming hand caught Bridget's wrist.

"Help," she wheezed. "All I wanted . . . was to help."

Medeoan shone brightly in her aunt's eyes at that moment, and Bridget could not tell who the words had come from. But Bridget had looked into the eyes of the dying before, and knew what she saw in Aunt Grace's face.

"We must hurry," she said to Sakra. "Have you the strength for this?"

"We have, if you will trust me."

She nodded.

Sakra did not waste time with another word. He reached for the red band that tied his hair back and pulled it free. The dozens of braids cascaded around his shoulders, the beads rattling and clacking against each other. Aunt Grace's grip convulsed painfully, digging her nails into Bridget's skin, but Bridget did not pull away. Aunt Grace needed contact now, needed the warmth of life to help her hold on.

Sakra took Bridget's free wrist and looped the red braid around it. Bridget made herself remain still, her mind open. She had some idea what was about to happen, and she strove to hold herself ready for it.

Sakra began to sing. His voice was deep and well trained and filled the dim little room with its richness, the strange syllables she could not understand rising and falling in steady waves. Winding the band around his own wrist he joined them together with the words and the silk. She felt the chill in the air and the deep current that came with the working of magic. Although she did not understand the words that evoked his magic, she felt their pull reaching under skin and bone, seeking the touch of her powers, her gifts.

She balked at first. She could not help it. The touch was too personal, too intimate, but she gained control of instinct, and reached inside, giving of herself to aid in this working.

Sakra's power accepted the gift of her own, and his song wove it with his, shaping it, turning it into a lifeline for her to hold, to follow. She could see it now, shining in the dim light. She felt the pull of it, as if it were a physical bond like the one about her wrist. It drew her down and into herself even as the song pulled her outward. She looked toward Aunt Grace, and she saw Medeoan.

It was a moment of stark clarity. She saw Medeoan's blue eyes, her greying hair, the deep lines of fury in her face, graven so much more starkly than the ones care had etched onto Aunt Grace's. The two were bound, more tightly even than she and Sakra now. She had expected to see that it was Medeoan's grip that held Aunt Grace so tightly, choking her, but Medeoan too was bound, and Aunt Grace clung tightly to the dowager's ghost, as if her entire soul depended on the presence of the spirit of a stranger.

The lifeline, the path created by Sakra's song and the weaving of their magics, led between these two, even though there was no way between. They were one, clinging together like two people drowning and dragging each other under, and yet Bridget knew she must follow. She must see the way. She reached for the place where her mind's eye was and willed it to open, willed herself to see what was hidden, what was true beneath the illusions and the bindings, to see Medeoan and be seen by her, and with that sight, with all the presence of self that she could muster, she followed Sakra's lifeline to that place where Grace and Medeoan walked.

She thought it would be something like entering the Land of Death and Spirit; the green light, the silence, the sense of some vital element missing from the air. She had been mistaken. It was like drowning. A cold heaviness rose around her, not parting to let her in, but yielding as she forced her way into its alien element. Image and light spread out, rippling and blending. Only the slender line she was pulled by remained clear.

I will see. I must. You cannot remain hidden from my sight. I do not permit it.

In her mind she heard again the strains of Sakra's spell song. She held them tight, weaving her determined thoughts into them, willing them outward to the watery blur of light and color that her world had become.

So slowly that her eyes strained and her head ached, the new world took shape.

To her surprise, Bridget found herself in the Long Gallery of the palace Vyshtavos. It was complete in every detail, with all the portraits in their places on the walls and fires crackling in the three fireplaces.

Medeoan and Aunt Grace stood before the center fireplace, clinging tightly to each other's hands and leaning together so closely and at such drastic angles that if one of them let go, the other would surely fall. Their heads were both tilted up in identical attitudes and they gazed at one particular portrait.

Bridget walked forward, Sakra's lifeline now no more than a shining thread wrapped around her wrist. Medeoan stirred a little, gradually becoming aware of Bridget's approach, although she made no noise. The dowager lowered her eyes to take in Bridget. Stiffly, puppetlike, Aunt Grace mimicked the dowager's gesture.

"These were my parents," said Medeoan, returning her gaze again to the portrait. Aunt Grace's head turned and tilted as well. "My husband murdered them."

"I know. I'm sorry." Bridget licked her lips. "Hello, Aunt Grace."

Aunt Grace did not look at her, nor did she loosen her hold on the dowager. It would have been comic were it not so appalling, two aging women in a gallery of portraits, looking back over the past, clinging only to each other.

"They're waiting for me, with Vyshko and Vyshemir." Medeoan spoke the words fatalistically. "I will have to answer for what I've done."

There was nothing Bridget could say to that. Grace leaned a little closer to the dowager. Her fingers dug into Medeoan's sagging skin.

If Medeoan felt any pain, she did not show it. She just tightened her own grip on Aunt Grace, leaving white circles around each fingertip on Grace's skin. "I didn't feel that way when I ruled. I felt I was right. I did what was necessary for Isavalta. There is not an emperor in the whole of history without blood on their hands. Most especially the blood of their family. I knew that."

"You knew a great deal," said Bridget carefully. She knew that she was seeing what was true, but only to an extent. The truths here were metaphoric, a representation of what was happening within Aunt Grace. The truth was the two of them were growing closer, not farther apart, and they were hurting each other to do so. Medeoan had no life left to lose, but Grace could still so easily lose hers.

"I did know so much. I still do." The dowager sounded wistful.

Bridget hesitated, uncertain of how to proceed. Part of her wanted to storm across the space between herself and the spirits and force them apart, but she held back. A hammer blow at this point might shatter all, and she must not forget they needed Medeoan who was weakening even as Aunt Grace was.

Aunt Grace rested her head on Medeoan's shoulder in a dreadful parody of affection. Somehow it was seeing that which broke Bridget's paralysis. "May I speak with my aunt?"

Medeoan shrugged. The gesture made Grace's head bobble grotesquely. "I am not the one who holds her silent."

"Aunt Grace?"

Aunt Grace turned her head, pressing her face against the dowager's neck, a child looking for comfort.

But it was Medeoan who staggered then, and Grace who steadied her. "It seems she has nothing to say to you." The dowager's voice grew breathier, as if she were also short of air.

"I don't believe that."

Medeoan's answering smile was thin and a little sad. "You doubt the evidence of your eyes at last?"

Anger finally made its way through Bridget's fear and hesitation, goading her into motion. She rounded the duo until her back was to the fire and the walls of portraits. "Aunt Grace, it's Bridget."

Grace lifted her head, looking about her curiously, as if she just found herself in this place, but it seemed to be of only mild interest. Yet her hands maintained their death-grip on Medeoan, and the two women swayed as if blown by a wind.

"I don't believe she can hear you," said the dowager, her voice was mild, but the tone fell flat.

Bridget reached out, uncertain whether she just meant to touch her aunt, or to try to grab her and shake her. Her arms would not reach. She could see the women, leaning together, less than two steps away from her, but when she stretched out her hands, she could not reach them. "Aunt Grace!" she cried. Grace continued to contemplate the paintings over Bridget's shoulder. "Is this your doing?" Bridget demanded of Medeoan.

"You did this between you." The dowager tried to shake her head, but she managed only a tremor. *Not much time left,* that thought and fresh fear stabbed at Bridget.

Fear banished thoughts of subtlety. "Will you let her go?"

"No." Bridget would not have thought it possible, but the dowager pressed herself closer yet to Aunt Grace, and Aunt Grace gathered her near.

"Why not?"

Medeoan looked at her as if she were simple. "We need each other to be."

Memories came crowding into Bridget's mind, thick and fast as she faced the dowager's mildness. She remembered the fearsome, frightened woman in the golden robes. She remembered seeing her crumbled on the floor beneath the Firebird's cage, and seeing the vision of Mikkel's murder at his mother's orders. She remembered excoriating Medeoan for what she had allowed herself to become. All the memories jabbed at her temper and her own fists tightened. *Stay calm,* she ordered herself. *Keep your wits together. Try to find out what's really happening in front of you.*

"Why does Aunt Grace need you?"

But Medeoan did not appear disposed to be helpful. Like Grace, she returned to the contemplation of the portraits. "You will have to ask her that."

"But you said she cannot hear me."

"Yes, I did."

For a moment, Bridget felt the absurd impulse to laugh. "I do not have time for this."

Both Medeoan and Grace leveled their gaze upon her. "Nor do we."

She felt the words hit her heart. They brought freshly home how weary, how hungry she was, and reminded her that she too was expending herself, as was Sakra. How long did any of them have? She glanced down at her lifeline. Was it dimmer than it had been, or were her eyes growing tired?

Concentrate, Bridget. "She said you were fading."

"Yes." By some common agreement, Grace and Medeoan walked a few steps farther down the gallery. It was a strange, limping, sideways gait that both kept them pressed together, and allowed them to keep their attention focused on the portraits.

"And you will take her with you." The fire at her back was too warm. Sweat prickled Bridget's neck under her collar. Or was it fever? What was happening to the body that she seemed to have shed completely? How long could it survive without her vital essence giving it care?

"She is my possession." Medeoan stopped to study one of the portraits that hung at eye level. "She gave herself to me. It cannot be helped."

"You could let her go."

"I told you, she will not let me."

"Or you will not let her."

"Yes."

There is a way. There must be a way. I need only to find it.

Bridget gazed at her surroundings, casting about for some sign that would bring her inspiration. She half expected the portraits to be moving, to be ghosts within this dream of ghosts and spirits.

The portraits did not move, but the shadows between them did. They flitted between the carved and gilded frames. They crossed into the paintings of long-dead nobles and divines and swept out again, leaving no trace of themselves. They clustered as if in conversation. They knotted and writhed as if in combat. They stood alone and silently sobbed.

Who were they? They had no place in the pictures of the high and mighty, no clarity in this memory or fantasy that held Medeoan's soul. Who could they be?

Who waited between the nobility?

The unknown. The soldiers and the clerks, the ladies-in-waiting and the ordinary people, the sorcerers in Isavalta and the children of the bureaucrats, the ones who were not there to sit for the portrait painters, but who were always there just the same, who made the paintings possible.

The ones whose lives were too short for them to be painted at all.

With those thoughts, Bridget found what she needed. A plan formed in her mind. Sakra had been mistaken in one thing. It was not Bridget who needed to convince Medeoan of what she needed to do. Medeoan had found someone else to cling to, even as she had in life clung to Avanasy, then Kalami, and then to the hope of Bridget.

"Such lovely pictures," she said, turning toward the portraits and folding her hands behind her as if she were in a museum. "So many faces, so many parents and sons and daughters." She tilted her head, feigning a casual attitude to match Medeoan's. "Where's your sister, Aunt Grace? Where's my mother?"

Grace stirred, forcing Medeoan to shift her balance, to lean a little less. Grace's eye swept back and forth, looking for something that was not there. Her mouth worked itself, struggling to form words though she apparently lacked the strength to lift her head from Medeoan's shoulder.

"I can't see her from here." Aunt Grace's voice was faint, but agitated. Shaking from the effort, she raised her head so she could crane her neck to see the portraits hung nearest the ceiling. Medeoan, as bound to Grace as Grace was to her, craned her neck identically. "I haven't seen her in years."

"I've seen her," said Bridget. "Not four months ago. She came to me."

Grace's eyes flitted back and forth again. Did she see the shadows? Her knuckles lost a little of their whiteness as her hand loosened its grip on Medeoan's arm. Her head wobbled on the stem of her neck, but it did not fall again. Her lips shaped a word.

Now Medeoan had to grip Grace more tightly. "You're upsetting her. You should not."

Bridget ignored the dowager. She circled around back of them so she stood on Grace's side. "I've seen her," she said again. "I know where she is. Would you like me to show her to you?"

Grace pulled farther away. It was a fraction of an inch, a bare loosening of hand and arm, but it was real. "Yes," she said so softly Bridget could barely hear her.

"You cannot show," snapped Medeoan. "You can only see."

You do not know what I can do. But Bridget did not say that aloud.

She did not have breath to spare. This must be a place of spirit, like the Shifting Lands. If that was true, then, like the Shifting Lands, strong desires, even wishes, could shape the world.

Bridget wished with all her heart to see her mother. To see her as she had when her ghost had come to Vyshtavos, full of love, full of the wish to help, and to let it be known that she did love.

Bridget's need then had been to free herself from what she held too tightly. It was Grace's need now, in an even more tangible way.

The portrait in front of them began to blur. The stiff-backed man in imperial blue with a crown of sapphires and a beard that hung down to his waist turned to a mass of undefined color. Then, like her surroundings when Bridget first came to this place, the portrait became clear once again. The image there was a woman, in a plain dress and apron, with auburn hair and a strong face that had seen both sorrows and joys.

It was Bridget's image of the mother she had seen only as a ghost and an old photograph. She had to pray it was close enough to the real thing for Grace.

In the next heartbeat, she knew it was. "Ingrid," breathed Aunt Grace. She tried to step forward, and this time, Medeoan had to struggle to hold her back.

Bridget concentrated on Grace. Wishes could shape the spirit world. Desire could shape it. She wished for her aunt's freedom. She wished for it with all the soul, with all the force of will Mistress Urshila taught her to bring to bear on a working.

"She forgives you, you know," whispered Bridget. "I forgive you."

"You do not," spat the dowager with such vehemence that Bridget feared she had badly misjudged the game.

Grace acted as if Medeoan had not spoken at all. "But do I forgive you?" she mused. Her hand rested only lightly on Medeoan's arm now, and if she did not stand straight, she at least bore her own weight on her own feet.

"Whether you forgive me is up to you," Bridget told her aunt. "Will you come back home and tell me if you do?" She must not sound too eager. She must not lose the focus of her need. Freedom. Aunt Grace must be free. She must see her sister. She must find her own mind. It was she who invited Medeoan into her soul. It was she who must force the dowager out again.

Aunt Grace was dreadfully pale. She stood alone, but she swayed on her feet. Bridget felt herself begin to waver in response. How long had she been here? Her wrist hurt where the lifeline bound it. Her head ached from wishing.

"Her home is here now, with me. I am the one who needs her." Medeoan drew herself up. She and Grace barely touched fingertips now, and Bridget could feel the pain, the struggle rolling off her in waves, but she could also feel the pull. It was almost as strong as the lifeline that brought her here. Bridget knew she would find it so easy to take one step, two, to wrap herself around Medeoan as Aunt Grace had. To no longer stand alone.

But this was costing Medeoan all of herself, Bridget could feel that as well.

"You're using her," Bridget said, slowly, clearly, biting off each word so not one syllable could be missed or mistaken. "You are using Grace as you used Avanasy, and your own son."

The words had either been exactly right, or exactly wrong, but they had hit home. The dowager stooped, seeming to become even older. "I needed them."

Still speaking slowly, still putting force of will and of wish behind the words, Bridget stepped forward. "The one died for your need, the other you almost killed." If she had been able to touch, she would have touched Aunt Grace now, rubbed up shoulder to shoulder with her. They could have even leaned together as Grace and Medeoan had done.

Medeoan's arm shivered, but did not move. Perhaps it could not move. "Are you going to allow the child to say such things to me?"

At that, Aunt Grace finally lifted her hands away from Medeoan. Bridget's heart soared, and she lost hold of her will and the portrait she had shaped began to blur. Aunt Grace just slammed her hands over her ears in the gesture of a child who can no longer bear what it hears.

"Please," she said, the word coming out as half a sob. "Please. I do not want this."

"You did. You do." Medeoan was crabbed, aged, diminished, but she was not yet defeated. "You were the special one. It should have stayed that way."

At first Bridget thought Grace was crying, but then she saw that her aunt's face was growing indistinct, like the portrait, like the world itself. "But it didn't. Whose fault is that?"

"You told me whose it was," hissed Medeoan. "You told me how she left you."

Grace lowered her hands, and she turned, slowly, hunched and shaking, as if she too were becoming an old woman, she faced the dowager. "I was wrong," she said, and Bridget knew that was the first time she had said those words about this thing. "It was my fault what I became, not Ingrid's."

Grace backed away, each step a battle, each step a victory.

"No," whispered the dowager. Bridget could barely hear her. Her skin was as white as her hair now, and the color had begun to drain even from her eyes.

Fading.

"Not like this," breathed the dowager. "I came to help. I only wanted to help."

It was this that Bridget had been waiting for. "Yes," she said. "You wanted to be a good ruler. I've been told that so many times." *But fear and pride and pain got in your way. Death brings great change and no change at all.* "I want to help Isavalta now. Tell me how to cage the Firebird."

"I cannot." Medeoan shrank away, growing young as she had grown old, a pale girl, scarcely a woman. A wraith.

"But you did cage it once."

"Oh, yes." The two words were filled with despair. "I did that."

I killed a man, she said with those simple words. *I killed so many.*

"Tell me how it was done," urged Bridget. Neither one of them had moved, and yet the distance between them had grown. Bridget strained her ears and strained her senses, but her whole being felt already tensed to the breaking point. The ache in her wrist had become a burn, distracting her and sapping vital strength. "Let me help Isavalta. That was what you brought me to Vyshtavos to do."

"The Firebird cannot be caged."

"Then what can be done?"

"Nothing. It is immortal. It has been granted vengeance." She lifted her head, for one heartbeat growing clear again in voice and visage. "You saw. You know."

"Medeoan, you told my aunt you wanted to help Isavalta, that you wanted redemption."

"They judge me, my parents, the gods. My spirit will be alone in the ice fields for all time."

Bridget faltered. The burn from the lifeline had begun to throb like a heartbeat, like her heartbeat, laboring in her chest, calling her back to herself, breaking her connection with this place. Confusion washed through her, robbing her of her voice. She had to concentrate, but she could not. Her strength was finally beginning to fail, and the gallery, Medeoan, and Grace were all receding like the tide.

Grace moved. She straightened her heavy shoulders and threw back her head. She lifted her hands that had clutched Medeoan so slightly.

"I call the spirits," she said, her voice deep and resonating. "I call the spirits to speak."

It was ridiculous, it was the cheapest sort of theater.

It was what Aunt Grace had done for thirty years and what she knew as she knew her name. It was second nature to her, and in this place, it had power.

"Speak!" she called out. "We know the pain of being trapped between. We bring you rest. Speak and tell us of your burden, and be absolved and forgiven of all wrong. Be gathered into the fold where you seek shelter, where there is yet room for your soul. Speak and know peace."

Medeoan moved forward, staring, her face filled with fear and wonder both. Her eyes were almost white now, as her skin, as her hair. The little girl, fading, all but gone.

"Speak to me," whispered Aunt Grace, gentle now, coaxing. She had solidified, grown taller and more stately, even as Medeoan had diminished. "Speak and be forgiven. Speak and be gathered in."

The little girl who was Medeoan stood up on tiptoe and whispered into Aunt Grace's ear. Aunt Grace listened, eyes closed, and at last nodded.

"Thank you," she said. "Thank you, Medeoan."

Medeoan smiled, a delighted child's smile. The two of them embraced, and slowly, like ice melting in the sun, Medeoan faded away in Aunt Grace's arms, and was gone.

In the same instant, the pain in Bridget's wrist became unbearable, robbing her exhausted mind of the last of its will to focus. The world became a blur of color and cold, and when it cleared, she was sitting on the bed, holding Aunt Grace, her face wet with tears.

In the circle of her arms, her aunt breathed easily, evenly, and without any sound except the healthy whisper of air through lungs that were whole and sound.

Grace stirred. Bridget meant to sit back, but she did not have the strength and instead slumped painfully against the brass headboard.

Sakra too gave up all pretense at dignity. His trembling hand plucked the scarlet band from his wrist, and he sat down at once on the floor.

Grace, though, Grace lifted her head, her eyes clear and a look of wonder on her face.

"What did she say?" croaked Bridget.

"It cannot be caged." Grace spoke the words slowly, savoring them as if they were a beloved memory. "The cage won't hold a second time, but if you can find the name of the man the Phoenix once was, it could be transformed."

Chapter Sixteen

Mae Shan watched her young mistress trot steadily down the hill toward the riverside town of Huaxing and tried to be glad. Tsan Nu, or "Anna" as she was now insisting was her proper name, had been full of energy and good humor since she'd done her last spell, walking the whole long way without complaint. Mae Shan wanted to be glad that the girl could keep up and that she was following without question. She wanted to ignore the distance in "Anna's" eyes and how only part of her attention seemed to be on where they were going.

Two things did lift Mae Shan's spirits. The first was that she had been able to pick out the red roof of Uncle Lien's house from the top of the last hill. The second was that no smoke rose from Huaxing, except for the benign white vapor from cooking fires.

The river itself was crowded with traffic. Boats of all sizes raced down its course, heading for the coast with all the sail they could raise. Mae Shan wondered where they were from and where they were bound, and if they knew for certain there was safety where they went. Uncertainty was beginning to tire her more than the journey, and she longed for answers.

They were almost alone on the hillside now. Most of the other refugees had chosen to flee deeper inland rather than take their chances on the river or at a town so close to the Heart. Or perhaps they had just been faster than Mae Shan and her charge, because although it was the middle of the day, Huaxing's gates were shut fast. Mae Shan, however, saw ordered movement on the battlements. This told her that unlike in T'ien, the guards here had not yet abandoned their posts.

She also saw, as they drew closer, that those same guards were armed with bows, and the four men on either side of the gate were stationed with arrows already nocked.

"Mistress, wait here," she said, pointing to a tangle of bushes at the roadside outside bow range. "Do not come until I call."

Tsan Nu's, Anna's, eyes went dim for a moment and Mae Shan wondered if the child was speaking to the father, or the father to the child, and what was being said. Whatever it was, her mistress ducked obediently behind the bush, crouching down so as not to be seen.

Well enough.

Mae Shan unslung her bundles and laid them beside those same bushes, certain the guards on the walls marked her movements. Then, unarmed and alone she walked down the center of the road to the gate.

"Stop there!" cried one of the guards on the left side of the gate when she drew within hail. "State your business!"

Mae Shan halted as she was ordered. "Lieutenant Mae Shan Jinn of the Heart's Own Guard stationed at the Autumn Palace at the pleasure and the service of the Son of Heaven and Earth."

Even from where she stood, she could see the man's jaw drop.

"You lie!" he roared. "No one survived from the Heart!"

"I did, as did my mistress." She held up her left hand. "I can show you my ring of service as proof."

The officer turned and said something to his subordinates that Mae Shan could not hear. Then he and another disappeared from the battlements in order to emerge from a side portal. Mae Shan stayed where she was and let them come to her. Their armor was brown and edged with green. The officer wore a green sash and his subordinate a brown one. The subordinate still had his bow at the ready. Mae Shan did not move except to lower her hand so they might see her sigil ring. She hoped they would decide to admit they recognized it. Sneaking into Huaxing once they were refused entry at the gate would not be an adventure to look forward to.

The officer, a lieutenant from the insignia on his green sash, touched her ring with one gloved finger.

"Goddess of Mercy," he whispered, a look of fear appearing on his face, as if he thought Mae Shan might vanish like a ghost. "We've been told no one survived. You must come with me at once. The mayor will want to speak with you."

Mae Shan bowed in salute. "I will willingly speak to the honorable mayor as soon as possible, but first I must see my mistress safely installed in my uncle's house."

"Lieutenant Mae Shan." The man dropped his voice. "Nowhere is safe. As the days pass without news from the Heart, the town is emptying out except for the looters. The mayor's villa is still guarded. You must come at once."

"My uncle is Lien Jinn," she said firmly. "Are you saying anyone will dare attempt his house, or will succeed in that attempt?"

"Lien Jinn?" repeated the guard, stunned. Mae Shan nodded once. She watched his face shift back and forth as some internal struggle played itself out.

Perhaps it will be the riverside after all.

He stared hard at her ring, now, she was sure, wondering whether she'd stolen it, but a soldier's bearing was not something a casual thief could fake, and the the hunger for news was strong. "You'll report to the mayor as soon as your mistress is safe?"

"I will come as soon as I am able."

"Bring her and enter then."

Mae Shan bowed in salute and thanks and returned to the thicket where she had left Anna—Tsan Nu and their gear.

"Come, mistress. We have been granted entry." She hefted her bundle. Tsan Nu looked accusing.

"You did not say your uncle was Lien Jinn."

"It is not a relationship I can acknowledge inside the Heart," she said, taking her mistress's hand. *Who is upset at this news? You or your father?* she wondered.

"My father says he is a pirate."

"He is also a sorcerer," Mae Shan told her. "And he is our only source of help right now."

Tsan Nu fell silent, and permitted herself to be led through the guard's portal by Mae Shan and the town's lieutenant. He presented them with a hastily written passport stamped with his name and the city seal giving Mae Shan and her mistress permission to be out on the streets. Mae Shan tucked it into her sash, while declining his offer of escort. She knew her way.

Mae Shan had only found out about Uncle Lien by overhearing a conversation between her parents. There had been a drought, and things were hard with them. Then, a messenger with a scar over his eye had arrived bearing a letter and a string of silver. Mae Shan, as the tallest of her siblings, had been given the job of stretching up on tiptoe to peek through the window as Father read the missive. The messenger stood there with his thumbs tucked in his sash and his jaw moving constantly as he chewed betel nuts, or something equally noxious. Father weighed the silver in his hand and looked at Mother. Without a word, Mother took the silver and handed it back to the messenger.

"We will take nothing from such a man as Lien Jinn," Father announced, dropping the letter onto the floor to show his total lack of respect for it. "He is a pirate and a rogue and I do not acknowledge him as family."

The messenger shrugged, tucked the silver into his sleeve, and went away, without even bowing once.

The speculation that night in the sleeping room had been intense. Wei Lin claimed she had heard of Uncle Lien from her teachers. He was actually their grandfather's brother. He was a sorcerer and a pirate and had a black beard two ells long that he could crack like a whip over the heads of his "nefarious" crew. Mae Shan wasn't clear what "nefarious" meant, but it sounded appropriately awful. Her brother Zhi told Wei Lin not to be ridiculous, but he had heard from some older boys that Lien Jinn had once beheaded fifty men in a single hour with his machete because they had tried to hide one pearl from him.

In their excitement, they had forgotten to keep their voices down. Mother and Father had woken up furious, and Father had forbidden the name of Lien from ever passing his children's lips again.

But Mae Shan's imagination was fired, and from that time forward, she kept the net of her ears spread for any stories she might catch concerning her mysterious uncle, especially when she accompanied her father and older brother on the boat to sell their produce to the brokers at the markets. At her mother's insistence, Mae Shan was forbidden to leave the boat, but that did not stop her from listening to the gossip that passed back and forth between the boats when Father and Zhi had gone to conduct their negotiations. It was amazing how much she could hear without leaving sight of the boat, or the warehouse door Father and Zhi had gone through.

All the various rumors and yarns she heard agreed about three things. The first was that Grandfather's brother, her Uncle Lien Jinn, was a pirate, smuggler, and thief. The second was that he was a sorcerer of great ability who had once served the Heart of the World. The third was that he had a house in town. The length and abilities of his beard remained in dispute.

When Father caught her whispering her latest tidbits of information to Zhi, he beat her black and blue for defying his order. After that, Mae Shan became determined to meet this fabled relation. She gathered all the information she could and stole out through the streets at night. She was big and she was fast, and she kept to the river's edge where the farmers moored their boats on market days. All of which probably saved her life, she reflected, now that she knew more about the streets of Huaxing. She had found the house, however, and she had scaled the wall, and then fell on her head.

The woman she would come to know as Auntie Cai Yun found Mae Shan wandering in a daze by the lily pool. Mae Shan remembered nothing of that. She did remember waking up in a strange, luxurious bed. Next to her sat a white-haired man with a beard that was nothing more than a tracing of neatly trimmed snowy hairs along the line of his chin.

"And now that the lily blossom has opened, perhaps she will reveal to us who she is," he said mildly.

Mae Shan's back had gotten up, pushed in part by the strangeness of being referred to as a lily blossom. That was the sort of thing people normally said to Wei Lin.

"I am Mae Shan Jinn, daughter of Menh Jinn and the great-niece of the mighty Lien Jinn, so you will tell him I am here to pay my respects. Please," she added, filial piety and headache rapidly wilting defiance.

The aged man blinked at her. "You are Menh's daughter? And you climbed my wall to see the mighty Lien Jinn?"

Mae Shan nodded, the feeling that she was missing something perfectly obvious beginning to dawn on her.

"You'd better tell me how you came to be here."

Mae Shan did, realizing by the time she was done that despite the disappointing length of his beard, it was Uncle Lien she spoke to.

"You are brave and you are audacious, Mae Shan, daughter of Menh," he said when she had finished. "But I sense also you do have some piety in you despite your excursion tonight. So. We will wrap your head in a vinegar bandage and you will stay here until dawn, when you will return to your father's boat with your cousin, Cai Yun. He does not know her and she will not give her right name. You will not speak of where you have been, and you will take the beating you deserve for your disobedience. You will from this day forward disdain our relationship as you should."

Despite his words, a light shone in his keen eye.

"And then?" Mae Shan ventured.

"Who am I to say what a stubborn girl will do then?" he replied placidly. "But I think a short ladder inside the wall is needed, just in case."

That was the beginning of a strange and surreptitious relationship. Sometimes during the fall trips, Mae Shan would sneak away in the night to visit her uncle, and sometimes she would only wander the garden, as the house was shut up tight. Sometimes she would glimpse Uncle Lien in one of the riverside teahouses, dressed as a merchant or a sailor, and she would in her casual way of eavesdropping overhear stories of her family and the wide world beyond the riverbanks and farms.

All that came to an end when Wei Lin was selected to enter the Heart of the World. Lonesome and disappointed, despite the fact that this was the thing everyone had prayed for, Mae Shan had argued with her father over some trifle and run to Uncle Lien's gardens, without even taking her regular precautions. As was his way, he heard her out thoughtfully, until she asked to be allowed to come live with him and be a pirate too.

"No, Mae Shan."

"Why not? I'm big, for a girl. I'm strong. I can learn to use a sword . . ."

"I know that," said Uncle Lien, "and you will, but not in my service."

"But why, Uncle? I want . . ."

He held up his hand. "Because you have the possibility of a good life ahead of you that dwelling on this connection would ruin. You must go home, Mae Shan, and you must not come here again. I will ask you to trust that I will still know of you and will be here if you ever have nowhere else to turn. But you are a young woman now, not a mischievous girl, and you must act like it."

Mae Shan bridled. "What life will I have? Wei Lin's going to forget all of us behind the Saffron Walls. They will marry me off to some fat farmer and I will raise fifteen children, each one rounder and more dirty than the last, and that will be that."

"That is not true," replied Uncle Lien.

"What do you know, old man?" shouted Mae Shan.

Uncle Lien did not blink or hesitate. "I know I am a sorcerer and that I have drawn a horoscope for my hardheaded grand-niece which says if she embraces her duty, she will stand against fire and death and be the salvation of the helpless."

Stand against fire and death and be the salvation of the helpless, Mae Shan turned those words over in her mind as she walked with Anna down the deserted streets of Huaxing. She shook her head. *Who knew one could be so tired on the day one's destiny came true?*

You have not saved her yet, Mae Shan. Keep your wits about you.

The silence of Huaxing's streets discomfited Mae Shan. The city was a prosperous place, as river ports generally were, and she was used to it being full of noise and life. In daylight she had only ever seen its thoroughfares full of pedestrians, carts, carriages, and sedan chairs. On this day, a single person here or there darted furtively between the houses. Guards marched in pairs, their square-toed shoes slapping hard against the cobbles. Mae Shan and Anna were stopped three separate times and ordered to produce the passport. She pictured the mayor huddled in his villa, staring up the river at the cloud of smoke still visible over the hills. Doubtless he wondered which rumors to believe, waited for his magistrates and envoys to bring news and feared what it might be, and tried to keep the people indoors to slow gossip and the panic it bred.

Mae Shan and Anna rounded a corner from the empty Street of Letter Writers onto the Street of Five Golden Willows. All at once, one of those furtive shadows plowed straight into Mae Shan, knocking all the wind out of her. She just had time to reach out and grab the elbow of a skinny, dirty boy whose eyes flashed fear and mischief before he squirmed away.

"Stay here!" shouted Mae Shan to Anna. She was on the boy in three running strides, catching his ear between her thumb and forefinger and dragging him to a halt.

"Ow!" he cried. "Ow! Please, mistress! Let me go! I didn't mean to run into you! I'm only trying to get to my grandmother! She's very sick, mistress, and my mother fears for her! Please, mistress!"

In no mood to be patient, Mae Shan pinched his ear harder, ignoring his cries. "You will return my paper, Master Thief, then we will discuss where you're going."

The boy slid his gaze sideways and got a look at her thunderous face. Seeing she was not even beginning to believe his story, he stopped his struggles and held out the grubby hand that clutched the now very wrinkled passport.

"Thank you, Master Thief." Mae Shan plucked the paper from his fingers and returned it to her sash.

Anna was staring at the boy who was no taller than she was. "My father says this boy is dangerous," she whispered. "He says you should kill him."

Her words startled Mae Shan badly, but she did not let that show. "Well, Master Thief?" She shook the boy by his ear. "Do you hear what my mistress tells me?"

"Ai-ah!" he cried. "Mistress, please, I swear, I'm sorry. Don't harm me, please! I was only . . ."

A new voice cut across whatever the boy had been about to say. "Only what, you monkey? You shame of your family?"

An old man hobbled out of the mouth of an alleyway, leaning heavily on a gnarled cane. He had more hair on his chin than on his head, and all of it was wispy and snow-white. He bowed deeply before Mae Shan.

"Mistress, this most undeserving and unfilial child is my grandson. I beg you show mercy to him. Return him to me and I will see he is well punished and such thievery will not happen again."

"No, Mae Shan." Anna grabbed her sleeve. "They are not human. They will tell on us to the Phoenix. Father says you must kill them both, right now."

Mae Shan swallowed against the tremor that ran through her. What was happening here? Could she trust this ghost that held possession of her mistress?

The old man bowed again. "I beg you, mistress. We are an old and respected family and we have resided long in this city. This child's disobedience has caused his father to tear out his own beard and his mother to weep tears of shame. Give me back this worthless youth and let me take him home. If the guards find him, they will surely give him

a hundred lashes. That is the penalty the mayor has declared for loot-
ing. Please, mistress."

"No, Mae Shan!" said Anna urgently.

The "grandfather" was probably lying, but what was the ghost doing? Mae Shan swallowed again, and pushed the boy into the old man's
arms.

"Take him then, Grandfather, and see that he does not thieve from
soldiers anymore."

"A blessing upon you for this mercy, mistress!" The old man
clamped his clawed hand around the boy's wrist and bowed three times
to show his gratitude. Then, with a kick, he sent the boy running back
down the alley, hobbling behind with surprising swiftness, even as he
waved his cane in the air to urge the boy on.

"Why did you do that?" demanded Anna. "You heard Father. Now
he's very angry with you."

"I heard," said Mae Shan solemnly. "I also know that mercy, especially in times of trial, goes further than the harshest punishment."

"But . . ."

"I have done what I have done." Mae Shan took Anna's hand again,
but did not look down at the girl. She feared to see the angry ghost looking out of her green eyes. "On my head be it."

Keeping her eyes straight ahead she hurried down the street toward
her uncle's house, forcing Anna to trot to keep up.

From the alley shadows, an old man and a young boy watched her
depart. Then they both resumed their shapes as foxes and slipped away in
the opposite direction.

There were no other such encounters as they worked their way
down to the riverside. From the bleary, grim faces of the soldiers they
encountered, Mae Shan guessed the mayor, from conscientiousness or
fear, had them patrolling through the night to keep such opportunists
on the move, if not actually in their hidey-holes. If the man and the boy
were not more cautious, they would suffer worse than a sore ear and
wounded pride.

Anna had not spoken one word since Mae Shan had let the thieves go, and that silence was as worrying as anything that had happened yet. Was the ghost whispering to her even now? What was it saying?

Be there, Uncle. This is far too much for me.

At last they reached River Street. The grandest houses with the highest walls lined its landward side overlooking the great river with its green-brown waters as full of boats as the streets were empty of people. Flat-bottomed barges such as she remembered from her childhood were poled close enough to the shore that she could see the owners, working steadily, numbly, fleeing as fast as water and muscle could take them. The fear of the fire, the mob, and the demons at the Left Gates returned to Mae Shan as she watched and she had to lower her gaze, lest that fear overwhelm her.

Three boats were tied up to the piers outside Uncle Lien's gates and Mae Shan was able to take heart again. If he were in his other house, or out on the sea, those would have been up on cradles on the muddy banks.

Unless he had already fled by the other means at his disposal.

Mae Shan turned from the water and picked up the baton for the bronze bell that hung beside the elaborately carved front gate. Uncle Lien had once told her the bell was enchanted and would not ring for any who wished him ill. She had sometimes wondered if this were true. Between Uncle Lien and Auntie Cai Yun, she had been told that practically every pale brick in the garden walls was enchanted.

Anna stared at the walls, her jaw hanging open. "Does he think he's the emperor to have woven himself so much protection?" The exclamation was awestruck. Mae Shan felt obscurely proud.

She struck the bell three times and its clear tone rang out across the silent streets and the noisy river. She held firmly to Anna's hand while they waited.

"I don't want to go in there," said Anna. "I'm afraid."

"You are or your father is?" Mae Shan asked, trying to keep her tone neutral.

"I am. I'm not sure I'll be able to hear Father inside the walls."

"If your father is truly safe within your heart, no enchantment can keep him from you." Mae Shan had no idea whether she spoke the truth, but the words seemed to content Anna for the moment.

Several dark figures moved on the veranda of the house, walking down the steps and the paved path toward the gate. Before long, Mae Shan recognized Auntie Cai Yun dressed in a simple black robe with a red skirt and sash, and carrying a stout cudgel. Behind her came two strangers, both men, both with the seamed, bark-brown faces and square hands of those who had spent years on ships and the open sea. The taller of the two had a series of red and blue knots tattooed on his rough hands and a long knife stuck in his coarse-woven sash. The other made do with a cudgel much like Auntie Cai Yun's, and a look that could have split wood.

As Cai Yun and her escort drew closer, Mae Shan could see her fine-boned face was drawn tight with determination so that the bones of her cheeks and jaw stood out in sharp relief. If Uncle Lien was sending her to the gate with two of his rougher sailors, things had been bad, or were threatening to become so.

Auntie Cai Yun was actually Mae Shan's cousin, but there was nearly twenty-five years difference in age between them, so Mae Shan used the more respectful title.

When Auntie Cai Yun reached the gate, Mae Shan bowed. "Auntie Cai Yun, it's Mae Shan!"

Auntie Cai Yun peered at her. "I do not know your face." The taller pirate fingered the hilt of his knife. Guarding the house had probably become quite dull, and escorting a nuisance away from the gate would provide at least some diversion.

Mae Shan did not ignore that knife, but neither did she let herself appear to be afraid of it. "It has been twelve years since we have seen each other. I was ten when I first stole away from my father who had come to trade at the market, so I could come visit my infamous Uncle Lien. I climbed a tree to get over the wall and fell on my head."

Auntie Cai Yun lowered her staff, but her face did not relax nor her eyes grow more open. The taller pirate looked disappointed. "Who is that with you?" Cai Yun nodded toward Anna.

Ask me a simple question, Auntie. "My charge, Anna. We've come from the Heart of the World and we need shelter and to speak with Uncle Lien."

The mention of the Heart of the World felled her suspicions. Her face paled. Even the shorter of the two sailors blanched. Cai Yun reached out to her younger cousin between the bars of the gate. "Heaven and Earth, Mae Shan, how did you escape?"

"With great difficulty, Auntie," quipped Mae Shan with a tired smile. "Is Uncle here? Will you let us in?"

By way of answer, Auntie Cai Yun produced an iron key that had been inlaid with silver. She unlocked the gate and pushed it open a crack, looking sharply this way and that as she did. At the same time, her escorts tensed, ready for action. Mae Shan urged Anna through the gate with a gentle hand on her shoulder. Inside the wall, the girl relaxed visibly. Evidently, none of Uncle Lien's protections drowned out her father's voice.

It could not possibly have been so easy to rid her of him, thought Mae Shan as she followed.

Auntie closed and locked the gate again before she turned to embrace Mae Shan. She said nothing, but Mae Shan could feel from the tension in her shoulders that things had not been easy in the house of Jinn, as if the presence of her uncouth companions were not proof enough of that.

Auntie released Mae Shan and turned to bow to Anna.

"Mistress, our house is honored by your presence. Let me make you welcome in my uncle's name and offer you such poor hospitality as we have."

Fortunately, Anna had not forgotten her manners. She bowed in return. "Thank you. Your hospitality does me much honor." Suspicion still gleamed in her eyes, but if Auntie Cai Yun noticed it, she gave no sign.

"Come." Auntie glanced back at the street. "We should be indoors, and Uncle Lien will want to see you at once."

She led them up the garden path, the sailors following silently behind. The years had obviously been good to Uncle Lien's fortune. His gardens were even more beautiful than Mae Shan remembered, and the house shone with new paint and gilding. Uncle Lien's pride was bound up in his houses. It was part of his great feud with the Nine Elders that he should live grandly and openly in the cities under their protection, and that there should be nothing they could do about it.

Four other sailors waited on the veranda and were waved back from the door by Auntie Cai Yun, but no servants came to greet them as they entered the house. Mae Shan suspected they had been sent away, but she did not remark on it to Auntie, who set her cudgel beside the doorway.

"If you will please follow me," was all she said, and she led them across the teakwood floor of the entrance hall to the carved screen that closed off Uncle Lien's personal study with its many shelves of scrolls and low rosewood tables.

Uncle Lien looked much as he had when she had seen him ten years ago, which was not surprising. Sorcerers aged slowly, unless, as her uncle once told her, they overreached their power. Then their lives would fade like the flowers in summer. Uncle Lien would never tell Mae Shan what he had done to turn his hair so white or put the wrinkles in his face.

"Mae Shan, my child." Uncle held up his hand in greeting as Mae Shan bowed. "Come and sit next to me. Tell me who this is with you." He gestured that Anna should take the seat across from the table.

Mae Shan sat beside her uncle gratefully. She could feel his warmth and sympathy even though he held himself in correct and dignified stillness and allowed no emotion to overcome him. They were, after all, not alone. His composure allowed Mae Shan to keep hers despite her tremendous weariness.

She introduced Anna as her charge from the Heart of the World. "She was guested there by her father, Kalami of Isavalta." She did not say the word "hostage," but Uncle Lien surely knew that was what she meant.

"My father is of Tuukos," Anna corrected her. "Not Isavalta."

"Of course, mistress."

"Kalami," said Uncle Lien. "Is he not lord sorcerer to the Dowager Empress Medeoan?"

"He was, but no more," answered Anna.

"I had not heard his fate." Uncle Lien shook his head once with regret, but Anna offered no more information. With difficulty, Mae Shan held her tongue.

"Uncle, times are going to be very bad now for Hung-Tse. What will happen to us at the Center of the World I do not know. I do know it will be worse for a child whose destiny is not ours. I mean to return her home. Her father will be able to help us." *Please do not ask how, Uncle.* "But we need shelter until he can do so."

"Of course, Niece. You and your mistress will have all the protection I can offer. Cai Yun will show you to a room where you may wash and rest. Food is being prepared."

"Thank you, Uncle." Mae Shan did not bother to hide either the gratitude or the weariness in her voice.

"Please come with me," said Auntie Cai Yun kindly.

Auntie led them up the wide, dark staircase to a tidy bedchamber. She began unlatching the doors to the second veranda that overlooked the garden, and opening chests to expose bed linens and fresh clothes.

It disturbed Mae Shan to see her refined cousin acting as house maid but she said nothing, because she knew Cai Yun saw it as part of her duties as mistress of the house, whether there were proper servants or not. While she bustled, Anna perched on the edge of one of the softly cushioned chairs. Mae Shan looked away to accept a jacket and trousers from Cai Yun. When she looked back, Anna had curled up in the chair and was sound asleep.

"Poor child," said Cai Yun as Mae Shan scooped the girl up and laid her on the bed, covering her up with a quilt from one of the open chests. "This all must be terribly hard for her."

"More than you or I can know, Auntie." Mae Shan smoothed Anna's hair back from her face. "I only hope the hardships are over soon."

Auntie's jaw tightened, but she made no answer to Mae Shan's hope. "I'll leave you to dress. Come down to Uncle's study again when you are ready."

She left. Mae Shan, moving carefully so as not to disturb Anna, changed out of her grimy nightclothes and into respectable black broadcloth trousers and a red undershirt with a black quilted jacket and red sash. She combed out her short hair and rinsed her face and hands in the white porcelain basin. Then, so she would not have to make a light later, she folded several of the soft linens and blankets into a pallet beside Anna's bed.

The clean clothes felt wonderful against Mae Shan's skin. She knew the sheets and blankets of her pallet bed would feel even better, but her own time for rest was not yet. She was reluctant to leave her mistress, but Auntie Cai Yun and the "servants" were diligent in the protection of this house and she felt with cold certainty Anna's father would not permit his daughter to be harmed. Not yet, anyway.

Rubbing her arms against a chill that came from inside as well as outside, Mae Shan stole softly from the room and down the stairs. Moonlight shone against the dark wood. The Greeting Hall was empty but she heard movement in the scroll room and smelled the sweet odor of burning incense.

Uncle Lien knelt before the ten polished spirit tablets on the camphor wood table. Each one had been dedicated to a particular ancestor and carried their name, their horoscope, and the prayers the priests had devised for them upon their crossing to Heaven. On the walls hung white silk scrolls with the history of those same ancestors and details of the family lineage and accomplishments. It was a stark room with only a straw mat on the floor. Nothing here was to distract one from proper contemplation of the ancestors.

Mae Shan knew how to move silently. Nonetheless, her uncle turned as if he could hear her very breath.

"Come here, child," he said, holding out one arm. "We are alone now."

Mae Shan rushed to him. As he pulled her close into his embrace, hot tears spilled from her. Now she could weep full for Wei Lin dead in the ashes of the Heart of the World. Now she could weep for the fear she felt of all she had seen and all she could scarcely imagine would come. She could weep for herself, her place lost, her world gone, and not even able to go home and find her family, if they were still on their land, if riot and fire had not taken them too.

When at last she had wept herself empty and had dried her eyes on the kerchief stowed in her sleeve, she was able to kneel back. Her uncle passed her a cup of tea and a branch of bitter willow. She set them both before the spirit tablets and bowed down until her forehead pressed against the floor.

"Honored Ancestors, your daughter Wei Lin walks to join you, her hair unbound and her feet bloody with violence. Please accept your daughter's prayers and take her kindly into your embrace. Let her drink from the wells of Heaven and forget the sorrows of her life. Let her be reborn where she may rejoice."

And please, Sister, forgive me. I wanted to save you. I truly did.

She said the prayer a second time, and a third, and a fourth, and slowly Mae Shan's heart began to ease.

Anna lay in the soft bed staring at the darkness. She was very tired, and she would have liked to remain asleep, but her father's voice warned her against it.

We must hear what Mae Shan is saying about us to her uncle.

"Mae Shan is my bodyguard," Anna whispered back. "She will always protect me."

When there was an emperor to make her do so, Anna, this was true, but now he is gone. We can't know what she will do.

"She didn't leave me in the fire. She could have. The others did."

She didn't know how bad the fire would be. Trust me, Anna. I am your father. Mae Shan has done her job very well, but she is just a soldier. We are heart and blood, you and I.

Don't worry, Anna, he added, and she felt the warmth of his love in her heart. *It surely is as you say. We'll just make sure, that's all.*

So Anna slipped out of her bed, and stood swaying on her bare feet for a moment. She was so tired.

Let me help, Anna.

Her father reached out from her heart, and her legs moved, quickly and soundlessly. Her hands cleverly found the door latch and lifted it so she could steal into the moonlit corridor. He made her legs do a quick little skip as they hurried down the hallway and Anna had to stifle a giggle.

Quietly now, Anna, said Father, but she felt a ripple of amusement in the stern thoughts.

The moon was waning so the house was nothing so much as vague shapes of shadow. The polished wooden floor was still warm from the heat of the day. She padded down the stairs, keeping to the deep shadows by the wall. But she saw no telltale lantern glow, heard no patter from other feet, nor the rustle of other cloth.

The first floor of the house was brighter than the second, for it had more paper walls to let in the fresh air and the moonlight. Anna, Father, hesitated, and she strained her ears and eyes instinctively. A faint gold spark shone to the left. Father stirred approvingly within her and took Anna's footsteps in that direction.

The light proved to be coming from the house's scroll room, the place where the lineage was recorded and the ancestors were venerated. Father took her to the edge of the threshold and pressed her against the wall, but at her own thought, she crouched down close to the floor. When Anna was still Tsan Nu, she didn't spend too much time with the other children in the women's palace, but she knew a thing or two about not being seen while on an expedition to the forbidden gardens or the kitchens.

Father lit her heart with his smile.

In the scroll room, Lien Jinn and Mae Shan bowed before the altar in meditation. Anna held very still. The room was silent except for the distant night noises beyond the house walls. The smallest sound would be heard.

Just as Anna was beginning to get bored and sleepy again, Mae Shan and Lien both straightened up from their prayerful attitudes.

"Now, Mae Shan." Lien took two more cups from the tray beside him and poured fresh tea for them both. Anna's mouth watered a little at the sight. "Tell me of your mistress and her father. In my study, your eyes spoke of something that is not right there."

Anna's heart thumped once.

Mae Shan sipped the tea noisily to show gratitude for it. "Uncle, I know nothing about magics other than what you have told me, but I believe the girl is possessed and I'm afraid of it."

Heed her not, Anna, whispered Father. *She does not understand.*

"Tell me," said Uncle Lien softly.

Mae Shan did. In the clipped, precise voice Anna had heard her use with her superiors, she told of their escape, and of Tsan Nu, now Anna, calling on her father. With each word, Lien grew progressively more still and more grave.

"This is a serious matter, Mae Shan, and you were right to tell me of it." Lien was silent for a moment. Mae Shan set down her cup and rested her hands on her thighs to show her willingness to listen with her full attention.

Now we shall see their true faces, Father told Anna. For the first time since she had taken him into her heart, Anna felt cold.

Uncle Lien also set his cup down on the tray, turning it slightly so the bamboo pattern faced him. "What is not commonly known is that almost thirty years ago, when Hung-Tse came under threat of invasion by Isavalta, the Nine Elders summoned the Immortal Guardian of Fire and the South, the Phoenix, to save us. What is even less well known is that by means of great magic, the then empress of Isavalta, Medeoan, was able to imprison the Phoenix within a golden cage and hold it hostage."

An image rose in Anna's mind with the strength of a spell-wrought vision. She saw the Phoenix, not as she had seen it before spread out across the sky, but much smaller, crouching in a cage with filigree bars of charred gold. The sacrilege of it bit hard in Anna's mind.

"I would not have thought such a thing possible," Mae Shan was saying, her voice filled with dread and wonder.

Uncle Lien's face took on a brief expression of grudging admiration. "It took great skill, and cost a life for the making of that cage. It took much of Medeoan's strength and sanity to keep it whole. Her judgment began to fail, as did her life. In her middle years, she took to her court a chief sorcerer, the lord sorcerer they called him, named Valin Kalami. He came from a province of their empire called Tuukos. The Tuukosov, however, hate the Isavaltans with a passion that will not die. The empress did not know that Kalami sought nothing less than the destruction of Isavalta.

"To help accomplish this end, he contacted certain representatives of the Heart of the World within the boundaries of Isavalta. Eventually, he was allowed to speak with the Nine Elders. He promised to free the Phoenix, so long held captive by Medeoan, and to facilitate an invasion of Isavalta by Hung-Tse, so that the threat to our northern borders would finally be ended.

"The Nine Elders of course wished to ensure his good behavior, and so asked that he send to them a hostage as a guarantee that he would do as he said."

Is this true, Father? What they say?

Some of it, Anna, but they do not know everything.

"Anna." Mae Shan's gaze flicked up to the ceiling, surely thinking of Anna where she believed her to be, asleep in bed.

Uncle Lien nodded. "Kalami was treacherous, and his only loyalty was to the land of his birth. How he met his end is uncertain, but there are those who say it was brought on him by the queen of the fox spirits. What is known is that his death was bound up with the death of Medeoan, and that these two things freed the Phoenix from its long imprisonment."

Father?

This is why I brought you here, to understand whose roof we are sheltered under and who your so-called protector is seeking advice from. Keep listening.

"But why raze the Heart of the World?" Mae Shan was asking, her voice coming close to cracking. "Why did it not take its vengeance on Isavalta?"

"I do not know. Who can say what such imprisonment would do even to one of the guardians. The great threat was always that Medeoan had found some way to alter the nature of the Phoenix. Perhaps she succeeded."

She did not. The Nine Elders underestimated the anger of their guardian at being left to languish.

Anna shuddered, remembering the heat and noise of the fire, and the sacred guardian presiding over it all.

Courage, Anna, whispered Father.

"And this treacherous spirit has rested himself in his daughter's heart," said Mae Shan and disbelief dropped Anna's jaw. Mae Shan couldn't believe what her uncle was telling her, surely? He was a pirate, a thief. How could she take his word for anything?

I'm sorry, Daughter, but you had to know.

"How powerful is the child?" Lien asked.

Powerful enough that all walk quietly around her. Powerful enough that ones she had thought she could trust must speak in whispers of her after dark.

Anna trembled. She did not want to think about that.

Be proud, Daughter, as I am proud of you.

Anna tried, but she just felt sick.

Mae Shan was looking down at her hands. "I don't know, Uncle. But I can tell you she saw what the Nine Elders did not. She knew the Phoenix would return for revenge."

Startled pride reached Anna from her father's place inside her. *Powerful enough that the Nine Elders ignored her and brought down their own destruction. Oh, my child, you are greater than I dared to dream.*

Lien sat silently for a long moment. "It was good that you brought her here."

"Uncle," said Mae Shan tentatively. "Is it possible the father's spirit means no harm? That he only seeks to protect his daughter and see her safely home? There are legends that speak of such things . . ."

Yes! That's how it truly is, Mae Shan. Anna's fists tightened. She longed to burst from the shadows, but Father held her steady.

"Indeed, but such stories do not involve possession, nor do they come of calling a spirit forth from the Shifting Lands. Such magics bring only grief."

"What do I do? I have sworn an oath to protect the girl with my life."

Another tremor shook Anna's frame. *You see? She wants to believe what is right. When I tell her the truth . . .*

Keep listening, Anna. Be strong.

"What do you know of the girl's mother?"

"Only that her mother is dead." Mae Shan paused. "I don't believe I've ever even heard her name."

I would have told you anything you wanted to know, thought Anna petulantly. *I would have told you her name was Kaija and that she died when I was born, and that my father sent me to the Heart of the World so I could learn the magics and ways of Hung-Tse so one day I could be ambassador between Hung-Tse and Tuukos.*

"Then you do not know if she has maternal kin in Isavalta or Tuukos."

Father remained silent and still while Mae Shan shook her head. Anna wanted to go. Surely they'd heard everything they needed to. They didn't need to stay here crouched on the floor and listen while Mae Shan kicked over the last part of what Anna thought of as her safe world.

Uncle Lien smoothed his sparse beard thoughtfully. "You are right that the child cannot stay here to face what comes now that the heart has been cut from the body of our country. In fact, now that it is full dark those . . . sailors who you saw manning my walls are now manning the boats and making certain pairs of eyes think I am already gone. I am not sure that I will permit even Cai Yun to stay, although I may not be able to order her away . . . and with the throne having changed hands in Isavalta, my name and word there will not be what it once was . . ."

"You served Isavalta?" said Mae Shan, shocked.

"I aided the Empress Medeoan on occasion," answered Uncle Lien calmly. "Do not look at me so, Mae Shan. You have known for years what I am. It is because of what I am that I can help you now."

Guiltily, Mae Shan dropped her gaze.

Why do you listen to this thief? Anna felt tears start to stream her cheeks.

Just a little longer, my brave child, said Father. *There is one thing more we must learn.*

"I must make some final provision for your cousin and several others of my household," Lien went on. "But as soon as that is done, I will take you and the child to the shores of Isavalta. You will have several letters and names with you that will be of help."

"And the ghost?"

Anna's mouth went dry.

"I must consult my texts for the most efficacious method, but I believe by dawn I will be able to free the child."

There, murmured Father deep in the back of her mind. *That is what I needed to hear. That tells us how much time we have.*

Mae Shan bowed again. "Thank you, Uncle. This was more than I could have hoped for. I hope . . . I want . . ." She stammered and tried again. "I will come back once Tsan Nu, Ah-na, is safe. I must go home and see that my parents are well, and then I must return to T'ien and do what I can. I hope . . ."

Come now, Anna, Father said within her. *They will not talk much longer and we cannot be seen.*

Anna ducked her head back, wiping her tears silently with her sleeve, something else Master Liaozhai would have chided her for, but Father remained silent about this as well. Back in the scroll room, Lien kept talking, unaware of her departure.

"Your heart is with your duty, Mae Shan, and it will steer you correctly. I will tell you this much, my grievance was old and long, and with the Nine Elders. They have been punished in a way I could not foresee despite my art . . ."

Whatever else Lien had to say to his niece, he said in private. Anna was beyond the range of his voice when she reached the stairs. She hurried up the steps and back into her room. Anna slipped into her bed and pulled the covers up to her chin. She lay there, staring at the ceiling.

Rest now, Anna. I'll wake you when it's time.

But Anna did not feel sleepy anymore. Too much of what she had heard was ringing through her mind. Mae Shan, who had saved her life and had seemed so nice, was talking about possession, even after Anna had told her that this was nothing like that. She was talking about stripping away Father's ghost and leaving Anna alone again with no home and no friends and no teachers . . . and Lien calling Father treacherous. And Mae Shan believed him! Her duty was to Anna, she'd sworn it, no matter what her family said. She should not have sat there listening to those lies. Why would Mae Shan listen to lies?

But she could find no answer, and if Father knew she asked that question, he said nothing. She listened awhile for Mae Shan's step and did not hear it, so she rolled over and closed her eyes. But as sleep reached its soft hand to cradle her, unbidden, one question repeated itself to Anna.

Why would Mae Shan listen to lies?

Chapter Seventeen

Through Anna's slitted eyes, Kalami watched the bodyguard Mae Shan enter the darkened room and come to the bedside to inspect her charge. Kalami shut Anna's eyes quickly. His daughter stirred a little in her sleep, but did not wake, although Kalami was startled to feel Mae Shan's light touch smoothing Anna's hair down.

When he heard her move away again, he risked another look through Anna's eyes. The body was so much easier to claim while she lay sweetly asleep, her mind occupied with her dreams. Mae Shan closed the latch on the man-sized shutters that opened onto the balcony and then considered the inner door, which had no means of being secured. At last, with a sigh, she shifted the pallet she had made up earlier and composed herself to sleep in front of the door.

Eventually, Mae Shan's breathing grew slow and even. Kalami lifted Anna's little hands and pushed the covers back. Mae Shan did not stir. He stood Anna up on the floorboards, cooling now in the night's chill. There was no interruption in the rhythm of the soldier's breathing. The woman was no doubt very tired herself, and despite her automatic precautions, she most likely knew how difficult it was for someone to enter a sorcerer's house unbidden or unwelcome. That sense of security dragged her into a deeper sleep than she might otherwise have known.

But he could not count on that, so he moved Anna gently and patiently toward the shuttered balcony. It was odd. He felt himself within her body, perceived the world through her senses, and yet he felt distant. It was not the feeling of life. The deeper he reached, to know again the beat of her heart and the surge of her blood, the farther those pulses of life receded. It vexed him for reasons he could not understand and distracted him constantly. But his life had been one of concentration and control. There was no need for concern yet. He would surely become used to this new mode of existence.

Under his guidance, Anna moved as deliberately and unconsciously as a sleepwalker. Her fingers quickly found the shutter's latch and eased it back. Lien's house was obviously well kept, for they came open without a creak. This was the dangerous part. Any change in the level of light would wake a trained bodyguard from the dead. He turned Anna so her body blocked the moonlight that tried to trickle past her shadow. He slipped her through the shutters quick as thought, closing them swiftly behind her. He held her there, listening. Her heart was surely pounding in her chest, and he longed to feel that beat, to know the press of breath again in his lungs. To feel warmth. He felt temperature only vaguely, although he could feel all other sensations through her hands, her skin. It was so strange that he should care about these things. As it was, he was well hidden and almost beyond harm. Very few magics could touch him, and his skills could keep Anna safe to shield and shelter him, and yet he did not want to remain as he was. He wanted with all his strength to be alive again.

No sound issued from within the room. Thankful, Kalami urged Anna forward.

The balcony wrapped itself around much of the second story of the house, a style favored by those in the south of Hung-Tse grand enough to have a second story. Kalami made Anna flit lightly along its length. He felt her dreams twist and crowd against him. He tried not to touch them. He did not wish to intrude, although he did itch to know what those dreams told her. He did not know the whole of his daughter's mind, and that worried him. He did not wish her to be able to hide from him.

Well, perhaps that could be dealt with, but there were other matters to be settled first.

The silver-and-shadow gardens spread out below the rail at Anna's left shoulder. The doors and windows on the right were flanked by terracotta images of various guardian spirits—dogs and dragons, cranes and horses, even soldiers, some as big as Anna. But the household did not rely too much on such protection because all the portals were securely shuttered. Annoyance rippled through Kalami and Anna's dreams stirred uneasily. Kalami calmed himself at once. This would all be easier if

Anna could remain asleep. Clarity of thought was more difficult when she was awake. It was as if her mind intruded on his, instead of the other way about.

I must come to a good understanding of this way of being or I will remain in danger.

A set of stone stairs led down to the lower floor of the house. At the bottom, it did not take much looking to see that the lower entryways were also shuttered tightly. In the distance, he thought he heard, or perhaps Anna thought she heard, the crackle of a fresh fire starting. Somewhere beyond the garden walls, someone shouted. Kalami suppressed his impatience. This was no good. The prospect of riots on his doorstep had made their host careful. It would have to be the garden. Together he and Anna were surely strong enough for what needed to be done. The little distance might give them a certain advantage.

Any sorcerer could feel a spell being created or destroyed, especially if it was being done nearby. Inside Lien's house there were surely tools for magic that would make what he had to do easier, but the risk of the old man's sensing the working was greater. Outside there was far less to work with, but the chances of discovery were also fewer.

Kalami turned Anna's path across the grass. The dew had fallen and her bare feet quickly grew wet. She must have felt the damp and chill, for Anna's own mind stretched and opened. She woke.

"Father? What is it?" She blinked, looking around her, her footsteps hesitating and a child's startled fear running through her.

Be easy, Daughter. It is time to arrange our escape.

"You said you'd wake me."

And so I have. I needed to get you out of your room before I did. I did not want you to make any sound that might have woken Mae Shan.

Anna accepted this answer. *Where do we go, Father?*

Down to the trees.

Light, swift, and strong, Anna ran across the lawn toward the grove. Her dexterous child's fingers quickly stripped the twigs from the tree branches Kalami indicated and she deposited them in her deep sleeve. Kalami found a moment to marvel in what it was to be a child again. His own boyhood was so far away and the visceral memory of it had been let fall wherever his body lay.

But there was no time to revel in this. Who knew how long the bodyguard would remain asleep, or whether diligent Cai Yun would take it into her head to make a midnight tour of the gardens now that the "sailors" had been sent away on other errands.

Now, we need a round stone and a sharp stone, and a place by one of the ponds or streams where we will not be easily seen.

A stream chattered and murmured beyond the trees. In the style of Hung-Tse gardens, it had been carefully routed in an auspicious direction, its bed worked over until the right mix of stone and sand gave it its particular pleasing song. Anna's eyes were as quick as her fingers and she picked up a knife-edged flint from the shallow edge of the stream and a water-rounded piece of sparkling granite from the bank. She retreated deep under the branches of an ancient willow and knelt down, spilling her finds out onto the grass that grew sparsely among the hunching roots.

Now, Anna, you must remain quiet and let me work. As I begin, you must draw on your magic for the shaping. Can you do this?

"I will try, Father."

You will succeed, Daughter. With these things, we will put the household to sleep. Let us begin.

Gently, as he had once reached out to encompass the shaping of spells, Kalami took his daughter's hands and the fibers of her voice. She was nervous, and he tried to soothe her, but he had little attention he could spare. He had to think now, to remember clearly. He knew this working. He only had to bring it to him again, but it seemed so very far away. Anna's hands shook a little as they began laying the twigs out in neat piles beside the granite stone.

"I am come into the dark night. I am knelt beside the flowing waters before the clean washed stone. I have taken the sacrifice of the forest and brought it to the earth."

Anna, holding herself still inside her own mind, felt the pattern inherent in the words and the laying out of the tools and reached within and without and drew up the magic.

Kalami almost lost himself in the rush of it. He had expected a stream, this was a torrent, a roaring flood. Had he lived, this would have drowned him. As it was he had to struggle to keep from being washed away. He could no longer move Anna's hands, he could only hold them frozen while he tried to grasp even the tenth part of Anna's power to shape into what suddenly seemed his pathetic weaving.

He had known himself to be strong in life. He had known Anna's mother carried a strength even greater, but neither of them could be compared to what they had created together.

What would Bridget have thought had she known?

"Who's Bridget?" asked Anna.

Kalami started and snapped back to himself, fighting to stay whole against the wild current of Anna's gift.

Help me, Daughter, we must concentrate.

Anna, schooled to obedience of her elders, immediately began to concentrate. In control of himself and her once again, Kalami reached for the flint. He pressed the fine edge against Anna's palm.

Anna balked, but Kalami held her hands still. *It is necessary, Anna. It is a small thing, but it is the only true power we have.*

"But it is blood magic. Master Liaozhai forbid . . ."

Master Liaozhai is dead and his understanding is over. If we do not do this, Lien will take me from you.

That silenced Anna's protests, and Kalami swiftly tore the soft skin of her palm, feeling her wince with the pain.

My brave child, he told her approvingly. To himself he thought there was a great deal his daughter had to unlearn.

But he must concentrate. The tide of her magic would ebb otherwise. He must bring his mind and her spirit to the task. Kalami focused on the world before him, on the blood that welled from his daughter's palm and on the shining stone.

"As my blood covers the stone, so shall my will cover the house of Lien." Anna's voice was light, almost a whisper, as he pressed her palm against the stone's curving surface. She winced again, although he held her still.

"As the stone is surrounded by the sacrifice of the forest, so shall the house of Lien be surrounded."

One twig from each tree, their ends overlapping to form the beginning of the pattern. Bitter willow, poison laburnum, chokeberry, bright fire maple, and all the rest. With Kalami's silent prodding, Anna found the pattern, laying down the twigs, making three rings of seven twigs each around the stone. This was not the sort of working she was used to, but with Kalami there to guide her hands, her power moved willingly to the strange shape, and her mouth spoke the words, adding another guide, another shape, another way to draw the power to the work. He found the rhythm of it, and the rhythm guided the current of the power, drawing in and down to wash into the working, and Kalami knew himself to be strong once again.

"I have made three walls of stone and three gates of iron and in them place the house of Lien. Let no creature stir, let no vapor enter or exit, let no thing that flies or creeps or walks find entrance or egress from the house of Lien . . ."

Again Anna hesitated. To her, the red palm print of her blood over the stone seemed to glow in the moonlight. Fear touched her spirit, raising her thoughts into sharp relief. This was too strong, too much. Her will trembled under the rush of her own power. Would this not smother them? She felt her power being drawn into the stone through the weaving, through her blood, and it frightened her, even as she realized this was a great working and she could complete it easily.

Kalami held back his anger with difficulty. He had to concentrate, had to hold the shape of the working.

No, no, Daughter. They will not smother. When we are gone, the wind will blow away the twigs and break the spell. We are only buying time to make our escape.

Her fear abated some and Kalami held tighter to her.

"I have made three walls of stone and three gates of iron." Anna's hands gathered up the last of the twigs and began to lay them down. "And in them I place the house of Lien. Let no creature stir, let no vapor enter or exit, let no thing that flies or creeps or walks find entrance or egress from the house of Lien . . ."

The whole world was the sticks and the stones, the bright red blood and the power that spilled forth, making the words true, shaping the world. Anna ceased to struggle or fear, caught up in her own strength and the delight of it.

How great his daughter would be when he returned her to Tuukos. What they would accomplish together!

"This is my word and . . ."

Motion flashed across Anna's field of vision, scattering the twigs and knocking the stone into the stream. Startled, Kalami lost his hold and Anna stared up into Lien's thunderous face.

"Did you think my house so poorly defended, Valin Kalami? Did you think I would not know what you do here?"

Anger rushed through Kalami, too swift to be contained. He thrust Anna aside and took hold of her voice.

"You know nothing, old man. Had you been willing to let me take my child and go, no threat would have come against your house." Such words sounded incongruous in Anna's high-pitched child's voice, but it was the only one available to him.

In the back of her own mind, Anna cried out, but Kalami ignored her.

"Do not waste your time with us," he said. "Hung-Tse is falling. Isavalta will fall. I only want to take my daughter back to the Holy Island so we will be able to aid our own during the time that follows."

"Were you a living man, I might take your word," said Lien softly. "But you are of the dead. You will drink up the life of this child, and then of any others who you touch. You will give all to the Old Witch because you cannot stop yourself. It is now your nature and your dictate."

"I have no dictate!" Kalami shouted. "Do not stand against me, Lien."

In response, Lien drew back his hand and tossed out a length of silken ribbon that shimmered in the moonlight. Kalami threw Anna to the ground before the stream, and the ribbon passed overhead. Her hands grasped the bloody stone and he heaved her to her feet so she could throw it hard. The effort made her scream, but the stone caught Lien squarely on the knee, knocking him off balance.

Kalami took command of Anna and together they ran. The gate would be locked, but its slats were spaced to prevent a grown man from creeping through, not a slender child. Anna's heart and lungs labored and her bare feet stung. Distantly, he felt her calling to him, wanting answers, wanting comfort, but there was no time for that now.

A pair of hands seized Anna's shoulders, jerking her off her feet. They turned her roughly around, and Kalami saw the bodyguard, Mae Shan, tall and angry in the moonlight.

"It's late for mischief, mistress," she said coolly.

Startled, Kalami's control of Anna slipped for a moment. "Help me, Mae Shan," she gasped, her tiny frame shaking. "I don't know what's happening. Lien Jinn tried to take Father away. Father . . ."

"I'm taking you back into the house, mistress," said Mae Shan. "It's not safe for you to be out."

"No!" cried Anna, struggling in Mae Shan's grip. But the bodyguard was evidently used to this, and she easily kept a firm hold of Anna while propelling her toward the house where a light appeared in the windows of the lower story.

"Mae Shan, he's going to try to take Father away," said Anna. "Don't let him do this. I won't be able to get to the Holy Island."

Mae Shan said nothing, she just kept walking, her hands heavy on Anna's shoulders.

"You're supposed to keep me safe!" wailed the child.

"I am, mistress," was all Mae Shan said.

A reply, Kalami realized, he had been expecting. The guard was unimaginative, but she was steadfast. Anna would not reach her through such pleading.

Hush, Anna, he told her. *Be still. We must wait our chance.*

"What's happening? Why are they afraid of you?" Anna whispered.

Your guard does not understand, so she fears. Her uncle . . . Anna's quick ears caught Lien's footfall coming up behind. *Her uncle seeks to curry favor with those now in power in Isavalta by delivering you to them.*

"But I thought the dowager . . ."

The dowager is no more, Anna. Her son rules Isavalta now, along with his wife who is of Hastinapura. The name of the southern empire sent a chill through Anna's mind and Kalami was pleased to feel it. *She has clever sorcerers to aid her, and they will be very glad to make use of you.*

"I don't want to go there," murmured Anna.

I will not let them take you, but we must be watchful and wait for our time to escape. Trust me, Anna, keep silent and let me help you when the time is right.

He felt her acquiescence and let her, in turn, feel his pride and approval. So much, so strange, and so fast, especially for such a young child, and yet she was still ready and able to obey her father. There was obviously much to be said for Hung-Tse's emphasis on filial piety.

He did not dare let them enter the house. There would be locks there that no working of his, or Anna's, could quickly undo. But the memories his daughter had shared with him showed him a way.

The bodyguard who paced behind her with one hand on Anna's shoulder carried a knife beneath her sash, and Anna knew exactly where.

They reached the stone steps that led to the back door of the house. For one brief moment, Lien was in arm's reach.

Let me work, Anna, murmured Kalami to his daughter, and he made Anna shrink, just a little toward Mae Shan.

Lien set his foot upon the stair. Kalami twisted Anna in her guard's grip and she snatched at the knife. Mae Shan shouted. Lien turned.

Kalami moved Anna's arms and plunged the knife deep into Lien's belly.

Lien's eyes widened in surprise, as the blood fountained out, spattering Anna and Mae Shan with bitter warmth. He did not pause to wrench the knife free again. While Mae Shan stood frozen, Kalami ducked Anna beneath her arms and ran, holding out her hands and arms that dripped red with Lien's life blood. Here was all the power he needed to make their escape.

In the back of her own mind, Anna was screaming. Terror poured through her in waves as he made them race back toward the trees, toward the stream, before the blood dried and hardened and became useless.

Anna, Anna, calm yourself. Calm yourself. I need your help.

But the child would not be calm and Kalami realized this much he would have to do himself. For him to cross back into the Land of Death and Spirit should be a fairly simple matter, what would be difficult was bringing Anna with him.

Listening to his young daughter scream in the back of her own mind, Kalami ran. He could not hear clearly, but there did not seem to be any footfalls behind him yet, and the brook was ahead, rippling in the light of the sinking moon. He paused Anna and on the bottom of her bare feet he smeared Lien's cooling blood.

Do not fight me, Anna. I need your magics.

But Anna had grown no more coherent, and now he heard running, he heard shouts to wake the house. Mae Shan was on her way.

Kalami steeled himself and reached. He reached into Anna's blood, and into her bones. He reached out through her skin and senses. He stretched the whole of himself, deep within and far without. He made her run, leaving bloody footprints on the grass, lifting her bloody hands to the wind, panting out the words of the spell like a frantic prayer.

"Beyond life there is a forest. Within the forest there is a river. At the end of the river is another shore. On the other shore, there waits the home of Valin Kalami. Breath and blood, carry Anna Kalami to the river. *Jukka* and *Keiji* carry Anna Kalami to the river's end. My heart's blood, my breath, my life, carry Anna Kalami to the home of Valin Kalami."

Anna's feet hit the running water, stumbling and skidding over the stones. Weak and disoriented, she was no longer able to keep Kalami from loosening the depths of her power. As mortal blood mixed with water, water's song, and words, Anna's power came flooding to the surface to be worked into the needed shape, to join the stream with the river Life that flowed through the Shifting Lands.

"Beyond life there is a forest," Kalami threw the words out joyfully, full of night and power and freedom. As the spell began again, the bodyguard charged through the grove like one of night's own demons.

Mae Shan! Anna would have cried the name aloud if she could.

Mae Shan lunged forward, but it was too late. The garden split open like a rotted fruit, and they were on another shore.

Anna vanished and Mae Shan stared openmouthed in a night gone suddenly silent. It was only gradually she was able to hear the chattering of the stream again. Training made her want to search the banks, to beat the trees and bushes looking for the fugitive, but she knew that would be futile. Wherever Kalami had taken Anna, the child was beyond Mae Shan's reach.

She had failed.

The realization crashed down on her. Mae Shan staggered. The solemn little girl was gone, lost to the possession of a restless ghost, and Mae Shan who had sworn to protect her with life and breath stood here, gaping like a fish. She should not have fallen asleep. She should have known even Uncle Lien's house could be breached . . .

Thinking of Uncle Lien turned Mae Shan around and she ran back to the house.

He was still alive when she reached him. Auntie crouched beside him, trying to stanch the blood with her bare hands, tears pouring from her eyes. The blood that oozed from his wound was dark and sluggish now. His eyes were bright with pain and his breathing was far too fast as his body tried to work muscles that had been torn by Anna's attack.

No. Not Anna's. Kalami's. It was Kalami that did this, never Tsan Nu . . . Anna.

Mae Shan rolled him out of the puddle that had formed and tore at his sash.

"You must get help. Who can we summon?" she asked breathlessly. She wrestled his jacket free and folded it, pressing it hard against the great well in his belly.

"I should stay," began Auntie. "You are faster . . ."

"I don't know anyone!" snapped back Mae Shan, forgetting manners and piety together. "Go!"

Auntie rose to her feet and dashed across the yard on bare feet, running for the gate. Mae Shan bent low over her uncle. The jacket was already soaked through, leaving her hands sticky with his blood. "Uncle, what can I get you? Have you a spell . . ."

Froth bubbled around Uncle Lien's lips. "No," he rasped. "The Last One is waiting. I am to go with him."

"No, Uncle." An unfamiliar wildness filled Mae Shan. "I need you. He's taken her from the world. How am I to find her without you?"

The light in Lien's eyes faded and Mae Shan pressed the back of her hand against her mouth to stop the cry, but for a moment, the old sorcerer rallied.

"My sash . . ." he murmured. Keeping one hand on her useless bandage, Mae Shan laid the broad black sash in her uncle's outstretched hand.

"Get me on my side," he whispered.

Mae Shan bit down all protests and rolled him so he could face the sash, and the blood, and his niece.

"Cai Yun," he breathed as the blood began to flow anew and he coughed, his chest heaving and spasming and yet more froth dripping down into his scant beard. Mae Shan was sure this must be the end, but with a groan, Lien reached out a trembling hand to his own blood where it spilled onto the grass. He trailed his fingers in the blood that smelled of iron and the sea. Lien touched his bloody fingers to his sash, tracing crude characters, writing some message to the gods. At the same time, he began to sing. His voice was high and broken and the words were meaningless to Mae Shan. But he seemed to gain strength through the singing, his eyes becoming clearer and his tremors easing. Maybe she would tie the bespelled sash around his waist and he would heal himself. Maybe he summoned another sorcerer to his side, or placated the Last One. He was a great sorcerer. He would not leave her alone.

Slowly, clumsily, Lien tied a knot in the sash. He coughed out one breath over it and pulled the ends tight.

"Mae . . ." he coughed again.

"I am here, Uncle."

He coughed again, pain racking him and more blood pouring onto the ground. It smelled foul, and Mae Shan knew his bowels had been punctured. He was going to die. If not now, then later after days of lingering, painful infection. Mae Shan felt as if her heart were crushed.

"Take this to my boat at the river's edge," Uncle Lien said so softly Mae Shan had to bend close to his mouth to hear. "You will know it by the signs painted blue on its side. Tie this sash to the mast and raise the sail, then undo the knot I have tied. The boat will sail you to Isavalta through the Shifting Lands. Speak my name in the court. You will find help. Do not . . ." His eyes lost their focus, but he spoke on, ever fainter while the tremors took his hands. "Do not leave the boat once you begin your journey. Invite no one on board with you. Give nothing away, accept nothing you are given. Believe nothing you see in the Shifting Lands . . . Pray, Niece, pray to Heaven you get through. I see the future here and Heaven must tremble at it . . . he must not keep hold of her. They must not be able to use her."

"I swear, Uncle," said Mae Shan.

But Uncle Lien had no more words for her. His eyes closed, and all his body went slack. In a moment, his eyes opened for the final time, still and staring, and Mae Shan knew the Last One had taken charge of him. Lien would now have his name written in the final records and all his deeds tallied. In three days, he would be led to Heaven so the gods could choose his next life.

Mae Shan's mind felt numb, but oddly clear. With deliberate care she lifted up her uncle's body and carried it to the scroll room, laying it out straight, folding his hands in an attitude of prayer and repose, mopping up the filth as best she could. Whispering apologies to her ancestors, she took the white silk lineages down from the walls and covered him over. She had no other shroud. She would not have her auntie return and find him left abandoned in the garden without reverence or regard.

She lit the incense from the charcoal in the covered brazier that still smoldered beside the altar. She touched her forehead to the floor five times, trying hard to pray, but her hollow heart refused to fill with any such words in this room where just a few hours before Uncle Lien had helped her mourn for lost Wei Lin.

Where was Auntie? When would she come back? Was she delayed in the streets? Did she believe there was still hope, or had she felt his spirit fly away?

Mae Shan went around to all the windows and doors and flung them wide open so that the wind would blow any malignant spirits through the house and they would not be trapped inside to work evil with the blood and bones of her uncle. Auntie Cai Yun would see this and know what had happened.

I am sorry, Aunt. I cannot wait for your return. One more wrong. One more time she must choose duty over blood, and Goddess of Mercy, there was so much blood . . .

Stop this, she ordered herself. *Realign your heart and your fool head. You heard what Uncle Lien said, and your duty is still before you.*

But neither head nor heart would clear for such urgings. She picked up the knotted sash and her spear. Staring at the blood for a long moment, another slow thought formed and she went upstairs and reclaimed her bow and arrows. Her knife she left where it had fallen in the grass outside. She could not bear to touch the thing again.

Such a soldier, such a guard. Perhaps the Phoenix meant me to die with the rest. Perhaps I should use that knife to make the last apology for my uselessness.

Even as she thought those words, she realized she might have done so, but Uncle Lien had laid a charge upon her.

She had to try. She could not do otherwise.

She shut the gate firmly behind her as she left the garden, with the idea that if there were any remaining spells of protection in the walls, that might help them hold. There was still no sign of Auntie.

Praying for the dead and apologizing to the living, Mae Shan headed down to the river. Dawn was coming up, staining the water pink and gold and outlining the boats and barges running as fast they could away from disaster, and perhaps toward more disaster yet.

Uncle Lien's boat still waited at the end of the dock, all rigged and ready. Mae Shan was a little surprised. She would have thought this far too tempting a target for a thief or refugee to pass by. Perhaps those who had come down here to make their escape knew it belonged to a sorcerer, and a pirate, who might be able to track them down no matter how far they went.

The boat itself was a small, shallow thing, with a mainmast and a bowsprit, seemingly made for short trips up and down the river. The gunwales had been painted with blue symbols in some writing she could not read, any more than she could understand the spell-song Uncle Lien had formed with his last breaths.

She clambered aboard. The rocking of the deck beneath her feet felt instantly familiar, but at the same time she was at a loss. This vessel was very different from the flat-bottomed barge that she had helped her father and brother pole up to market and back home. She had never learned to handle any other sort of vessel. As a soldier, it had been presumed that should she need to go anywhere by water, there would be sailors to transport her where she might need to go.

Calling on old memories of Huaxing's wharfs and docks, she undid the lashing on the sails and then the mooring on the boat. She found the pole and pushed off from the dock into the river's current. Then she angled the steering oar to take the boat out toward the middle of the river. The wind caught her skin, drying tears she did not realize she had shed and bringing the scents of water and garbage, and very faintly, the smell of smoke.

The boat slid into the stronger current near the middle of the river, and Mae Shan drifted, feeling the weight of Uncle Lien's sash in her sleeve.

She could escape this now. She could pole herself home, find her family. Their village had stood flood, famine, and disaster before. It had seen emperors and empires rise and fall again. Surely she'd be safe there.

Before those thoughts could take a more tenacious hold, Mae Shan found the main line to hoist the sail. She hauled on it, lashing it around a block she assumed was there for the purpose. The snow-white canvas caught the wind and drew taut. The golden dawn light showed her that the canvas was not just plain white cloth. Woven into its surface, white on white, were patterns and symbols she could scarcely make out.

Standing and staring did not seem a luxury she should take right now. Mae Shan pulled out the sash and tied one end to the mast. With fingers made warm by her work, she undid the knot Uncle Lien had tied so tightly. Then she stood on the bench by the steering oar, pointed her gaze down the river, gripped the oar shaft, and waited.

Mae Shan had heard of the Land of Death and Spirit, but as she had no magic about her, she had no expectations of crossing it until the Last One led her to Heaven. She knew stories, of course. Everyone knew the tales about sages and clever children dealing with monsters who had emerged from the Shifting Lands. Her brothers and sisters told other stories about those monsters, who also ate those foolish sages and children who turned out to be impious, or not so clever after all. There were stories told around the fire or the stove at night, of ghosts and possessions, betrayed loves, or heroes who took their battles beyond the bounds of the world, right up to the shores of Heaven.

Her uncle had never told her a single one of these stories.

The banks slipped by in the brightening dawn. Dark figures, alone or in crowds, moved in and out of the deepest shadows that remained. Other boats scudded down the broad river, but they ignored her. Mae Shan stuck by her oar, trying to steer a straight course and watching the boom swing slightly in the wind and wondering if she should bring the sail in a little, and when she would move beyond the world.

As the sun rose higher, the sky became covered with a grey haze that seemed too lazy to gather itself into clouds. The wind blew cold and Mae Shan shivered under her quilted jacket, wishing for her padded armor.

They say in Isavalta it is so cold that people wear their coats to bed.

Movement on the bank caught Mae Shan's eye. A figure, this one brighter than the others had been, dashed down the bank. The sleeves and hems of her robe streamed out behind her. Clearly a woman of good family. Behind her ran a cluster of thick armed thugs, and they were gaining.

Don't look, said part of Mae Shan's mind. *Don't dwell on it. You have a greater errand.*

The woman on the bank stumbled and it was clear, even from this distance, that she would soon fall. Mae Shan cursed, and groped for the boat's anchor. She tossed it into the river. It splashed into the water, and then Mae Shan noticed what was truly wrong.

The splash made no sound. It was as though she had been suddenly and completely deafened. The woman on the bank stumbled again. Her hair had come loose and fell like a curtain over her eyes. Her feet were bare. The thugs drew closer. The boat swayed at anchor, and in all the world there was no sound, not even the slap of waves against the boat's

hull. Mae Shan stared as one of the thugs snatched at the woman's flowing sleeve, and remembered how another name for the Land of Death
and Spirit was the Silent Lands.

Believe nothing you see.

Cursing again behind clenched teeth, Mae Shan hauled the anchor
stone up. The rope was completely dry. The stone made no noise as it
dropped to the deck. Current and wind took hold again and pulled the
boat forward. On the bank, the woman tripped and finally fell and the
thugs descended. Mae Shan looked to the steering oar, and decided it was
useless to try to steer a river when you could not trust what you saw. She
sat herself down on the bench and gripped the rail, grimly pointing her
gaze forward and trying with all her soul to trust to Uncle Lien's spell.

The banks around the river changed slowly. What had been a house
when she glanced at it a moment before became a hoary tree, its branches
heavy with ruby fruits. Mae Shan's stomach rumbled. What had been a
temple became a palace, its doors open and inviting and faintly seen figures waving welcome to her. Her exhaustion doubled. What had been
other boats turned to beasts, great swans and cranes. She glimpsed a
horse with a fish's tail broaching a wave. A scaly back that could have belonged to a dragon slipped past the hull.

Mae Shan squared her shoulders to attention and pointed her eyes
ahead, calling on all her training and discipline. *Believe nothing you see,*
she repeated to herself. Motion and fantasy tugged at her vision, but she
held herself still, despite the scents of broiling meats and fresh fruit that
drifted on the soundless wind.

It's just another long watch. It will soon be done.

But from the corners of her eyes, she could see the banks change
again. They grew closer. They grew darker, rising high above the boat to
become cliffs of limestone hung with vines and dotted here and there
with bright clusters of flowers. Something moved among the vines. Mae
Shan's gaze flickered upward before she could stop it. Tiny figures
climbed up and down the vines like monkeys, but the figures did not
have monkeys' faces. They had the faces of dogs, or devils, or humans
with wide, white eyes. They pointed and mocked at her, and she knew if
she could hear, she would be surrounded by raucous laughter echoing
through the stone chasm.

A gout of water erupted in front of the boat. Mae Shan started backward. Another gout leapt up to starboard, and two more to port. Something dark whizzed past. Mae Shan ducked. The thing bounced off the rail and landed in the water, raising another silent splash.

The grotesque creatures had stopped laughing and were now throwing stones, leering openmouthed at her in their anger.

She felt the wind of the eerily silent missiles as they breezed past her ears to splash into the water or glance off the rails or the bowsprit. They came from all sides. Mae Shan ducked down, covering her head with her hands, but it was no good. The missiles breezed past her knuckles and elbows. The little boat had no hold. There was no place for her to take shelter. She huddled in the bottom of the boat, feeling it shudder as the rocks bounced off rail, bow, and stern. Her back felt naked, but she could see no canvas or other covering she could use.

Mae Shan?

The sound of a voice was so startling, Mae Shan looked up. The monkey demons gaped and grinned, and hurled more of their dark missiles at her, but above them, on the edge of the cliff, Mae Shan saw a slender woman dressed in fine silks standing beside a youthful figure robed entirely in white.

Wei Lin. Even from this distance, even as the boat drifted farther away down the current, Mae Shan knew it was Wei Lin. Of course. It was the third day. Wei Lin's deeds had been recorded and now the Last One was taking her to Heaven.

Was it the nature of the land that made her feel the boat moving, without Wei Lin drifting farther away?

Why are you here, Mae Shan? Wei Lin's voice reached Mae Shan through the windows of her mind, not through her ears. *You are not dead.*

"No," she said and her voice sounded loud and hollow as it rang through the canyon. It seemed to enrage the monkey demons. They swarmed lower on their vines, baring their long fangs, lunging out as far as legs and arms would stretch. They swung down low, shaking fists and waggling tongues. Some jumped from vine to vine, swinging ever lower. Mae Shan saw hunger in their eyes.

You are a divided, living soul, Mae Shan. You are bringing danger to yourself. Go. Leave here.

"I'm trying, Wei Lin." The sail was full, the current moved, the boat stayed in the middle of the river, but the missiles rained down, splashing up the river water on all sides.

"Wei Lin . . . I'm sorry . . ."

I know. Let go of regret, Mae Shan. It holds you to me. I love you, my sister. Do not seek after me anymore.

Seek after you? Mae Shan closed her mouth around the words. Had she been? Was it possible her own desires guided the course of this river and her boat? These were the Shifting Lands as well as the Silent Lands, who knew what might shape them?

The Last One laid a slender hand on Wei Lin's arm.

I must go, Mae Shan. Hold to your duty, Sister. Do not try to follow me.

The Last One turned away, and Wei Lin, folding her hands into her sleeves, followed peacefully and obediently behind.

Mae Shan could not take her eyes from her sister's retreating form. *Wait,* she wanted to shout. She had so much more she wanted to say. She wanted to touch her sister's hand once more, to bid her farewell properly, to ask her to thank Uncle Lien for all he had done when he too reached Heaven.

But the demons left her no time to gather herself. The missiles and the leering redoubled. The winged creatures swooped low, pelting the deck with their stones and making huge, teary eyes at her in mockery as they clutched their chests and beat their breasts, wagging and sobbing. The boat sailed on, but they followed behind, laughing at her grief, throwing their rain of stones down.

Mae Shan could stand no more.

I'll teach you to keep your distance at least.

She picked up her bow and removed the silk casing from the string. She strung the weapon and selected an arrow. Her actions seemed to amuse the demons, because they wagged their heads and bodies even more furiously, swooping close to the masts and rails, laughing their silent, jeering laughs, mocking Wei Lin's piously folded hands and bowed head.

Mae Shan sighted carefully along the arrow shaft, picking out one of the largest demons with the biggest grin. *Let them watch him fall and see how much they laugh then.*

She loosed the arrow. The big demon threw up its arms as the shaft approached, and sank deep into its chest. Its jaw went slack and its eyes went blank, and its wings folded and it plummeted toward the river.

But before it reached the water it spread its wings again, swooping up to the deck, and landing neatly on the rail. With one clawed hand, it pulled the arrow from its own chest and snapped the shaft in two.

For a moment, Mae Shan could only stare. Other demons settled on the rails, on the mast, on the bow.

Give nothing, Uncle Lien had said. *Take nothing.* And this was why. Until she had given these creatures something of herself, they did not, perhaps could not, touch her. But memory came too late, and they were all around her now, landing on mast and rail. They smelled of corrupted flesh, and their eyes glowed like golden lanterns.

The largest demon bowed in mocking thanks and hopped lightly onto the deck. Mae Shan tossed the bow aside. The demon grinned and slunk closer. Mae Shan snatched up the spear and swung it wide, sending the demons scuttling quickly back for a single heartbeat.

Wait for me, Wei Lin, she thought grimly. *I won't be long.*

The Vixen sat on her high, green hill, waiting. Foxes and kits frisked in the grass at her feet, snapping playfully at each other's noses and tails. The Vixen lifted her nose, and the playing stopped at once. All ears pricked up. All muzzles turned.

A white fox and a red kit trotted through the summer-green grass. The other foxes parted for them, recognizing this pair as two of their own. The new arrivals fawned at the feet of the Vixen, rubbing their chins against her paws. She lapped the forehead of the elder, and gently nuzzled the younger.

"What did you see?" she asked.

"The dead man has hidden himself within his daughter," said the white fox. "He looks out of her eyes and tells her what to do."

"And she obeys?"

"She tries."

"Pity," said the Vixen. "But if he chooses to involve an innocent, there is little that can be done. Has he brought his daughter into the homelands?"

"Even now."

"Very well." The Vixen's eyes glinted in the green light and she stood, her tail whisking to and fro.

"Mother, there is more to tell."

"Speak, then."

"The girl has a bodyguard, who treated us fair and showed mercy, despite the urging of her own mistress and the dead man."

"Did she?"

The white fox nodded. "She has come into the homelands and is even now in danger."

"Foolish woman. Do you beg a boon for her?"

"Mother, I do."

The Vixen considered. She looked first one way, and then the other, and not even the *lokai* who waited on her word and her pleasure could tell all that she saw.

"So many fools," she sighed. "The father seeks to use up the daughter and the mother who freed the father seeks the child she doesn't know she endangered, and all forget the true danger and ignore the true blessing." She considered a moment longer. "Very well, my child, we will grant your boon. There may be advantage here yet."

"And the dead man?"

"He will run about for a time." She snapped her teeth. "But he cannot expect to escape because of a pair of careless eyes. Come." She trotted down the hill and her children followed, eager to learn what new game their mother played.

Chapter Eighteen

Mikkel stood on one of Vyshtavos's many balconies and looked out over the gardens. Just this morning they had been silent and empty. Now they were a sea of mud and people. They huddled in makeshift encampments. Children ran back and forth, calling to each other or their parents. The blue coats and gilded helmets of the house guard flashed here and there. They moved through the crowds, measuring out bread and cold soup from kettles to people lined up with bowls or pots, some with nothing but their empty hands.

The cobbled courtyard was full of the earliest arrivals. Every hand that could be spared was clearing out the palace's lower rooms. Commander Chadek was on the verge of apoplexy, but Mikkel and Ananda had held firm. They would bring as many people into the palace as they could, if for no other reason than a mob on the grounds thinking it was warmer and drier inside might become tempted to try to take what they wanted. People who saw they might at least get a turn at shelter would be more patient.

He could still see the green robes of the god house acolytes moving among the people, cheering them along, listening where needed, praying, singing. Bakhar's people were devout, and strong.

Mikkel found himself wondering if the gods they all worshiped were as good and strong, and a moment later cursing himself for doubt.

It was going to be night again soon. The sun was just three fingers above the horizon. Lord Daren was dead. Mistress Urshila was dead. They had severed the head of the murderess from her body not an hour ago. The Tuukosov woman had laughed as the ax came down. Bridget and Sakra were a world away, if they were that close, and Ananda was trying hard to be strong, but she felt the lack of one of her most loyal servants.

And here he stood—imperial, detached, magnanimous, hungry, frightened, and useless. He had sat with the Council of Lords all morning, and had accomplished exactly nothing. The only answer was they had to wait. They had to let the sorcerers, those who remained alive, work. They had to pray. There was simply not enough known about the Firebird or what it had done, and even an emperor could not change that.

Or could he?

Mikkel looked down at the crowd. This was just the beginning. This was two days of darkness. How many would there be after three, after a week, after a month? How soon could they find new sorcerers to come to court and help the four who struggled through the ancient texts, arguing with themselves? When would the first news come that people had started to die?

Patience, Imperial Majesty, they said. *It is not bad yet. We have time.*

It is not bad yet, but it will become so, Mikkel protested inside himself. *And we only hope we have time.*

The sun had dipped a little farther down. The blue of the sky deepened its hue. Mikkel thought of spending another night staring into the darkness, feeling Ananda pretending to be asleep beside him, hoping that would coax him toward unconsciousness. He thought of waiting and watching that crowd who came to him for help swelling until even the imperial grounds could not hold them all.

No. Mikkel straightened himself up. No.

Walking so quickly his entourage had to scramble to catch up, Mikkel headed down to the god house.

The chamber was a masterpiece of gilt and murals made to house the images of Vyshko and Vyshemir who stood in white robes on their pedestal of black and red marble. The doors to the library and its windows had been thrown open, but the light was dimming quickly in here. He could, however, still see Vyshemir as she held out her cup and her knife and Vyshko who held his pike high over his head, his face fierce and triumphant.

Mikkel kissed the hem of Vyshko's robe reverently, and then looked up into the god's eyes.

Were you afraid? he asked silently. *When you stood on the walls and knew it would be the last thing you ever did? Who did you pray to, you who were about to become divine?*

309

"Imperial Majesty?"

Bakhar, keeper of the emperor's god house, stood diffidently beside the little door that led to the vestments room. He was a portly man with a white beard that flowed down his chest like foam. Mikkel had never known anyone more devout and more humble in the sight of the gods.

As Mikkel looked toward him, Bakhar knelt.

"Forgive me, Majesty. I did not mean to intrude, but I wished to know if there was anything I could do to help."

"Please, stand," said Mikkel. "And there is," he added as the keeper got to his feet with the swiftness of a much younger man. "I need Vyshko's pike."

Bakhar's face went blank with surprise. "Majesty," he began carefully. "If I may ask . . ."

"No," said Mikkel, and he knew he sounded more tired than anything else. "But I need the pike. You will get it from the cask, please."

He was Vyshko's heir. The holy artifacts could not be withheld from him. Bakhar reverenced deeply and went to the golden casket that lay in the largest of the god house's alcoves. Unlit candles surrounded it, waiting for the moment when the fire returned. Bakhar bowed three times before the casket, murmuring prayers. He raised the lid and lifted out a long package of pure white silk. Cradling it in both arms like an infant, he crossed the floor and knelt before his emperor, holding out the silken package with head bowed, lips still moving in prayer.

Mikkel took what he was offered and unwrapped the silk. He had seen the pike before, when he was declared an adult and when he ascended the throne. So he was ready for the fact that it was a battered, unimposing weapon with spots of rust and chips out of its wooden shaft. But the tip was still sharp, and when he took it into his hands, he could still feel, or imagine he felt, the thrum of the god's power inside it, waiting for the time of danger, waiting until it was needed, as it had been once before.

The god house door eased open. Mikkel looked up, expecting to see one of the guards or a page. Instead, Ananda walked into the dimming house.

"My Husband Imperial, I was told . . ." she began. Then she stopped, staring at the kneeling keeper, and at the ancient pike and the white silk draped across Mikkel's arm.

She kissed the goddess's hem without looking at it. "What are you doing, Mikkel?"

Mikkel nodded to Keeper Bakhar, who hesitated a bare instant, probably thinking he might offer himself as mediator for whatever might come next. He quickly thought the better of it, though, reverenced hastily and removed himself back to the vestment room and his private offices.

Ananda came closer. She held out her hand over the holy artifact, but did not touch it. She just closed her fingers into a fist above it and lowered her arm until that fist was clenched at her side.

"What are you doing?" she asked again.

Mikkel draped the white silk over one of the nearby pews. "I'm not going to wait."

"I don't understand."

To his surprise, he found himself smiling. "It's what always happens in the ballads, isn't it? The hero waits until everything else has been tried, until his whole family, or thousands of his people, or at very least his two older brothers, have died. Then and only then does he go out to fight the battle that was his in the first place. I do not have older brothers, and I am not going to wait."

Understanding robbed her face of color and expression. "Mikkel, this is not your battle."

He turned the pike over in his hands, feeling how the place where one's hands would naturally grip had been worn to butter smoothness over the years. "How can it not be? It was my mother who brought this on. That creature will punish the whole of Isavalta for what she did."

"But how can you fight such a thing? You are not a sorcerer."

"No," he agreed. "I am the emperor."

Ananda looked at him, fear filling the whole of her. He wasn't sure he'd ever really seen her afraid before, although he knew she had been many times. She'd told him all about what had happened to her while he was in durance, and they'd held each other and wept for each other's suffering.

"Mikkel, this is nonsense," she said flatly. "The sorcerers have barely begun their studies. We do not even know the extent of what is happening." He knew what she was really saying. She was really saying, "I have just found you. Don't leave me again."

What answer did he have to that love? "The grounds are full of people too frightened to stay home, and you are talking about handing a child over to the sorcerers for their use should their own power fail them. How much worse should it get before I try to act?"

Ananda pulled back, wounded, and he wanted to erase the words at once, but he could not, because they were the truth. "Is this because of what I said?"

The god's weapon lay warm in his hands, but dead. He wanted to cast it aside and embrace Ananda's living form. He wanted never to have to speak a hard word to her, ever. She had suffered for him. Hers had been the first face he had seen when he came back to himself. Hers was the only true touch of love he had ever known. "I'd be lying if I said it was not in part because of that. But it is more." He set the butt of the pike gently against the polished floor. "Ananda, I have been told all my life that the emperor is bound to the land, that he is its first and last defense. That there is a power in him that is beyond magic. It is akin to how a person may become divine."

Ananda wet her lips and tried several times to speak, but failed. At last she forced the words out. "Do you seek to become a god, my husband?"

"No. I seek to become a whole man."

She stood before him, swaying on her feet, uncertain what to do, she who had kept herself alive and powerful for three years with no one to trust but Sakra. Mikkel held out his arm, and to his relief, Ananda rushed into his embrace, throwing her arms around him, pressing her whole self against him as if trying to meld the two of them into one creature.

After a time, she said, "Will I be making myself ridiculous if I ask to come with you?"

"No, never that." He loosened his hold on her reluctantly. "But you cannot come. You have to be here in case . . ."

"In case you die." She spat the last word as if it were a curse. He understood that her anger was not for him. It was for the circumstances that pushed them both to this place.

"In case sacrifice is all the Firebird will accept," Mikkel amended gently. It might be that his life was the only thing the immortal power would accept. He was the first and last defense. He was ready for that. He had been through worse.

Ananda, however, was not ready to make such concession yet.

"Mikkel, what good can I do here? Alone? No one trusts me, and those I could trust have . . . are gone." She looked over her shoulder, as if she hoped Sakra might suddenly appear. "It is you the lords look to. If I am left behind, they'll be plotting my death before your ashes are cooled."

Mikkel looked at the floor. They were both the children of monarchs. They had both grown up in palaces. They knew well the schemes that could breed in gilded corridors. She was not exaggerating, only saying what needed to be said between them, but it was so hard. "Because you, by the fact that will-they nil-they you are empress, will be able to hold the court together long enough for Lord Master Peshek to be recalled from Tuukos. Peshek is esteemed. He can set up a board of regency to govern and choose a new emperor. Then, you can stay . . . or you can go home, if you want."

Ananda moved away from him, cupping her arm where his had touched her. Was she already imagining what it would be like to never have the hope of such a touch again? "Have you thought of anything but this for the past day?" she asked, exasperation coloring her fear.

"I have thought I would be very sorry not to live long enough to meet your children."

And Ananda was in his arms again, and he was kissing her as if it were the first time, as if it were the last time, as if it were all that mattered. The Firebird could have come and burned the world down around them at that moment, and nothing would touch them. There was only their kiss and each other.

When at long last they separated, Ananda, as was her wont, returned immediately to the practical. "The Firebird could be anywhere. How will you know where to look?"

Mikkel smiled and nodded toward one of the murals that showed a landscape crowned by deep summer-green trees. "I believe I know who to ask."

The Vixen paced delicately along the empty shore at the edge of a great blue sea. Once again she had abandoned her fox's shape to walk as a woman, her red hair cascading down the back of her simple shift. A small smile played about her lips as she turned toward the ocean to observe the spectacle upon the surging waves.

On the green waters danced a ring of women. They were each of them naked except for their headdresses and girdles of pearls around their waists. Each of them held something in their hands—a white flower, a bowl, a sword, a living bird. These things they passed among them, tossing them back and forth in flashing patterns that no mortal juggler could have matched. Their feet stamped on the water, disturbing it, roiling it, sending their dance forth on the tides of the water over and over again. Always changing, yet always repeating, closed and open at the same time, the shining brown women danced together and alone. Because while they flashed around in their perfect circle, sometimes there seemed to be seven of them, and other times there seemed to be only one.

The Vixen arched one eyebrow.

Though there was no music to this dance, there was no escaping the rhythm of it. Even the Vixen felt its power. This dance, these goddesses, reached out to shape and reshape the world they ruled. The Vixen felt those shapings buffet her, pulling and compelling, seeking the truth and seeking to bring it new forms. Beneath their feet the mortal world churned in the waters of the ocean. Its very tides answered their compulsion, and those tides in turn shaped their dance.

"Very cyclical. Quite lovely," the Vixen murmured. "But don't you find the damp a bit much at times?"

As she spoke, one of the women caught the bowl tossed to her by her fellows. Her headdress was a filigree of gold and dripped with diamonds. She lifted the bronze vessel high and swung it low, catching up some seawater and scattering it as she spun. The drops flashed in the pale light of the green sky. All at once, where there had been one woman, there were two; the one who danced in the ring, passing on the bowl and receiving instead the white bird, and the other, identical, except she was draped in silk that was the color of the sky and of the water. She trod as lightly and steadily on the ocean as if she walked on a marble floor. She approached the Vixen and regarded her with eyes that were dark as night, but seemed at the same time filled with light.

The Vixen returned that fiery gaze calmly.

"As you have taken the trouble to come all this way, I suppose I should give you greeting," said the goddess.

"Never let it be said that Her Majesty Jalaja, the Queen of Earth, is not the epitome of all that is gracious." The Vixen dropped a curtsy and held the pose.

Jalaja looked down her long nose at the Vixen and said nothing. Eventually, the Vixen straightened up and folded her hands in front of her, waiting patiently.

A spasm of annoyance crossed Jalaja's perfect face. "Will you sit?" she inquired. Because her words were part of the dance of shaping there were at once two thrones on the empty sand, one carved of wood behind the Vixen, and one formed of gold behind Jalaja.

"Ah, yes." The Vixen examined the chair for a moment before she sat, reclining on one elbow. "This indeed is the courtesy and welcome I remember from five thousand years ago. I don't know how I've stayed away so long, my sister."

"I am no sister to you," snapped Jalaja. "My sisters are makers, not destroyers, and if you remember your last welcome, do you also remember how your children bedeviled our chosen and tried, by your word, to throw our lands into darkness?"

As she spoke, an image formed on the rippling water. A young man ran through an orchard, his eyes wide with terror. At his heels ran dozens of foxes, some white, some red, some grey, some the size of wolves, and some tiny kits just out of their burrows. They yipped and snarled. Blood ran down the young man's back and legs.

The Vixen considered the image.

"That was no fault of my sons . . ."

"No, it never is, is it?" said Jalaja coldly.

The Vixen's gaze faltered for one sliver of an instant. "As I recall, they were not your lands at the time, but shall two such as we quibble over details?"

"Why have you come?"

"To talk of this and that." The Vixen gestured dismissively and the scene in the ocean waves vanished. "To renew the bonds of sisterhood that have so long been severed between you and I."

Jalaja heard these words and only looked sour. "It has been five millennia since you were banished from my lands by my servants. Do not think you will gain entry again so easily."

The Vixen's smile grew sharp. "Such a thought never entered my mind, I assure you."

"You should look to your own lands. The Firebird is there now, wreaking its vengeance."

"My lands?" The Vixen laid her hand on her bosom and arched her brows in surprise. "You are mistaken, Your Majesty. I have no lands. I have only my poor family to give me comfort as I wander from place to place. Denied entrance by so many . . ."

Jalaja's expression again turned sour, but the Vixen's smile only spread wider.

"I ask you again, what do you want?"

"I have come to claim the favor you owe me." The Vixen smoothed her skirt down. "One so schooled in all arts of courtesy and diplomacy such as yourself will not have forgotten such a promise."

Jalaja hissed through her teeth. "The promise was made by my sister. Ask her your favor."

"But it was you she promised I should have it from." The Vixen's words took on an edge. "When she came a-begging for a pretty toy that had fallen into my hands so that this game of guardians, cages, and vengeance could begin."

"You had stolen the heart of the Old Witch and trapped her in her house. Had she been able to roam the world, the man Yamuna would have been her prey for his transgressions, and the Firebird would not have been released."

"Perhaps, perhaps not." The Vixen smiled again. "Perhaps if fish could fly they would mate with the birds, and then what good would all our nets be? But even you and I may not rewrite what has happened. The Firebird was brought into being, and you owe me a favor."

Jalaja's face was hard. Her hand curled on her thigh. From the corner of her eye, the Vixen saw a sword cut through the shimmering air, swinging down into the water and slicing the waves in twain. That sword was sharp enough to cut a mortal soul from its body without troubling its flesh, she knew. She also knew Queen Jalaja noted the glance she gave it.

"What is it that you want?" Jalaja asked at last.

The Vixen sighed and looked down at her hands. "Oh, it is a small thing. A trifle. I am almost loath to trouble you with it, but there is this promise between us."

"A small thing, from you?" Jalaja laughed grimly. "I doubt that greatly. What is it?"

"It is a matter of timing. There is a living soul who needs your aid."

"The soldier? That does seem a paltry thing. You could easily do what is needful yourself."

"Alas, I cannot." The Vixen's careless tone was strained.

"And why is that?" Jalaja cocked her head. Diamonds rang against gold. The Vixen said nothing, and Jalaja raised one finger and pointed it at the fox woman. "Because she is a child of Hung-Tse. You cannot touch her life, despite your sneaking." Again the Vixen made no reply and Jalaja threw back her head and laughed. "So! You have found your limit! I never thought I would see this day."

"I am not the one who claims to be the queen of all creation," muttered the Vixen. "Will you honor the bargain between us?"

Jalaja's face grew calculating. She saw that there was some game underneath the Vixen's words, and she sought to see the way the pieces waited on the board. "The soldier is none of ours. You should be speaking with Szu Yi."

The Vixen sighed, and looked down at her hands. "The Goddess of Mercy is rather busy at present. I do not wish to trouble her."

Jalaja's eyes shone with a knowing light. "You do not want her to know that your progeny have snuck back into her realm."

The Vixen lifted one hand languidly, studying her perfect fingers, and still avoiding Jalaja's burning gaze. "She will see for herself, as soon as she looks."

"And what will she do then?" Jalaja leaned forward, trying to catch the Vixen's eye, but the Vixen looked quickly out over the waters, apparently watching the dance. "She and her kin will be furious," Jalaja answered her own question. "You are risking the anger of a goddess, but you come to use the debt between us for the life of one soldier."

The Vixen sighed. Out on the ocean, the dance continued, sword, bowl, lotus, and bird flashing from hand to hand as the goddesses spun out their eternal pattern. "Despite the things that are said about me, I do have some understanding of my place. No matter what the favor, you would not help the likes of me against a fellow goddess."

Jalaja lifted her own brows. "Would I not?"

Slowly, as if it took a moment for Jalaja's words to sink in, the Vixen turned back toward her. "What is it you are saying?"

"Tch, and you are the one with the reputation for such subtlety."

Jalaja sat back in her throne, curling her hands lightly around its golden arms. "Her people have been harassing those I protect for too long. Now, I myself could not interfere in her lands in such a fashion . . ."

The Vixen's eyes narrowed. "But if it were I who asked, you could assist in her, shall we say, distraction, and claim it to be against your will."

"It would of course be against my will," said Jalaja evenly. "But what could I do? I am in debt to you, as you point out."

Now it was the Vixen's turn to sit back and take on an air of calculation. "And what of the soldier? She guards a thing I require."

"So you do have some care for Isavalta after all." Jalaja watched her sisters and herself dancing upon the waters. "One of our own will soon be going that way. He could still help, were he in the right place at the right time."

"But you would not arrange that for nothing," said the Vixen blandly.

"No." Jalaja's smile burned like her eyes did. "You would be bound in debt to me."

"Such majesty bound with such a creature as I? No, I hate to see what is so perfect sullied. I was wrong to come." The Vixen rose to her feet.

"Now you admit you are wrong!" Jalaja laughed. "This is a time of miracles such as to astonish gods. But stay awhile yet." She held up her hand and her smile softened, just a little.

The Vixen sank back into her chair, watching Jalaja closely as if waiting for the trap to be sprung.

"You can have your entry into Hung-Tse and the life of this soldier, if you acknowledge the debt bond to me, here and now, aloud. It is everything that you wanted, and more than you came for, and as a debt, it is after all a small thing."

"For you, perhaps. I do not enter into debt bond with anyone. I have never done so."

Jalaja shrugged. "Very well. Then you may have the life of the soldier, which you have asked for, and I . . . well, I must speak to Szu Yi from time to time, must I not? I fear I cannot promise that I may not make a passing remark about your family's new travels."

The Vixen looked quickly inland, toward the mist that gave the illusion of true distance to the shifting world. Her tongue protruded slightly between her red lips as she considered her options and her normally calm face grew drawn and anxious. Then, at last, the Vixen hung her proud head. "Yes, I acknowledge there is now a debt bond between us. You need do nothing. You do this as a favor to me, and may lay claim to that which is mine in return if I do not fulfill the debt in good order."

"Very good." Jalaja rose, as did the Vixen. The thrones vanished and again there was only shore and sea and the eternal dance. "Go then. Your request will be granted."

The Vixen turned away, and was a red fox again, very much out of place on the seaside, slinking away into the dunes with head and tail lowered. Behind her, Jalaja laughed and rejoined herself in the dance.

But as soon as she topped the dunes, the Vixen paused and looked back on the dance through the screen of thin grasses, her green eyes gleaming.

"What is mine is yours, O Queen. And since you lay claim to what is mine, I must deliver it to you, in your land, must I not?"

It was not until Bridget woke to the full light of morning that she had a chance to be surprised at how easily she had fallen into unconsciousness after limping back to Grace's sofa with a spare quilt and pillow.

Her hair was a rat's nest. She was abominably hungry and thirsty as well.

Sakra was still asleep in front of the cold stove.

Matches, food, something to drink, return at once to Isavalta to tell them what we've learned, and set off again as soon as can be to find Anna. Bridget shook her head at the absurdity of her list of tasks. She wondered how things were in Isavalta, if Prathad and Richikha were managing all right, and how Ananda was coping. It was odd to feel a yearning for the place that had only been her home for a few brief months, but there was a comfort and welcome there she would not quickly find again.

And yet, she was not there. She was here in Bayfield again, calling back ghosts of the dead, and the living.

God Almighty, she tried unsuccessfully to smooth her hair back. *It was supposed to be over and done. It's time for the happily ever after, for new life and beginnings. Why are all the dead coming back to us now?*

Oh, Anna, I didn't meant that. I didn't.

To get away from uncomfortable thoughts, Bridget got up and began rummaging through the drawers of one of Aunt Grace's little curio tables, looking for matches. It was early enough in the spring that the chill was uncomfortable.

Although she tried to be quiet, the noise of her movement woke Sakra. He pushed himself up into a sitting position.

"How are you feeling?" he asked by way of morning greeting.

"Better." She held up the box of matches. "I thought I'd light the stove. We may not have such a luxury when we return to Isavalta."

"A good thought," he said, but his gaze strayed toward the window, as if looking for something.

"What is it?" asked Bridget, although she found she was afraid to know the answer. She did not want there to be any more of this. She did not want to be tired again, frightened again, planning and scheming again. She wanted to rest.

"I was thinking of Medeoan," said Sakra gravely. "I was thinking how it is that she is really gone." He paused. "After you returned last night, did you look at your aunt closely, with both eyes?"

"Yes."

"Did you see the ghost? Did you see any reflection of Medeoan at all?"

"No." Sakra's eyes were strange and distant, almost frightened. "Surely she's at rest now. Even she deserves that much." But he looked away again. "Sakra, what is it? Tell me."

His face tightened, as if in pain. "The promise of the Seven Mothers is that there is no true ending. Life and death, the mortal and the immortal, are wheels within wheels, always turning, coming together and separating again. Your death leads to your birth which leads again to your death, and again to your birth. The dance is forever, the pattern changes but is not broken. But . . . there have been . . . rarely, but there have been those who chose to step outside the pattern, who gave up the dance to leave all to someone who could continue within it, to win a great battle or heal a great wound. There is only oblivion then. No eternity, no rest, no rebirth or Heaven. It is the greatest sacrifice. I think that is what Medeoan has done when she held on long enough to pass on what was needed to you and Grace." His brow furrowed in distress. "I have hated this woman since I laid eyes on her, hated her for all the long, cold years

320

I have been in Isavalta even as I pitied her, even as I tried to forgive when she lay so broken at the end. But . . . the things she did to Ananda, to her own son. You know only some of it, Bridget. But now she has done this. I don't know what to think." He stared past her, seeing only his own confusion. "Part of me wants to believe this is a trick, a perversion, one more evil to add to Medeoan's name. But if you cannot see her shade within your aunt . . ." He shook his head. "May the Mothers help me, I don't know how to forgive so much."

The pain in his face was real. That fact reached her, even though what he was saying had yet to really sink in.

"We know my eyes are not infallible." She offered the words tentatively. Sakra only shook his head again.

"It took the Shifting Lands to deceive them. I do not think a single ghost here could manage so much."

Bridget looked down at her hands. She had tightened her fist around the matchbox, crumpling its paper. "We need to get back. I can't think about any of this here. There isn't room for this sort of miracle in Bayfield."

Sakra's mouth quirked up in the suggestion of a smile. "I think this miracle began in Bayfield."

"Perhaps." Bridget pushed her snarled hair back again. "But I've never known how." She shook herself. "I do, however, know how to light that stove, and I'm getting cold."

"If my lady would do the honors." Sakra bowed gracefully and stood aside for her. In spite of the uncertainty of his feeling of what had happened to Medeoan, he too seemed healed even after so short a rest. His bruises had faded at least a little, and his placid demeanor had reasserted itself. "I fear I am not familiar with this particular variety of luxury." He frowned at the stove as if it were a strange dog in the yard.

Bridget found herself smiling as she brushed past him, giving the cold stove a small pat to show him it really was a well-behaved creature. Sakra laughed a little and Bridget grinned. Despite all, they could find a moment for each other, just as they had from the very beginning. They were at ease together again, and she was grateful for it.

She knelt in front of the stove, layering tinder and kindling on top of the ashes. After a moment, she became acutely aware he was watching her, taking in each movement of her hands, each turn of her head. She found herself wishing she'd gone through the bother of braiding her hair last night so it was not such a mass of snarls, and then laughed at herself for her vanity.

The match struck against the hearthstones. The tinder took on the first try, and the fire blossomed readily, so Bridget was able to lay on the larger sticks of fuel and close the slatted door.

"And there you have it." She stood, wiping her hands on her stained and rumpled skirt.

Sakra was only a few inches away from her. She felt the heat from his skin more acutely than she did the heat from the stove. Seeing her discomfort, he made to move away.

"Wait," said Bridget, coming to one more decision.

Sakra stayed where he was, so close she could reach out to touch him without any effort at all. "Yes?"

She kissed him, slowly and cautiously, as uncertain as any half-grown girl who was afraid of being too bold. He stiffened in surprise at the first brush of her lips, but softened in the space of one short breath, leaning toward her, helping her, wrapping his strong arms around her. He tasted of cinnamon and cloves. He smelled like life itself.

The doorknob rattled. Bridget started like a guilty child, but Sakra only smiled and stepped back a respectful distance. By the time the door opened to reveal Aunt Grace, shawl over her head and market basket slung on her arm, there was no hint of impropriety anywhere but Bridget's blush.

Grace, thankfully, busied herself with hanging up her shawl, which gave Bridget time to compose herself and pick the basket up from the floor where Grace had set it. A dozen fresh eggs waited underneath a blue-checked cloth.

"I thought we could all use some breakfast," announced Grace, as if she expected a challenge. "Good, you have the stove going. There's a frying pan hanging by the basin in the other room. Fetch it out, Bridget, would you? You'll find the drippings can as well."

Bridget shared a glance with Sakra, who gestured with open palms, saying silently they must obey. Bridget agreed.

By the time she returned, she saw Aunt Grace had set Sakra to work cracking eggs into an ancient earthenware bowl she had brought out from somewhere, while Grace added milk from a bottle that must have been delivered on the doorstep.

Bridget had never pictured any such scene taking place in the over-fringed and perfumed parlor, but she realized Aunt Grace had no stove in her living quarters, and she had to do her cooking somewhere.

"While we're at this, Bridget, you can make use of the time, I'm sure," Grace said. "The lavatory's down the hall." Sakra cracked the last egg into the bowl, and Aunt Grace commenced whisking them with a battered fork. She pushed her hair back from her face, and Bridget saw the thin scab on the wound she had caused.

"I'm sorry, Aunt Grace," she blurted out. "About, before. I didn't mean . . . I lost control. I don't know what I'm doing very well yet."

Grace sighed, but did not look up. "I think that's a hazard of our family. Always rushing into things when we don't know what we're really doing." Our family. Not "my sister," not "you." Us.

"Aunt Grace—" Bridget began again.

"No," Grace interrupted. "I'm not ready yet."

So, Bridget held her peace. The lavatory was cramped and none too clean, but it had water that ran clear after a minute of rust-red, and Bridget made a brief wash with the cold water and harsh soap. As Sakra left to do the same, Bridget sat on the sofa and put her hair into some semblance of order with a comb and pins borrowed from Aunt Grace. Other than that, Grace did not pause in her shuttling between the stove and the sideboard that, it turned out, contained her mismatched china and aging silverware.

Bridget let her aunt have her silence and as much space as she could. There was so much to readjust to, she was not sorry for a little time to herself.

Breakfast was the eggs cooked in bacon fat eaten with thick slices of toasted bread spread with new butter and last summer's blueberry preserves, and a most unladylike brew of coffee so thick and black it satisfied even Sakra's taste.

When the last crust had been consumed, Aunt Grace pulled her coffee mug toward her and clutched it with both hands. She stared into the depths of her cup, as if she meant to work one of her divinations from what she saw there. Her whole frame slumped forward, seeking to curl in on her heart, to protect herself. Bridget felt Grace's weariness and worries dragging her down toward the comfortable place in her where nothing had changed, where the old excuses and old refusals were still valid and necessary. Part of her longed to sink back to that place inside herself.

Desiring change, but not to be changed.

When Grace straightened back and shoulders, her carriage became completely that of the woman Bridget had always known, and her heart constricted.

"You'll be leaving now, I suppose," Grace said in her familiar, acerbic tone.

"I've got to finish this thing," said Bridget. "I've got to find Anna."

"Of course." Aunt Grace's gaze returned to her cup. She was struggling with something inside her, something old and strong, Bridget was sure.

"Did . . . that man . . . the one who took your mother away . . ."

"Avanasy," whispered Bridget.

"Yes. Did he love her? Did he truly?"

Which was not at all the question Bridget had been expecting. "Yes," she answered. "Truly, and deeply, beyond the time of his death even."

"You don't know this?" Sakra asked Aunt Grace.

Grace sipped her coffee before she answered. "I know Medeoan loved him," said Grace. "And that he couldn't return that love, and it broke her heart." Memory, so old and yet so new, dimmed her eyes. "Part of her understood he loved Ingrid, part of her could never accept it," she murmured, closing her eyes. "I'm too old for this."

"Aunt Grace, I think *I'm* too old for this." Humor and determination reestablished themselves and Bridget found it easier to breathe. "But we haven't been given the luxury of choice."

"Nor of time," said Sakra, lifting his head as if he had just caught an unfamiliar and unpleasant scent.

"What is it?" asked Grace, before Bridget could.

"I don't know." Sakra glanced about him, looking for the source of whatever it was he sensed. When he did not find it, he frowned. "Nothing, perhaps, but it is a feeling, an intuition. I do not think we should linger here." He looked down at Bridget. "Do you think you are strong enough to make the crossing now?"

"If I must be."

"I think that you must."

Bridget nodded once, accepting his word. She turned to her aunt. "I'm sorry, Aunt Grace. I'd stay longer if I could."

Grace wrapped her arms around herself as if warding off the cold. "Yes, I know."

"All right." Bridget reached out and touched her hand so Aunt Grace would look at her. "When this is over, I'll come back. I swear it."

Grace nodded, but Bridget knew she did not believe. Bridget wanted to speak some words of reassurance, but before she could find any strong enough, Sakra pushed back his chair. Seemingly unable to sit still a moment longer, he got to his feet and began to pace, peering out between the shutter slats, looking for the reason for his sudden restlessness. "No time left," he murmured. "Why? What's coming?" He shivered. "And we still must create a spell for our return."

At that, Aunt Grace drew herself up. "I think I can help."

Bridget stared. She could not stop herself.

"There were advantages to having Medeoan in my head. She really did live her life over again for me, and I managed to retain a few things. Roll back the carpet so we can get ready. Excuse me."

Grace vanished behind her curtain. Bridget looked from the curtain to Sakra and back again.

"I don't know," he said in answer to her unspoken question. "But we can hope."

Grace watched them through the space between the curtain and the threshold. As soon as she was gone, they moved close together, heads bowed, talking in confidence. Anger she did not want stirred inside her. She knew now Sakra was from a place called Hastinapura, and that Medeoan's treacherous husband had been from the same place. As a result she had for years nurtured a hatred of all such people, even though she had married her son to a woman of the same realm, even though she passed on the regret of that blinding hatred with all the other things she had given to Grace.

It was so strange. It was as if she were seeing double. Thinking double. She stood both inside and outside every action. She knelt and pried up one of the floorboards by the bed and pulled her money box out from under it. She unlocked the box with the key she kept in her pocket and dumped the money back into the empty hole. The box was all she needed for now.

Grace's hands opened her jewelry box and set aside the paste and gilt and plucked out the two necklaces that were genuine silver. The first held a locket that Ingrid had given her when she turned sixteen. She had not looked at it in years, and yet she had never given it away. Not even when the wolf was at the door and she could have pawned it for a meal and a down payment on the back rent. She slipped the locket off the chain and pocketed it.

The other was a slim chain hung with garnets given to her by some admirer professing his love. Had he purchased some of her rapidly diminishing virtue with this gift? She stared at it, and could not remember. All at once, Frank's face appeared before her mind's eye. She found herself wishing she could explain things to him, but that wish dissolved in an unexpected eagerness as she planned what was needed, a feeling of finally doing right, of being of good use. She checked the jug on the stand and found it full of water, so there would be no need to go down to the lavatory. She tucked the open money box under her arm, picked up the water jug, and returned to the parlor.

Bridget and Sakra had finished their private conference and begun moving the furniture and rolling up the rugs to expose the scuffed and warped floorboards underneath. Her newly critical eye noted this last with approval. The pattern of the carpet would only confuse the pattern of the spell.

Bridget straightened, dusting off her hands. "Well, Aunt Grace, what next?"

Grace set down the jug on her worktable that had been pushed back against the wall. She handed Bridget the silver chain, and told her, pulling the instructions out of the depths of her new knowledge, not knowing what she was going to say until the words tumbled from her lips. Bridget took it all in, uncertainty bordering on disbelief plain on her face. When Grace finished, Bridget turned to Sakra, her brows arched.

"It could well work," he said. "With sufficient power behind it."

"All right, then." Bridget tucked her skirts up into her waistband and set to work.

Bridget set the open money box in the center of the room, with the key in the lock. She pulled the chimney off one of the lit lamps and trimmed the wick low so it began to smoke and the scent of mineral oil grew sharp. This she set beside the money box. Then she picked up the jug and took a deep breath.

"At the end of the world there burns a lamp. Beneath the light there is a door that is locked with a silver key. Beyond the door there is the river whose name is birth, whose name is death, whose name is life. Beyond the river is Eternal Isavalta." Bridget dipped her fingers into the jug and sprinkled the water onto the floor, walking in a tight spiral working outward from the box and the lamp. "I, Bridget Loftfield Lederle, daughter of Ingrid, daughter of Bridget, have lit the lantern. I have opened the lock with the key of silver, I have opened the door. I have marked the way with water from the river whose name is birth, whose name is death, whose name is life. I will walk the path that is the riverbed and I will set my feet on the ground that is Eternal Isavalta. This is my word and my word is firm."

The room grew cold and the air turned prickly, as if a thunderstorm drew close overhead. The hairs on Grace's arms and the back of her neck rose slowly and her skin shivered with goose pimples. It was getting hard to breathe. The air felt thin.

Bridget began the chant again. She did not look in the least cold. Instead her cheeks were flushed with warmth and her eyes shone brightly. She began the spell again, her voice trembling from effort or from eagerness, it was hard to tell. Grace swayed, pulled by some force she could not name. She wanted to walk, to run, to dance to the rhythm of Bridget's words and the patter of water drops she scattered from her fingertips. The two sounds, the only sounds, and yet somehow they filled the whole world and wove themselves together becoming one indivisible thing, a single command that reached inside to Grace's heart and sinews and would not let her be still.

Bridget repeated the chant again, and then again. The spiral grew to encompass Sakra. The words wound round with the sharp-scented smoke and the patter of the water. Grace felt herself growing lightheaded. Her eyesight grew dim, or was it the room itself blurring, softening, melting into Bridget's words? The photographs on the wall seemed to move, turn, and stare, the images becoming grey ghosts to see her off on this bizarre journey.

The air had grown so cold, Grace was shaking. She could barely breathe. Bridget wound one of the silver chains around Sakra's wrist.

Her face was pale, her gaze distant, her words unceasing, but softening, drifting down into barest whispers.

Bridget's lips moved, but Grace could no longer hear what she was saying, and she began to walk forward, continuing the spiral she had begun with the water. The world around her was melting like butter, slumping, spreading, running out into endless, undefined whiteness.

Bridget led him into whiteness, her eyes wide open.

Then, they were gone, and Grace was alone in her parlor, with only the rolled-back carpet, disordered furniture, and the washing up for three to show that anything had happened.

She let out a breath that she did not know she had been holding, and inside her something loosened. On impulse she got up and walked over to one of the little mirrors that hung between the photographs to help create dim but eye-catching reflections during seances. She studied her own face, and noted that her eyes were sunken a little deeper than they had been when she had given herself over to Medeoan's ghost, her hair touched with a little more silver.

"Well," she said to her reflection. "You're free. Once again. What are you going to do this time?"

Chapter Nineteen

Anna's eyes opened, and for the first time, she saw the Land of Death and Spirit.

The Land of Death and Spirit is a land of part truths, Master Liaozhai had said. *It is not Heaven and it is not Earth, it is only the pathway between. It is a place of memories and remnants and the creatures that are welcome no place else. You cannot see the whole of a thing there, and so must beware of all that you do see.*

Anna had been told often enough that her greatest gift was her ability to see truly. She had never thought what that would mean in a place where everything was partly hidden. Her eyes saw too much all at once, and they saw nothing at all. She saw the world try to show her a deep forest of pine trees with trunks that were wider than she was tall. But at the same time, she saw things that her mind could scarcely understand. She saw fear, she saw love and jealousy, happiness and sorrow, she saw the hundred million memories of the dead swarming like bees. She saw time encasing all like golden ice, not moving at all. She saw a river of voices and worlds cutting its swath through all. She saw its countless winding tributaries weaving through the land like roots beneath soil. She looked up and saw the high blue dome farther away than the sky had ever been and knew it was Heaven.

She saw the ghosts, as thin and fragile as veils of tissue. She saw the spirits flit between them, unnoticed. She saw everything at once, piled on top of one another like sheets of rice paper, for there was no true time or distance to separate one thing from another.

It was too much. Anna clapped her hands over her eyes and moaned.

A hand closed gently about her shoulder. Anna jumped, looked up, and saw her father. He stood out clearly from the chaos around him and he looked exactly as he had the last time she had seen him tall and smiling, wearing his high-necked black kaftan with its bright blue sash. His dark eyes shone with the pleasure of seeing her again.

"Father!" Anna threw her arms around him. The embrace he returned was strong, but it was cool. Now that he was dead, he had no warmth to give her. It didn't matter. He was beside her now and she could see him. She wasn't alone.

"We must hurry, Anna," he said after a time that felt far too short. "It is not safe here."

Worry tightened his voice as it never had while he was in her heart.

"I can't." She squeezed her eyes shut. "I can't see."

She felt him crouching down. "Look at me."

Anna shook her head, feeling suddenly tiny and miserable. She did not want to be assaulted again with all those things that were impossible to see and yet showed themselves to her anyway.

"Look at me, Anna. It's all right." His voice was gentle but firm. Anna swallowed, and slowly peeled her eyes open.

Father's face was still clear and present in front of her, and she found if she focused on his eyes, the lands behind him became nothing but a watery blur, and while it was unsettling, she could at least stand it.

Father searched her eyes and in his own she saw unease. "Yes," he said. "You have your mother's gift of sight, and you are seeing too much." Anna nodded. "All who cross here must concentrate, Anna. You will have to concentrate twice as hard as anyone else. You must pick an image and hold it in your mind. What do you see that troubles you least?"

"You," she answered promptly. "And there's a forest."

"Good. Think about seeing the forest, and seeing me. Think about it as if you were concentrating on a question for an oracle, but hold it inside."

"I'll try." To prove it, Anna peeked over his shoulder and concentrated on seeing the evergreen forest.

The golden ice of time and the swirl of emotion and memory fell back almost at once, allowing the dark trees to show through. They were only a shell, Anna knew, and she still saw the flicker and flash of the spirits and the ghosts that moved as quick as thought between them, but there was always movement in a forest and her mind accepted this easily. Her fear ebbed and her father straightened up.

"Good. Let us go." His voice was tight with strain. "This is not a place either of us can stay."

Anna took the hand he held out to her. That too was cool. Father looked this way and that. They stood on a dirt track beside a trickling brook. Anna squinted to blur her vision and concentrated on not looking any deeper. She'd have a headache soon, like she did after a hard lesson.

"What do you see, Father?" she asked.

"Hush," he said irritably. "I have to think."

Anna closed her mouth immediately. To her distress, Father seemed to be growing more confused. She didn't like seeing him hesitate. She wanted him to pick a direction. She wanted to be in Tuukos, like he promised. She wanted to be somewhere that didn't swim and shift in front of her eyes. She wanted to go home.

"This way," he said, turning to his right down the path.

Anna trotted obediently behind, trying not to see. His grip on her wrist was tight to the point of painful, but she tried not to squirm. All the stories she'd ever been told about how easy it was to become lost in the Shifting Lands echoed through her memory, making it all too easy to see the confusion behind the forest again. So, she held on tightly to her father and was glad he held on tightly to her.

"Hurry, Anna," he said. "We have a long way to go."

Anna obeyed, trying to keep up although she was soon short of breath, and trying not to see the deepening worry on her father's face.

The Shifting Lands opened before Bridget and Sakra as a carefully groomed garden. The grass was soft underfoot. Flowers of every shape and color blossomed in rich beds, inviting a passerby to pause and admire them. Groves of trees heavy with sweet-scented fruit swayed silently in the wind.

Every pleasant sight invited Bridget to relax, to slow her pace and stay awhile. She knew better. The Land of Death and Spirit itself could take an interest in the living who were brash enough to walk through its precincts, even if the spirits and powers that dwelled there chose to ignore them. She wondered where her rabbit was, and if it was still free, and tried to put the thought from her. Even though she still believed she had done someone in distress a favor, she did not want to call anything toward her. There was no telling whether she'd call the rabbit, or the dogs.

Stop. Stop. Think of Isavalta, now. Think of Vyshtavos, and your room. Think about Richikha and Prathad and finding out how they are weathering this.

Think about how much you need to be home.

As she focused on her memories, she began to feel Isavalta. It had a weight and presence to it. She could feel the path that wound toward it beneath her feet. She tightened her grip on the chain that bound her to Sakra. He kept his eyes straight ahead, and his stride was long and quick. She had to stretch her own legs to keep up. He did not even glance down at her, or at the fragrant, peaceful garden that surrounded them.

Sakra knew even better than she did the dangers of paying attention to any of the fleeting visions of the Shifting Lands, and at first she thought his unwavering gaze was only a manifestation of his concentration on their goal rather than their surroundings. Gradually, though, worry threaded through her own attempts to keep her mind looking beyond the Silent Lands to Isavalta.

"What is it?" she breathed as lightly as she could. "Sakra?"

"I don't know," he answered tightly. "Something. There is something out there for us." He did not slow, did not hear the import of his own words, he who had warned her so many times of the dangers of walking in this place.

What was he hurrying toward?

Bridget tried to follow Sakra's gaze, willing herself to see, but all that happened was the garden blurred, replaced by nothing at first, and then by too much. The brook they followed was also a river, the flowers were whole gardens themselves, and each tree was a forest as full of eyes as it was of trees, each one swiveling and searching.

Searching for them.

Sakra froze in midstride. "Do you hear something?"

"In the Silent Lands? Surely not." But even as she said it, she strained to hear instead of see. The world around her became a meadow of knee-high grass shaded by mountains made misty by a blue haze. Isavalta's direction shifted, and it seemed to grow a little farther away. Sakra turned his head this way and that and his eyes widened. There it was, the only thing that could make a sound to break the perpetual silence of the Land of Death and Spirit. A living voice.

"My God, there's someone out there." She said the words in a whisper, afraid of attracting more attention than they already had.

"Which way?" asked Sakra, turning his head this way and that. "Can you see?"

The voice gave Bridget something to concentrate on and her sight grew clear. The meadow fell away down a gentle slope to the river, and she saw that on the river floated a boat, with a single mast and billowing white sails.

"There." Bridget took Sakra's wrist and wished for him to see. The land obliged and lived up to one of its many names, shifting around them. But Bridget felt unease as it did so. There were all those hidden eyes. What did they see?

The river at first seemed far away, but as Sakra began to move in their direction, it grew rapidly closer. Before Bridget could blink twice, they were on its shore.

The boat must have been snagged, because despite the swift current of the river, it stayed in place. A woman stood on its deck wielding a long spear and facing down the Devil.

Bridget had never yet seen the Devil in any vision, and now she felt she did not need to. This creature was twice Sakra's size with scarlet skin and a muzzle like a dog. Fangs curled from its lower jaw. It swung a bright sword to counter the woman's spear. She parried, feinted, feinted again, and stabbed, straight into the heart of the demon.

But the demon did not fall, it shattered, becoming a thousand smaller, winged creatures that circled the boat like a flock of birds from a nightmare. Bridget wasn't even sure the woman could see these smaller creatures. She kept staring straight ahead. Then, they mobbed together and merged, becoming one great monster again, settling onto the rocking deck behind her.

"Ai-ya!" the woman cried in anger and desperation, and the demon raised its sword and the dance began again.

She kept her back to the mast, but she had no room to move. The demon pressed her, slashing left and right, making her use every inch she had. The sword swung for her head, and she ducked just in time so it hit the mast, cutting the decoration hanging there in two pieces. The woman straightened and she moved grimly into the fight again, with practice and concentration, but how long had she fought already, and how much longer could she go on? Surely she had already seen she could not kill this thing. Why didn't she use her magic? What . . .

Bridget's gaze leapt to the far bank. Among the pine trunks, she saw another woman. This one wore black armor that blended with the shadows, leaving her barely visible, but Bridget could just make out height and breadth, the high cheeks and the straight line of the jaw.

"God Almighty," breathed Bridget. "Sakra, I think she's a divided soul. I see her other half across the river." Divided souls were untouched by any gift of magic. Who had brought such a person undefended into the Shifting Lands? Worse, who had left her here?

Whatever fascination had held him before evaporated as Sakra watched the desperate battle on the rocking boat. His face creased, torn between fears, fear for a living soul trapped in the Shifting Lands, and fear for them being drawn into a trap from which there was no escape.

"What do you see, Bridget? Tell me exactly."

She described the woman, and the still figure in the shadows that mirrored her, or mirrored what she ought to be. She described the demon and the deadly dance they danced together on the deck of the boat.

Sakra's jaw moved back and forth, once. Something pulled at the fibers of Bridget's heart. Was it the spell, or the motion of the Shifting Lands around them? Was it the current of the river, or some other thing altogether? Bridget had no way to tell, but she knew she would not be able to stand still much longer.

Sakra reached up and touched one of his dozens of braids. His mouth moved, whispering something Bridget could not hear. With a tug, he loosened the silver thread that held one braid. The lock of hair fell free, and Bridget felt a soft wind, like a living breath pass across her skin. Sakra's mouth still moved, but he shook, and to Bridget's dismay, began to unwind the chain that bound them together.

On the river, the woman had dropped to one knee, stabbing upward. The demon evaded the stroke easily, and lifted its head to laugh as she stumbled to her feet, only alive because he was not done playing with her yet. The despair on the woman's face said she knew that too well, but she had no escape and no choice. She certainly had not seen Bridget and Sakra on the shore.

Sakra stepped away from Bridget. The loose chain slapped against her wrist. Sakra raised his arms, spreading them out above his head, and a sword took shape in his hand. Not a straight sword such as Bridget was familiar with, but a great, curving machete with a pair of wicked points.

"Demon!" he cried out, his voice echoing in the all-encompassing silence. "Leave her alone! Do you wish a fight? You will have one here!" He whirled the blade smoothly over his head, bringing it slashing down across his body, and then stabbing outward, straight for the demon's heart.

For a moment, everything froze; the great scarlet demon, the beleaguered woman, the waters of the river itself, and Bridget, to her horror, had time to wonder how Sakra thought he could kill this monster with a sword when a spear had done no good at all.

The spell he loosed must give the blade some power. That must be it.

The demon looked to Sakra and back at the woman, who was gasping for breath and holding her spear in both hands, waiting for the monster to move again. Her short black hair fluttered in front of her pale face. Bridget could not see her eyes, and did not know if they flickered to the riverbank to see she had help. But her mirrorself, the other half of her soul, stared at them from across the river, and Bridget thought she saw hope there.

The demon leered at the woman and blew her a kiss in a chilling parody of a lover's promise. It took one stride and it was on the shore with Sakra. Its fangs glistened as brightly as the blade of its sword.

Sakra did not waste his breath on words, but swung his own sword out and around, slashing for the demon's belly. The monster blocked him easily, and their dance began.

Bridget had never envisioned Sakra as a warrior. She had known he could be dangerous, but his danger was in his mind and in his magic. Now she watched him as he moved with a graceful precision. His blade seemed to float on the air as it whirled and slashed. Sparks flew to either side as he parried the demon's blade in a clash that should have sounded like a hammer on an anvil, and yet was completely noiseless.

It was a long, terrified moment before Bridget thought to look toward the woman with the spear, and saw that whatever had held her boat in place had come loose. The little craft was starting to drift, its sails completely slack. The woman realized it too and stared about herself in panic.

Bridget sprinted to the riverbank. "The line!" she called out, praying the woman could hear and that hearing would bring sight. "Throw me the line!"

The woman did see her, but she did not move, she only stared, the spear still in her hands.

"The line!" called out Bridget again. At the very edge of her vision, Sakra wove and darted. He courted death and she couldn't even stand witness for him. The boat was almost out of all possible range now. "Love of God, woman, throw me the line!"

Finally, the woman reacted. She dropped her spear, snatched up a coil of rope, and swinging her body in a practiced motion tossed it toward Bridget. It uncoiled in the air, playing out and out. Bridget lunged forward and caught the very end a bare handspan above the water, almost overbalancing into the river. Immediately, she wrapped the rope about her wrist, dug her heels into the bank, and began to pull. The boat was light, but the current was strong and the pebbly bank offered little for her to brace herself against. She strained with all her might, not yet softened by her time in an Isavaltan palace, and was able to pull the boat a painfully small distance toward the shore. The woman recovered her wits, grabbed a long pole from beneath the gunwales, and dug it into the river bottom, pushing toward shore. They pushed and hauled, and at last they were able to beach the boat on the bank of mud and gravel.

The woman began to clamber over the gunwale.

"No!" cried out Bridget. "Stay there! Don't get out of the boat."

The woman stared at her as if she were speaking a foreign language. Bridget took her first careful look at the other's skin the color of golden tea, her dark, almond-shaped eyes, and her straight black hair and wondered if that was exactly what she was doing.

"Stay." She gestured "stop" with both hands. The woman's eyes narrowed, but she lowered her foot and stepped back toward the mast. Bridget instead climbed into the boat with her. The woman picked up her spear, but her hand shook. Bridget, both to show she was not afraid and that the woman had nothing to fear from her, turned her back to watch Sakra again, praying that she would not have to set the boat out into the river again. Praying that he would not fall to this monster. Praying for a miracle in a place of marvels and phantoms.

Please. Help me. Help him. Please, God, this once, hear me.

The fight raged on. The weapons were little more than blurs as they struck, flew apart, and struck again. Sakra's motions were spare and expert. There was nothing flowery, nothing without purpose. But the harder he fought, the broader the demon's leer grew. Sakra struck home, and struck again, an arm, a wrist, a shoulder, but his blows had no effect. The demon didn't even flinch. Bridget's heart turned to ice.

Oh, God, God, please, don't let him die.

They were not alone anymore. Bridget had been told time and again life in the Shifting Lands attracted attention. She had been told passions, desires, wishes, roused the curiosity and the greed of the inhabitants of this place, and they would come to see what new thing passed among them. She had never seen evidence of this before, though, not as she did now.

They came down from the hills and emerged from the grass. They stepped out of the rocks on the bank and appeared out of the sky and thin air. They came from everywhere but the river itself. They were minute creatures, hump-backed, crooked, and brown like tree roots. They were tall and impossibly thin with gossamer wings. They were knights on horseback. They were wolves, crows, and ravens. They were men and women clothed in silk and gold, or completely naked. They were mighty birds of prey perched on rocks and on shoulders.

Their attention was all on Sakra and the demon. Bridget felt their eagerness, waiting for one to fall, waiting to claim the loser's body and whatever other spoils their natures permitted them to take hold of. They crowded the far bank now, and there would be no way to launch the boat back on the river again without being seen, and even now some of them were turning their voracious eyes on Bridget and the woman in their beached craft.

The demon seemed to have wearied of the game and began to attack in earnest now. It was far taller than Sakra, and its reach was longer. It moved with the speed of lightning, its blade seeming to vanish as it swung down, only to reappear when Sakra made one more parry. Slowly, relentlessly, he pressed Sakra back, and it was all Sakra could do to angle his steps toward the river, toward the boat.

Some of the creatures around them grinned, some looked bored, others greedy. Not one frowned. Not one moved to help.

Sakra missed his footing and stumbled. The demon's blade slashed at his head. He brought his sword up in a desperate parry, but the weight of the impact loosened his grip. His sword slipped and he rolled out of reach, only barely keeping hold of his weapon. Bridget snatched up the boat's pole, ready to jump onto the bank. She could at least distract the thing, at least get Sakra into the boat . . .

Beside her, the woman cried out and pointed overhead. Reflexively, Bridget looked.

Over their heads, birds took shape, huge scarlet and blue forms. They spread their great wings and opened their curved beaks to let out cries that no human ear could hear. Sakra raised his free hand to the splendid winged creatures and shouted a word Bridget could not understand. The whole brilliantly plumed flock descended upon the Devil. The creature shattered into its hundred pieces, but each piece was now gripped tightly in the beaks and talons of Sakra's birds. In the next moment, the birds rose into the air, bearing the struggling demons away with them into the emerald sky.

The woman watched with open mouth. As the sky engulfed the birds, her knees crumbled and she dropped to the boat's deck. On the bank, the fabulous audience that had gathered began to stir. Bridget saw one great grey fox look straight at her.

"Help me!" cried Bridget to the woman, digging the pole into the riverbank. "Hurry!" The last was for Sakra. She did not dare call out his name where all these things could hear it.

Again, the woman showed she was quick to recover. She reversed her spear in her hands and jammed the butt of it into the riverbank. Sakra crawled to his feet, abandoning his sword in the mud, and launched into a stumbling run. As the current caught the boat again, he vaulted over the gunwale, and dropped into the bottom. Bridget thrust the pole into the other woman's hands, and the woman continued digging it into the river bottom, pushing them out toward the center of the river. Bridget grabbed the steering oar and, relieved to find it handled much like the tillers she was used to, guided them into the current. The creatures on the bank swayed as if caught by the wind. Wings rose, ears flattened, mouths moved, hooves and paws stamped. One of the gossamer-winged beings launched itself into the air, rising shining into the emerald sky, inviting all to stop and stare, to stop thinking of what they were doing.

Bridget could barely feel the breeze. Her experienced eye spotted the

main line and hauled the sail up, unfurling all the canvas. The snowy sail
billowed for a moment, fell slack, and billowed again. The woman's mouth
moved, whether praying or swearing Bridget couldn't tell. She wanted to
do both. She wanted to collapse next to Sakra and make sure he was all
right.

*Think of Isavalta. Think of getting him home. That's all that matters.
Think of getting him home.* She gripped the tiller tight with both hands,
feeling honest wood under her palm, feeling the familiar rush of water
beneath the keel of the boat. She had lived most of her life around boats.
She knew and trusted them. This was a good boat, well built, light but
steady beneath her hand. It would take them home. The rigging was unfamiliar, but she could probably work it in a pinch.

Think of Isavalta, she told herself, and she did, with all her heart
and mind.

But something was wrong. She felt no weight. She felt no path.

Oh. No.

The woman apparently knew something was wrong. She staggered
to the mast, and looked down at the deck, at the scraps of cloth that had
been a decorative cloth hanging from the mast, but which had been
sliced in two by the demon's sword. The woman picked up a scrap of
cloth in each hand. As she looked at the shreds, the last of the color
drained from her face.

She spoke, quickly, softly. Bridget did not understand the words,
but she understood the fear. It came to the woman haltingly, as something she was not familiar with, but perhaps had seen too much of far
too recently.

"She says this was a spell," Sakra translated. He took one of the
scraps and ran it through his fingers, looking at the sigils on it. "She says
it was to take her to the court of Isavalta."

Bridget swallowed. Her throat had gone completely dry. She reached
out, concentrating fiercely on any memory she could draw up. She had
walked this road before, alone. She could do this. She thought of her
apartment in Vyshtavos, of walking through the house she had been
given, of the first time Sakra had made her laugh. She remembered how
she felt when she walked herself to Isavalta before, how her heart had
been full of hope and anticipation.

"Can you find it?" asked Sakra.

Bridget swallowed again and the words turned to dust in her mouth. "No," she said. "We're lost."

The forest closed in tightly around Anna and her father, leaving barely room for them and the silent brook that sparkled over rounded stones of red and grey. Movement and light still flitted between the trees, catching Anna's eye, distracting her. She tried squinting, but that just made her eyes hurt worse. She was thirsty. She was tired. She wanted her father to say they were almost there. She wanted to be safe and home.

The path took a deep bend following the meandering brook. Father frowned, casting about, looking for what Anna could not say, but the expression on his face did not invite questions. He held her tighter, pinching her fingers together. It was hard to keep still. She tried looking at the brook, which she knew was the river. Maybe if she only looked a little, she could see where they were going, and how far it was.

Movement on the opposite bank made her look up, and Anna saw two people. A man and a woman, as clear and substantial as Father was. The woman was tall and strong-boned. She had auburn hair that tumbled over her shoulders and a kind face, with the skin and eyes of someone from northern climes. She wore a plain black dress. Beside her stood a man with dark gold hair, dressed in a high-necked black coat such as men of Isavalta wore.

"Who are they, Father?"

Father's gaze flickered from the way ahead for an instant. "Ghosts, Anna," he said, shaking her hand a little. "Only ghosts."

They're not like the other ghosts, she wanted to tell him, but before she could speak, a woman's voice rang through her mind.

Your mother lives, Anna.

"What?" Anna twisted in her father's grip, trying to see behind her better. The woman was reaching out a hand to her, her face sad, but filled with determination. "Father, they're speaking to me."

"They cannot. They are ghosts. They cannot touch you, Anna. We must keep going."

Now she heard the man's voice, deep and rich. As he spoke, the couple seemed to grow closer to her, even though Father strode quickly down the path. *Your mother is alive, Anna. She is crossing the Silent*

Lands right now. Her name is Bridget. You can call to her and she will hear.

Anna grabbed Father's sleeve. "They say my mother is alive."

"They lie, Anna," Father snapped. "They are trying to draw us off the path."

"But who were they? Father, do you see them?"

"No," he said without looking back. "They are menacing you because you are ignorant of the ways of this place. They hope to draw you to them and drink your spirit."

"Why?" she asked, and then she thought, *If you can't see them, how do you know they are ghosts?*

"Because they are the dead and the dead hunger for what they are not and can never be."

"Do you?" asked Anna very softly. She wasn't sure she wanted him to hear her.

"I am your father," was his only answer.

Anna snuck a glance over at the far bank. They were still there. They hadn't moved, but they had kept up.

You're ghosts, she thought at them. *Nothing but ghosts. Go away.*

Look for your mother, Anna, came the woman's voice again. *Look for Bridget.*

"Do not listen, Anna," ordered Father sternly.

But it was too late. The strange name rang in Anna's mind, and she remembered how she had heard it from Father as well. Her eyes flickered from the path to the world beyond and for a moment she forgot to see only the forest and her father. The forest faded and where there had been a brook beside her, she saw the great river flowing, cutting a swath between the forty thousand forms that filled the kaleidoscope landscape, on it floated a boat, and in the boat she saw three human shapes. Because she looked, because for a moment she willed, there was no distance and she saw clearly. There was a woman with hair the color of the lady ghost who spoke to her. There was a man of Hastinapura in clothing from Isavalta, and there was a third woman with straight black hair and a black and red jacket, sitting in the bottom of the boat and clutching a spear.

"Mae . . ."

"No!" Father clapped a hand over her mouth.

Anna looked up at him, startled.

"Call no names here. You don't know what you will bring." He looked frightened and his face had gone pale. Not pale, thin. Anna blinked, and for an instant Father flickered in her sight like the other ghosts.

Anna shook her head. "But it's my bodyguard. She's here! She came for me!"

Father crouched down in front of her again, so his face was all she could see. He was still too pale, but at least he was solid again. He completely blocked her view of Mae Shan. "She's serving her uncle, Daughter," he said earnestly, angrily. "Not you. You've seen that." He punctuated his words with a shake. "You killed her uncle. She will want revenge for that."

"No, Father. Why . . ."

Father did not let her finish. He stood again, and again grasped her hand too hard. A wave of dizziness swept through Anna's mind and brought a fog of tears to her eyes. "We must go before she finds us."

He strode away. Anna ran to keep up, but the air was thin in her lungs and she was soon gasping. She could not keep her mind on how to see things anymore. The world was a blur, with too many images to focus on. She could see everything, but she could make out nothing. There was nothing for her to anchor herself to except a strange name and the river, and Mae Shan, who Father called a liar, and who she did not wish to see again, but did not wish to abandon.

Call your mother. Call Bridget. She will hear you.

Why did the ghosts tell her this? Mother's name was Kaija and she was dead. They must be lying, trying to trick her as Father said. She must close her ears. She must focus on duty and obedience. She must not be persuaded by things that were false.

But why would these false ghosts come to her when her mother did not? Where was her mother to protect and guide them in this place?

And why were they speaking the same name Father had?

Our ancestors reside in Heaven with the gods, Master Liaozhai said. *We are like the goldfish in the pond to them. When we pray or have need of instruction, they will descend into the Land of Death and Spirit to stand at the riverbank and touch our lives in its waters.* They had sat in the Moon Garden, watching the silver carp in their round, brown pond.

But sorcerers can walk in the Land of Death and Spirit, Anna had pointed out. *Couldn't I go there to speak with the ancestors?*

Only in the gravest of emergencies. It is a reversal of the natural flow of the forces of the universe, and must not be undertaken lightly.

But they were here already, and beset. Surely this was an emergency.

"Father," she began carefully. She barely had breath left to speak. "Why don't you . . ."

"Do not question me now, Daughter. I must concentrate. I feel . . . the river calls, but others call . . . I don't understand . . ." Father lapsed into silence.

But why don't you call Mother to help ward away the false ghosts? asked Anna in her own mind. As soon as the thought of Mother came to her, she saw again the woman with the auburn hair and her companions in the boat, and she saw Mae Shan, who looked tired and frightened, and not at all like she was looking for revenge.

That is not Mother! shouted Anna to herself. *Mother is Kaija Kalami, and she has blue eyes and black hair and she is living in Heaven with the gods, and she watches me as if I were a goldfish in a pond!*

She strained her eyes, staring through the flashing, flying, turning, riotous images that surrounded her, that decked the evergreen, eternal forest and the crooked riverbanks. *Kaija!* she shouted in her mind. *Kaija Kalami! Mother!*

But she only saw the stranger with Mae Shan, looking down the river, seeing her own destination, and then they were gone, and the river was empty again.

"Keep up, Daughter!" ordered Father.

"But I can't see Mother!" she cried, tears stinging her eyes and sweat breaking out on her cold forehead. She couldn't breathe. She couldn't get enough air.

"Stop that nonsense!" His heavy hand cuffed the back of her head. Anna stumbled, stunned. No one had ever hit her, not Master Liaozhai, not the Minister of the North, not Mae Shan, no one. She couldn't catch her breath for shame, and began to cough. Tears ran from her eyes, and where they fell, small flowers sprang up from the dirt.

Father didn't look at her, he only tightened his grip on her hand and strode on.

"Something," he muttered. "Someplace . . . we must leave here, or she will find us, don't think, just walk, hurry, hurry . . . I feel it, I hear it, but where, *where?*"

Anna swallowed. She was busy worrying about lying ghosts and Mother when Father told her what was happening, and she was not attending to her duty. No wonder he'd gotten angry.

"I could try to see for you, Father . . ." she said meekly.

But Father did not seem to have heard her. "There!" he cried. "There! That is our way!"

Anna looked hard in the direction of Father's gaze. She tried to focus, tried to shut out distraction, to relax her mind as she would open hand or an eye, and to only see what Father saw, and she looked . . .

. . . And she saw a path through the pines with their black trunks and their limbs endlessly swaying in the silent breeze. The path was dirt and it ran through the moss and pine needles to the riverbank. The river here was deep and swift, running with barely a ripple across its surface, and as she saw the surface, she saw past the surface and down to the stones and sand, and the stones and sand were person and place, as the river water was life and memory, and she saw a place of dim and flickering light, where the stone wall was stained with ancient blood and a wizened, half-naked man sat in the midst of the heat and red stone and called, and called.

Fear stabbed at Anna's heart, and she tugged at her father's hand. "No, Father, that isn't . . ."

Father's hand came down again, hitting her hard and making the whole world spin. He scooped her up into his arms and ran, jolting her with each step as the tears ran fast down her cheeks. She wanted to speak, wanted to warn him, but she was afraid.

He must see. He must know something, but we can't be going there! That's not Tuukos. It can't be.

But she did not dare speak. She did not want Father to think she was questioning him again. She did not want to earn another blow.

They reached the pebbly shore. Father stopped right at river's edge, the toes of his boots just touching the rippling water. He set her down and she folded her hands and bowed her head, as she had done when Master Liaozhai was angry at her. She wanted to show him she was obedient and understood her duty perfectly so he would not be angry anymore.

But why could she not see Mother? The question would not leave her.

"You must lead me into the river," Father said. "Here and now. I cannot go farther as myself anymore."

"Yes, Father." She took his hand, screwed up her courage, and walked forward into the river. It was not truly water. It was the route back to the living worlds, and it was dry and cool and dimmed the light of the Shifting Lands. As she walked and the world blurred, whispers began in her ears, telling secrets, lies, truths, nonsense, and deep sense. All the voices of life surrounded her, growing louder, growing stronger as the world around her grew darker. She could feel nothing under her feet, and the touch of Father's hand melted away.

She tried to cry out but could not. Her footsteps faltered. She was blind and there were only the unintelligible voices around her.

But one voice called clearly. "Come. Come to me."

The voice grated in Anna's ears. It sounded wrong, although she could not have said how. She did not want to follow it, but she had nowhere else to go.

"Come. Come to me."

She could feel Father inside her heart again. He did not speak with words, but she felt him urging her toward the voice. This was the way he intended her to go. It could not be wrong then. She must not think that.

Gulping back her fear and confusion, Anna followed the low, grating call.

Chapter Twenty

Sakra pushed himself up slowly from where he lay on the deck. Bridget did not look at him. She stared out at the river. The banks changed on either side, shrinking and shriveling until they were nothing but barren rock, grey and lifeless. The thin wind blew straight through her, but gave her no air to breathe. Shadows drifted across the green sky like clouds. They were being watched. She felt that through every pore in her skin.

She set her fear aside. She thought of Prathad and Richikha. She thought of Mikkel, Ananda, and the lord master Peshek who had known her parents and had come to stay at Vyshtavos for several weeks in the middle of winter to talk to her and help her get settled. She thought of Sakra, of walking with him and talking late into the night, of him teaching her the names of the Isavaltan stars and the plants in the gardens and the streets of the town.

But there was nothing. The boat drifted down the river as boats on real rivers did when there was no guiding hand.

She tried again. She thought of the woods and gardens she had seen, of laboring over the elementary language and reading lessons Mistress Urshila set her and how she had struggled through them, sometimes late into the night, furious at her teacher for treating her like a child, and furious at herself for not being a better student.

Where are you? she thought to the whole world.

But the world did not answer. Another shadow scudded overhead. Something hunched and grey scuttled behind the rocks.

The woman was talking to Sakra, low and tense. Anger and fear warred with each other in her features. She tried to struggle to her feet, but the rocking motion of the boat robbed her of what little balance she had and she fell panting and coughing into the bottom. However long she had been here, it was too long. Her lungs were feeling the lack of air and her strength would soon ebb.

Sakra touched her arm, and said something else in her language.

"I will try to find what is left of the spell here to guide us," he told Bridget, but his words and breathing were heavy.

Bridget bit her lip. She scanned the banks, searching for some sign. Stretching out with her sight to see past the jumble of grey stone. There had to be something. Something real and true she could see in this mist of illusions. There had to be.

On the right bank she saw the mirror image of the woman crouched beside her. She leaned heavily on her spear, and held out her hand, beckoning wearily.

On the right bank, she saw a withered, brown man with a great, ragged hole in his sunken chest. He grinned at her as if she were the funniest joke he'd ever seen. She saw other forms, indistinct and fleeting, behind and between the rocks. They watched and they waited. She could not see them, oh, no, not even with her vaunted, precious eyes, but they could see her quite well, her and Sakra and this stranger she had thought she was saving.

Something flashed overhead. Bridget winced, but did not look up. She dropped her gaze to the river water, willing herself to remember, to think only of Isavalta, but fear already nibbled at the back of her mind, and the knowledge that she had failed began to burrow into her heart. She felt Sakra's magic writhing fretfully beside her like a sleeper caught in a nightmare, but it could not take form.

Again something flashed, in front of her this time, above the horizon, like a bird gliding above the waters. Bridget turned her mind inward, trying not to see. There was nothing to see. Mistress Urshila had been right. She had trusted too much to her eyes. She did not have enough learning. She had forgotten what little she had known and she had lost them. Lost Sakra, lost herself, lost this poor stranger and was trying to sift truth from illusion as if it were gold dust mixed in sawdust, not willing to believe, even now, it simply wasn't there.

The woman spoke, Sakra answered, his magic stirred again, and fell still.

Flash. A shining form swooped over the river. A bird. A gull, but not a living gull. The bird wheeled closer, and Bridget saw it was a creature of crystal. Each feather was perfectly shaped from glass. It was a beautiful thing to watch as it dipped and dove, and rose again to circle overhead.

Stop, Bridget. Stop. She squeezed her eyes shut. *It's another trick. It wants you to follow it.*

The woman was speaking again. Her words coming in gasps. Bridget's eyes snapped open. The crystalline gull had landed on the prow of the boat. Sakra had planted both hands on the bench and was trying to heave himself to his feet.

The gull was clear glass with smoked glass on the cap of its head and the tips of its pinions. She could see the river right through the heart of it, blurred and distorted, green and brown and grey and white. Its eyes were onyx beads, and it looked at her first through one and then the other, and Bridget felt her mind stir, and a sensation—part inspiration, part power—unfolded, stretched, turned, and wheeled.

The gull opened its beak and threw back its head in soundless cry and launched itself into the air.

"Urshila." Bridget lifted her hands away from the gunwales so she could shade her eyes and watch the flight of the crystalline bird as it turned overhead.

"What?" gasped Sakra.

"It is. It's her. She's come to show us the way home."

"Bridget, do you see her?"

"No." She shook her head, grinning absurdly. "She's shown me. Sakra, please, trust in this."

Sakra only looked defeated. "We have no other choice."

Bridget clambered back to the steering oar and gripped the smooth wood again. Her skin seemed extra sensitive. She could feel each line of the grain beneath her palm. She turned her gaze overhead, catching hold of the glass seagull with her eyes and held it, willing her mind's eye open for whatever it had to show her.

The gull hovered motionless for one moment, glinting in the clear green sky, and then folded its wings and dove fearlessly into the river depths, and with mind, sight, and soul, Bridget followed.

It was like plunging into a thick pool. The world went mossy green, then brown flecked with gold, then black, and with her mind's eye wide open, she saw the gull leading them on.

And she saw Mistress Urshila cold and dead on a flagstone floor.

And she saw Valin Kalami standing before the Old Witch, Baba Yaga.

And she saw the woman, the stranger in the boat, but she was running through streets filled with smoke and ash, clutching a young girl to her, and the girl had black hair and green eyes, and Bridget knew the child with all her heart.

And then the world opened up around them, and the prow of the boat slapped hard against a wave that sent up a shock of salt spray, and a thick, honest wind filled with the smell of salt blew Bridget's tousled hair forward over her face and caught the sail, snapping the canvas out and singing through the lines. Ahead, breakers roared against a sandy beach that rose to form an island of winter-grey stone and spring-green forests.

Bridget grabbed hold of the steering oar, relief making her weak as water, and only instinct putting her hand to the line to haul the sail down before the wind drove them straight into the breakers.

They were in the living world and they themselves were alive and all of them dragging in great gulps of rich salt air.

But wherever they were, it was not Isavalta.

Grey stones stuck out of the earth like bones. Wind whipped her hair in front of her face, bringing with it the roar and the salt tang of the sea.

Where the world was not grey, it seemed to be all shades of green. Deep black-green for the moss on the boulders and cliffs, pale lime-green in the cups of the little flowers that grew in the shelter of the stones. Vivid emerald in the grass and the new leaves of the trees flashing out in the clean spring sun. The low hills that curved around in a cluster in front of her joined together to become one great mountain that rose up almost to the sky.

It was a place wholly different from any Anna had ever seen and as she gazed out at it, she felt her father's love rising in her mind like mist from still waters. This was the place of his boyhood. He knew the names of the tiny flowers—veridian, maiden's cup, moth's heart. The hill at her right shoulder was Urho's Barrow, and as the name came to her, so did the story of the giant buried beneath it. The forest that covered its broad slope was the perfect place to find whiteback mushrooms, pitcher moss, and everheart root for tea, for sleeplessness and easing a cramped stomach. Everything she could see caused meaning and longing to well up in her mind.

But at the same time, Anna could only blink stupidly at it all. *I'm tired, Father.*

Of course, Anna. Let me take you. The Holy Island is generous with food and shelter. I'll show you.

She did not want to walk. She just wanted to sit down where she was, but she did not struggle. Under Father's will, her feet moved lightly and all but ran her up Urho's barrow until the trees engulfed them, turning the bright day into twilight, and reminding Anna, for all she saw everything through the warmth of her father's love for each detail, of nothing so much as the deep woods of the Land of Death and Spirit.

Was Mae Shan all right? she wondered. Should she even be thinking about her? Would Father be mad?

But if Father knew her thoughts in the back of her own mind, there was no stirring, no touch, and best of all, no scolding. And he did not lie about the food. He knew where the squirrels kept their winter nuts and just how to crack them open. He knew about the tender hearts of reeds that grew by the streams of snowmelt that tasted tangy and salty. The whiteback mushrooms were peppery and the fiddlehead ferns were crisp and juicy. She wished for rice and tea, and a sweet cake, but she wasn't hungry anymore, and Father wasn't angry. The moss sheltered by old trees and new ferns was damp where she lay down, but she was cradled by memories of doing this a hundred times before and it didn't seem so bad. Maybe the bad part was over now that they were on the Holy Island where Father always wanted to be. Maybe he'd be happy now and live contentedly in her heart and they'd have a home by the sea and he'd teach her to swim and to sail a boat . . .

Filled with the hopes of finding a life to replace the one she'd lost, Anna was able to settle deeply into sleep.

Anna, wake up.

Anna sat up, staring all around her, trying to remember why she was here in the woods. Her stomach felt sick. Her head was light.

Memory came back slowly. "What is it, Father?"

We are called. We must go.

Anna pushed her hair back irritably. Dead leaves fell onto the scuffed moss beside her. "I don't hear anything."

Anna, don't argue. Let me take you.

Anna didn't want to. It suddenly all seemed wrong. She didn't feel good. She wanted tea. She wanted Mae Shan and Master Liaozhai. But Father pressed her to one side and made her legs stand up and start climbing up the hill. Anna tried to feel warm and safe. Father would take care of her. But all she could do was watch, and try not to feel the way her feet hurt, and the way her stomach ached.

Father made her climb steadily. If he could feel her discomfort, he ignored it. Memory of the blows he had given her in the Silent Lands kept Anna quiet. *I must be good,* she told herself. *I must be good.*

The slope got steeper. Rivers of stone ran between the tree roots, and great outcroppings jutted from the mountainside. One of those outcroppings had split open to make a cave, and Father took them straight inside.

The world went dark in an instant, and even Father had to stop. In charge of herself again, Anna swayed back and forth on tired legs and tried to catch her breath. Her heart pounded hard against her ribs. There were splashes of bright light in the back of the cave, but she couldn't see straight.

Slowly, though, Anna's vision cleared. Light and shadow resolved into sense, but her heart still pounded. She saw now that the orange glow was light reflected off damp stone and off a still pool worn into slick rock. The fire burned before an old man, naked to the waist, sweat shining on his skin the way the water shone on the cave walls. But where the walls were dark, he was pale, pale as death, pale as the bellies of the fish who lived in the depths of the ocean and never saw the light while they were alive.

Anna realized she should have felt scared, but she only felt sick.

As the old man seemed to take shape in front of her, the rest of her senses seemed to clear, and she knew what else was wrong. This place was filled with magic. It was as full of power as it was of air. It was not being drawn or called, it simply was, a whole great pool of magic unformed and unshaped, constant. How could that be? Magic had to be called. It required an act of will. Even in the most sacred spaces. And it had to be shaped, or it dissolved. It could not simply be captured like water in a bath, could it?

The old man spoke. His voice was high-pitched and broken. She didn't understand his words, but Father did, and she heard them ring in her mind through him.

"Welcome, Daughter. Welcome, Son," the old man said.

Kneel, Anna. Kneel.

She hesitated but Father bent her knees for her and bowed her head. Sounds filled her mind, and she realized they were words, the language of the Holy Island that Father had always said he'd teach her one day.

"Holy Father," she said, awkwardly, for her tongue wasn't used to shaping these sounds. "Bestow your blessing on your poor daughter."

Anna looked up at the wrinkled creature before her. His cheeks and mouth were sunken in and his black eyes protruded. His hair hung in twisted clumps like snakes and his skin was loose on his bones. The kilt that was his only clothing was leather scraps sewn together with gut and smeared with soot and grease. His hands were black with ash and there was a stench that reminded Anna sharply of the city of T'ien while it burned.

This was a holy man? Anna thought about the clean temples, the monks and priests with their shaved heads, and the white faces of the gods and goddesses. They did not leer like this man. They did not grin with sunken gums. Anna trembled.

Do not be disrespectful, Daughter, warned Father sharply.

"You fear this old man?" the "holy father" lisped, and Anna saw his tongue was stained as black as his hands. "You fear what you do not understand."

Father gave her no words, and Anna was glad. She tried not to shake. She tried to remember that power, and holiness came in many forms.

"You have neglected this child, Valin Kalami," said the old man. "You have given her education over to foreigners."

Anna shrank back gratefully to give Father room to speak. "It was a matter of necessity, Holy Father. But she is home now."

"Yes, yes." The old man peered forward. His eyes were pale with cataracts and Anna wondered that he could see at all. "She is as you promised. New in her learning, great in her power. She will be a great seer for Tuukos."

A thrill of fear ran through Anna at those words. A seer for Tuukos?

What did that mean? Hesitantly she moved to touch Father, but the old man began to sway back and forth and she retreated again.

"Will be, will be," he crooned. "Come from water, come through fire to call fire back again." His whitened eyes stared into the darkness of the cave, but his hands began moving, like creatures with minds of their own, working among the bones and stones that surrounded him.

And Anna saw. A hundred images, a thousand opened in front of her. She saw a young man, tall and proud wearing a crown of horn with people kneeling at his feet. She saw the years parade past and the crowned man becoming shrunken, bitter, and mad. She saw the madness in waves and storms, a vision within a vision.

She saw the Phoenix in a golden cage.

She saw Father in a palace of stone talking with an old woman, urging her to something . . . she could not hear.

She saw Father in the dark lifting an infant from a cradle and wrapping a blanket around it as it slept.

She saw herself. She saw herself in the cave with a crown of horn on her head. She saw herself beneath the spreading wings of the Phoenix, her mouth open wide to scream. She saw herself beside a woman with auburn hair and green eyes in a plain grey dress. The woman wrapped her arms around Anna and wept.

She saw herself beside a golden cage, her arms lifted to the sky. She saw Father looking out of her eyes and calling the Phoenix down. She saw the Land of Death and Spirit open up around her. She saw a woman and a man holding hands in a little boat on a wide sea.

What is this? Anna, what are you doing?

"Nothing, Father. I swear." Before her, the old man only swayed back and forth, lost in his visions or his madness, she couldn't tell which.

Stop this at once!

"I can't," Anna cried. *I can't help seeing.*

These are shadows and fables. Your power is confused by the presence of the Holy Father.

But she didn't believe him and she felt his realization that she knew he lied and Anna bit her lip. She did not want this. She wanted to obey, to believe, to be dutiful and good. She did not want to see by the power of a madman. She closed her eyes, but she knew it would do no good. While the Holy Man called the visions, Anna must see.

She saw Mae Shan holding a demon at spear's length, a real one this time, not a ghost of ash.

Then, the Holy Father shook himself, laughing and crying all at once at whatever he had seen.

In the next heartbeat he frowned hard at Anna. "No, no, no," he spat. "It will not do. You are too much for her. Come, come, Daughter. Learn now the craft and power you are heir to."

The old man got himself to his feet and scuttled like some huge crab toward the back of the cave, beyond the reach of the firelight. Something lay there in the dark on the stony floor. Anna did not want to move toward it. She didn't want to see anything more this madman had to show her. Father's anger washed through her, and tears began to trickle from her eyes. He didn't wait, he didn't even ask, he just took her body and moved it forward until she stood beside the Holy Father, and looked down at what he had to show.

It was a man of glass, laid out straight on the bed of stone. It was perfect in every detail, down to the lines on its knuckles and the shape of its nails. It was dressed simply, in a loose brown tunic and trousers. Its eyes were shut, but the artisan had even given it eyelashes.

"It was made many centuries ago, when we were great." Spittle flecked the Holy Father's lips. "See it now? See the fire, the earth, and water that went into its making. See the blood and the metals that painted it and made it whole."

And Anna did see. She saw the fire in the great crucible, she saw the sorcerers crowded around with their buckets and their knives.

Stop, please. I don't want this.

Father paid no attention.

"Strike it, hear it ring." The old man knocked his knuckles against the statue's torso, and it rang like a bell. "Does it not call beautifully to you?"

Yes, said Father in the back of her mind. *Yes.*

"Lay your hands here, Daughter." He indicated the statue's heart. Anna obeyed. What else was she to do? The glass was smoothly contoured underneath her palms. It felt exactly like a man's chest, only cold and hard as death and ice.

The seer picked up a knife. It too was made of glass, but this glass was as black as coal. The edge was so keen, Anna could barely see it in the dim and flickering light. He lifted his left hand just long enough for Anna to see it was thick and twisted, not only with age and calluses, but with scars. His face was almost peaceful as he drove the tip of his knife into the tip of his first finger, setting the blood free to run in scarlet threads down his hand.

Anna felt the magic this place held twist and shiver. She felt the blood call it and it obeyed, eagerly. The old man murmured his charm, as lightly as a woman would hum a lullaby. The magic here was so rich and so ready, he needed no more force than that. He leaned across the statue and began smearing its face with his blood. Slowly, Anna saw that he was painting eyes on it.

Anna's heart tore open and she screamed, falling to her knees. Father rushed out of her with all the breath in her lungs.

The statue's eyes opened, and they were Father's eyes. Its hand moved, and it was Father's hand. He sat up and pulled his knees up under him, slowly, stiffly, like someone waking from a long sleep. Anna felt her eyes bulge in their sockets. It was Father. Truly. He was perfect in every way, just as she had seen him in the Land of Death and Spirit. For all her staring, she could see nothing false about him, except the tiniest glimmer in the light, that might have been a sheen of perspiration on his light brown skin.

"Father," she whispered, reaching out to touch him. To her relief, his skin felt warm beneath her fingertips, not cold like the glass.

The seer was grinning. Anna tried not to look at him.

Father moved his lips experimentally a few times, then he spoke. "This is not life."

"No." The seer shook his head. "That is beyond what even the greatest of us could give. But you need no longer exhaust your daughter with your presence." He turned the smile to her, and she saw all his black gums. "She needs to be nurtured and cared for, not used up."

"No." Father looked at her, but there was nothing kind in his gaze. Anna told herself it was his new eyes. He was not used to them yet.

He had a body of his own now. Now he would be able to be with her as she had always dreamed. They would have a house, and he would teach her all the things Master Liaozhai hadn't yet, and they would live together for a hundred years if they wanted to. It would be all right. She would be a good daughter, and he would never have to hit her anymore.

He was only angry with her because she did not understand the things that were important to him. That must be it. She would learn, though. She would.

"Now." The seer sank back onto his haunches. "We must talk, your father and I, of such things as are not fit for the ears of one not yet bound by her apprenticeship oaths."

Father gestured to her. The motion was fluid, but the smile that accompanied it was brittle. "Go outside, Anna. Play for a bit. Stay in sight of the cave."

"Yes, Father." She was glad enough to obey. She wanted to be near him, but she also wanted to be away from the seer. She did not like his greedy, greasy looks, and she did not like his casual use of blood. Father did not truly mean to apprentice her to him. He would explain that when he was finished.

She remembered to bow, and hurried out into the sunshine.

Anna breathed the fresh air and stretched her shoulders with a feeling of relief. The cave was an unwholesome place, she was sure. She was not surprised that the Holy Father's mind wandered swimming constantly in so much power that was unformed and unused. Master Liaozhai would never have done such a thing. Perhaps, if he seemed in a good mood, she could talk to Father about it. Perhaps if the seer moved, he would get better, and not be so crooked and . . . so frightening.

Anna shivered and set out to explore to get away from the feeling. Father's release had been painful, but now she felt much better, as if she had put down something heavy she'd been carrying for too long.

She found she didn't want to think about that either.

It looked like there was a small plateau above the cave mouth. She could probably see out to the ocean from up there. Picking her way carefully on her bare feet, Anna climbed the slope. It was good to just be alone for a while under the trees, to see the mosses and the mushrooms, to collect the leaves of some of the trees, to see how the rivers of ancient rock, all speckled black and grey ran between the trunks of trees that were as crooked as the seer's arms.

Father had once told her that in ancient times the gods had cracked the mountain open so that it poured living fire down its slopes and melted the stone and sand it touched, and in this way showed the people of Tuukos the properties of glass and the secrets of its making.

She reached the plateau and stood up straight on the shelf of ancient stone. Her skin became gooseflesh in the cold wind that blew down from the mountaintop, but she didn't head back to the shelter of the trees. She had been right. From here she could see the long green and grey slope of the mountain like a quilted skirt, with the ocean spread below it as clear and blue as the sky above. She could even see a little boat with a snow-white sail bobbing on the waves, and just make out the three people moving about on its deck.

Anna froze. She had seen this boat in just this way before, in the split second before the Silent Lands had shifted for her sight and shown her that the boat was occupied by Mae Shan.

Mae Shan had followed them out of the Land of Death and Spirit. Mae Shan had found them, after she'd . . . after what had happened. Anna remembered the warmth of the blood on her hands. The breeze from the ocean smelled like the blood had. She wanted to run down to Mae Shan, to explain to her that it had been an accident, really, that Father had been afraid and needed to escape. He hadn't meant it, not really.

Father will want to know she's here. The thought sent a jolt through Anna. He didn't like Mae Shan and would not be glad she was here. She hadn't found a way yet to explain to him her bodyguard was just doing her duty, that they were friends, that Mae Shan was just worried about her, like Father himself worried.

But if Mae Shan found them before she had a chance to talk to Father, or if Father found out she was here and then realized Anna hadn't told him . . . anything could happen. Anna bit her lip. It would be best to tell him. He'd want to see the boat and she could bring him up here where the seer couldn't hear them and then she could explain things properly to him.

Anna jumped back down onto the slope and ran to the cave mouth. She stopped herself just before the line of shadow inside. She would not run in like a barbarian. She would walk in, humble and composed, and speak in a polite manner. She would show Father that she did know how to behave properly.

Anna smoothed her rumpled coat and folded her hands neatly. Then, taking small, tidy steps, she walked into the cave, following the sound of men's voices. The unused, omnipresent power was as stifling as the heat, but she gritted her teeth against it. She would not complain. She was not a baby.

Anna stopped while she was still in shadow. She would wait for a pause in their conversation, as was polite, and then she would excuse herself and ask to talk to Father. That was the right way to do things.

Their voices echoed oddly off the stone walls making it difficult to hear the individual words at first, which was fine with Anna, she did not want to be accused of eavesdropping, but gradually they cleared, and she could understand that they were talking about Father's new body and the nature of the spell that held his spirit confined. Before she could decide whether or not to move back a few steps so as not to overhear anything she wasn't supposed to, Father said, "You should not have taken me from her. I cannot control her so well now."

No. That was not what she heard. She had misunderstood that.

"It was necessary," the seer replied. "You would have killed her shortly, or driven her mad."

"I would not." *I love her! She's my daughter!* "I need her."

"You are dead. Your needs are greater than can be met by the living."

"I was very close to life with her."

"And that is why you came very close to draining it away. You are of more use as you are now, and she is in less danger. There has not been one such as she born in a thousand years. She will bring us to greatness once we have achieved our freedom."

She should leave now. She should go back outside. She should run down the mountainside and back up again until she exhausted herself and forgot what she heard.

"I failed you, Holy Father, and I'm sorry."

"You did not fail. You died before the completion of your work. That is why I have brought you back here."

"How may I serve?"

"By finishing what you have begun. You will cage the Firebird."

"Holy Father, if I had that knowledge, I do not have the means. Mortal breath is needed."

"It will be supplied."

"Not Anna . . ."

"Oh, no, no, my son. Her mother."

"Bridget? Bridget is here?"

"She comes. You will call the Firebird and shape the cage and she will seal it with her life, as her father did before her."

"Holy Father, the danger is severe."

"There is no danger too great for this. We will be free! I will be free!"

"Without question."

"The woman will give her life gladly, because if she does not, her child will die."

"Yes, Holy Father."

Moving as carefully and quietly as she knew how, Anna slipped out of the cave. She wanted to be sick. She couldn't even think, or see straight. She didn't know what to do besides run down the mountainside, crying as she ran.

Kalami sat cross-legged in front of the holy seer of Tuukos listening with both delight and trepidation as the ancient man gave his prophecy.

"The old ways will emerge from darkness. The new light will be ours. I see it even now." The seer's eyes grew bright and distant. His reed-thin body rocked back and forth and his lips drew back over his naked gums. Kalami waited until he could wait no more. Stillness came hard to him in this new way of being. He would have thought it would be easier, but with the stillness came fear from deep within. Fear of the darkness and the change, the teeth and the eyes. He felt hollow, a shell within a shell. He needed motion to supply what heart and lungs and blood had once given him.

When he could stand it no longer, Kalami said, "It will be as you say. But forgive me, Holy Father, how will we know how to create the cage?"

"When the dowager was gone, they thought to seal up the chamber where she had done her work, but a servant of the True Blood was there first. She placed in it a poppet and a witch's eye, and I was able to see and to understand. You will receive my instruction."

Kalami bowed his head. "Yes, Holy Father." *Finally, finally, I will do this thing. I will save my people after all. I will set all to rights, and then I will have payment for my death. Yes. I will have that too.*

The seer looked at him as if he could read his thoughts. Perhaps he could. Kalami had no true notion of the magics that could be called up from this place. He tried to move his mind back to more pious thoughts.

The seer just cackled. "Call the child back now. It is time she hear the role she is to play."

"Holy Father . . ." Kalami did not want to speak of this, but there was little choice. "There may be difficulties. There is much my daughter has not been told."

"That was your mistake then. If you had prepared her, there would not be this trouble now."

Again, Kalami bowed his head, accepting the rebuke. "As you say, Holy Father. I will make sure she is ready to hear her future."

Kalami rose, and walked to the mouth of the cave. He wore this new body lightly. He had thought it would be heavier than flesh and bone, but to his surprise, he found he had to force himself to move slowly. His senses were dull, colors dim, scents vague, and of touch there was almost nothing at all. This was not life.

What's more, it was vulnerable. Every spell that could be cast, could be broken, especially by the one who shaped the original spell, and in this poppet, as ancient and powerful as its shaping was, he did not have the sword and shield of Anna's power instantly available to him. At any time, the seer, the Holy Father, could cast him out and leave him with nowhere to go but back into the Land of Death and Spirit, where Baba Yaga waited for him, and the Vixen's sons ran freely.

No. He would not stay as he was. He would cage the Firebird, and he would use Bridget to do it with pleasure. After that, he would look into Bridget's eyes as she died and after that . . . well, life could not be granted, true, but life could be claimed.

He would not have long to remain like his. The seer had seen that Anna was the future of Tuukos, but had he seen clearly whose soul was within Anna's body and wielding her power?

Outside, the sun shone, but his eyes did not need to blink. The mossy clearing before the cave mouth was as dim as twilight to him, although the sun was still a full handspan above the horizon.

"Anna!" he called. His voice sounded too smooth, too light to his new ears. "Anna!"

There was no answer. He looked about him with his weak eyes and called again with his weak voice. "Anna! Come here!"

But there was still no answer.

Damn the girl, this was not the time for carelessness, or for mischief. With the other understanding he had to impart, he would make sure she knew better than to disobey his instructions in future. He had thought her instructors in Hung-Tse had taught her better.

Kalami began a search of the woods nearby, but he did not find Anna anywhere. He called and called with a voice that did not grow weak or hoarse, but there was no answer.

Damn the girl! But worry overrode the anger and Kalami returned to the cave and the seer's chamber.

"Holy Father . . ." he began, dropping to one knee.

The seer was bent over his gazing bowl. Fresh blood dripped from his brow and his thumbs.

"She has fled you."

"Yes, Holy Father. Where . . ."

The seer's cackling laughter echoed all around the cave. "Down to the shore, down to meet the ones who she believes will save her from her father's wickedness." The seer looked up, grinning to show all his diseased gums as if that were the greatest of all jokes. "Her mother comes on the tide, with the bodyguard Mae Shan and the sorcerer Sakra. You should go down with her to meet them and escort them here."

Kalami got to his feet once more. He felt warmer than he had since he returned to the living world. "Yes, Holy Father."

"You will need this." The seer held up his obsidian knife.

Kalami closed his fingers around it and for a moment felt the power that filled the cave reshape itself around the blade. This knife had known the greatest sacrifice before. He placed it reverently in his pocket.

Kalami left the cave. He stood poised for a moment on the mountainside. Then, he began to run. He ran fast as a mountain sheep, fast as a horse. He flew down the slope, without weight, without impediment. He ran like thought, like the first flash of sunlight in morning. He laughed as he ran, until the ground leveled out, and he saw Anna wading through a thick patch of fern. She must have been very tired, for she did not run. She trudged.

She also had not heard him coming, for she did not look back.

Kalami held himself still a moment, deciding how to proceed. He remembered what the seer had told him. If she had overheard any of their conversation, he would have to work very, very carefully.

"Anna," he said.

Anna jerked and whirled around. She stared at him with a look of utter horror.

Carefully, gently, Kalami walked up to his daughter. She stood poised on the edge of flight, but seemed mesmerized at his approach.

"Anna, I'm sorry." He knelt down so his eyes were even with hers. "I did not mean to frighten you."

She had been weeping. Her eyes were red and swollen and her cheeks were white. She said nothing, just looked back over her shoulder, trying to decide whether to run.

"You heard me talking with the Holy Father, didn't you?" he asked.

Anna sniffled. "You said . . ."

"I know, I know." He held up his hand. He did not touch her, not yet. She was not ready for this yet. "I'm so sorry, Anna, I should have found a way to warn you as soon as I realized what was happening."

Anna made no reply, but she was listening.

"The seer is mad, Anna. Things are very bad here. I had to speak as I did or he would know I doubted him. He's very powerful and if he became angry he could hurt us both."

Anna licked her lips. She wanted to believe. He could feel how badly she wanted to. He wanted to pull her close, to feel her heartbeat and her blood rushing beneath her skin. He wanted to drain all the fear from her into himself and know what it was to feel as she felt.

What it was to live.

"We should get away from here," she said, breaking his reverie. "Please, Father."

"We will, Anna," said Kalami soberly, "but we have to plan carefully. If we don't, he'll break the working that holds me in this body and I'll be gone forever."

Anna swallowed visibly. She had not thought of that. "What do we do?"

Kalami sat back on his heels. "For the moment we pretend to obey him. It will be very difficult. He wants us to bring the people who are coming in the boat to him."

"Mae Shan?" Her voice was a whisper. He could barely hear it over the wind. He leaned close, and that was a mistake, because now he caught the scent of her skin and even of her tears, and he wanted to touch her, to pull her to him, to return again to her mind, to own it this time.

"Yes, I'm afraid Mae Shan too."

"And . . . Bridget?"

"Yes."

Belligerence appeared in Anna's face for the first time. She must be very close to the edge. "He said she's my mother, like the ghosts in the Shifting Lands."

Kalami looked away, pretending to search for words in the patterns of the fern and the tree limbs. "Anna, I'm sorry, I had to lie to you. I meant to tell you the truth when you were older. She is your mother."

Anna said nothing to that. Nothing at all.

"She is a cruel and pitiless woman, Anna, and very powerful. It was she who killed the dowager of Isavalta."

"Killed?"

He nodded. "She was in the pay of the dowager's mad son."

Anna ducked her head.

What is she thinking? Kalami knew if he held her close, he would find the answer. He would reach inside her and know her blood and heart, and they would be his. Life would be his.

Stop. Stop. Control yourself.

"You killed Lien Jinn," Anna said.

Anger rose in him, and Kalami pushed it aside with difficulty. "Anna, listen to me. I did not know at first how very bad your mother was, and by the time I did . . . you were already born, and all I could do was protect you from her. That was part of the reason I had to send you to Hung-Tse. The Heart of the World was one of the only places where the magic was powerful enough to hide you from her."

"My mother." Anna whispered the words as if she had never heard them before and was trying to understand what they meant.

"Anna, I'm so sorry, but there's no time to lose." Kalami laid a hand on her shoulder, careful to be gentle, careful to be reassuring. She was afraid, and that would not do. He needed her trust. He needed all of her. "You must be strong, Daughter. This will all be over soon, and then we will be truly together, you and I. I swear it to you."

Anna bit her lip. She must have fallen as she made her way down the slope, he now saw, because her chin was scraped, and there was a small split in her lip. He watched the red blood as if he had never seen anything so beautiful.

Anna did not seem to notice. She was too absorbed in making her own decision. He was able to refocus himself on her eyes, and her white, white face before she looked up at him again.

"What do we have to do?" she said.

Kalami smiled. "All you have to do is come with me. I need your mother and the others to see you are with me. It will stop them from trying anything dangerous while we take them to the seer so he can take care of them. I will have to say some very bad things. I will have to threaten you."

"To kill me?"

"You will be safe, I promise you. I won't leave you alone for a second. You must trust me. I am not going to let anything happen to you."

"Because you need me?" Fresh tears trickled down her cheeks.

How much had she overheard? Far too much, damn the disobedient girl. Kalami forced his temper down again.

"Because I love you, Anna, because you are my child." He gathered her to him, hugging her, stroking her hair. Distantly, he felt her tears wetting his shirt. He held her for as long as he dared, then he gently pushed her away, standing her upright, with both his hands on her shoulders. "Are you ready to be strong now, Anna?"

She nodded, wiping at her face with her sleeve. Kalami reached out and brushed away a tear that she had missed.

"This is the last thing, I promise. Once the seer has these three, he will be distracted and we will be able to escape. Now, it will be very hard for you to hear me lie to Mae Shan, but you must remember she wants to take me away from you. You must not forget that for a second."

She nodded slowly. "I will remember."

"Then let us go, Anna." Kalami straightened up and with his hand still on her shoulder, he steered her down the mountainside.

Chapter Twenty-one

The Foxwood was only half a day's ride from Vyshtavos. Mikkel's great-great-grandfather had insisted his palace be built nearby, to show that he was not afraid of any power, mortal or immortal. Mikkel had always noted he had not built it *too* close, however.

For the past hour, Mikkel had been alone on the roads. People had passed him, heading toward the palace, looking for news or solace from the emperor. No one recognized him. He rode alone, carrying nothing but the battered pike, wearing nothing finer than a coat of good brown wool sashed with a broad band of deep blue.

"You should have some hint about you," Ananda had said as she tied the sash around his waist, her eyes lowered to hide the tears. "That is the way it always is in those ballads."

The roads were still sloppy with the *rasputitsa* rains, and the horse at times had more waded than trotted. The poor animal was on the verge of exhaustion now, despite the fact that Mikkel had gotten off and walked what felt like half the way. His boots were solid mud up to his calves.

It is a damned damp time of year for the Firebird to plague us, he thought wryly as he pulled his foot free from the muck yet again. *You'd think it would come in autumn when the fields are being burned.*

The first shadow of the Foxwood fell across his horse. The creature whickered and danced a little, signaling its extreme reluctance to walk under the ancient trees.

Intelligent animal. Mikkel dismounted. He did not tie it. Today he would force no one to do anything they did not want to do. Not even a horse.

He shouldered Vyshko's pike, and walked into the woods, being very careful to keep to the middle of the road. The trees were huge, and hoary with moss. No woodsman, no charcoal burner, no hunter had ever roamed between these trees. This was not the emperor's wood, nor did it belong to any lord master. This wood was wholly the property of another. Not even his mother had forgotten that. Undisturbed for thousands of years, the trees grew so thickly their branches intertwined, blocking out all the remaining sunlight. Mikkel wished for a lantern before remembering that as things were, it would do no good.

Mikkel had not gone fifty yards down the wooded road when he saw the flash of wild, green eyes. A red fox about the size of a small dog stepped up to the edge of the road. It paused with one forepaw raised, as if ready to flee. Then, it set that paw down and bowed its head in what Mikkel realized was a parody of a courtly reverence.

Mindful of where he was, Mikkel reverenced in return.

"Emperor of Isavalta," said the fox. "What do you seek here?"

"I seek an audience with the V . . . the queen of the *lokai*," replied Mikkel, pulling out all his best court manners. "If Her Majesty should deign to grant so impertinent a request."

"She has in fact been expecting you." The fox's right ear twitched, although Mikkel could hear nothing. "She sends her apologies for not being here to greet you herself, but has sent me to see to your needs."

"Then she knows why I have come?"

"She does." The fox nodded, a vaguely ridiculous gesture on such a creature. Mikkel had long years of practice at not laughing during an audience, and it stood him in good stead now.

"Does Her Majesty then know where the Firebird is?"

"I am to take you to it," replied the fox. "If His Majesty Imperial will follow me?" It turned itself around and raised its paw again, preparing to set off into the trees.

Mikkel did not move. "Master Fox, forgive me, but it has long been the agreement between our peoples that the forest is yours, and only the road is ours to travel freely." The trees were home to the *lokai*, and very few could walk into the forest and walk out again. This place had almost taken Ananda from him. Only Sakra having the foresight to arm himself and some of her guard with cold iron had saved her life.

Was that light in the fox's eye humor? Or was it memory? Mikkel suppressed a shiver. What if this was one of the foxes that had nearly taken Ananda?

It does not matter. You have already gone too far. You cannot let it matter.

"I have been instructed to grant you safe conduct, Majesty," the fox said. "No one of our people will harm or hinder you while you are in our lands and I myself will see you return safely to your road."

No spirit power would lie about an obligation, Luden had said. Mikkel hoped he was right.

"Thank you, Master Fox." Mikkel shouldered the pike again. "If you would please lead the way."

Mikkel thought the fox's gaze lingered on his hand that was clutching the pike so hard his knuckles had surely gone white. The creature, however, said nothing. It only trotted away into the ancient trees and Mikkel followed.

It was even darker between the trees than it had been on the road. He could not see anything clearly. All the trees were the same, and Mikkel soon felt dizzy trying to keep track of direction. He could not tell whether he had walked a short way very slowly or a long way very quickly. He soon realized that the only way to keep his wits from spinning was to keep his attention on the fox. For all it moved swiftly, its feet making no noise on the pine needles and decaying leaves, it seemed to be the only fixed point in a world where distances alternately compressed and expanded around him like a concertina.

Then, for the first time in days, Mikkel smelled smoke. The fox led him out of the trees, and Mikkel knew if he turned his head, he would see the forest had vanished. Ahead of him waited a small hill that had perhaps once been wooded, but now its slope was nothing but ash and char. At the very top remained the burnt stump of what had once been a tree thicker around than his waist. On the jagged lip of that stump perched the Firebird.

Mikkel had heard the Firebird was enormous, that it could blot out moon or sun when it flew across the sky, but this creature atop the hill was no bigger than a wren.

"I thank you for your pains, Master Fox." Mikkel reverenced to his guide. The fox bowed its head politely, and settled down into the tall grass at the edge of the burned patch to wait for Mikkel to come back, or not, as the case might be.

Mikkel shifted his grip on the pike and began to climb. The ash was still warm and slippery underfoot, and it was hard to stay upright. More than once he had to use the Holy Means of Isavalta's Deliverance as a walking stick, and he hoped if he met Vyshko soon the god would forgive him. Heat and ash rose up around him with each step, getting into eyes, nose, and hair.

At last, hot, sweaty, and filthy and feeling more like a pig keeper than a prince, Mikkel gained the crest of the hill and stood before the Firebird. It seemed hardly bigger than a candle flame. Yet, its living fire burned so brightly and so steadily that he soon had to look away and blink back his tears. It was as painful as looking into the sun.

This tiny, beautiful creature was the thing so brimming with hate it would condemn his people to darkness and starve them all to death.

It was surveying the valley and seemed to take no notice of him. Mikkel knelt. The ash was hot enough to sting his knees through the cloth of his trousers, but he stayed as he was with his head bowed, waiting to be acknowledged.

At last, the Firebird spoke. "You are her son."

"I am." Mikkel raised his head. The Firebird's eyes were blue, he saw, like the sapphires in the imperial crown, or the very heart of the hottest flame.

The Firebird looked at the pike. "Do you think to kill me with that?"

"I do not want to."

The Firebird blinked its blue eye, and the pike's wooden shaft burst into flame. The fire bit into his skin at once, and Mikkel dropped the pike, scrambling backward, holding his hand.

The Firebird watched the weapon burn. After a time, the fire simply winked out, and there was nothing left of Vyshko's pike but the metal tip.

The Firebird again turned its blazing blue eye toward Mikkel, and Mikkel bowed.

"I am sorry," he said. "I should not have brought a weapon here. It was presumptuous, and one more thing for which I must ask your forgiveness."

The Firebird seemed to have to consider that for a moment. "You have come to beg for forgiveness?"

"Yes."

That did not seem to be the answer the Firebird was expecting. It hesitated a moment before giving its answer. "No." The word flared like a fresh coal. "There can be no forgiveness for what you and yours have done."

Mikkel drew his shoulders back. He did not want to speak these words. *Ananda forgive me. I am no clever peasant boy. I am only myself.*

"I offer my life in apology."

"Do you?" it whispered.

The Firebird began to grow. It rose up like a sheet of flame from the stump. It became the size of a hawk, of an eagle, of a swan. The heat from it was more than Mikkel could bear, but he made himself stand his ground. The Firebird spread out its wings to embrace him in flame. "Do you offer your life to me?" it roared.

Mikkel fell to his knees. *Vyshko grant me your strength. Ananda forgive me.* "Yes!"

Flame was all around him. Mikkel screamed but somehow, against all instinct, did not run. He smelled burning, closed his eyes, held his breath, and waited to die.

And then the heat was gone. Mikkel's eyes opened. The Firebird, once again the size of a wren, sat before him. His hair felt singed. His face hurt. His hands hurt, but he was alive.

"Why?" demanded the Firebird. "Why would you come here? You are the seed of my captor. Why would you ask my forgiveness if you were not afraid of me?"

The urge to run washed over Mikkel even more strongly. The pain was growing, as if his body was only slowly beginning to realize how close the fire had come.

He made himself sit down in the ashes. It was not dignified, but it would keep him from bolting.

"I dreamed once," he said. "I dreamed I saw a beautiful bird in the garden outside my window, but I couldn't reach it. I tried and I tried, but I couldn't reach it, and the bird was crying, in my dream, because its leg was tangled in some twine that had gotten wrapped around the branch it was sitting on." He sounded mad. This was ridiculous; this would do nothing. But it was all he had. "And I wanted to free the bird, but I could not, because I was in a cage myself, and when I woke, I was blind." He lifted his head, and dared to look the Firebird in the eye. "She caged me too. I know something of what you suffered, and I am sorry. I am here to do whatever you want, to earn forgiveness. I am the last of the blood that wronged you. Spare my people. Take your revenge on me."

Tentatively, hesitantly, the Firebird stretched out its neck. "You would do this?"

"I would."

But before he could speak another word, the Firebird screamed. It was a sound like tearing metal. It launched itself into the air, becoming again the curtain of flame. Mikkel fell backward, crying out in pain and in fear.

"No! Liar! You lied!" It screamed with an anguish that stopped Mikkel's heart.

And it was gone.

Mikkel was on his feet, looking around for enemy or attacker, but there was none. He was alone on the burnt-out hill, his own burns setting their pain more deeply into his skin and the horrified scream of the Firebird echoing in his soul.

The fox who was his guide began to pick its way up the hill, stopping frequently to shake ashes from its paws.

"What happened!" Mikkel cried.

The fox did not answer immediately. It nosed the stump where the Firebird had perched and sniffed around the charred and blackened roots. Then, it looked into the sky.

"Someone is trying your mother's trick," said the fox. "May their gods help them."

Mikkel thought of the beautiful bird, of the heartache and how close it had come to believing him, how very close, and now it was gone again to someone who wanted to drive it back into captivity.

He bent his head, and then his knees, and the emperor of Isavalta so recently freed from his own bondage began to cry.

Chapter Twenty-two

Mae Shan and the sorcerer Sakra hopped into the surf and each grabbed a gunwale to help beach Uncle Lien's boat while the woman, whom Sakra had told Mae Shan was named Bridget, took in the sail and lashed it down. When she felt the press and shift of dry sand under her shoes, Mae Shan thought she might cry or faint from relief. She had not believed she would live. She had not believed she would ever see the sun or the shore again.

She had spoken to old soldiers and heard about the things one did after battle. The moments of insanity, elation, or unbearable sorrow that could seize hold of one who had been pressed to their breaking point despite years of training. She had not at that time truly understood the feeling with which they spoke, and had dismissed much of it. Perhaps one day she would be able to return and apologize. If any were left alive.

Mae Shan swallowed and closed her eyes, feeling the sun on her face and listening to the surge and roar of the ocean at her back.

Your battle is not over yet. Not yet.

She opened her eyes. Sakra was helping Bridget out of the boat. She had her hems gathered up almost to her knees, revealing a pair of thick black stockings and tattered shoes that had once been fine slippers. She didn't seem to need the hand the sorcerer held out to her, as she jumped down easily into the water and waded to the beach without hesitation or thought of modesty. Surely she was a fisherwoman, or the daughter of farmers as Mae Shan was. Whatever she was, she was used to hard work and boats, as well as magic.

She was saying something to Sakra, her hand clutching his arm tightly. Her face was white, and Mae Shan thought that if she could hear her there would be a tremor in her voice. She hoped Sakra knew where they were. It was a beautiful place with the great mountain rising green and grey to meet the sky, and the strange sand of the beach glittering around them black as well as gold. She was thankful beyond words for their rescue of her but she still hoped they knew how she might best find a representative of the emperor of Isavalta. As much as her blood burned to undo her uncle's murderer with her bare hands, she was not such a fool. She needed magic, and she needed other soldiers. She would get down on her knees before the gods of Isavalta and forswear herself if she had to, but she would get what she needed and she would drive Valin Kalami back into the Land of Death and Spirit, and if need be she would follow him there herself to make certain that he stayed this time.

For now that she was in the real world and on solid ground, now that shock and nightmare were over, her anger spilled out of her like blood, and only blood would assuage it.

Sakra approached her. Mae Shan took a deep breath and calling on years of discipline pushed that anger to the back of her mind. She bowed to the sorcerer, her hand clasped around her fist in salute.

"Sir, this one most humbly thanks you and the Lady Bridget for all you have done. This one's life is in debt and service to you." She spoke in the most formal dialect she possessed.

The Hastinapuran bowed. "This one salutes the bravery of Mae Shan. Certainly she has borne herself honorably through grave dangers. If a question may be permitted."

Mae Shan glanced over Sakra's shoulder and saw Bridget. It was not only the black sand that made her look so white. She watched Mae Shan's every move with anxious eyes. "Of course. I will help in any way I can," she said, switching to less formal phrasings.

"Do you know a girl child named Anna?"

Mae Shan felt as if she had been struck. "What is this?" she demanded. "Who are you? What do you know of Tsan Nu . . . of Anna?"

Sakra held up his hands and pressed them together, a gesture asking for peace and patience. "Forgive me, forgive me, but I doubted for a moment what I had been told and I should not have . . . will you come with me? There are stories to be told here."

This I readily believe. Mae Shan followed him to where Bridget stood. He said something to her in the language they shared, and her hand flew to her mouth to stifle a scream or a sob. For a moment Mae Shan thought the woman was going to lunge forward and shake her, but she only swayed on her feet. Then, she said something to Sakra.

"The Lady Bridget asks your forgiveness for her emotion," Sakra said to Mae Shan, though Mae Shan wondered if the Lady Bridget had said any such thing. "She asks me to tell you she is Anna's mother."

Mae Shan stared in open and frank disbelief. The woman met her gaze, but it was clear she was at the end of some harrowing adventure of her own. Mae Shan tried to see any of Anna in her. The coloring was wrong, and the hair, but there was something familiar in the shape of the face. Mae Shan took two steps forward, and now that she looked closely, the eyes, the eyes were the right pale shade. It could be the truth.

"How is this possible?" Mae Shan asked Sakra.

"I don't know." He shook his head. "We are in the hands of the gods in this, all of us."

Mae Shan looked at Tsan Nu's mother, who looked to be Isavaltan, and at the Hastinapuran who stood beside her and obviously had to restrain himself from taking her hands to comfort her. *But in the hands of whose gods in this tumult when our gods distrust each other as much as our emperors do?*

"Tell Lady Bridget I was Anna's bodyguard for five years as lieutenant of the Heart's Own Guard in the Heart of the World. Tell her I helped bring Anna out of the Heart when it burned down. Tell her when last I saw Anna she was alive in my uncle's house. Tell her . . ." Mae Shan faltered. "There is too much to tell."

"Will you permit this one to make it possible for Lieutenant Mae Shan to speak in her own words without this one's fumbling?" asked Sakra with another bow.

The return to high formalities told Mae Shan all she needed to know about what he wanted to do. The thought of yet more magic made her sick inside, but she nodded her aquiescence.

The spell itself involved taking one of the beads from his braided hair, rinsing it clean in seawater, and speaking over it in the manner of sorcerers. He then gave it to her to swallow, a possibility Mae Shan found she had prepared herself for. It was not as difficult as she feared. Sakra then pressed two fingers against her lips and spoke three more words. Mae Shan felt cold for a heartbeat, then hot, and then that too passed.

Sakra stepped away, bowing in thanks or apology, Mae Shan was not sure which. "You will be able to speak freely now," he said in words and cadences that were alien to Mae Shan's ears but no longer so to her mind or tongue.

She turned to Bridget, who had knotted the fingers of both hands into her skirt in a search for something to hold on to.

"Tell me," she said to Mae Shan. Her voice was a whisper, barely audible over the waves, and it brimmed with fear, with hope, with love and sorrow and forty thousand other things that Mae Shan could barely begin to guess at. "Tell me about my daughter."

There on the black and gold sands, Mae Shan told her story. They sat out of reach of the waves. There was water and a little food stowed in the boat so they were able to find some refreshment as she spoke. Mae Shan reclaimed her spear and sat with her back to the water so she could face inland. She was a soldier still, whatever else happened. Her training had kept her alive this far, she would follow it even if they were in the middle of nowhere.

She was glad to be able to tell this woman that Anna was a good child, that she was clever, kind, obedient, and happy, that she had been well cared for and had known affection from her teachers and nurses.

She spoke of the burning of the Heart as quickly and as sparingly as she could, to save the mother's feelings, yes, but also her own. She did not want to dwell on what was not there anymore. She was too worn down by that enormity to be able to fend off a fresh attack from her own memory.

She was, however, glad to speak of Valin Kalami and what he had done. She wanted every moment carved deeply in her mind. She wanted these two to be as furious as she was. She wanted their help without question or delay, and letting them know exactly what Kalami had done to Anna seemed the best way to secure that agreement. It was the only weapon she had for this fight.

When at last Mae Shan finished, Bridget said, "Thank you." She rose, bread crumbs and sand scattering from her skirt, and walked back to the edge of the waves. She stood staring out at the sea for a long moment, rubbing her arms.

Mae Shan thought Sakra would go to her then, but he did not. Instead, Sakra told Mae Shan Bridget's story, and it was as fantastic as any fairy tale told at fireside after the children had gone to bed. Although he did not move toward her, he watched Bridget as he spoke. She stood with the waves lapping at her torn shoes. She did not look like any great sorceress, until one saw the stony resolve tightening her features and sparking danger in her eyes that were so much like Anna's.

Bridget must have been able to hear at least the rise and fall of Sakra's voice, because as soon as he had finished with their tale, she strode back, head and shoulders erect, her jaw hard.

"We will find him, Mae Shan," she declared. "For you and for my daughter."

"Your magics are great," said Mae Shan. "But do you even know where we are?"

"Yes," Bridget answered. "I recognize the mountain. This is Tuukos. Kalami has come home." She glanced at Sakra and obviously saw some question there. "I had Richikha read to me about it after . . . everything. I wanted to know what had driven Kalami to do what he had done. All I knew he had done at that point." She looked away, attempting to collect herself. "The good news is Lord Master Peshek is here, in the city of Ahde. I had a letter from him before this all started saying he had arrived. He will help us."

Sakra nodded. "Ahde is on the coast, if I remember correctly. Do you think you can handle the boat in these waters?"

Bridget looked toward the rolling blue ocean, puffing out her cheeks in calculation. At the same time, Mae Shan glimpsed movement among a pile of rocks a few dozen yards down the beach. Not caring if she appeared too nervous, she shot to her feet. Sakra and Bridget turned to look.

A form stood on a boulder, small and slender, with long hair blowing like a banner in the ocean wind.

"What . . ." began Bridget.

But even at this distance, Mae Shan recognized the form of the child in her borrowed clothes. "Goddess of Mercy, it's Anna."

"Anna!" screamed Bridget, and before anything more could be said or thought, she was on her feet, tearing down the beach with Sakra hard on her heels.

Mae Shan swore and snatched up her spear. *Stop!* she wanted to yell, but it was too late. They were already running full speed into whatever trap had been set, as Kalami had surely known they would.

There was no cover beyond that jumble of rocks. No way she had not been seen, nowhere to slip away and take up position. This was Kalami's home. If he had brought allies, all efforts were futile now, but she had to try.

Mae Shan angled for the tree line. Allies or no, perhaps she could lose them in the tangle of the forest, watch and see where Bridget and Sakra would be taken to, if they weren't killed outright . . .

"Mae Shan!" A child's scream rose high over the ocean's roar, like the call of a hunting bird. It jerked Mae Shan's head around before she could stop herself.

On the boulder, beside Anna, stood a man, and the man held a knife at the child's throat. Mae Shan skidded to a stop, spraying black and gold sand up around her.

"Mae Shan!" called the man. "No farther!"

There was the trap. She should have seen it as soon as Anna appeared. Their boat had been spotted as it came to land. It had been too late before they even set foot on shore.

Mae Shan gripped the shaft of her spear with both hands and raised it high over her head. She would not drop it unless ordered to do so. Even a trapped animal might find a chance to bite.

"Very good. Now, come here. I would speak with you!"

Keeping her spear held high, Mae Shan slogged through the loose black and gold sand. Patches of black stone stood out here and there. Scoured clean by wind they looked like dark pools of oil, or bottomless holes waiting for someone to make an unlucky step.

Already done, she thought toward her own fancy.

She was close enough now to start taking in details. *Waste not one breath when you are looking for your opening,* her trainer had said. *One breath may be all you have.*

A flat black rock, speckled with lichen, thrust out of the sand, making a kind of natural platform. Ocean or mountain had tumbled clusters of man-sized grey boulders around it in a complex and disorderly jumble that left only one corner of the platform rock clear for easy climbing. A man, who was tall and wiry, stood with his back to the jumbled stones and his face toward the opening. Anna stood in front of him, as still as a statue, her face blank, but her eyes filled with fear. He had one hand on her shoulder. To the left side of her throat he held the point of an obsidian knife.

Mae Shan had seen one of these once, in the home of one of the imperial doctors who favored it for surgeries. He said there was no steel so sharp.

Mae Shan looked hard at the man. He seemed to have lived soft. His arms and long, brown face were without scars, or the whipcord lines of muscles. His clothing was simple. He wore no armor or protective gear. There was no sign of any weapon save that black and glistening knife beneath Anna's chin. His hands were nearly doll-like in their smoothness, yet he held the knife with confidence. He kept his eyes steadily on Mae Shan's progress. If he had confederates, he was sure of them, because he cast no glance in any other direction looking for signs of readiness or arrival.

He remained silent until Mae Shan drew abreast of Bridget and Sakra.

"Excellent," he said. "You can stop there."

"Kalami," spat Bridget.

Mae Shan started, but stilled herself quickly, concentrating on her watching and on alternately tightening and loosening her grip on her spear so that her hands would not grow numb. So this was Valin Kalami. She did not ask how he found this body. He was a sorcerer and a barbarian. It was their way to perform such blasphemies. She was only glad he was no longer inside Anna. Now she would have a chance to kill him without harming her charge.

Kalami was smiling at Bridget. Smiling, he should have been a handsome man, in his way, except for the cruelty in his eyes.

"Yes, my dear. So good of you to come and finally meet your daughter."

Anna also looked to Bridget, bewildered. She had thought her mother dead and her father a kind savior. What did she think now?

"Anna, has he hurt you?" asked Mae Shan.

Anna began to shake her head, but felt the knife. "I'm sorry, Mae Shan," she said softly.

"It is of no matter, mistress." *Squeeze. Release. Squeeze. Release. Keep your hands ready. Keep your eyes on him. Don't let him see the way you stand. Don't let him know your readiness.*

"Let her go," said Bridget. "I will do anything you ask, just let Mae Shan take her and go." She swallowed. "I beg you."

"Yes." Kalami's smile grew broader and sharper. "You do, and you will. But our child should be with the parent who did not give her away as an infant, don't you think?"

Which was too much for the woman. "You stole her!" she cried as if her heart were breaking afresh. "You stole her in the middle of the night and you made me think she was dead!"

"What else was I to do?" Kalami shrugged. "You were not going to let me take her, were you?"

Which story is it? Mae Shan watched confusion growing in Anna's eyes. *You should stick to one lie, Valin Kalami. What is the matter with you?*

Apparently Sakra noticed as well. "You were a better liar when you were alive, Kalami. The Vixen would be disappointed you learned nothing in her company."

"Quiet!" Kalami's whole body stiffened with fear and for one moment his whole attention was on the sorcerer.

Mae Shan swung her spear into her right hand and cast it out, straight for Kalami's exposed chest and watched with elation as it flew straight and true.

The spear struck the sorcerer with a high ringing noise as if it had just struck a bell made of glass and fell clattering to the rock, rolled away, and thudded onto the sand.

Inside herself, Mae Shan howled to shake the Heavens. Anna went paper-white. Kalami did not even stagger. He just turned his head to look down at the weapon with an oddly inhuman fluidity.

"Pick up your toy," he said to Mae Shan, his voice brimming with satisfaction. "And do not trouble me with it again."

Slowly, carefully, so the sorcerer could see each movement, Mae Shan walked forward to the base of the rock. It came up to her shoulders, too high for her to make any sort of leap. Any such attempt would be too dangerous for Anna, who did not seem to have blinked this whole time. Mae Shan held up her right hand as she retrieved the spear with her left, and raised it over her head as she had before, and slowly backed away to stand beside the others.

"I understand you had to try," said Kalami magnanimously. "And I am glad we have gotten that out of the way. As for you"—he looked toward Sakra, but this time Mae Shan could see he kept her in his peripheral vision—"I caution you, Southerner, I might decide you are not needed after all. There are plenty of bodies to spare." His hand clamped down tighter on Anna's shoulder and the child winced in pain.

Bridget bit her lip. Her hands twitched. It seemed to Mae Shan that the air grew a little colder.

"We must climb the mountain now," Kalami went on, visibly forcing himself to relax once more. "You will walk in front of me. Mae Shan, you will go first, as you are. The other two will follow you, with their hands folded behind their backs. You will all remember that I have this knife at Anna's throat, and her only purpose here is to prevent attack. Should attack come, she will no longer be of use to me."

"I swear, Kalami," said Bridget hoarsely. Tears glistened in her eyes. "Whatever you want, just . . ."

"No, no, my dear Bridget. Whatever I want, and then." He smiled. "Go. You will see the path. Do not one of you look back."

Mae Shan turned to face the mountain. She did see the path, thin and snaking up the hills that blended together to become the mountain. It was far more green than brown, apparently a lightly traveled route. Still working her hands to keep them limber, Mae Shan marched toward it, keeping her shoulders and arms relaxed and loose, remembering to breathe. There would be some chance. There would be some way. She traveled with sorcerers. She still had the spear. There would be some way.

To believe otherwise was to despair, and she had not come so far, she had not witnessed so much to give way now.

She did not hear Sakra and Bridget fall into step behind her. The sound of the ocean was too loud to hear footfalls on sand, but neither did she look back to see they were there. The path of the dead from Hell this might be, but she would not make the mistake the poems spoke of and look back to see where she had been and thus lose her promised freedom. Kalami would not kill Anna on this path. He needed her yet to control her mother, and Mae Shan, and through them Sakra. What chance she would have lay ahead of her.

The path up the mountain was steep and winding. The trees were stunted, but they grew together in tight clumps, leaving room for little between them but bracken, or a patch of grey or black stone. The cool of the ocean breeze soon fell behind them. Mae Shan began to perspire freely, and her lungs strained to keep her supplied with air. Now she could hear the others moving behind her, the rustle of cloth, the crackle of sticks and last year's leaves, the hiss of labored breath. Anna's whisper, then Kalami's. She almost forgot the orders not to look back, but caught herself in time.

Gradually, the trees grew taller and straighter, cutting off the sunlight. Clouds of tiny, black insects swarmed around Mae Shan's face, settling on her neck and behind her ears to drink their fill. She did not let go of her spear. She did not look back or shake her head to try to clear them. She thought she would go mad with itching, but she did not want Kalami to become tense and wary again. She wanted him to think they were cowed.

The path steepened. Despite her efforts, the feeling in Mae Shan's hands began to drain away, replaced by an aching in her elbows and shoulders. Her feet felt leaden and the cloth of her shoes was damp with sweat.

"No, Anna," said Kalami suddenly. "Not there. We have a way to go yet."

So they kept climbing.

The path wandered through the trees and the thickets that sprang up wherever there was a patch of sunlight. That sunlight was steeply slanted now, and the forest was dimming toward twilight. Hunger cramped Mae Shan's belly and thirst made her throat itch as badly as her face and neck did from drying sweat and insect bites. A dozen times she thought she saw a place where she might dive out of sight, and turn, spear at the ready. But who would she kill like that? He had already shown her he had no reason to fear her weapon. She could turn, throw the spear to distract attention, snatch Anna and run away, vanish into the forest and wait for darkness, but could she do any of that before the black knife flickered?

Patience. Patience. It is still ahead of you. Keep walking. You will meet your chance.

Eventually, the trees began to thin and shrink again. Mae Shan emerged, blinking, into the deep golden light of evening. The forest spread out behind and below her now. Ahead, the ground rose steeply enough to become jagged walls of grey veined with black. Here and there she saw the white forms of mountain goats, looking calmly down at the humans, and knowing themselves to be perfectly safe. There was no climbing these cliffs.

"To your right, Mae Shan," called out Kalami. "Go carefully. These screes are treacherous."

Her arms ached as they never had. Her legs were weakening as well, and still, Mae Shan turned as she was bidden, putting the cliffs on her left side and the open, stony slope on her right. She let her eyes dart quickly to the side as she did, and managed to glimpse Kalami, who was—oh, thank Heaven he had that much compassion—carrying Anna now. The exhausted child lay limp against his chest. Her color did not look healthy.

The knife still glittered in his hand.

Sakra and Bridget marched grimly between Mae Shan and Kalami, with Bridget closest to her child. Their shoulders were slumped and they stumbled against the ridges that centuries of wind had carved in the stone. Her own balance was none too certain, and she wobbled and skidded like a clown on stepping stones in a bad comic play. The light was dimming rapidly. Soon she would not be able to see at all.

Soon I will break my neck, and at least I will be able to wait for Kalami in the Land of Death and Spirit.

Forgive me, Anna.

"Look sharp, Mae Shan," called out Kalami. "Watch for the marking stone of obsidian. Turn toward the cliffs when you see it, and walk straight ahead."

Her eyes were bleary, her head ached, and the light was only getting worse, but Mae Shan gritted her teeth and tried to obey. Stones clattered underfoot and behind her. Overhead, a goat let loose a tiny bit of scree, and a pebble bounced down in front of her, startling her and almost robbing her of what little balance she had left. The wind blew cold against her exposed and bloodless hands. She stumbled, and stumbled again.

Then she saw something glint in the last rays of day. A finger of black and glassy stone thrust itself out of a rock fall. As she had been ordered, Mae Shan turned to face the cliff and trudged forward, wondering sardonically to herself if Kalami would be happy once she had broken her nose against the solid wall of stone.

Then, in the fading light, she made out a narrow crack hidden in a cleft in the cliff face. There seemed to be a grey twilight shining through, and she realized this was a passageway, through to . . . somewhere.

"That's far enough, Mae Shan. Stand aside."

Mae Shan did. She fell back with Bridget and with Sakra. They were as disheveled, as exhausted and filthy as she. They let Kalami pass them, able to do nothing more than glare at him. He cradled Anna against his chest and held the knife pressed against her back. He couldn't cut her throat quickly from this position, but if such knives were as sharp as she'd heard, he could sever her spine and leave her to die slowly.

"There, there, Anna," he said in a mocking parody of father's love as he passed Bridget. "We're almost done." He kissed the half-sleeping child on top of her forehead. "And you will all please remember, I know what is on the other side of this, and you do not. I still hold her life as I hold her body. If you do not all come through before a man may count to one hundred, she will die within moments and your only consolation will be that it will be quick. Mae Shan, you will come first."

Kalami vanished into the crevice. Mae Shan looked to Bridget. Her face was wet with tears but if anything, her expression had hardened.

You had better pray I get to you before she does, Valin Kalami.

Mae Shan faced the cliff. The only cold comfort this moment offered was that she had to lower her spear in order go through the low, narrow passage. Her shoulders screamed in protest but she did not take the time to listen. She turned her body to fit through the crevice.

As she did, Sakra caught her eye. "They shape glass," he murmured.

What? Mae Shan did not take time to speak the question. She did not want to risk being overheard. She instead squeezed as quickly as she could into the cramped darkness.

To Mae Shan's relief, once inside the opening, the stone was smooth and the way was short. The evening light opened before her, and she was through in a space of time measured in heartbeats.

Once she had straightened up, the first thing she saw was Valin Kalami holding Anna close and watching Mae Shan with his sly eyes.

Then she saw the valley.

It was a perfect bowl shape with the teeth of the cliffs rising high overhead. Where outside there had been scrub and rock, here there was grass like a verdant carpet. Even in the twilight it glowed with color. Clusters of daffodils broke the green here and there to shine with a gold that rivaled the setting sun. Small brown birds like quail, and larger ones with red heads that might have been gulls of some sort nested in the short grass, undisturbed by their arrival, for by now Sakra and Bridget had come through the crevice. The white mountain sheep and goats grazed serenely on the lush vegetation, or settled together in knots, preparing for sleep.

The only things that rose higher than the heads of the sheep waited down on the smooth floor of the valley bowl. A circle of trees grew down there, where it was closer to night than day, but Mae Shan could still tell those trees were scarlet red, branches, trunks, twigs, leaves and all. They were perfect in their shape, with thick, straight trunks and beautiful spreading branches. They must have been tended as carefully as the trees in the gardens of the Heart, and for as many centuries. As she stared, however, she saw how they gleamed unnaturally in the last rays of day, as if they were made of red ice.

As if they were made of glass.

"They destroyed the crucibles where we wrought our greatest shapings," Kalami said. "They smashed our creations and took our artisans to be their slaves. They slaughtered our sorcerers, our teachers, our leaders. But they never found their way here. Never." His smile was positively wild as he gazed out at the great valley. "Did your emperor make the Heart of the World? The gods themselves made this heart for us."

How could such things be made? Mae Shan could not take her eyes off the trees. They were too big for any crucible. They were too perfect for any human craftsman. From this distance, only the tiniest sheen showed them to be other than creations of nature.

Only the tiniest sheen.

Mae Shan looked again at Kalami, as he stared over the top of his daughter's head. His skin shone as well. At first she thought it was perspiration from his exertions, but now she looked again. She saw the smoothness of his arms and face and hands.

Glass. They shape glass.

It was this that shook Mae Shan back to herself. Anna was watching her. The child's skin was grey, and yet she seemed flushed with fever. Ordinary concerns touched Mae Shan, the daughter of a large family. When had the child last had a proper meal? When had she last slept? There was something beyond plain worry or confusion in her face. Mae Shan had seen her look this way before. She wanted reassurance. In her father's arms, she was looking to Mae Shan to give it to her.

But Mae Shan had none to give, not yet, so she would find a way to give her what she could. She would let the child know she still cared, that she knew it was not Anna who had done what had been done.

And she would give Anna her mother as well.

"Anna, you are not well," she said succinctly in the language of Isavalta. Beside her, she felt Bridget stiffen.

"My daughter is fine," returned Kalami. "She is only tired. If you care for her"—this was said to Bridget—"you will see that we conclude our business quickly."

Anna was looking at Bridget again. Wondering, surely, who this woman who bore the title of mother actually was. Her mind was not completely made up yet, or it had been changed, and that was something else.

There were dark, lumpish shapes in the center of the ring of scarlet trees. Only one of them moved. It paced back and forth in a pattern of ritual, or of working. Someone below them was preparing for their arrival and a light burned low and orange on what looked to be an altar.

"As you were before," said Kalami. "Let us go."

Mae Shan thought her shoulders would break, but she swung the spear high over her head again.

"Your mother saved my life," she said to Anna as she did.

Kalami answered before Anna could. "That one traitor saves another is not surprising. We know who you are, Mae Shan."

"Yes," Mae Shan said as she turned away to march down the steep slope of the valley. "I know you do."

Fortunately, the dew had not yet fallen. The way would have been nearly impossible if the grass had been slick as well as soft. By the time they reached level ground, night had truly arrived. Birds and sheep had fallen silent. The wind blew through the grass without sound. It might have been the Land of Death and Spirit, except for the sky. The sky above was indigo and black, and the stars, the landscape and inhabitants of Heaven, came out in their millions to witness whatever thing Kalami had in store for them, and for his daughter.

Ahead of them, in the grove, someone was lighting lanterns that hung in the tree branches. Tiny lights like infant stars shone through scarlet leaves and branches, making them dance as if they swayed in the night breeze. It was beautiful and it was eerie for everything was the exact color of fresh blood.

As the ring of glass trees grew nearer, Mae Shan expected them to seem less real, but they did not. The lines of the trunks were rippled and grooved, as tree bark was. Each red leaf had its own individual shape and color. She could see no join where leaf met twig, and she wondered almost hysterically if they fell in the autumn and needed to be swept up with special brooms. The wind freshened, and Mae Shan heard a new sound. As the leaves shivered, they sang, ever so slightly, high, fragile, almost painful notes, making a song of knifelike beauty that set all the senses on edge.

Mae Shan walked into the grove of trees the color of blood surrounded by the singing of ancient glass, and faced a monster. A brown and wasted man hunched in a robe that had once been white, but that age had turned yellow, belted round with a leather braid those same years had stained black. He had a long taper in his hand that he had been using to light the lanterns, that Mae Shan now saw were also made of glass, clear instead of scarlet. By their light, she saw the greed in his eyes at their approach.

"Kneel before the Holy Father," barked Kalami, as if they should have known what to do. Mae Shan knelt in the cooling grass, with Sakra and Bridget following suit. Kalami set Anna down on her feet, keeping her close, but not, she noticed, with the knife immediately at her throat. He felt safer here, more sure of them, weakened as he knew they were. Neither he nor Anna made the obeisance.

The one Kalami called Holy Father laid the taper aside on what Mae Shan had taken for an altar. She saw now it was a squat, square crucible of black stone, its fire burning so brightly, it was painful to look at. Beside it lay a heap of ore speckled with gold, and beside that lay a perfectly round pool that reflected all the stars in the darkening sky.

"Welcome," said Kalami's Holy Father, his tongue slipping against gums that had no teeth left. "Now you see what not even all those of the True Blood have looked upon. Now you see the Holy of Holies. It is from here you will be the means to shape our salvation."

The holy monster shuffled up to Mae Shan, and took her spear in his skinny hands. Mindful of Anna and the knife, Mae Shan let it go. Her arms fell painfully to her sides, and she wondered if she'd ever find the strength to lift them again.

"Good," he said, surveying the shaft and the honed tip as if he meant to purchase it. "A soldier should die with her weapons beside her."

"Are we all to die, Holy Father?" inquired Sakra.

"Or just Mae Shan?" added Bridget.

"Keep quiet!" snapped Kalami.

Mae Shan risked another glance at Anna. She seemed to have recovered a little now that she was on her feet. Her eyes were clearer, and they were watching Mae Shan, and they were watching the stranger who was her mother, and they were determinedly not watching the knife in her father's hand.

Where is my chance? It is here, I know it is. Where?

"Tonight we finish the work begun by our most loyal son," the Holy Father went on, smiling broadly, so the firelight played across his wet gums.

He waited, letting the words sink in, waiting for comprehension, and it came.

"God Almighty," said Bridget hoarsely. "The Firebird. You're going to try to cage the Firebird and keep it for Tuukos, like the dowager kept it for Isavalta."

"The *murhata* have had a taste of its power now," said the holy madman. "They know how well they should fear it now. They will bow before the ones who gave them their gods, as they should have all these long years. Their blood will shape our workings as it did before, and they will understand our greatness afresh."

Mae Shan looked at the scarlet trees, and realized what blasphemy had made them. Her stomach, which she thought must now be beyond such delicacy, turned over inside her.

"I can't cage the Firebird," Bridget was saying.

"A pity," said the madman, smiling serenely. "If that is the truth then when it is called here, it will kill us all." He nodded significantly toward Anna.

It was a gesture Bridget could not miss. She flung herself down on the grass. "Please. Please, not the child. I don't know how to do this thing you ask. Let Kalami take Anna away from here. She is one of your people. She does not deserve to die because I don't know what to do."

Those words, that gesture, must have cost her everything, and yet Mae Shan knew she made them freely, even gladly, if it would help. If it would save Anna.

But did Anna know it? With only the flickering lights of the tiny lanterns and the bloody reflections of the trees, Mae Shan couldn't see her silent, solemn face well enough to know for sure.

"You can stop this pretense," Kalami said. "Anna knows you for the false mother you are. No show of devotion will undo what you have already done."

Slowly, deliberately, like one who was no longer concerned for consequences, Bridget climbed to her feet. "What I have done?" she whispered. "What *I* have done!" she shouted, her voice rising to a shriek. "Why are you holding a knife at her throat, Valin Kalami? If my heart is so hollow, why is her life the only card you have to play against us all? Where are your magics, your bribes, your compulsions? Where is all your power, Sorcerer? Why is threatening my daughter all you can do to be sure of me if I don't *care*?"

"Disloyalty, disobedience, and dishonesty. Of these, which is the worse fault?" murmured Mae Shan in the language she and Anna shared for so long. It was one of the many lessons they had both been taught, reciting dutifully with the other children in their classes. *Dishonesty is the worse fault, for dishonesty encompasses the other two.*

Her father was a liar and he was using her. Did Anna understand that yet or did she, in the way of a child, try to reconcile her father's behavior with the fact that he said he loved her?

Mae Shan didn't think Kalami even heard her whisper. He was facing wild-eyed Bridget. "You are nothing. A receptacle for power, for seed. You are a thing to be used, and you will be used."

Bridget went so still she might herself have been made of glass. Mae Shan had seen such anger before. It was the place beyond fury where everything in sight becomes a potential weapon. It was the moment where one knows quite coolly that one will destroy another, and the only thing holding Bridget still was the presence of her daughter.

"Remember this, Anna. Whatever happens next, whatever you come to think of me, remember what was said and done here."

Bridget turned to the Holy Father, monk or madman, whatever he was. "Will you let my daughter go?"

"No," he answered. "If you wish to save her, you will help us fashion a cage for the Firebird."

"I don't know how." Bridget bit off each word.

This did not disconcert the ancient and wizened man in the least. "You do not have to. Kalami does. All that is required is your living power and your mortal breath. You will play the role your father Avanasy played for Medeoan. Your life will seal the cage."

Sakra opened his mouth.

"And here is the southerner to say he also is a sorcerer, he will do this thing in her stead," said Kalami before Bridget could speak. "Oh, no, Sakra. Your life has other uses."

"Am I to know what these uses may be?" Sakra asked evenly.

As Kalami shifted his attention to Sakra, Bridget bowed her head, turning minutely toward Mae Shan.

"What is the Firebird's name?" she breathed.

Mae Shan held herself still, hoping to convey with silence and rigidity that she did not understand.

"Hung-Tse has fallen. Isavalta will fall," Kalami said to Sakra. For a moment he was lost in his dreams for his future and his people. He did not see his daughter turned toward the prisoners, watching, listening. "We cannot permit Hastinapura to stroll north and take all it wants, can we? We must understand their minds and their magics. We must talk for a very long time, you and I."

"His name. He was a man," hissed Bridget urgently. "What is his *name?*"

"Xuan, Minister of Fire . . ."

"No," whispered a small voice in the language of Hung-Tse. "Seong. His name was Seong."

"Anna!" Kalami's hand came down hard and heavy upon her shoulder. "I have told you what that woman is, you will not speak to her. I will not let her lie to you anymore."

"Kalami." The Holy Father lifted his head to the stars and the waning quarter moon. "This is the time that was foreseen. Now you will call the Firebird. Now it will all begin."

"Watch, Anna," said Kalami, his smooth, light voice shaking with eagerness. "See again what power you are to be heir to."

The old man, the Holy Father, picked up Mae Shan's spear, and grinning like a monkey, he hunched down between Mae Shan and Anna.

"Do not mistake me, soldier," he said softly. "This place is my place, my power is here. It has been my place for hundreds of years. I am faster here than you, and far, far more deadly. Try to reach the girl and you will die, and the one beside you will die. Our daughter is more valuable than either of you."

"The glass is beautiful," said Sakra, conversationally. "Your people can indeed work miracles."

"We will again." The Holy Father grinned. "We will be whole again and we will rebuild."

Kalami was laying the gold ore into the crucible fire. Bridget was watching Anna watching her. Light flickered over her face as if over polished marble.

"But glass is fragile. There is much it cannot endure," Sakra went on. "Sudden heat, then sudden cold, it may shatter like a dream of the future."

"This is no dream, Southerner," hissed the old man. Beyond him, Anna stared at her parents, her glimmering father, her stony mother. "I have seen what will be. I have nurtured it and readied it. I knew all would be as it is now. I did not even mourn the death of my most loyal son, for I knew he would return to me as he is now, to finish what was begun."

Sakra shook his head slowly, without ever taking his gaze off the madman. "Visions show what may be. Visions change. Visions break like hot glass plunged into snow."

The old man sat back, laying the spear across his bony knees. "Your words are meaningless, Southerner. They are without power or shape, but they may distract. You will be silent now."

Sakra closed his mouth.

"Mae Shan," Kalami called her name. "Come here."

Mae Shan, feeling detached from herself as her thoughts swirled into fresh understanding, stood and walked to the crucible. The heat was great, breaking out fresh sweat on her forehead. Bridget too dripped in perspiration, but hers was mixed with tears of anger, Mae Shan had no doubt. She tried to catch Bridget's eye.

Did you hear? Did you?

"Hold out your arm."

Mae Shan thought she knew what was coming, but she was unprepared for the swiftness and the brutality of it. The black knife slashed out, cutting through layers of cloth as if they weren't there and down deep into the flesh of her forearm. Blood poured forth, spilling onto the fire and the melting gold, pumping her life out to the rhythm of her own frantic heart. The pain came a moment later and Mae Shan cried out, falling to her knees clutching the wound she knew could be fatal, and her blood flowed onto the grass, forming a stream to surround the crucible.

"You will shape the gold and the fire, Bridget Lederle, breathe deep and bring us the cage."

The world throbbed. Mae Shan tried to tighten her sleeve around her wound, but she did not have the strength left in her hands to tie any knot. Her vision began to fail, becoming a fog of blood and pain. Overhead, she saw Bridget plunge her hands into the fire of the crucible. Was this new thrumming in the air Bridget's power, rising to do her bidding? Bridget had a plan. Mae Shan tried to think what it could be, how she could help. She was dying. There was nothing left for her to fear either, and she was ignored, and it was her chance, her chance had come and she was too weak, too hurt.

What is his name?

Shattered, like hot glass plunged into snow.

I'm sorry, Mae Shan.

"Your time is now, my son. Declare yourself. Call the Firebird to us."

Kalami stepped forward, his face and eyes shining with triumph. He flung his head back and raised his arms to the sky.

"Come! The fire of the earth, the fire in the stone, calls you! I, Valin Kalami, call you! You know me! Come to me!"

So much power poured through those words, even Mae Shan could feel it. It was power cold as death, power of soul and memory without reservation. Sorcerers who spent themselves too freely would die. Kalami had passed that danger and shaken it off and now had no reason to hold anything back. It felt as if he reached into the sky and beyond. Kalami who had once stood before the sacred guardian and declared he would hold it forever imprisoned for his own ends now called it to heel like a dog.

And it came.

It spread its fire overhead, blocking out the stars. Heat seared Mae Shan's eyes and blistered her skin. It was beautiful. It was holy. Its white beak opened in a scream of rage that burned her soul as its heat burned her flesh, rocking her with fresh pain, boiling the blood that ran down her arm.

Goddess of Mercy, forgive me, forgive me. I am too weak. My understanding too small.

Then as her mind and vision swam, she saw Bridget raise up her arms. Fire ran from her as blood ran from Mae Shan, leaving only her skin, only her hands, only her will.

Kalami staggered, and the Holy Father rose up and gripped the spear. Kalami shouted and whatever he said, Bridget's hands were forced down slowly, fighting for every inch, but still they plunged again into the flames.

The Firebird spread its wings over them all, screaming in its fury, and on the ground where Mae Shan crouched, her blood ran away into the pool of stars. And there was the heat, the terrible raging heat, and Kalami shone like a god, and Mae Shan's weakening mind thought she was back in the Heart of the World, watching it burn, and seeing Wei Lin burn and longing only for cold water.

And she knew.

The Firebird screamed its rage. Bridget shaped the gold into bars with her bare hands and trapped power, and Mae Shan staggered to her feet. With the last of her strength, she threw herself against Valin Kalami, and fell sprawling into the grass. Kalami staggered backward, and fell into the pool of stars.

Kalami shattered.

The enchanted glass burst into a thousand jagged pieces, merging with the water, and vanishing. Someone screamed over the metallic roar of the Phoenix. Maybe it was Wei Lin.

No. It was Tsan Nu leaning over Mae Shan.

"I'm sorry. I'm sorry. Don't die. Don't leave me. I'm sorry, Mae Shan."

"Help your mother," Mae Shan told her. It was the most important thing in the world. It was the only thing left. "Help her."

Then she was running away, like water, like blood, running down the passages of the Heart of the World, looking for Wei Lin, and finding only darkness.

Anna watched Mae Shan's head fall onto the grass. The Phoenix soared overhead, and she didn't even look. The whole world had gone red, gold, and orange, and she remembered the stink of burning from before, and she couldn't see it.

Mae Shan wasn't moving, and she didn't know what to do.

Anna.

It was Father. Mae Shan had broken the glass body that held him, and now his spirit was trapped again, but in the pool this time, for ghosts that died suddenly could be trapped where they were, especially by water. And he called to her.

Anna, help me.

Power ran everywhere, straining, shaping, reshaping. Mother was reaching up to the Phoenix, trying to encompass it with her power. She'd needed a name. Names were used in transformation. Was she trying to change it?

Anna, I can't stay here. You must help me, or we'll fail.

Father. He loved her. He'd saved her.

The seer was on his feet, screaming and waving his spear. Anna couldn't even understand him. The Hastinapuran launched himself forward without even bothering to stand up and knocked the seer down, and the two of them rolled on the ground, wrestling for Mae Shan's spear.

All because of Father, of what he'd done and made her do.

Remember this, the woman, Bridget, her mother, had said. *Whatever happens next, remember this.*

He'd cut Mae Shan's arm. He'd held a knife to Anna's throat. He'd told her he would have to do these things and why. He'd warned her.

Help your mother, Mae Shan said. *Help her.*

Mae Shan was almost dead, bloody and almost dead, lying with her own blood around her, like her uncle Lien Jinn had.

Help me, Anna!

Anna catapulted herself forward, colliding with the woman Bridget, with her mother. Too angry, too frightened, too broken-hearted to think, Anna reached. She reached outside to pull the magic down, and there was so much, she could have suffocated in it, but she held, and she rode the current of it, shaping it by wish and need, with fire and air and love. She wrapped her arms around Bridget, and poured the torrent of her magic into this stranger, her mother, her only hope to save her friend.

Stop him, stop him. Don't let him kill Mae Shan!

Bridget reached out, catching up the tides of magic, the generations of life and death, hope, fear, breath, and stillness. The cup of her soul filled and strained and cried out from the pain of such power. She could not grasp it all. She had no choice. She must hold, must shape, must weave the pattern of nothing more than air and will. She must call the fire down.

Her body's eyes were blind. There was too much fire. She could not see. But her mind's eye, her second sight, saw the Firebird, wailing aloud for vengeance and betrayal.

She tried to fling the net of her will around it, but it withered and fell before the strength of the fire.

It's too strong, too huge. I'm not strong enough.

Fear broke Bridget's nerve and let the power spill out useless and un-formed and she felt the terror of death. But then, something caught at her. Thin arms wrapped tight around her waist, and power, bright, vivid, strong, and frantic, poured into her, launching her spirit high, catching her up, ordering her to try, try, keep trying. She must. She must do this thing. She must live. She must save Mae Shan.

Anna. She must save Anna, and she knew what was happening. Her daughter had made her choice, and was now loaning Bridget all the power she had to give so Bridget could save her friend.

The knowledge of Anna beside her gave the final strength she needed. With her soul, her hands and vision, and all the magic that filled them she reached out into the living fire. The guardian screamed in pain, and Bridget echoed that scream, but she closed her will and spirit around the heart of the Firebird. She felt it beat, she felt it burn. It was wildness, it was vengeance, and yet, and yet . . .

Inside, at the core, there was a place that was still cool, a place that was lost and lonely and tired. Bridget bolstered by her daughter, reached to that single cool place amid conflagration of the Firebird heart.

I am here to bring you home, she tried to say. *I am here to bring you to safety.*

She cupped herself around the coolness and felt it tremble.

Now, Anna. Pull.

She felt her daughter tremble, but she also felt her call out, and she pulled. Slowly, as if she were a great weight, instead of a thing of air and fear, Bridget felt herself slip away from the fire. The cool spark, the essence she held struggled. It cried out. Bridget tightened herself around it. Anna's pull faltered.

I bring you freedom. Freedom!

But the essence cried out in its fear and lunged against her. The shell of will that was Bridget cracked.

Anna!

Anna pulled. Bridget clamped herself tight against the essence of the Firebird heart with the last of her strength. The fire burned through her, seeking what she stole, but Bridget began to shape the essence. She drew on the fire that surrounded her. The flames felt soft as clay under her hands. She made two arms, a trunk, two legs, a man's head. She indented hollows for eyes. She drew out a nose and ears.

Remember, she willed the cool spark at its center. *You once wore this shape. Remember.*

Her second sight showed her the man. He was small and slender, he had fine hands and a long face and a snubbed nose and chin. He had thick brows and long hair worn in a queue down his back.

Remember. You were Xuan and you were Seong.

She did not understand what this meant, but Anna did, and through the power, through the will to help and hold, her knowledge came to Bridget.

You began as Seong, but you became Xuan again. Over and again, you were Xuan. You always returned to Xuan.

There were tattoos. They swirled and wove their patterns on arms, on torso, on legs and face. There were robes, as heavily woven with symbols as the flesh was colored with them. There was the life, given in sacrifice, but always sought again, always returned to.

Remember.

That is gone, wailed the Firebird. *That is no more.*

It is here. Remember. See. Let me show you.

She gathered the flames together, shaping them with care, hands obeying the vision before her mind's eye. Pain made her weak, but need held her to her work. To lose this was to lose life, to lose Anna, to lose Sakra, to lose herself. No. Not again.

Remember. It is here. I'll show you.

And Anna pulled and Bridget held, and slowly, the flames shrank from around them and solidified. Cooled by the human heart that was still within the guardian, and became flesh. Painfully, Bridget felt her heart beat, her lungs stir. Slowly, she found the eyes of her own body again, and was able to will them to open. She looked into the dark eyes of a stranger in robes of red and orange with the Firebird, harmless in gold thread, embroidered across them.

She fainted at his feet before the pain could reach her.

Chapter Twenty-three

The Vixen stalked toward the sacred grove, she paused, one foot raised, ears turned forward. Nothing moved. Seemingly relaxed, she trotted forward, pausing to nose around the bases of the scarlet trees, taking in the scents of the past and the future.

The grass did not even rustle beneath her feet as she came to the aftermath. Human bodies lay scattered in every direction. The child collapsed against her mother. Before them huddled Xuan, the Minister of Fire, small, middle-aged, and merely human once more. The woman soldier lay sprawled beside the rainwater pool, staining its waters red with her blood. The two sorcerers, one old, one young, fell side by side, the younger still with his hands on the shaft where it protruded from the chest of the elder.

The spring wind blew. The Vixen sneezed. "Dear me," she murmured to herself. "How very untidy."

Picking her way between the fallen humans, the Vixen walked up to the edge of the pool. She paused once, briefly to breathe across Bridget Lederle's face, and once to lap at Mae Shan's wounded arm. She sat down by the edge of the pool, and scratched her chin with her hind foot.

"Valin Kalami," she said. "I think you had better come out of there."

The ghost rose from the pool of night, naked and shivering with the cold and fear of his second death.

"No!" he wailed when he saw her and her fangs and hungry eyes. "No! You have no more claim on me!"

"Nor has she."

The Vixen cocked her head, baring her fangs as she did. Behind her, Baba Yaga leaned on her pestle, her two great mastiffs at her sides.

"You are wrong," the Vixen flattened her ears against her skull. "He shed the blood of my children, there is no renouncing that claim."

"Your children lost him, he came to me. Will you fight for him?" The mastiffs too laid their ears back, baring their teeth from under curling lips, and their teeth were sharp as razors. "Will you take him back from me?"

The Vixen looked at the dogs, growling and straining against their mistress's invisible hold. She looked at the Old Witch with her iron teeth and her pestle stained by ancient blood. She knew by scent which gods, which powers, had belonged to that blood. She looked at the eyes older than Grandfather Death.

She looked at the thin human ghost that would have killed her sons for his games of power.

"Very well," she sighed. "Take him."

The ghost tried to scream, but with a snap of her long fingers, Baba Yaga choked off the sound. Then, she reached out and plucked him up, and stuffed him into the leather sack at her waist.

"Very good," said the Old Witch. "Remember this the next time you want something that is mine."

She vanished. The Vixen whisked her tail back and forth a few times. "Oh, I shall, you may be assured."

One of the humans stirred. Bridget. The Vixen trotted over and sat on her haunches.

Bridget's eyes fluttered open. "You," she began.

"Yes." The Vixen scratched her chin.

Displaying a laudable mother's instinct, her hand went immediately out to her child. She felt the warmth of the girl's skin, and the rise and fall of her chest. *Alive,* she thought. *My child is alive.*

Only then did other thoughts come into her mind, her gaze darted to the bodyguard and the sorcerers. "What about . . . ?"

"The others?" The Vixen scratched her chin. "You have done a few services for me, whether you knew it or not. I have reason to be grateful. So, I have decided those with you will live."

She swallowed. This, the Vixen saw, was only partially welcome news. Still, the woman was sensible enough not to argue with the current position of herself and her family. "Thank you."

The Vixen inclined her head. "You're welcome."

Bridget gently moved her daughter's head and arm so she could stand, test her strength, try to make herself ready. For surely, something else must happen. The woman was not yet ready to believe nothing more would happen to her. "What about Kalami?" she said, gazing into the sacred and bloody pool where shattered glass now glimmered in the mud.

The Vixen showed her yellow teeth. "He will not trouble you again. Baba Yaga has him."

Again proving her basic sensibility, fear took hold in Bridget at the mention of the Old Witch. "She . . . ?"

"Yes." The Vixen plunked back onto haunches, nosing her tail, setting her fur in order. "You see, she is wise in many things, the Witch with the Iron Teeth, although don't tell her I said so." The Vixen flashed her open-mouthed grin. "She told me once that my children were unsafe guardians for Kalami, that they would grow bored with the chase and careless in their hunt. Valin Kalami would have been free from us, eventually. She was right.

"The Old Witch, however, does not grow bored, and she will not ever let go of what is hers."

The Vixen's fangs shone briefly as she laughed, and then she was gone, leaving Bridget on her own to cope with the living and the dead.

In the end, it took them two days to climb down from the mountain. They went slowly, trying to regain their strength, but it was not easy. Food was scarce in the early spring, even with what Anna remembered of her father's teachings. Anna would only speak sporadically on the way down from the forest, and mostly kept close to Mae Shan, who tried to find ways to comfort and cheer her, while at the same time supporting Xuan, who, while strong, seemed bewildered at having only a human body and human mind again.

The boat was still on the shore. Now that Sakra knew its nature, he was able to work with the enchanted sails and take them round the coast to the city of Ahde. They made it to shore safely, but could make it no farther. Tuukosov fishermen found their boat stuck in the harbor mud, dirty, bloody, worn from hunger and thirst, and recognizing them as foreigners, called the Isavaltan guards, who in turn called for carts to carry them to the high house, and Lord Master Peshek.

When Bridget at last awoke after a full night's sleep in a clean bed, with nothing more hanging over her than the weight of memory, she closed her eyes, and then opened them again, to be sure she was not dreaming.

She did not ache. If she was hungry and thirsty, it was with the usual proportions of waking up first thing in the morning after a long sleep. It felt . . . luxurious, like something to be celebrated. There was so much to do, so much to try to understand and reconcile, but now, for this moment, she could just be.

Bridget swung her feet out of bed. Feeling positively wanton, she threw on only the lightest robe and slippers that had been provided. Half-dressed by Isavaltan standards, she slipped out into the grey stone hallway and down the winding stairs to the spring garden contained by the high house's daunting stone walls.

The air smelled of flowers, mud, greenery, and distantly cooking porridge. There was no scent of ash, of burning, of blood. There was only the world coming to life. Bridget stretched up her arms, spreading her fingertips out toward the sun as if to cup it in her hands and bring it to earth to admire. She was alive, alive!

Bridget swung her arms down with a satisfied sigh, and saw Anna standing in the shadow of a bush laden with lavender buds, and staring.

Caught between embarrassment and the strong desire to run to the girl and wrap her arms around her, Bridget settled for closing her robe a little more decently.

"Hello, Anna." She managed to say the words fairly smoothly.

Anna started to bow, but then stopped. "I'm sorry. I don't know what the custom is here."

There was something in the way she spoke, half confusion, half frustration, that made Bridget smile. "Between you and me, I think hello will do."

"Oh."

She was beautiful. Her hair hung in long, black ringlets, badly in need of a comb. Her eyes were wide, and slightly slanted above her high cheekbones. Oh, she was going to break hearts with those eyes one day. She was going to be tall too.

Bridget's knees quivered, and she knew she wasn't going to be able to stand up much longer. The garden was studded with stone benches, the nearest one still damp from the night and partly moss-covered, but Bridget sat down anyway, and searched desperately for a neutral topic of conversation.

"Have you seen Mae Shan this morning?"

"She is with Minister Xuan in the other wing of the garden." Anna looked over her shoulder, seeing if they had company or looking for a way to escape this conversation, Bridget couldn't tell. "Shall I go get her for you?"

"No, that's all right." *Don't leave. Stay here. Let me look at you, my beautiful, beautiful child.* "Is she well?"

"She says she's much better."

"Good." The wind blew hard for a moment, making the heavy, gaudy flowers nod and bow. Anna fidgeted. Bridget tried not to knot her fingers together.

"And you," she said, hoping it was not too daring, that she wouldn't frighten her child away. "How are you feeling?"

"I'm much better too, thank you." It was polite, a reply she had been probably taught to make. It told Bridget nothing except that her daughter had manners, which was good to know, but not what she wanted. She wanted to reach out, to end this feeling of Anna being directly in front of her and yet a thousand miles away.

Because there was nothing else for her to do, Bridget decided to be honest.

"Do you have any questions, Anna? I don't know where to begin to talk about everything that's happened over the past few days, let alone how . . . we came to be here."

Anna dug her toe into the lawn and looked down as she did. Maybe she had no questions. Maybe she didn't want to talk. Maybe this was the exact wrong thing to do, and she had frightened the child.

God Almighty, how am I to know what to do?

But at last, Anna looked up. "Is there . . . where am I to go?"

Of course. Bridget found she could breathe again. *Of course you'd want to know that.* She smoothed the skirt of her robe down, hoping to look casual, and fairly sure she was failing utterly. "Well, I have a house near the imperial palace where there's more than enough room. I thought we might go there, until full summer at least, then we might go stay in Vienska when the emperor and empress go traveling. It's very pretty there, they tell me. There's a large lake for swimming in." An idea struck her. "Do you know how to swim?"

"No."

Carefully, afraid of frightening her, afraid of frightening herself, Bridget said, "I could teach you if you like, and how to sail a boat. On the lake, anyway." She added, "I'm not much of a hand on the ocean."

"Is there a difference?" asked Anna, a little genuine curiosity showing through.

"Oh, yes, a big difference."

Her brow furrowed. Her toe continued to worry at the grass. "Did my father know how to sail on the ocean?"

Bridget swallowed. A bird was singing full-throated welcome in the tree. She wished she could point that out instead, or say something about how good the porridge smelled. *She will have questions. You are the only one left to answer them.* "Yes, he did."

Anna went back to watching her toes again. The one working at the grass had found the dirt beneath and was beginning to dig a small hole. What was it looking for? "Did he love me?"

What reply could she possibly make to that? "Anna, I don't know."

The hole grew a little bigger as the toe worked at it. Then the toe stopped, the foot withdrew, and Anna looked up. "Did you?"

Bridget's throat seized up and for a moment she was not sure she would be able to make a single sound. When she could finally speak, it was only in a hoarse whisper. "Yes, I did." Very much. "When I thought you had died, I didn't think I'd ever love anybody so much again."

Anna contemplated this very seriously for a time. "Did you?"

Bridget nodded. "Yes. The minute I saw you and knew who you were."

Anna looked away, watching the flowers bowing to the wind. She stared up in the trees, trying to see the bird, who was joined now by a rival, or perhaps it was a mate. Her toe began worrying at its hole again, spreading it out, making it just a bit deeper. "I think I would like to learn how to swim."

Bridget's heart swelled until she thought it would burst. She allowed herself to believe a small smile would not overwhelm Anna. "I'm glad to hear it. It's lots of fun."

"Master Liaozhai said it is only when we are learning something new that we truly understand the beauty of what we know," her daughter volunteered.

Bridget arched her eyebrows. "I think you must tell me more about Master Liaozhai one day," she said, meaning it. She wanted to know about every second of Anna's life up until now.

"All right." Anna looked up to the trees again, and back over her shoulder. Bridget, half amused, half distressed that her daughter could find something more interesting than her mother, decided the interview was probably at an end.

Bridget mustered a brisk tone. "Right now, however, I'm not fit to be seen in public." She stood, adjusting her robe so it more fully covered her nightdress. "I'm going to go get dressed so I can go in to breakfast and thank Lord Master Peshek for his hospitality. I'll see you there, all right?"

"All right." Anna bowed again, stopped midway through the gesture again, and straightened up. "Good-bye."

"Good-bye." Bridget turned with forced calm back toward the little winding stairs, congratulating herself on not fleeing as fast as her feet would carry her. Movement in the arched window overhead caught her eye, and she saw Sakra's face looking down at her.

Eavesdropper, she thought primly, even as she gathered her hems to hurry up the stairs to meet him. If she could not talk to someone about her meeting with Anna, she felt she would suffocate on unspoken words.

Sakra seemed to realize this. As soon as she reentered the drafty, stony hall he said, "Did it go well?" He held out his hand.

Bridget took it and held it tightly, letting out a long breath. "Yes. I think so. We made some sort of start, anyway. I don't think the idea of coming to live with me terrifies her, and she has agreed to swimming lessons."

Sakra smiled his quiet smile. "Then I would say that the conversation went very well indeed."

Bridget looked out the window, seeing the garden, seeing the future, plans, observations, hopes, and fears crowding her mind, and all of them trying to tumble out her mouth at once. "I'll have to have Prathad make up a room for her. I have no idea what she's used to. I hope I can get her to tell me. She's so . . . polite."

"Courtesy is very important in Hung-Tse," Sakra told her. "She will have been rigorously schooled."

"Schooling, that's something else we'll have to see about. Won't Mistress Urshila be pleased. There'll be two of us to put up with." She stopped herself. "If Mistress Urshila is still alive." She pressed her free hand against her forehead. "She was right, you know, about more than one thing, and I'm sorry I didn't learn that sooner."

"Starting life over is difficult."

It was then it dawned on her that she had been standing here holding Sakra's hand for several minutes, and she'd barely been aware of it. It was so natural, so comfortable and comforting. But with awareness now came a flush to her cheeks. His hand was warm, slightly callused, and strong. It would have been improper for her to be seen holding this man's hand back in Bayfield, in Isavalta it was scandalous.

Bridget did not let go. She just looked down at their two hands, fingers locked together, her white skin and his brown. "I seem to be about to start over again."

"Yes," he said simply, but she heard how his breath had quickened.

She looked up into his autumn eyes. "Will you help me?"

In answer, Sakra cradled her face gently in both his hands and bowed his head, giving her a kiss that was full of more promises than either one of them could speak. Neither noticed Anna's small, serious face watching them from the garden below.

Anna turned away from the sight of her mother and Sakra kissing in front of the garden window, embarrassed, uncomfortable, but not, she found, very surprised.

The garden was very different from the ones she was used to. It was crowded and wild, except for the razor-straight paths cutting through it. There were fountains, but no streams, and huge, bright flowers, cups of red and white, great splays of yellow, trees heavy with pink and white blossoms. Nothing she knew the name of.

It did look like it held plenty of secrets though, under the broad-leafed plants and between the poorly groomed trees, and that made Anna curious. If they were going to stay here a little while, it would be interesting to explore. And safe. She looked at the grey stone walls. She didn't think they'd protect against magic, but there were other things out there and they were at least strong.

She wondered what Bridget would do if she told her she was scared of this town that had only one wall ringing it on the outside. She didn't think Bridget would scold, but she didn't know. Maybe later.

Right now, Anna smelled porridge, and some kind of meat, and something sweet that might have been roasting vegetables or stewing fruit. Her stomach rumbled, and she ran across the garden, heading for the wing of the high house that held the kitchen. No matter where you were, Cooks could be begged from, she was certain.

Following her nose, Anna didn't pay attention to where else she was going, and she nearly collided with Mae Shan and the Minister of Fire, but Mae Shan held her hand out and Anna was able to pull up short.

They had removed Minister Xuan's formal garments and dressed him in a warm robe of fur and velvet, but he walked stooped over as if it were too heavy for him. The bones of his face seemed to stand out sharply, and everything he saw seemed to startle him, for his eyes blinked constantly.

Anna bowed hastily, with the deference due to the old, the sick, and the frightening. "I'm sorry. I didn't mean to intrude." She glanced at Mae Shan just long enough to see her guard wasn't mad, and turned to run the other way.

"W-w-ait," said Minister Xuan. He stammered heavily. Anna supposed his new mouth was trying to learn how to shape words. Or was it his old mouth? Had they given him back his old body or made him a new one? She would have to ask Bridget . . . Mother.

Mae Shan was frowning at her. Anna gathered her manners back together and bowed again. "Sir."

"M-mm . . ." The effort of speech made him sway on his feet. Mae Shan turned him toward one of the crude benches that littered the garden and sat him down as one might an elderly relative. Once he no longer had to stand, his speech became a little more smooth. Probably because he had less to think about. "Mae Shan tells. Tells me. You helped."

Anna bowed once again, humbly acknowledging her part. She didn't really want to be reminded of it. She didn't want to remember the heat, and the blood, and Father breaking into a thousand pieces.

"It was Anna's help that brought you back, Minister," Mae Shan was saying.

Minister Xuan straightened his back a little beneath the burden of his robe. "I am back. The guardian has gone to Heaven." He closed his eyes as he said that, and a look of profound relief softened his sharp features, and then his head bowed and his shoulders slumped and his lips parted. Anna's breath froze in her throat. Had he died? Was it something she did? But then a small snore escaped him.

Mae Shan smiled ruefully, and shifted her position minutely so the minister could lean against her shoulder. "I fear being human is tiring. The minister has much healing to do."

Anna realized there was a very important question she hadn't had a chance to ask yet. "Where will you go, Mae Shan?"

Mae Shan smiled gently. "I will go home, mistress. My charge is done. You are safe now."

"Oh." Anna kicked her heel against the flagstones.

"I must take the minister back to Hung-Tse," Mae Shan continued. She was trying to make sure Anna understood. Anna did, but she felt sick to her stomach anyway. "He is the last of the Nine Elders. With him there, we can begin to rebuild what has been lost. He has the authority to choose the new emperor, before . . . the worst comes to be."

Anna thumped her heel against the stones a few more times, trying to bang away some of the sinking feeling inside of her. "Are you glad you will be going home?"

"I will be sorry to leave you." Mae Shan said in her most serious voice, so Anna knew it was true. The pain in her stomach eased a little.

"Oh," she said.

Mae Shan was looking at her. Embarrassed, Anna stopped kicking the stones, and tried to study them instead. They were all different sizes, cut to fit close together, but there didn't seem to be any pattern to it, like the stones in the walls.

"Do you like her, your mother?" asked Mae Shan.

Anna squinted up at her. "Do you?"

Mae Shan nodded once. "Yes. I do."

Anna found she was glad to hear that. She was able to look into Mae Shan's eyes, and she saw, just by looking at this person she'd gone so far with, who she'd save and who had saved her, that if she'd said no, Mae Shan would have found a way to take her back to Hung-Tse too.

"She's going to teach me to swim."

Mae Shan smiled and Anna thought she would have relaxed her

shoulders, but she didn't want to disturb the minister. "That will be fun."

"That's what she said." Anna paused. Mae Shan looked down at the minister leaning against her. Asleep, he had a nicely shaped face. His tattoos obscured most of his features, but the dragons and the phoenixes made him look strong. She hoped he'd be all right. She hoped Mae Shan would too. Her face had turned serious and tired.

She wanted to say how she'd miss Mae Shan, but the only words that would come out were, "Are you sad?"

Mae Shan sighed. The wind strengthened again, rustling the previous year's leaves and this year's flowers. "I'm afraid. I don't know what's happened to my family. I don't know when I will be able to find them."

"I didn't know you had a family, aside from Lien . . ." Anna stopped. If he was Mae Shan's only family, then she had none. He was dead, with Father and with the holy madman and almost with Mae Shan. She bit her lip. When would she be able to stop thinking about that?

"I have five . . . no, I have four brothers and sisters." Pain crossed her face, and Anna remembered her bowed in prayer in the scroll room with her uncle. She had never asked her who she'd been praying for.

"You should go home then," Anna said out loud so she wouldn't think about that anymore either. So much to think about. So much not to think about.

"Thank you, mistress," Mae Shan said solemnly, but there was a light in her eyes that made Anna want to smile.

"You're not my guard anymore." It made her both sad and happy to say that. "I think you can call me Anna now."

Mae Shan inclined her head. "Thank you, Anna."

"Will you be at breakfast?"

"If the minister wakes in time." That was Mae Shan, always taking care of someone else. She was very good at it. The minister would be fine as long as she was with him. Anna had reason to know.

"I'll bring you some food if you're not there," Anna promised.

"Thank you, mistress . . . Anna." Mae Shan smiled.

Anna smiled back, turned, and ran down the path, not toward the kitchen, but toward the dining hall, where her mother would meet her. It would be all right. It was spring, and her mother had a house where they would live together, and they'd talk and she'd learn to swim and write letters to Mae Shan. The air smelled of spring and breakfast, and Anna ran as fast as she could toward her new life.

Ten thousand *li* away, in the city of T'ien, a red fox padded through the streets and where it passed, emerald grass, bright with dew, began to sprout between the stones.

Epilogue

The summer's night had thrown its quilt over Bayfield, turning the air thick with heat and damp. Mosquitoes whined outside Grace's screened windows, trying to get inside to find their supper. Grace sat up beside her lamp, mending her gypsy skirt. She needed to get back to work soon. There had been some gossip about the time of Bridget's ... visit. How anyone had found out her niece had returned was beyond Grace. Frank would not have said a word.

Frank. He'd been by to see her several times, and he had gone again, without answers to his many questions. She wanted to speak, but she couldn't, and she couldn't even say why. It was as if she were waiting for something.

Perhaps she was. Grace lowered her sewing to her lap with a sigh. She stared at the worn green satin shining in the golden lamplight. No, there was no perhaps. She was waiting. No matter how many times she had tried to tell herself there was nothing to wait for, she could not stop.

She got up and went to the window. If she turned her head just so, she could see the lake and the sparks of the lighthouses marking the safe way out past the islands. She counted them and found the Sand Island light. It burned as bright and steady as the others. The new keeper was in residence with his family, and the work of the place had resumed. Had anyone told them about Bridget? Surely. But what had they said? Did his wife's face pucker with disapproval when she heard the rumors the town had to offer? Or did she shake her head with pity? What would the keeper and his family do if Grace marched up to their door and told them the truth?

A knock sounded on Grace's door. She jumped, pressing her hand against her heart as it pounded hard against her ribs.

"Who is it?" she called.

The answer came and it had a smile in it. "It's me, Aunt Grace."

Grace ran to the door and threw it open. Bridget stood there, looking neat and normal in her grey shirtwaist dress and white apron. Grace felt her mouth drop open. "You came," she said, amazed. "You came." *You kept your promise. You remembered.*

"I'm sorry I was so long, but there are . . . issues of time in these things. May I come in? If I'm seen, there will be talk, I'm sure."

Grace stepped aside. Her head was awhirl. She did not know how to name what she felt. It was close to elation. She had not wanted to believe Bridget would simply vanish again, but part of her was sure that was what had happened. That was the rift in her that would not heal.

She closed the door, and latched it, as if she thought Bridget might suddenly change her mind and try to flee. "I . . . I was just thinking of you," she stammered. *Collect yourself. This is ridiculous.*

"I'm not surprised." Bridget brushed at her apron. "In order to . . . make my crossing I had to call to you, in a way."

"I see," said Grace, although she did not. "Will you sit? Would you like some tea?"

Bridget laughed, and Grace found herself smiling at the sound. This was absurd, but she did not know how else to act. Bridget did sit, how-ever, perching herself on the edge of Grace's horsehair sofa.

"How are you, Aunt Grace?"

A quick, meaningless reply came readily to Grace's tongue. She forced it back. Now was not the time to fall into the old ways. "I hardly know." She set her sewing in her work basket and took her own seat again. "I . . . I think I've been recovering. Getting used to being myself again. Trying to make up my mind about what to do with myself." Her fingers knotted themselves together. "But I haven't been able to."

"Well." Bridget clasped her own hands together, leaning forward, working up her courage, Grace thought. "You could come with me."

They sat there, face-to-face in the dim, overcrowded parlor with all the paraphernalia of Grace's profession and deception surrounding them. For the first time in her adult life, Bridget held out her hand to her aunt.

"I wanted to ask you before but . . . it was so uncertain. I wasn't sure there would be a place to invite you to. But it's all done. The Fire-bird's . . . gone, and Anna . . . Anna's safe."

Grace felt her heart constrict. "She is alive then?"

Bridget nodded and Grace thought she had never seen anyone glowing with such happiness. "Alive and well, and running a bit wild, I'm afraid." She shook her head, but her expression was all mother's pride. "Will you come back with me, Aunt Grace? Come and meet your great-niece?"

This was it. Grace knew it. This was the moment she had been waiting for all these months. For Bridget to speak the words that Grace had wanted with all her soul to hear from Ingrid and never had. This was the conclusion of all that had begun so many years ago.

When Grace straightened back and shoulders. "What would happen if I did?"

"Well, you would stay at my house, at least at first. Then we'll see about finding you a place, or you can just keep house with me, with us. Whatever you'd like."

"You have a house there?"

Bridget colored a little. "As it turns out, I'm quite rich. My father, Avanasy, was elevated to the nobility by Medeoan's father and he got some . . . appertanences to go with his title. Medeoan held on to the estate . . . she had planned to give it to me, but things got complicated. Anyway, the current emperor declared Avanasy's property and fortune to be my rightful inheritance, and there turned out to be rather a lot of it."

Bridget stood, her hand still outstretched, and crossed the room to where Grace sat. "Come with me, Aunt Grace. You'll have a home and we can finally be family."

But we are, Bridget. We are.

Grace looked at her niece, and took her hand. The weight of years of anger slipped from her back, and Grace knew she was truly free at last. Now she could make her choice, without a score to settle, without an imagined slight to redress, without fear of what her mind held or her eyes saw.

"No," she said. "I don't think I will."

"You'd be welcome." Bridget squeezed her hand. "I promise. By the others, and by me."

"I believe you." Grace felt herself smile. "But I've spent almost fifty years in this world hiding from what I am, and what I have been. I think it's high time I found out just what I've been hiding from."

Bridget expelled a sigh that did not not sound either relieved or melancholy. She sounded . . . satisfied.

"Then, will you come with me as far as the lakeside?"

Grace's eyes narrowed. "To say good-bye?"

Bridget's smile grew wistful. "Among other things. Please walk with me, Aunt Grace."

Grace peered searchingly at the younger woman for a moment, but her niece's face gave nothing away, not even to Grace's experienced eye. *Well, if you're going to learn to trust, you'd best make up your mind to do it, hadn't you?*

"Let me get my shawl," she said.

Wrapped lightly in the warm summer night, the two women walked down the empty streets under the light of the full moon. Bridget steered them away from the wharf that was crowded with the noise of men's voices even at this hour. Instead, they walked down beneath the shelter of the bluff to where the grass turned to sand. Grace found herself remembering her girlhood, so long ago, standing on the island sands, telling Ingrid all the fine things she planned to do with her life. She was going to Madison. She'd go to teacher's college. She was going to Chicago. She'd become a nurse. She'd marry a millionaire who would take her to New York City and maybe all the way to Europe. There was more than one young man in Bayfield, she'd boasted, who would take her as far as Madison, and then she'd be on her way.

But the ghosts and the voices had been too many, and the young men had been as false as she, and she had shut herself away from them all.

Ahead of them spread the great black and silver lake. Above stretched the sky with the moon and the millions of silver stars. This had been the edge of the world for as long as she could remember. She was not surprised to hear Bridget say this other place, this Isavalta, lay beyond it.

Bridget put a hand on Grace's shoulder, silently urging her to stay where she was. Bridget herself walked forward, right to the restless edge of the water. Careless of her boots and hems, she took one more step so that she stood with one foot in the water and one on dry land. She pulled what looked like a small ball of yarn or twine from her apron pocket. Looping one end around her wrist, she drew back her arm and hurled the ball out toward the center of the lake. The slender line payed out, shining silver in the moonlight, and finally drifted down to the water, and promptly sank into the darkness.

"I have come to the edge of the world," she said in the strange, singsong voice she had used to work the charm that had taken her away that last time. "I stand with one foot in the world of my birth and one foot in the world of my blood. I weave the line of silver, of moonlight, and of blood and I make the great cry. Let the wall be breached by this my command. Let the breach be healed by my further word. Let my mother pass the breach and let her stand forth. This is my word, and my word is strong."

Grace felt the hairs rise on the back of her neck. At the words "my mother," her tongue froze to the roof of her mouth. Something was happening, she had no doubt of it. She felt it in the fiber of her soul, but what that was she could not have said, and she was afraid to guess.

Around them, the moonlight seemed to blur, as if her eyes had suddenly filled with tears. She wiped at them, and when she lowered her hand, Ingrid stood on the waters before her.

Not Ingrid aged as she should have been, but Ingrid as she remained in Grace's memory. Tall and straight, with their mother's auburn hair, and her working dress and apron tidy. It was impossible that she should be there, but she was real just the same. Grace had no room for doubt in her.

With a cry, she ran forward, splashing into water up to her knees, both hands flung out to embrace her sister standing so calm and smiling in front of her. It had been so many years, she had lost count. It had been the measure of Bridget's life and longer, and . . .

And Ingrid was long, long dead.

Grace pulled up short, up to her knees in the lake that was still icy cold despite the summer's warmth. Still, she did not shiver.

"You're a ghost," she said to Ingrid.

Ingrid nodded once.

"But you're true. Bridget brought you here."

Again, Ingrid nodded. A wind blew, and it did not stir a hair on her head or ruffle her apron hem.

"Can you speak?"

Ingrid smiled. *A very little. The gift of our family has always been sight.*

For a moment, she stood and did nothing but stare. Here it was, the moment she'd wished for. Ingrid was back. She could say anything, ask anything. A thousand imagined conversations poured out of her memory, but none of them moved her voice.

Instead, she said, "I'm sorry, Ingrid."

Forgive me, Grace. I wanted to come for you.

Grace embraced her sister. It should not have been possible, but it was. From deep memory she knew the warmth of Ingrid's arms in the featherlight touch of her ghost. The bitter years washed away in the waters of the lake, and she was seventeen again, and she cared for nothing, and she loved her sister.

After a time, Ingrid pulled away, a warm breath of spring passing Grace's cheek.

Bridget is growing tired.

"Yes, of course." Grace wiped her cheeks. This time the tears were real, and they must have flowed freely for some time. Her face was as damp as if she'd dipped it in the lake. "This can be no small thing she's doing."

No, but she is very strong, my Bridget.

"I would expect that of any daughter of yours."

Pride rolled in waves from Ingrid's shade. *Be happy, Grace.*

"I will," she said, and she knew it to be true. "Good-bye, Ingrid."

The ghost's attention turned briefly from Grace, and back on the shore, she saw Bridget nod.

"This is my word," said Bridget. "And my word is firm. I draw back the silver line, and I heal the breach. This is my word."

Slowly, as if it were a heavy towline instead of a slender thread, Bridget drew the string from the water, inch by inch. The lake's cold finally soaked into Grace, and she realized that if she did not move now, her feet would be completely numbed and she would not be able to move at all. She cast a last glance toward Ingrid, but the ghost had already faded into moonlight. It was all right. They had said all that had needed saying, and no parting look was truly required.

Clumsy, cold, and wet through, Grace hiked up her hems and waded to shore. She minded none of it. She felt seventeen again. No. At seventeen her heart had been callow and careless. Now it was full to the brim with a strength and security she had never thought to claim as her own.

On the shore, Bridget drew back from the water, and stowed her reel of thread in her pocket. Even in the moonlight, Grace could see how she shivered.

"Let's get you home," she said at once, as if Bridget had been the one in lake water up to her knees while Grace had just wet one boot.

Bridget shook her head. "I need to get back to Isavalta. If I don't go tonight, it will be months before I can try again."

"But you're exhausted. How can you manage . . . ?"

"Sakra is . . ." Bridget broke off with a wave. "Suffice it to say someone is holding the door for me. I will be fine, Aunt Grace. You must trust me in this."

"I do, but . . ." She reached out, letting the gesture finish the sentence for her.

Bridget understood. "I will be back, Aunt Grace, and don't worry. I will be able to find you wherever you've gone."

"Good."

There did not seem to be any need for another word. Grace embraced her niece, a true, warm, strong living embrace. Then Bridget turned away and cast out her line again. This time it did not fall into the water. It stayed straight and taut as if it had been caught by someone in the darkness Grace could not see. Bridget walked out across the waters, and she was gone.

Grace took a deep breath and let it out slowly. The night was warm, but she was cold, and her whole future waited with the dawn. She would go see Frank as soon as it was light enough. This time, she would tell him the whole long, complex truth that had held her apart from him for all these years. He would believe her. She knew that now. He would believe her and he would understand and then . . . well, then they would see what would come of that understanding.

Grace turned her back on the lake and began walking home.

About the Author

Sarah Zettel, author of three fantasy and five science fiction novels, has won the Locus Award for the Best First Novel, for *Reclamation* (1996), and was runner-up for the Philip K. Dick Award for the best paperback original SF novel, for *Fool's War* (1997). *The Firebird's Vengeance* is the third fantasy novel in her Isavalta series. She lives outside Ann Arbor, Michigan.